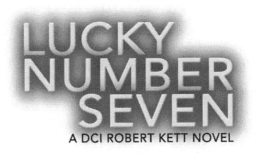

A DCI ROBERT KETT NOVEL

ALEX SMITH

RELENTLESS
M E D I A

LUCKY NUMBER SEVEN
Published Worldwide by Relentless Media.
This edition published in 2023.

Edited by Hanna Elizabeth

ISBN: 978-1-913877-13-2

www.alexsmithbooks.com
relentless.media

ALSO BY ALEX SMITH

The DCI Robert Kett Thrillers

Paper Girls

Bad Dog

Three Little Pigs

Whip Crack

Run Rabbit Run

Stone Cold Dead

Every Mother's Son

Sweet Briar Rose

Jaw Breaker

Knock Knock

King Rat

Knuckle Bones

Lucky Number Seven

Cry Baby: A Novella

The Softley Softley Thrillers

The Harder They Fall

Hard Luck House (Coming Soon)

Other Books

Six Days, Six Hours, Six Minutes

*To Christopher / Gramps,
with so much love
and potatoes.*

We miss you.

PROLOGUE

Monday

SOMEBODY HAD TAKEN A MONSTROUS SHIT OUTSIDE THE office.

Again.

Gloria Easterman—*not Gloria Estefan!* she would tell people, as if there could be any hope of mistaking them— smelled it before she saw it, the creep of sewage tickling the back of her nostrils as she rounded the corner from the car park. And sure enough, there it sat, grounded like a Viking longboat on the short access ramp that led to the front door, its brave crew of sweetcorn chunks clinging desperately to the sides. It was being besieged by an army of flies, the sound of them like kazoos. It seemed too big to be real, almost as long and as thick as her forearm.

In all her fifty-five years, she'd never once produced a poop a quarter of that size. Even Phil, God rest him, hadn't managed anything quite so gargantuan, even on those rare occasions he'd come to her and confessed that he'd blocked the downstairs loo, necessitating a length of bamboo from the garden and a sturdy pair of rubber gloves. Whoever had squatted there last night with their trousers around their ankles must have been twelve foot tall.

She approached it like she would a wild animal, her clacking heels echoing off the sides of the buildings on the other side of the wide street. That was the trouble about having an office at the bottom of Prince of Wales Road, she knew. It was the busiest street in the city for pubs and clubs, a veritable Roman orgy of booze and lechery and violence and kebabs from Friday night to Monday morning. There hadn't been a day in all her time here where she hadn't had to sweep bottles and chip trays from the stoop or wash the bright orange vomit from beneath the windows.

And if that wasn't enough, apparently the office was now a toilet, because this was now twice in two weeks that somebody had released the Kraken outside Reed, Barnham and Crabbe Insurance.

"Well?" she said, looking at the shit like it might take it upon itself to slope away down the hill and deposit itself in the river. It didn't, of course. It just sat there, the stench of it reaching her sinuses, hanging on the back of her tongue. The gag took her by surprise, her stomach clenching hard, her sourdough toast and jam halfway back to daylight before she managed to swallow it back down.

She threw the pile of shit another disapproving look before skirting around it. Reed, Barnham and Crabbe occupied a Victorian house that was impressively stately on the outside but utterly unsuitable for an office once you entered. It was microscopic inside, like a reverse Tardis, and dry rot had chewed away most of its supporting walls and floorboards. She'd mentioned this to her boss more than once, but Ben Reed was a man who put money before everything, just so long as he was putting it in his own pocket.

She slid her key into the lock but it didn't turn, and when she turned the handle, the door opened. *Which is weird*, she thought, because she was always the first person to arrive at the office in the morning.

"Hello?" she called out as she walked into the downstairs room.

The big front window seemed to suck in the early summer sunshine like a hothouse—which was kind of ironic considering every single one of the dozen or so plants on display was fake. Gloria glanced at the street and noticed how streaky the glass was, making a mental note to call the window cleaner. She hadn't seen him in weeks, and she wondered whether Ben had cancelled the contract to keep the costs down.

"Hello?" she said again. "Ben? Asif?"

"Morning, Gloria," came the reply, and she followed it down the short corridor that led to the narrow kitchen. Ben —the only member of Reed, Barnham and Crabbe to still be part of the band, as it were—was hunched over the coffee maker, the expression on his face that of a monkey trying to work out how to fix a rocket ship. He glanced at her, his forehead knotted into a frown. He was wearing a white shirt and a woollen tank top, which must have felt unbearable in this weather, and his corduroy trousers were an obnoxious shade of red. "Can't get the bloody thing to work."

"You've switched it on at the wall?" Gloria asked, taking off her coat and hanging it on the peg next to Ben's ancient Barbour. There were six pegs there at the moment, but there were seven of pretty much everything else. Seven desks and seven chairs, seven mugs and seven sets of cutlery. Ben liked to keep things concise, and when Justin had left the office last month—permanently, another cost-cutting measure—Ben had literally unscrewed his peg from the wall. He was a man of unwavering precision, and was fond of saying it.

"I've switched it on at the wall, Gloria," he said. "I know it's early, but I'm not an idiot."

Gloria wiggled the coffee machine out a little, discovering that Ben had plugged in the toaster instead. She switched the plugs without a word and the little red light came on.

"Weird," Ben grunted. "Somebody's bust a grumpy on the doorstep again."

"They've bust a *what*?"

"Taken a shit," Ben explained. "You saw it?"

"Hard to miss," Gloria replied. "I've seen smaller dogs."

"Can you do something about it?"

For the first time in a long time, Gloria felt an unpleasant rush of anger towards her employer. It wasn't so much that she was expected to clean up the mess. She'd long ago accepted that she was the bottom rung of the ladder here, and she'd spent too many years as a nurse to be at all bothered by human waste. It was more the fact Ben had felt the need to ask her. *And* the fact he'd stepped over the same shit that morning and not thought once about sorting it out himself—him or his wife, presumably.

"Millie here?" Gloria asked.

"Upstairs," he said.

"She didn't fancy it?"

No reply. Ben prodded the coffee machine with a fat finger and it started to chug.

"I fixed it," said Ben. "Don't worry."

"Of course," said Gloria. "Well done, you. I'll handle the shit."

These weren't the same words she was thinking, not even close. Ben didn't even look at her again, his gaze lost in the coffee pot.

He looks knackered, she thought, *stressed.* It was no secret the company was having problems, but the weight of it seemed to sit a little heavier on his shoulders every single day. It made her grateful, in a weird way. Because there would always be jobs for people like her, people who weren't afraid to clean up the shit. But dusty old farts like Ben Reed, with their father's money and their red trousers and their crumbling Land Rovers, were slowly going extinct.

"Now, please," he said. "We've got clients at nine."

I know that, she thought as she opened the cupboard beneath the sink and pulled out a carrier bag. *I bloody booked them.*

But it was better to remain silent, and she bit her tongue as she headed back through the building. By the time she'd entered the front office again, Asif was there, hanging his expensive coat on the back of his chair.

"Morning, Glores," he said in his Mancunian accent, flashing her a smile that was so bright it was almost blinding. That was Asif in a nutshell, dashingly handsome and still irritatingly young, but he didn't seem real. He was like one of those plastic dolls that kids played with. "Somebody's heaved a Havana on the step."

"Really?" she said with as much sarcasm as she could muster.

"Yeah? How did you miss it? I needed a stepladder to get over the bloody thing."

"I'll see to it then, shall I?"

"Good lass," said Asif, crashing down onto his chair. "We should get some CCTV or something."

"No room in the budget," called Ben from the kitchen.

"Big spike, then," Asif said with a grin, swinging back and forth on his chair. "Get 'em right up the jacksie."

There are a number of things I could do right now with a big spike, thought Gloria as she walked outside again. Compared to the greenhouse heat of the office, the day was almost chilly, and she shivered as she studied the turd. It seemed even sturdier than it had five minutes ago, and more flies had gathered as the word spread. The sound of them was louder than the passing traffic.

"We meet again, old friend," she said quietly.

"What's that?"

Will Talion was gliding down the street, controlling his wheelchair with the same finesse she always marvelled at. He spun neatly onto the ramp, his arms thick with muscle as he shunted himself upwards. He stopped on the other side of the poop, his eyebrows rising.

"How could that thing even fit inside a human being?"

Gloria shrugged, the bag flapping in her hand.

"There's a public toilet literally right there," Will said, looking across the road to the public car park and its neat row of 24-hour public restrooms. "How lazy do you have to be?"

"Judging by the size of it, I'm guessing he didn't have a lot of time," she said.

"Fair enough. It does look like it might have just clawed its way free. You ever seen *Alien*?"

At this, Gloria laughed. She liked Will, and not just because he'd started here at roughly the same time she had, years ago now. He was younger than her by a good decade, but he had the eyes of somebody much older, somebody who'd experienced life. He was handsome too, a kind of Brad Pittiness to him, if that was a thing. All of that was massively undermined by the fact that he was a massive nerd, his wheelchair covered in stickers from sci-fi shows on the TV, most of which she'd never heard of.

"You want me to do it?" he asked, and she was genuinely grateful to him for even suggesting it. "Or we can do it together. I'll wait at the bottom of the ramp in case it makes a break for it."

She laughed again, and in doing so inhaled a fresh wave of intestinal stench. She gagged, doubling over, finding herself even closer and gagging again. By the time she'd straightened up her eyes were watering so much that Will was a wet mess in front of her. But she could hear him heaving too.

"Oh God," he said. "Don't do that. I can handle a dirty biscuit but I can't do—"

He made a noise like a broken cement mixer.

"I can't do sick, sorry."

She couldn't stop herself gagging again, one hand in front of her mouth. For what had to have been a full twenty seconds the pair of them heaved, making more noise than an overenthusiastic children's percussion orchestra.

"Sorry," said Will eventually.

She stood to the side as he wheeled carefully over the chocolate truncheon, manoeuvring himself through the door. He held it open for Sephie Newton, who was running up the ramp with so much urgency she almost put her foot right in it. Gloria had to step in front of her, waving her arms.

"Jesus Christ," said Sephie. "Did a *person* do that?"

"We're all asking the same thing," Gloria said.

"It's so *solid*," said Sephie, her fingertips to her mouth. "Give me the bag, I'll do it."

And she would, bless her. Sephie was a good girl, barely out of her teens but ready to help with anything.

"Go on in," Gloria said. "I've got it."

Sephie pulled a face and disappeared into the gloom of the hallway, shouting back as she went.

"Thanks, Glore, you're a rock star!"

Yeah, right, I'm Gloria Estefan, she thought. She was pretty sure that no rock star in the history of the world had been asked to scoop up a giant turd from outside the front door of a crappy little insurance firm which paid less than minimum wage, if you counted the overtime.

"Right," she said, addressing the log. "I'll go easy if you do."

She put her hand inside the carrier bag the way she did every time she walked her dog, Taffy—a Chihuahua cross whose deposits were never larger than a treat-sized Toffee Crisp—covered her mouth with her free hand, and bent down for the kill.

It was so much worse than she'd expected it to be. It was like picking up a lump of soft clay, one end detaching itself from the bulk and releasing a fresh wave of hell stench. Gloria groaned, grabbing great handfuls of whatever she could, her eyes full of tears again. The shit still felt warm, like it was fresh.

"Nope," she said, her breakfast once again threatening to punch its way up from her stomach. "Nope, nope, nope."

She stood up, holding the bag away from her like it contained a feral badger. It had serious heft, heavy enough to bludgeon somebody to death with, surely. She was tempted to walk back into the kitchen to find out. Instead, she wiped her eyes on the sleeve of her blazer until the world swam back into focus, seeing a man standing at the bottom of the ramp. He'd appeared so suddenly and so silently that it startled her. His face was that of somebody who'd just watched a grown woman pick up a monstrous human shit.

"Oh," she said. "Sorry."

"No worries," he said, still grimacing. "You missed a bit."

She had, but there was no way she was going back down there.

"Help yourself," she said. The smell of the bagged shit had lined her nose, her mouth, her throat, and she still felt like she was one hiccup away from projectile vomiting. "You need something?"

The man didn't reply immediately. He was her age, she supposed, mid-fifties, his greying hair hidden beneath a navy-blue cap. His beard still held most of its copper colour, though, shaped into a point that sat neatly between two enormous neck tattoos—one of the Virgin Mary praying, the other of what could have been a pair of breasts, although Gloria couldn't be sure. He was wearing overalls that were the same colour as his cap, and when she clocked the white van that idled on the road she realised he was a delivery driver.

"Reed, Barnham and Crabbe?" he asked, watching her every move.

Gloria nodded, still holding the bag at arm's length.

"Got some parcels for you. You okay to take them?"

She glanced at the office, the window full of darkness from this angle. Asif would be sitting right there, probably watching her with that big, shark-like grin on his face. She felt the same ripple of hot anger rise inside her, and she belched acid.

"I'll take them," she said. "Give me a second."

She carried the turd around the side of the building into the little car park at the back. The wheelie bins stood like soldiers against the wall, and she lobbed the shit into the closest one. The thud it made when it hit the bottom seemed to make the ground shake. She sniffed her fingers as she returned to the front door, but the smell of faeces was so deeply ingrained in her nasal passages she couldn't tell if her hands were clean or not.

"Here you go," said the driver. He was holding a little stack of rectangular packages, each one roughly the size of a gift-boxed wine bottle—four in all. They were wrapped in plain brown paper and practically mummified with parcel tape. "Got two more in the van. You manage?"

"They heavy?"

The driver nodded, awkwardly bundling the parcels into her waiting arms, close enough to huff morning breath all over her. She recoiled, tripping on the lip of the ramp and practically tap-dancing to the door. There was nobody there to open it for her, of course, and she almost dropped the boxes as she struggled through.

True to form, Asif grinned up at her from his desk by the window.

"You alright there, Glorie-worie?" he said, and she wondered whether she should have kept hold of the giant shit and made him floss his teeth with it.

She dumped the packages onto Sephie's desk, although there was no sign of her. By the time she'd returned to the door the driver was halfway through, the two remaining boxes in his hands. She took them from him, adding them to the pile. There was a smell coming from them, something sweet and almost almondy.

"Quick sig, please," the man said, pulling a pen from behind his ear and a folded scrap of paper from his pocket. Gloria did as she was asked, passing the pen back and wiping greasy earwax from her palm. The driver lifted a calloused hand in thanks as he made his way out of the door.

"What are these?" said Sephie as she walked into the front room, a cup of tea in each hand. She set them both down on her desk and picked up the closest parcel, turning it around. "Doesn't say who they're for. Doesn't say anything."

Gloria lifted another box, checking the four long sides and the two short ones. There were no labels of any kind. It was about the right kind of heavy for a bottle, she thought. Maybe chocolates, too, given the smell.

"Looks like wine," said Asif from his chair. "Probably from Montaigne for the boat jobs."

"Montaigne sent a hamper," said Gloria. "A really cheap one."

Asif shrugged.

"No idea, then. One of those brews for me, Sephie?"

"No," Sephie replied. "Get your own. This one's Glore's."

Gloria gave her a genuine smile of appreciation and Sephie returned it.

"Six boxes," the young woman said. "Six of us. Doesn't take a genius to work that one out."

"Thank God," said Asif. "Or you'd be in trouble."

Sephie stuck up her middle finger, then passed the parcel she was holding to Gloria.

"You can have this one. I'll take a couple upstairs and check with Ben."

"I'll help," said Gloria, collecting two more boxes.

Sephie made her way up the rickety stairs and Gloria walked into the middle room, a windowless office that was barely big enough for Will's desk and his wheelchair. He glanced up, his serious face illuminated by his computer screen. Gloria dropped the box in front of him and he studied it.

"What's this?"

"No idea. Wine, maybe? Came in the mail. Six of them."

"Thanks," he said. "You opened yours?"

"Saving it," she said. "Nine's a little early for a tipple, even with the day I've had."

He smiled at her.

"You should open it. Christmas is a long way off."

She left the room, the stairs creaking beneath her as she trudged to the upper floor. There were two offices on this floor, a big one at the front where Ben and his wife pretended to work, and Gloria's cramped, mouldering dungeon at the back where she kept the whole operation going. In between was a bathroom that looked like it had been installed when the house had first been built, as if it was being kept as a museum piece. Sephie was coming out of the front office and rolling her eyes.

"Somebody's in an even worse mood than usual," she said quietly before trudging down the steps.

Gloria poked her head through the door to see Ben at his desk, the parcel already forgotten. Millicent Reed sat at her desk on the other side of the room, a vape in her hand even though she knew full well she wasn't supposed to smoke inside. She was an attractive woman in every way except the ones that counted, because her face was always screwed up into such a look of disgust and misery that she instantly filled anyone she spoke to with a strong desire to hurl themselves off a bridge.

"Did you deal with it?" Millie asked, directing the question at the parcel she turned back and forth in her hands. It took Gloria a moment to understand she was talking to her.

"Deal with it?"

"The *thing* on the ramp," Millie went on, still not looking up.

That same bubbling stew of anger was back, and Gloria felt a sudden and unexpected hatred for this stupid little office with its stupid little people. But she didn't speak the thoughts aloud because she was here too, after all, and she was the stupidest and littlest of the lot.

"Yes," she said. "It's in the bin."

"We should get cameras," said Millie, picking at the tape with her pinkie nail. "Get them arrested."

"Can't," said Ben. "No money."

"You know what these are?" asked Gloria, holding up her own box.

"Probably Montaigne," said Ben.

"Montaigne sent a hamper."

"Burley then," the man went on, staring at his screen. "It'll be cheap champagne, I wouldn't touch it with a barge-pole. But go ahead, treat yourself."

Treat myself to the stuff you wouldn't touch with a bargepole, Gloria thought. *Well, fuck you very much, your highness.*

Millie had ripped the paper off her box, but Gloria didn't stop to see what was inside it. She stomped towards her office, shouldering the swollen door open and trying not to breathe the damp air. Towers of box files blocked the passage to her desk the way they'd always done, and she squeezed through them, her back aching by the time she'd twisted herself into her chair.

Taking a moment to centre herself—*calm thoughts, Gloria, it's only 322 days until you go on holiday*—she set the parcel down on the desk and set about opening it. Ben could go to hell. She *would* treat herself, because ever since

Phil had passed, God bless him, she'd not had a single present to open—no kids, of course, no siblings, and it hadn't occurred to the dog to do something nice for her even though she fed and watered it every bloody day. It was about time she had something nice.

The parcel tape was ridiculously tight, but with the help of the nail file she kept in her drawer, she prised it free. The paper came away in a spiral, like orange peel, but the box beneath was as plain as the packaging, the cardboard marked with three words hand-printed in clumsy capital letters.

LUCKY NUMBER ONE.

She worked open the lid, catching a strange and unexpected whiff of the beach—not salt, but that unpleasant, crabby tang you got sometimes when you were close to the water. She tilted the box and jiggled it until its contents scattered over her desk.

Stones, maybe fifty of them of various shapes and sizes and colours and patterns, sitting there in a puddle of sand.

"What on earth?" she said.

The floor of the landing squeaked as somebody walked across it, and Ben appeared in the door.

"Did you book the Aviva folk in for ten?" he asked, his brow folding inwards like origami. "I told you not to talk—"

It was the strangest thing. The light in the hallway seemed to burn like an old-fashioned flash bulb, turning Ben into a perfectly dark silhouette—only for a fraction of a second, barely long enough for Gloria to even notice it, let alone work out what was happening.

Then the fist of God punched its way into her office, a concussive blast that hurled Ben into the desk, that shunted the desk into Gloria, that blew out the window behind her in a hail of glass.

The world roared, a noise of pure, unbearable fury that was the very worst thing Gloria had ever heard.

Then it fell into a silence and a darkness that was a million times worse.

She struggled against it, *railed* against it the way she would have done against a physical attacker, hauling herself up to her feet as reality blinked its way slowly back on. The sound came first, a terrible ringing in her ears, then the light —so bright she couldn't look at it. All she could see was the silhouette of Ben in the door. Only when she tried to walk did she realise she wasn't standing after all, she was still lying down, and it took every ounce of strength she possessed to sit up.

When she turned her head it took the world a moment to catch up, everything swaying wildly. She was downstairs, she realised, in the middle room. And she was wondering if she'd somehow made her own way down here when she looked up and saw that there was no ceiling, just *her* ceiling, the one in her office overhead. Paperwork drifted down like falling snow, some of it burned to still-glowing embers.

There was no sign of Ben, but a Will-shaped lump lay slumped beside his desk, his wheelchair overturned beside him. He was trying to roll himself over, his hands grasping at the air.

"Will?" Gloria said, the word exploding out of her mouth as a cough. There was smoke in the air, a *lot* of it. It billowed down through the hole in the ceiling, great waves of it that clawed into her lungs and made her feel like she was drowning. Past the ringing in her ears she could hear the roar and crackle of a fire. There was something else, too, a sound she'd never heard before.

Somebody was screaming.

It was a proper scream, so laden with grief and pain that

it filled Gloria with horror, made her want to bury herself in the smoke and the debris just so she wouldn't have to listen to it.

There was pain in every single part of her. Not the dull, relentless pain she'd grown used to over the last few years, but something sharper, scarier. All she wanted to do was lie there so the agony didn't get any worse, but she understood that if she did that, she'd never leave this building.

The very last thing she'd have done in life was scoop up another man's dung.

No, she thought. *Not today*.

She didn't think she could stand, so she worked herself onto all fours, crawling towards Will. He craned back, saw her coming.

"What...?" he croaked, and then something else that she couldn't make out.

She kept moving towards him, the little room so much bigger than it should have been. Every time she blinked she could see Ben's silhouette in the doorway overhead, as if it had been seared into her retinas for all time—then she realised there actually *was* somebody in the doorway, a dark, hunched shadow.

"Sephie?" said Gloria. Then she said it again, louder.

The shape stumbled through the door, took form. Sephie was sobbing, her words tangled into wet clumps.

"What happened? What happened?"

Gloria tried to answer and her lungs resisted, the pain in her chest like her heart was cramping. She pointed through the door, hoping Sephie would understand. The young woman nodded, grabbing Gloria and helping her to her feet.

Will had managed to climb back into his chair but he wasn't going anywhere, the floor a mountain range of joists and bricks, debris still raining down on them. The little building shuddered like it might die at any second, burying them alive.

"Help me," Gloria said, the coughs exploding from her.

She stumbled to Will and took hold of one arm, Sephie taking the other. The guy was built like a brick shit house and he was as heavy as one too, but Gloria had spent her life hauling patients between beds—including Phil—and she took the brunt of his weight, taking one painful step at a time until they'd reached the door.

There was no sign of Ben or Asif in the smoke that filled the front room, but she didn't have the strength to call for them. She put one foot in front of the other, Will's arm around her neck making her feel like she was trying to haul a double-decker bus.

There was no ceiling in here, either, just rafters that jutted from the blackened walls like broken ribs. Fires burned freely up there, too bright to look at. There was too much debris in front of the door that led into the corridor, but the window had been reduced to splinters of glass, the street visible beyond. A gust of sweet, fresh air parted the smoke, calling her onwards.

The building groaned as they went, a death rattle. Inch by inch, they crossed the room until they reached the window, lowering Will gently onto the wide sill. He dropped down the other side by himself, commando crawling away from the building.

Asif stood on the pavement, holding one of the parcels in one hand and using the other to film the scene on his phone. Gloria waited for Sephie to climb out of the window, then she followed, the drop further than she'd expected. She walked to the others on legs made of seaweed, legs that gave up on her when she reached the road, depositing her on her backside.

"You okay?" asked Asif, aiming the phone at her.

You fucking left us, she wanted to say, but her smoke-damaged lungs had been switched to core systems only.

Somebody was running over from the newsagent's, more people making their way down the hill. She thought she could hear sirens. Will was propped up against a post box, his chest heaving with every breath.

"Where's Ben?" said Sephie, who had crouched down beside her. "Millie?"

The answer couldn't be good, could it? Their little Victorian building was a pyre, the roof blazing, a pillar of smoke as thick and as high as Nelson's Column. Gloria could feel the heat coming off it from where she sat. She wondered whether she should go back in and try to find them, try to help them. Then she thought about what *they* would have done if they were out here and she was in there, and she stayed where she was.

Besides, the sirens were louder now, and when she glanced up the street she saw a fire engine careening down the hill. It thundered up to them so hard and fast she almost screamed, its brakes hissing as it came to a stop. The firemen were out in a heartbeat, a clamour of noise as they went to work. One of them dropped onto his haunches beside her, the sun right over his shoulder and making her feel like there was an inferno blazing inside her skull.

"Anyone inside?" he asked, his shout reduced to a whisper by the ringing in her ears.

"Two people," she told him. "Ben and Millie Reed."

"What happened?"

She opened her mouth, but nothing came out. She didn't know what had happened. All she could remember was Millie in her office, pulling the tape off her parcel.

"Something exploded," said Sephie. "I don't know what, it just went..."

Boom, Gloria finished silently. *It just went boom.*

"We..." she started, her voice a witch's croak. She cleared her throat. "We had a delivery, six boxes..."

"It wasn't them, was it?" said Sephie. "It can't have been."

"What did they look like?" asked the fireman.

Gloria struggled to find the words before realising she didn't need to. Asif was standing right there, one of the parcels clenched in his fingers. She had no idea why he was holding it, but it stung more than a little that he'd taken *that* thing with him and left them behind to burn.

"He's got one," said Gloria, pointing. "Right there."

Asif seemed to remember what he held in his hand. His eyes grew wide, and he hurled it to the ground.

"No!" yelled the fireman, and the rush of adrenaline that blazed through Gloria's body was so fierce it felt like another explosion. Asif staggered away, backing into the fire engine.

"What the fuck is it?" he said. "A *bomb*?"

"Everyone clear the street," the fireman was shouting. "Get back, all of you."

Gloria wasn't going to argue with that. Sephie helped her up and they limped towards Will, who was being tended to by the man who ran the kebab shop on the corner.

She looked back only once, seeing the parcel on the ground. Asif must have taken the top layer of paper off because she could make out the same big, blocky letters written there, almost exactly the same as her own.

LUCKY NUMBER FOUR.

"Hey," yelled the fireman. "You know where these came from?"

"A driver dropped them off," Gloria shouted back. "Just this morning."

"You know what it means?" he went on. "Lucky Number Four?"

She shook her head and turned her back on him, every part of her body aching as she walked up the hill. The air was still full of smoke, gunshots exploding inside the building as the fire chewed its way through the roof. She couldn't remember a time when the sky had ever been so blue, when the birds had sung quite so loud, when every single thing she looked at seemed to shine with utter clarity —like she'd been watching TV on her nan's old set her whole life and suddenly upgraded to 8K.

She was lucky, she knew, and she said it out loud.

"Lucky. Lucky. Lucky."

"What's that?" asked Sephie.

Gloria didn't answer, she just let her heavy body collapse onto a wooden bench outside a nightclub, putting her head into her smoke-scented hands. She thought about Millie opening that parcel. She thought about Ben, his silhouette still seared into her retinas, right there every time she blinked. She tried to feel some kind of sadness for them and realised she couldn't feel anything at all.

Lucky, she thought again, as Sephie slumped down beside her. *Lucky for some.*

But not for everyone.

CHAPTER ONE

"You do realise they've all seen him before, right, Pete?" said Allie Porter from where she sat in the driver's seat of her Ford Fiesta.

DI Peter Porter stood at the open rear door doing his best to unclip the belt of the car seat. Squirming beneath him in a fit of giggles and dribble was Robert 'Bobby' Porter. It was the baby's four-month birthday, and he seemed to be celebrating by trying to fit his entire fist into his mouth. He gazed up at his dad with those enormous blue eyes, chattering excitedly through his chubby fingers. The unreality of it, the joy of it, the sheer terror of it, seemed to kick Porter right in the solar plexus—the way it did at least a hundred times a day.

Holy shit, we had a baby.

He squeezed the buckle but it wouldn't release, the clip notoriously stubborn. He switched to his other hand, then tried them both together, grunting with frustration.

"Just leave him here," said Allie. "Nobody wants to see the baby anymore. They've had enough of him."

"How could anyone ever have enough of this little guy?"

said Porter, grabbing the strap and giving it a good tug in the hope he might be able to rip it open. The car seat wobbled and Bobby's laughter grew. It was addictive, and Porter found himself laughing alongside his son.

My son, he thought, and that same cold wash of adrenaline coursed through him. *Holy shit.*

It had taken him a while to work out what that feeling was. Love, the purest kind, a kind he'd never felt before because it was so different to the love he felt for Allie, for his parents, or for anyone else. It was a painful kind of love, one that left him reeling.

Allie grunted her frustration, reaching through the gap between the seats and unclipping the belt with a gentle twist of her fingers.

"How do you do that?" Porter asked.

"They're designed not to be opened by babies," she replied, and left it at that.

Porter wiggled his fingers under his child and hefted him gently out of the car. He clutched him to his chest, marvelling at the solid bulk of him, at the impossible heat that seemed to pour off him.

Bobby fussed in his rainbow all-in-one, not sure about leaving the car, less sure about the blinding early morning sun, still not quite sure about the giant man who held him. He was his mother's son, for sure. He tolerated Porter for cuddles and bedtime lullabies and walks around the park, but he didn't like to be away from Allie for any amount of time.

"Just for five minutes," said Porter. "Just to say hi. They love him. You can wait here if you like."

"A five-minute break," Allie said, stifling a yawn with the back of her hand. "Lucky me."

Porter carried the baby through the car park, which was

filling fast as the morning shift rolled in. He had to keep hefting Bobby up, he was so heavy, cradling him in an arm that was already trembling. A PC held the door open for him and he squeezed inside, heading for the Major Investigation Team's offices. By the time he'd carefully shouldered his way through the door, Bobby was starting to squirm, making the little baby-panda whines he used when he missed his mum.

"You're alright," Porter whispered, hoisting him up and offering his free hand. Bobby grabbed his finger in his clammy fist—a grip that felt far too strong for a baby—pulling it towards his mouth. "No," Porter told him. "Daddy's not for eating."

Bobby's bottom lip trembled.

"Sorry," he said. "Sorry, you can eat me if you like."

"I wouldn't if I were you," came a voice from the bullpen. PC Duke was standing beside the door to Clare's office, one of only three coppers in the enormous space. He was holding something in his hand, something wrapped in tin foil. He smiled through his dark, bushy beard. "You don't know where he's been."

Porter would have replied, but he was distracted by the fact that all of the desks and chairs had been pushed to the sides of the bullpen, leaving an empty space in the middle of the room.

"Somebody playing cricket in here?" he asked as he made his way towards Duke.

"Something like that, sir," Duke said, still smiling. "How's my little namesake doing?"

Porter sighed, wishing for the millionth time that he hadn't used Aaron for the baby's middle name. It wasn't that the big PC didn't deserve it—he'd saved Porter's life in the Knuckle Bones case, and it hadn't been the first time—

it was more that he mentioned it every single time Porter saw him. Duke tickled Bobby's bare foot with his little finger.

"How's little Bobby Aaron?" he said in a ridiculously high-pitched voice. "How's my cutesy-wutsey wiggly babykins?"

"Dear God," muttered Porter, pulling a face. "Where is everyone?"

"Kate's in with the boss, sir," said Duke, nodding to Clare's open door. "Nobody else has shown up yet."

"What have you got there?" Porter asked, looking at the foil-wrapped package in Duke's hand. It smelled almost like cake.

"Nothing, sir," said Duke, pulling it away. "It's not for you."

He tickled the baby's foot a little more with his free hand, Bobby's giggles like chuckling birdsong.

"Haven't you got work to be getting on with, Constable?" Porter asked, pulling Bobby away from him for a reason he couldn't quite put his finger on.

"I'm on the Extreme Crime Task Force now, sir," he replied with a shrug. "We haven't had any extreme crime this morning."

"Apart from your face," Porter said beneath his breath.

"What, sir?"

"Nothing. Go put the kettle on, will you?"

He pushed past Duke before the PC could answer and peered into Clare's office. The Superintendent sat at his desk with a face like a constipated gargoyle. Savage stood next to him, both of them studying something in her hand. They turned together when they heard Bobby coo.

"Morning, sir," said Savage, walking over. "And Bobby! I haven't seen you for two whole days. I missed you."

She opened her arms and Porter passed the baby to her, shaking some of the discomfort from his biceps.

"How has he got so heavy?" she asked.

"Takes after his dad," said Duke from the door.

"Kettle," Porter ordered, glaring at him.

"Actually, I was hoping to give you something, Superintendent."

Clare frowned.

"What are you planning on giving me, Duke? A headache?"

"No, sir," said Duke, stepping into the room. He held out the object wrapped in foil, and when Clare didn't take it, he dropped it onto the Super's desk. "It's for you. I made it."

"You made it?" said Clare.

"To say thanks for letting me on the Task Force," said Duke.

"He was up all night doing it," said Savage, jiggling Bobby. "This was the third attempt."

Clare looked horrified. Duke peeled up a corner of the foil, revealing a slab of pale sponge cake flecked with white chunks. The smell of it was delicious, and Porter licked his lips, moving in.

"No, sir," said Duke, like he was talking to a dog. "Bad Porter. Not for you."

"You're about three words away from a beating," Porter said.

"What is it?" asked Clare, gurning.

"It's a Bounty, sir," said Duke.

"I can assure you it's not."

"A Bounty cake. A homemade one. I call it my Bounty Surprise."

"I don't like surprises."

"I made it, sir. At home. It's coconut cake with a coconut cream centre, sprinkled with coconut flakes and some coconut oil. I know you like coconut, sir. I wanted to do something special. To say thanks. With coconuts."

Clare stared at the cake a little longer.

"You can eat it, sir," said Duke, struggling. "It's a cake."

The Super prodded the cake the way you might prod roadkill to see if it was still alive, releasing the sickly sweet aroma of coconut. It did smell just like a Bounty, Porter thought with some irritation.

"I'll eat it later," said Clare, folding the foil around the cake and dropping it into the pocket of his suit jacket.

"You definitely will?" asked Duke. "Because I made it. For you."

The atmosphere in the office had grown decidedly awkward, but fortunately Bobby was cooing gently.

"You're such a sweetie," said Savage, tickling the baby's chin. "How's he sleeping? Like a baby?"

"Yeah," said Porter, the mere thought of last night making him yawn so hard his jaw cracked. "If by 'like a baby' you mean he woke up seven times, shit himself then cried a lot. Allie does most of it, though. I'm on the sofa."

"Haven't you got like three spare rooms in your house?"

Porter shrugged. Clare was out of his chair and shambling towards the baby like he meant to eat it. Bobby watched warily, his little brow concertinaing with uncertainty.

"Robert Aaron *Colin* Porter," said Clare. "It's good to see him looking so healthy."

"They didn't call him Colin, sir," said Savage, but Clare ignored her, holding his hands out and beckoning with his fingers.

"Come on, Detective, my turn. Little Colin wants a tossing cuddle."

"So wrong," said Savage, passing the baby over.

Clare bounced Bobby in his arms like he was preparing for some kind of Highland caber toss. The baby was not enjoying it—the same way Bobby never seemed to enjoy being manhandled by the Superintendent. His face crumpled and he started to sob, holding his hands out not to Porter but to Savage.

"Is that mean old Duke scaring you with his big beard and his awful cake?" Clare said, bouncing the kid even harder. "I'll fire him. Oh yes, I will."

"I didn't do anything, sir," said Duke. "I don't think he likes y—"

"Nasty Duke," Clare went on. "Scaring little babies with his horrible hairy face. Oh yes he does."

Bobby's sobs were now screams, his face beetroot red and slick with sweat.

"I'll take him, sir," Porter said, reaching for his son. "He just doesn't like being away from his mum." He shrugged. "She has boobs."

"To be fair, sir," said Duke, "so do you."

Porter jabbed a finger at him.

"Put the kettle on, Constable, or you're going to be wearing it."

Duke lifted his hands in surrender and retreated. Bobby's cries were almost hysterical now, the baby trying to twist himself out of Clare's hands. Porter prised him away and held him to his chest, feeling the strength of the kid as he fought to get free. His screams were so loud they were physically painful. Clare was shaking his head with disapproval.

"You've made him cry, Porter," he said.

"I didn't—"

"Get him back to his mother, man. I can't hear myself think."

He ushered Porter and Savage out of his office and slammed the door shut with such force that the rising pitch of Bobby's cries could have shattered windows. Savage was speaking, but Porter couldn't hear a word she was saying.

"Hang on," he said, making his way back to the corridor, the cooler air and the movement doing a little to quiet Bobby. "You're alright," he told the baby as he crossed the lobby and walked into the car park. "You're okay, buddy."

He was surprised to see Allie standing right outside the main doors, her arms folded over her chest, her foot tapping. She looked like she was fretting, and she clicked her fingers impatiently when Porter appeared. He passed the baby to her, the last of Bobby's cries whimpering into silence as she held him. His little face was plastered with tears and snot, his breaths hitching.

"What did you do to him, Pete?" she said.

"It wasn't me. Bloody Clare held him. Again."

"Poor little thing," she said. "I could hear him crying all the way out here."

Porter doubted that was true, but he also knew that Allie possessed the same sixth sense all mothers had when it came to their children. She'd have heard Bobby crying even if he'd been in a locked room on the other side of the world.

He bent down and kissed the baby on his sweaty forehead.

"Sorry, mate. I should have left you in the car."

He gave Allie a kiss on her forehead too, although she turned her head away like she almost always did.

"You gonna be okay?" he asked her.

"We'll be great," she said, heading back towards the car. "We always are."

Porter watched them go, feeling the same way he always did when his child wasn't with him—imagining the vast, churning, grinding machine that was life, and all the ways it could hurt their little boy if he wasn't there to watch over him. It took every ounce of restraint he possessed not to run after them, to climb back into the car and lock the doors. Robbie had told him once that having a child was like pulling yourself inside out, everything hurt, all the time. He hadn't got it then, but he understood it now. It was love, the simplest, rawest, oldest kind you could get.

He watched Allie buckle Bobby into his seat, watched her climb behind the wheel and start the engine.

But he couldn't face watching them drive away.

With a sigh that came from the very heart of him, he walked back inside.

CHAPTER TWO

DCI KETT CAUGHT UP TO PORTER AS HE WAS CROSSING the lobby, calling his name three times before the DI turned around.

"You okay, Pete?" he asked, opening the door that led into the warren of HQ. "Away with the fairies?"

"Sorry, sir," Porter said, walking through. He waggled a finger in his ear. "Bobby was screaming so loud I think I've gone deaf."

"Yeah, I heard him. He okay?"

"Clare held him," said Porter, and Kett grimaced.

"Did he do the thing where he looked like he was going to throw him through the window?"

Porter nodded.

"You'd think after having six kids of his own he'd know how to hold a baby."

"You'd think," Porter said as they reached the bullpen. "You know what all this is about, sir?"

Kett walked into the open-plan office to see that someone had rearranged the furniture. All the desks had been lined up around the walls, leaving a cavernous space in the centre. Duke was on his knees in the middle of the room marking out lines with masking tape, Savage perched against her desk watching him work.

"I have absolutely no idea," Kett said, mystified. "Kate, what on earth is going on?"

Before she had a chance to answer, Clare's office door swung open and the Superintendent lurched out of it.

"I'll tell you what's going on," he said, as if he'd been waiting for his cue. "You lot are supposed to be the Extreme Crime Task Force, is that correct?"

Nobody answered him, in case it was a trap.

"The elite unit inside the Norfolk Constabulary, yes?" Clare went on, undeterred.

Again, the question was met by silence. Kett met Porter's eye and he knew they were thinking the same thing.

Brace yourself.

"Elite," said Clare, pointing his finger at Porter, then swinging it towards Kett. "Elite my arse. Look at yourselves, you're a disgrace."

"*What*, sir?" spluttered Kett.

"We've got one officer who looks like he needs a Zimmer frame to make it from the car park to his desk."

"Is he talking about me?" Kett asked Porter.

"Yes, Robbie, I am talking about you. You walk around like the Tin Man from Oz after he's had a hernia removed."

"Oddly specific, sir," muttered Kett, watching Clare do a reasonably good impersonation of him shambling around the office. "I have been through some stuff," he added as a defence. "You know, being stabbed and shot and all that."

"No excuse," Clare said. "I've been shot too, remember? You don't see me slouching about. I have a tossing regime, Detective."

"I really don't want to know, sir," said Kett.

"A tossing *exercise* regime, it keeps me fit, keeps me healthy, keeps me regular."

"Oh Christ," said Kett.

"And as for you, Pete," Clare said, eyeballing Porter. "I've ignored it for long enough."

"Ignored what, sir?" said Porter, sucking in his stomach. It didn't do a lot of good, the bulge still visible over his waistband.

"Ignored this," said Clare, waving both arms at the DI. "You've swollen up like that girl from *Charlie and the Chocolate Factory*. You look like a giant blueberry. You look like you've eaten a Fiat Panda, and it's just sitting there inside you, slowly digesting. I'm worried other officers are going to start orbiting around you because of your gravitational pull."

Duke was trying not to laugh, but his wheezing chuckles were the loudest thing in the room.

"How much weight have you put on in the last year, Pete?" Clare asked.

Porter gasped, frantically doing up his suit jacket.

"You can't ask that, sir," said Savage.

"I bloody well can," said Clare. "And you can't hide it under that jacket, Pete. You'd need a bloody tent to cover it up."

Porter gasped again. Duke was positively howling now.

"Go easy, sir," said Kett. "He's just had a baby."

"He looks like he's *having* a baby," said Clare. "I'd guess he's about nine months in. And you haven't just had a baby, Porter, your *wife* has. I don't know what's going on with you, but this ends here. No more vanishing into the broom cupboard to munch your way through a six-pack of Snickers."

Porter gasped for a third time.

"I've been watching you, Porter," said Clare. "And I found the wrappers in your desk. The snacks have to stop, and no more driving to work."

"But—"

"You live over the road, Porter. I can see your house from the windows on the top floor. You can bloody walk here. And from tomorrow, we're starting every single day with a bit of exercise."

Kett groaned.

"Which is what we're doing this morning," the Super said. "I need a way to gauge your fitness levels, so we're going to do a *bleep* test."

"A bleep test?" said Kett.

"Yes, so called because it will *bleep* you the fuck up," said Clare.

"That doesn't make any—"

"Duke here will explain the rules. He's going to be your new physical trainer."

"He's going to be *what*?" said Porter, shaking his head. "No way, sir, he's no fitter than I am."

"Porter, he's basically Arnold Schwarzenegger," said Clare. "You're one of the Krankies. The little one."

Porter couldn't even manage a gasp this time, his mouth just hung open. Duke was grinning, his chest puffed out.

"You're just letting him off because he made you a cake," said Porter.

"A cake?" asked Kett.

"Took him all night," added Savage.

"Over to you, Duke," said Clare.

"Right," said the PC. "Listen carefully. You line up at one end of the room and when you hear the bleep, you start running."

"Gonna run my boot up your arsehole," muttered Porter.

"Porter!" snapped Clare. "He's in charge, you hear? Those are my orders."

"And you have to reach the second line before you hear the next bleep, okay?" Duke went on. "Then start running back. The bleeps get closer together every time, so you have to speed up as you go."

Porter was shooting daggers at the big PC.

"There are twenty stages, with a set number of shuttles in each round. The number of times you can make it to the next bleep in time is your score. I did it earlier, and I reached Level 19 with a score of 8. That's pretty good."

"That's pretty good," mimicked Porter in a croaky falsetto.

"Kate beat me, though," Duke said, giving her a smile. "She's a lot faster than I am. Hard to run with all this muscle, I guess."

"Hard to run when your head's so big," said Porter.

"Enough!" said Clare. "Porter, I want you to give it a go."

"I don't have any trainers, sir."

"Bare feet, then," said Clare. "Like I said, no more excuses."

"But—"

"Get your toss on!" Clare roared, making everyone jump.

The Super's phone was ringing, and he marched into his office.

"I don't have to do this, do I?" Kett asked.

"Afraid so, sir," said Duke. "But Porter's up first."

The DI looked like he was about to cry.

"Just do your best, sir," said Duke. "I'm here with you. We'll get you into shape."

"I'm already in shape, Constable," growled Porter.

"Yeah, sir, you're *round*. I mean a better shape."

"You little—"

Porter threw himself at Duke, the PC darting backwards out of his reach.

"That's it, sir," he said, avoiding another lunge. "Get some speed up, get your heart racing."

Porter tried again but Savage got between them, one hand planted on Porter's chest.

"Enough," she said. "It'll be good for all of us to get a little fitter. Just give it a go, sir. It can't hurt."

"It'll hurt *him* alright," said Porter, standing down and jutting his chin at Duke. He was out of breath already, and a sad look settled on his face. "Fine," he said. "I'll do it."

"Good man," said Duke. "I'll set it up."

"Don't," said Clare, marching out of his office. "We need to go. There's been an explosion."

"Thank God," said Porter.

"An explosion, sir?" said Savage. "Where?"

"Bottom of Prince of Wales. It's just happened, that's all I know. We'll find out on the way."

He opened the door for them, giving Porter one more disapproving look.

"And Pete, I want you to jog to the car park."

"But—"

"Go!"

CHAPTER THREE

IT WAS ONE OF THE FIRST THINGS YOU LEARNED WHEN you joined Norfolk Constabulary: Prince of Wales Road was a battleground, especially at the weekends when the pubs and clubs emptied out.

But as Savage drove the IRV down the hill and the bottom of the street came into view, Kett realised it had become an actual war zone.

The first thing he saw was the tower of smoke rising from a burning building, polluting the crisp, blue morning sky. Two fire engines blocked the road, their hoses forming rainbows in the shimmering air. There was no sign of an ambulance yet but it was clear that there was walking wounded. A crowd had formed further up the street, held there by a couple of constables and a firefighter. One man around Kett's age sat propped against a shopfront, his face streaked with dirt and blood. Two women, one younger, one older, sat on a wooden bench, both of them caked in soot and smoke.

"Jesus," said Savage.

"What happened?" Duke asked from the back. "Gas leak, maybe?"

There was no way past the fire engines so Savage pulled up behind them, cutting the engine. Kett got out, seeing Clare's enormous Mercedes glide to a halt in their wake. Porter stared miserably through the windscreen—Clare had made him ride with him so he wouldn't be tempted to snack on the way. They both clambered out, their heads lifting as they followed the trail of smoke into the sky.

"You know what happened?" Kett asked.

Clare didn't answer. People were still evacuating the buildings along Prince of Wales Road, half of them taking photos and videos on their phones. Two more constables were walking up the hill. The first, an older man, took off his hat as he neared. He was sweating buckets, and it was no surprise. Kett could feel the force of the fire even from where they were standing. The roar of it filled the street, firework cracks setting his nerves on edge.

"Prescott," said Clare with a nod of welcome. "What happened?"

"Not a hundred percent sure, sir," said the PC. "Just got here. Smokies are too busy to talk but they think it was a bomb."

"A bomb?" said Kett.

PC Prescott nodded, holding his hat against his chest like he was at a funeral.

"That's all I know, sir. They think there are still people inside, but..."

He didn't need to finish. The building was a shell, the street decorated with shards of glass and chunks of masonry. If it had been a bomb, it had gone off with some force.

"What is this place?" asked Clare.

There was no sign anymore, the front of the building

blackened beyond repair. It had been a house at some point, one of the older buildings along the street that had survived a century of development. It was sandwiched between two much more modern buildings, both of which were in danger of going up with it.

"Insurance place, I think," said Savage. "Can't remember the name, but I'm pretty sure it was an office."

"How do you remember that, Encyclopaedia Jones?" asked Porter. She shrugged, then clicked her fingers.

"Had crab in the name," she said. "I'm sure of it."

"Reed, Barnham and Crabbe," said Duke, looking at his phone. "It's an insurance broker."

The building let out a deep, almost subsonic groan as the roof collapsed. A wave of smoke and dust and blistering heat billowed into the street, hiding the fire engines from view. Kett put his sleeve to his mouth as the stench of it reached him, his eyes watering. They all moved back a few feet as the cloud billowed outwards, borne on a breeze that blew up from the river.

"Why would somebody bomb an insurance broker?" asked Porter, coughing hard.

A shape emerged from the cloud, one of the firefighters. He removed his helmet as he ran up to them, and Kett recognised the angular face and shaved head of Angus Croll.

"You fellas might want to back off," he said, his voice like a man who'd smoked a hundred cigarettes a day since he was a kid. "We don't know what we've got in there."

"It was a bomb?" asked Clare. Croll glanced over his shoulder.

"Don't know for sure yet, but it seems like it. Detonated in the front upstairs room about thirty minutes ago. There's no gas feed into this building, all electric. No sign of anything else that might have gone off, and the pattern of debris and the spread of the fire tells me this was something small but very powerful. Everything about this says IED."

He shook his head.

"Thought I'd seen the last of them when I was in Iraq."

"Anything we can do to help?"

"No. Just stay back. Witness told us there were six packages delivered. We think the bomb might have been in one, that leaves five others."

"Christ," said Clare. "Where's the witness?"

"Over there," said Croll, nodding up the street. "The two women and the guy."

He pulled on his helmet and jogged back. The cloud had started to dissipate as the smokies won their battle with the fire. But that wouldn't mean a thing, Kett knew, if there were more explosives. If one IED could take out a building, five could demolish half the street.

"This doesn't make any sense," he said.

"Not yet," said Clare. "You and Porter go talk to our witnesses. Savage, with me. Duke, I need you on crowd control. Get those cars moving."

"Traffic duty?" said Duke. "I thought I was on the Task For—"

"Now," said Clare. There was a calmness to his voice that was almost scarier than when he was yelling.

Duke nodded, bounding along the street to where a tail of traffic stretched into the city. Kett followed Porter up the hill. It wasn't exactly steep, but thanks to the smoke he was breathing hard by the time they reached the crowd. So was Porter, and the pair of them shared a sheepish look as they struggled for air.

"Maybe he's not wrong about us getting in shape, eh, sir?" said Porter.

"Yeah, maybe."

Kett nodded to the constables who stood like bouncers in front of the crowd. He pulled out his warrant card and held it up.

"Okay, listen up," he shouted, loud enough to be heard at the back. "My name is DCI Robert Kett, with the Norfolk Police. I need to speak with anyone who saw what happened this morning, anyone who was inside the building. Everyone else, get lost, unless you need medical assistance."

It was pretty obvious who'd been inside the building. The three people he'd spotted when they'd driven past a moment ago all looked at him, the man raising a hand in the air from where he'd collapsed against the shop window. Everybody else started to drift away and Porter walked over to help the stragglers.

Kett approached the two women first. They sat huddled together on the bench, both of them shivering. One was in her fifties, dressed in a smart, dark skirt suit, her hair plastered over her face and her makeup so thick that Kett could see it beneath the soot. The other was maybe thirty years her junior, and blood still ran freely from her nose. He ducked onto his haunches in front of them.

"Are you okay?" he asked, knowing full well how ridiculous he sounded. "There's an ambulance on its way. We can help you, if you're hurt. My name's Robbie. Can you tell me yours?"

The older woman cocked her head.

"What?"

"You'll have to speak up," said the other woman. "Can't hear anything over the ringing."

"Sorry," he said, raising his voice to a shout. "My name's Robbie. Who are you?"

"Sephie," said the younger woman. "This is Gloria."

"Easterman," said the older woman. "Not Gloria Estefan, if you were wondering."

He wasn't, but he offered a small smile at the attempt at humour.

"You work in the building?"

They both nodded. The dirt that covered Gloria's face was streaked with rivulets, and she was crying again now. She tried to cover it with her hands and Kett saw that one of her nails had been torn away.

"You're okay," he said. "You're safe. Are either of you injured? Seriously, I mean?"

They both shook their heads, although Sephie had to pinch her nose to stop the blood from flowing.

"Gave 'em a look over," said the nearest constable. "Nothing life-threatening. Paramedics must be on holiday."

"Are they dead?" asked Gloria, peeking through her fingers.

"Who?"

"Ben and Millie. Reed. They're married. They were still inside. They... I don't know if..."

She slapped her hands onto her knees.

"Oh, God."

"I don't know," said Kett. "But those guys are the best. They're doing everything they can to get them out."

It didn't seem to give her much relief. Kett glanced at the man who sat against the shop a dozen yards away.

"Was he with you?" he asked. "You think he could come over?"

Sephie shook her head.

"He can't walk."

"Because of the explosion?" said Kett.

"No, he's always been in a wheelchair," she said. "I

mean, not now, obviously, he had to leave it behind. He can't walk."

"How did he get out?"

"We carried him," said Sephie. "Me and Glore. That fucker, Asif, just bolted. Coward."

"Asif? Where is he now?"

She shrugged.

"Let's start at the beginning then," he said. "If you're okay to talk."

Neither of them replied, and he took that as a sign to carry on.

"You were inside the building when the explosion happened."

The women both nodded, Gloria screwing up her face in pain. She put a hand to her neck.

"It's my fault," she said. "I took them in, I..."

"The packages?" Kett asked, and she nodded so hard her hair fell over her face. "There were six of them?"

"Yeah, but no labels," she said. "I figured there's six people in the office, six boxes. I thought they were gifts."

"We get sent stuff all the time," said Sephie. "Because we do a lot of corporate jobs."

"Looked like wine," Gloria went on. "But I opened mine and..."

Her face creased up like she couldn't quite remember. Kett gave her all the time she needed.

"Stones," she said. "It was full of stones."

"Stones?" said Sephie. Gloria nodded, still confused.

"They were from the beach, I could smell it. I..."

"I didn't open mine," said Sephie, almost apologetically. "Don't drink wine, was going to take it home for..."

She stopped, her eyes growing wide.

"I was going to take it home for my sister," she said. "God, her kids, it could have..."

"But it didn't," said Robbie. "They're okay. Can you tell me who was in the building? You two, the guy over there."

"Will," said Gloria.

"Right, Will. Asif was there, and Ben and Millie? Anyone else?"

"No," said Sephie.

"Those are the only people who work in the office?"

"Used to be seven," said Gloria, sniffing. "Justin was with us until last week. Ben fired him."

"You know why?"

"Bit of a livewire, big temper."

"Justin who?"

"Hope," said Sephie.

"You know where he lives?"

"It's on my computer," said Gloria. "I'll check for you when..."

And she seemed to remember the fact that her computer was now gone, along with the rest of her office.

"He lives in the city somewhere," said Sephie. "Asked me out once and told me. It's not a house, it's like a flat or something. I can't remember."

Kett could hear the faintest trace of a siren, and he hoped it was the ambulance. His knees were aching so he stood straight, his joints cracking louder than the burning building. Porter was making his way back over, his eyes on the newsagent's across the road as if he was planning to make a mad dash for a Twix. He caught Kett's eye, a guilty look flashing across his face.

"Were there labels on the parcels? A name? A delivery note? Anything?" Kett asked the women.

"Nothing," said Gloria. "It was weird. They were just wrapped in plain brown paper."

"What about the driver?"

"Just a delivery guy. He, uh…" Her eyes searched the sky. "He had tattoos on his neck. A Virgin Mary, maybe, and… I remember thinking he had… *breasts*."

"The driver had breasts?" asked Kett.

"No, his tattoo, on his neck. They looked like breasts."

"My age? Younger? What kind of van was it?"

"Your age, I guess?" said Gloria. "Early fifties?"

"I'm 45," said Kett, somewhat defensively.

"*Really*?" said Sephie.

"You've had a hard life," said Gloria with genuine sympathy.

"Right," Kett said. "Can you walk me through what happened after the parcels arrived?"

Gloria shrugged. Sephie wiped her hand across her face, smearing blood from her nose to her ear. She seemed to notice it for the first time.

"Shit," she said.

"Paramedics are almost here," said Kett, and when he looked up he was relieved it wasn't a lie. The ambulance was doing its best to get through the traffic, Duke looking like he was trying to physically push the cars out of its way. "You're going to be okay. But anything you can tell me now could really help."

"Glore put the packages down on my desk," said Sephie. "I took two up to Ben and Millie. They're in the front office."

"Upstairs?" said Kett, and she nodded. "They think that's where the explosion happened. You were downstairs when it went off?"

"I was," said Sephie. "Just got down the stairs, was in the

kitchen at the back and... felt like somebody picked the whole street up and shook it. Ceiling came down, almost brained me, and I..."

Her eyes roved in their sockets so wildly that Kett thought she was about to start fitting.

"Back door was locked, so I went through the front, saw Glore and Will in the middle room and we helped each other out."

"You were downstairs too?" Kett asked Gloria.

"No, I was *upstairs*. My office is at the back. I was sitting there and Ben was at my door. He was asking me something and..."

She swallowed hard.

"I can still see him. When I blink. I can still see him right there, burned into me. It was so bright. I don't know what happened. I think the floor must have given way because I ended up in Will's office."

The ambulance had cleared the jam and its engine roared as it gunned its way towards them. Porter flagged it down and it bumped onto the kerb, the siren dying. The paramedics were out in a flash, one heading towards Kett, the other veering in the direction of the man who sat by the shop.

"I'm sorry," said Kett. "I really am, but is there anything else you can tell me?"

The paramedic, a young woman, ducked down beside Gloria.

"Sorry," she said. "We've got about three ambulances for the whole city at the moment. It's a nightmare. What happened?"

"An explosion," said Kett.

"A bomb," added Gloria. "It was a bomb, I know it. You say it happened upstairs? In Ben's office?"

Kett nodded.

"He was talking to me, but Millie was opening her package right before the bomb went off. I saw her. She was tearing off the wrapper. It was hers, I know it. She's... she has to be, doesn't she?"

Dead, thought Kett, but he didn't reply.

"Can we finish this later?" asked the paramedic. "We could really do with getting you both to the hospital."

She'd moved over to Sephie, and she looked concerned.

"You okay to walk?"

Sephie nodded, and Gloria burst into tears again. She was holding the younger woman's hand in both of hers.

"Can either of you think why you'd be a target?" asked Kett. "You or the company. Anything at all. A grudge, anything like that?"

"We sell insurance," said Gloria. "There's no reason."

"Go get yourselves sorted," said Kett. "I'll be in touch."

He backed off, glancing at the fire to see that the last of the flames had been doused. He could hear shouts from inside as the firefighters searched the ruins.

"Mr, uh..."

Kett turned back. Gloria was on her feet, looking more than a little unsteady—partly to do with the fact that she was only wearing one shoe.

"When I opened my parcel, there was something written on the box inside. Lucky Number One."

"Lucky Number One?" Kett echoed. "That was it?"

"Just that. I saw Asif's as well, though. His said Lucky Number Four."

"You know what it means?"

She shook her head.

"Lucky," Kett said. "Thanks."

He watched the women limp towards the ambulance,

then he went to join the second paramedic. He'd wheeled a stretcher over and Porter was helping him lift the man called Will onto it. Will was a big guy, his arms thick with muscle, and the paramedic was struggling.

"Need a hand?" Kett asked, but they managed to ease him onto the stretcher.

Will reached down and lifted both of his legs into place. Then, incredibly, a weak smile appeared beneath the crust of blood and filth on his face.

"Thanks," he said to the paramedic. "Sorry."

"You're doing great," the paramedic replied.

"Will?" Kett asked, and the guy nodded. "You okay?"

"I've been better," he said. "Head feels like there's a buzz saw in it. You found Ben yet? Millie?"

"Not yet," said Kett. "Before you go, can I ask you a question?"

"It'll have to be quick," said the paramedic. "Very quick."

"Just one, I promise. Did you take one of the parcels that got delivered this morning?"

Will nodded.

"Did you open it?"

"That's two questions, pal," said the paramedic, wheeling the stretcher across the pavement. Will craned his head back as he went and nodded.

"What did it say?" Kett shouted.

"Lucky Number Three," said Will. "It was full of rocks. Go figure."

CHAPTER FOUR

It was Monday morning, and Prince of Wales Road had a hangover. The businesses were almost all pubs, clubs or kebab shops and they were shut up tight, as if they were trying to catch up on some sleep. There were security cameras everywhere, some pointing over the road at the office, which still belched smoke. But no matter how hard DC Savage knocked on the doors—and she knocked *hard*—nobody answered.

"Come on," she muttered as she reached the junction where the road joined with Rose Lane. Directly across a triangular green was a school, but there was no CCTV in sight. On her right was a small row of shops, the nearest of which was a kebab place that looked like it hadn't been opened in decades. Next to that was a mobile phone shop that seemed equally deserted. This one, at least, had a little camera pointing towards the street. The sign above the door said Cell Blasters, which made absolutely no sense.

Savage followed the line of the camera to where the fire engines sat. It would have had a clear line of sight to the front door of Reed, Barnham and Crabbe.

If it worked, of course.

"Feeling lucky?" she asked herself as she approached.

The door was so filthy she couldn't see through it, even when she cupped her hand to the glass. Five J2O bottles were lined up on the step, a sixth on its side and at least thirty cigarette butts along for the ride. She hammered on the frame, then stood back.

"Police!" she hollered. "Open up."

If anyone answered her, it was drowned out by a paramedic rapid response car that was making its way up from the direction of the river. It parked in front of the fire engines, the siren snapping off. Savage walked along the narrow front of the shop, seeing a display of old phones in a glass case and a couple of laptops that looked like they ran on steam power. She thumped her fist on the window three times.

"Police!" she called again.

Something moved inside, a flash of shadow behind the sun-drenched glass. It was heading for the door, and Savage heard a key being turned. She pulled her warrant card out and held it ready, but the door didn't open.

"Hello?" she said, as the shape slid out of sight.

She put a hand to the door and gave it a shove. It opened reluctantly, a tinkling bell announcing her arrival. The shop was tiny, barely bigger than the living room in her flat, and a man was shuffling across it towards a small counter on the far side. The way he was moving, not to mention his diminutive size—he couldn't have been taller than five foot —put him somewhere well into old age. The smell that hit her as she entered was pure body odour, worse even than the sulphurous stench of the fire. It seemed to ooze from every single particle of this weird little shop.

"Uh, hi?" Savage said to the man's back. "Hello?"

If he heard her, he showed no sign of it. He reached the counter and cocked his leg, farting loudly.

"Better," he said quietly.

"Excuse me," said Savage, moving closer. The smell of the man was mixing with the ripe aroma of the room, making her feel lightheaded.

He still didn't reply, scratching his head with one hand as he stepped behind the counter. Savage was close enough to touch him, and even though she really didn't want to, she reached out and tapped her finger on his shoulder.

The man actually screamed, whirling around with both hands clutched to his chest. He fell back into the space behind the counter, only the wall holding him up, and stared at Savage with eyes that were as big as saucers.

"Jesus Holy Mother of Christ!" he said in a high-pitched voice that had more than a little Irish in it. "You almost killed me!"

"Oh, sorry," said Savage, holding up her warrant card. "I really am. I was calling out."

The man kept his hands on his heart, watching Savage like she might *actually* be about to kill him. From this angle, everything about him still seemed to belong to an old man—his hair almost gone, the rest of it grey, his back bent to accommodate his weight, his glasses hanging around his neck on a cord—but his face was surprisingly young. From the front, he didn't look any older than thirty.

"What's this?" he asked, studying her warrant card, some of his composure returning. "What are you showing me?"

"I'm police," she said, shaking the card. "DC Savage. Norfolk Constabulary."

He frowned at her, shaking his head.

"Police!" she said again.

He nodded, then shook his head, then nodded again. Savage sighed, taking in a little more air than she intended. She couldn't help herself, pinching her nose for a moment.

"I'm here because of the explosion," she said, putting her warrant card away and pointing through the open door.

The man reached into his pocket and pulled out a hearing aid crowned with a lump of yellow wax the size of a jelly tot. He flicked the wax to the floor and slid the earpiece into place, blinking at Savage.

"Can you hear me?" asked Savage when he didn't say anything.

"I can now," the man said. "You're police?"

"I'm here about the explosion over the road. Did you see it? Hear it?"

The expression on his face told her he hadn't noticed a thing.

"It happened half an hour ago," she said. "In the Reed, Barnham and Crabbe building."

He stared at her as if she was speaking a foreign language.

"The camera over your front door, does it work?"

The man nodded.

"Have to have it or the young folk'll shit everywhere," he said. "Happens every bloody weekend. There was an explosion?"

She could almost see his brain warming up.

"Yes, this morning. They're still putting out the fire."

"Was anyone hurt?"

"I don't know," said Savage. "The camera feed, can I take a look at it?"

The man nodded, then his face grew tight.

"I forgot, it's broken," he said. "Sorry."

"It's broken?" Savage replied. "Look, Mr, uh..."

"Hawker," he said. "Phil. I'm sorry, but unless you want to buy a phone, I can't help you."

"Do any of these phones even work?" Savage asked, studying the motley collection of devices on offer. "I need to see the footage from the camera, Mr Hawker. It's important."

"Broke," he said again, sniffing. "Like you said, everything in here is broke. Sorry."

Savage didn't move, rapping her knuckles gently on the countertop.

"Would it work if I got a warrant?" she said. "If I came back with a few friends?"

Hawker pulled his hearing aid out again and laid it on the counter.

"Something tells me it must be pretty hard to pay your business rates selling ten-year-old Nokias. What else are you up to?"

"I can't hear you, sorry."

"Mr Hawker, I'm—"

He shrugged his shoulders.

"Literally can't hear a thing, sorry."

Savage eyeballed him for a moment, then backed away from the counter. To the right was a door and she pushed it open.

"Hey!" squawked Hawker. "You can't go in there!"

She instantly wished she hadn't, because the smell rushed out at her like a charging rhino, enough to make her double up.

"Oh God," she whispered, feeling the acid start to burn up from her stomach. "What *is* that?"

Hawker was waddling after her, pushing the hearing aid back into place. She pushed on, entering a room that was no bigger than the one she'd just left. On one side was a desk with an old computer, and on the other a mattress covered in bedding that was so dirty it was almost standing upright of its own accord. A dozen or more pornographic magazines were scattered across the floor like a collapsed house of cards.

"Ew," said Savage, her skin crawling.

"Stop!" Hawker cried, pushing through the door after her. "This is my personal space, you're not allowed in here."

"Believe me, I want to be here as much as you want me to be. That computer connected to the camera?"

"Get out," he hissed at her back. "I'll call the…"

"Police?" she finished for him. "You're very welcome, but they'll send out the nearest available officer and that will be me. Because I'm already here. Look, Mr Hawker, I couldn't care less about your choice of reading material."

Her eye caught the title of the closest magazine —*Gorgeous Grannies*—and she almost ate her words.

"Just like I couldn't care less about the fact you're obviously squatting inside a building that is not suitable for domestic purposes and which doesn't, as far as I can see, even have bathroom facilities."

"Got a bucket," muttered Hawker, but his head had dropped. He stood in the middle of the room like a sulking teenager.

"All I care about is finding whoever delivered a bomb to the building across the road," she said. "I get that, I'm gone."

Hawker sighed, and Savage almost felt a little sorry for him. He veered around her, dragging that fug of BO smell after him, and gave the mouse a shake to wake up the computer. Savage pretended not to look while he closed a browser window that she had absolutely no desire to look at. Then another one.

"Sorry," he said.

And another.

"Gets lonely in here."

He clicked a few more times, then cleared his throat.

"Not the best camera in the world."

He loaded up the CCTV software and took two big steps back so that she could get to the desk. On-screen she could see the street, including the fire engines and the rapid response car. She could also see Superintendent Clare, who had wandered into shot. He was standing outside the shop and he looked like he was in the middle of an argument.

"This thing have sound?" she asked.

"Camera does, but I don't have no speakers," said Hawker.

The Super was definitely arguing with somebody, his face twisted into a look of fury, his finger jabbing the air. She thought he might be on his phone, but then he turned and his other hand came into view, clenched into a fist by his side.

"What are you doing, sir?" she asked quietly.

"You know him?" said Hawker, who had crept a little too close for comfort. "He looks mad."

Clare suddenly ducked, his hands on his head like he was being attacked. Savage was ready to run to his aid when something else appeared in the shot.

"Is that a *seagull*?" said Savage.

It was, and it flapped around the Superintendent's head like it was trying to land there. Clare's arms wheeled manically, his twisted face visible between the bird's wings. After a handful of seconds the seagull vanished off-screen and Clare ran after it.

"That was... weird," said Savage.

She reached for the mouse, then stopped, remembering

who'd been using it before her. Hawker seemed to sense her reluctance.

"It's a little sticky, sorry."

She felt her stomach roil again, a cold sweat breaking out on her face. She reached into her pocket and pulled out a pair of evidence gloves, pulling them on. Then she pulled out a second set, double bagging her hands. Even then, touching that ancient mouse was a struggle.

She worked as quickly as she could, rewinding the footage. The PC tower beneath the desk groaned in protest, a wheel of death appearing while it struggled to keep up with her. Eventually, though, she saw Clare reel backwards, then herself retreating out of the door, then the paramedic's car reversing up the street, and the fire engines vanishing.

The explosion itself was unmistakeable, the entire screen blazing white, the camera shaking with the force of the shockwave. She couldn't help herself, letting it play out, seeing that flash of light again, seeing pieces of brick and shards of glass scatter across the street, seeing people run for cover. Even without sound, she could hear it.

"That's real?" said Hawker, leaning closer. His round, wet eyes reflected the horror on the screen. "That happened today?"

She didn't reply, she just scrubbed backwards, past the explosion, until she saw a van pass right in front of the shop she was now in. She kept rewinding, seeing it stop outside the office across the road, then back out of view.

She stopped, pressed play, and the van idled into the shot again. The driver got out, too far away for her to make any sense of him. He walked out of sight behind his van and Savage clenched and unclenched her fists as she waited.

It was a good thirty seconds later that the driver appeared again, climbing back into his seat and closing the door. The van pulled away, taking a right and passing Cell Blasters.

Savage paused the feed. Across the street she could see the office, shapes moving behind the dark window, six packages sitting on a desk.

That's the bomb, she thought, and the temperature in the room dropped twenty degrees.

She turned her attention to the van, the driver a little clearer now that he was up close—but not much, because the windscreen was full of the reflected street. Savage clicked the footage forward one frame at a time, finding the best shot. He was in his fifties, bearded, his hair hidden by a cap and his neck covered with tattoos. She could see ink on his knuckles, too, as he gripped the wheel. His mouth was open wide and there was no mistaking the expression on his face.

He was grinning.

He looks wild, Savage thought. *He looks insane*.

She reversed the feed, shot by shot, until the front of the van came into view.

There was no registration plate.

"Dammit," she said.

She rewound again to the point the van started moving, pulling out her phone and starting a timer. The van drove past, people moved behind the large front window. The timer counted and Savage braced herself.

The building exploded again—there in one frame, literally obliterated by light in the next. She stopped, because she couldn't bear to watch the destruction again.

"Four minutes and twelve seconds," she said.

"What?" asked Hawker.

She didn't reply, rewinding the footage again and pausing it on the clearest shot of the driver's face. She took a couple of photographs with her phone, then a wider shot of the van. Then she texted everything to the Superintendent.

"There are going to be a few people coming to watch this," she said, sliding her phone into her pocket. "So I'd say you've got about ten minutes to clean up the room, and delete your internet history."

Hawker nodded his gratitude. Savage made her way across the tissue-strewn room like she was navigating a minefield. Only when she reached the door did the man call out to her.

"You're welcome to stay, if you like?" he said, gesturing around him. "Hang out for a bit?"

"Uh..." said Savage, utterly blindsided.

"I've got Pot Noodles," Hawker added with a hopeful smile.

Savage had no idea what to say to that, so she crossed the shop and escaped into the morning, pulling off her gloves as she went.

CHAPTER FIVE

KETT WATCHED THE AMBULANCE PULL AWAY, ITS SIREN pleading mournfully as it fought through the gridlocked traffic. His eyes were red raw from the poisonous air and he rubbed them with his knuckles before blinking his way back down the hill.

The smoke was starting to thin, at least. The hoses were still on, raining water over the ruin of the office and drenching the two buildings on either side of it.

Evacuations were still in progress, people scattering through the doors of the accountancy bureau next door to Reed, Barnham and Crabbe, and the school over the road emptying itself in a flurry of blue and yellow uniforms. Kett saw a lot of tears, and when he glanced back to make sure Porter was following him he was surprised to see them on the DI's face too.

"You okay, Pete?"

Porter nodded, scrubbing at his face. There was still a faint scar there from when he'd been in the tunnels during the Knuckle Bones case, four months ago. Another explosion, just as deadly—although thankfully it hadn't been Porter who'd died.

"Little too close to the bone, sir," the DI said. "The smell, everything, just puts me right back down there, you know?"

"You can sit this one out. It's no trouble."

Porter waved his words away like they were smoke, and walked on with gritted teeth. They'd reached the front of the first fire engine, thirty yards from the remains of the office, when one of the smokies blocked their path.

"Sorry," he said. "Can't let you get any closer."

"Fire's out, isn't it?" said Kett.

"Could be more explosives inside," said the fireman. "Got the 11th EOD Regiment on their way."

"The army?" said Kett.

"Not like the Met, is it, sir?" said Porter. "No bomb disposal in Norfolk."

"You know how long they'll be?" Kett asked.

"Coming from Colchester," said the fireman. "Shouldn't be long. We're pulling our—"

A barrage of shouts interrupted him, two more fire-fighters tripping and slipping their way out of the wreckage of the office. There was somebody strung up between them, their head hanging limply, their feet dragging across the ground.

"Shit," said Kett.

He started to move only for the fireman to plant a gloved hand right in the middle of his chest, hard enough to knock the wind out of him.

"Go round," he said.

Kett did as he was told, making his way along the outer flank of the fire engines. He reached the paramedic's car at the same time as the firefighters, who laid their burden on the pavement as gently as they could.

It was a man, although it was almost impossible to say any more than that. His skin was a tapestry of burns, cuts and smoke, the blood fused into tribal patterns by the heat. He wasn't wearing a shirt and his red trousers had been shredded, both shoes missing.

"Whoa," said the paramedic, dropping to his knees, his fingers on the man's throat. "Where'd you find him?"

The closest firefighter removed her mask, struggling to catch her breath.

"On the kitchen roof," she said. "Blast must have knocked him clear out the window."

"He alive?" asked Kett.

"Yeah," said the paramedic. "But only just. That ambulance still up the street?"

"No," said Kett.

The man swore, opening his bag.

"Anyone know his name?"

"Ben Reed, I think," said Kett.

"Ben," shouted the paramedic. "Ben, can you hear me?"

There was a rumble of thunder from inside the building as more of the roof collapsed, and the firefighters moved towards the street—gesturing for Kett and Porter to step back as well.

"Gotta clear out," said the one who'd been carrying Ben.

"Did you see anyone else inside?" Kett asked her as he retreated onto the street. "A woman?"

"Dead," the firefighter said.

"You're sure?"

The look she gave him was full of quiet horror, and it told him everything he needed to know. She bolted, her equipment rattling as she ran back up the hill.

"All the times I think this job is shit," said Porter, watching her go. "I just remind myself how lucky I am I'm not a smokie."

Kett nodded. His sinuses felt like they had acid in them, his throat raw. Down the hill, a crowd had settled on the bridge, held there by a row of uniformed officers. In the other direction the bulk of Prince of Wales Road was now deserted as Duke directed traffic onto Rose Lane. A cordon had been set up there as well, this one being battered by a hail of reporters.

"There was another man in the office this morning, wasn't there?" Kett said. "Asif? Where is he?"

Porter shrugged.

"And where's Clare?"

"He ran off after a seagull, sir," said the DI.

"He what?" said Kett. "*Why?*"

Porter opened his mouth to answer, then hesitated, frowning.

"I'm not entirely sure."

"Sir," came a cry from behind him, and he turned to see Savage running across the road.

"Any luck?" he asked her.

"Yeah," she said, pulling out her phone. She grimaced, wiping it down her suit jacket. "Sticky," she said by way of explanation. "That place was gross."

She pointed at a shop that sat on the small stretch of road that joined Prince of Wales to Rose Lane. Cell Blasters.

"That name doesn't make any sense," he said.

"Yeah, sir, but they've got a camera."

"Tell me it works," said Kett.

"It works. Van driver stopped here, handed the packages to one of the women from the office."

"Gloria Easterman," said Kett.

"The van was blocking the office so I couldn't see much," said Savage. "He drove off sharpish, went right past the shop."

"You get a plate?"

"Didn't have one, sir," she said. "Not on the front, anyway. But this is him."

She held up her phone and Kett and Porter leaned in to see a grainy photograph of a bearded man in his early fifties, a cap on his head, his neck heavily tattooed.

"He looks happy," said Porter.

"He looks nuts, sir," said Savage. "Right?"

Kett slipped on his glasses and took the phone from her, holding it close. The man was grinning, his mouth twisted open weirdly like he was in the middle of shouting something. There was a gleam in his eyes, a mad excitement.

"The bomb went off four minutes and twelve seconds after he pulled away," said Savage. "At 8:51, according to the timestamp on the camera. He drove up Eastbourne Place, past the shop, and then he would have had to go right, up Rose Lane. There will be more cameras there. He might have had a plate on the back of the van."

"Good work," said Kett. "You know what kind of van it is?"

Porter took the phone from him, studying it for a good half a minute.

"No," he said when he finally handed it back.

"It's a Vauxhall," said Savage, reclaiming it from Kett. "An older one."

"Well, I knew *that*," said Porter.

"Good place to start," said Kett. "You seen the Super anywhere?"

"I saw him on camera," said Savage. "He looked like he was fighting a seagull."

"But *why*?" asked Kett.

"I have no idea."

"We should make the most of him being gone," said Porter. "Shop over there, I can grab some snacks?"

"No," said Kett and Savage together.

Porter spluttered out a sigh.

"I'll get somebody in to copy the footage from the camera, sir," Savage continued. "But I promised the man ten minutes to clean up."

She actually shuddered.

The fire engine beside them roared to life with such urgency that Kett thought it was another bomb going off. His body tensed, his heart revving. The fire crew was boarding and the lead officer, Croll, yelled to them from the window.

"We need everyone back, including you lot, okay? You don't want to be standing here if another IED goes off."

The fire engine pulled up the hill, followed by the second one, both stopping another fifty yards away. Only the paramedic was left, working on his patient with an intense focus. The air was full of sirens and Kett saw another ambulance crawling over the bridge, the crowd of people blocking its way. A chaos of constables attempted to clear the path and lift the cordon, allowing it to crawl towards them.

"Did you see the other guy anywhere, Kate?" asked Kett. "Asif."

"No, sir. You know what he looks like?"

"Like this," said Porter, holding his phone up. He'd found the website for Reed, Barnham and Crabbe and a young man grinned out at them, smartly dressed and even more smartly manicured. "Asif Nasir. Says here he's been with the company four years. In sales."

"Where the hell did he go?" said Kett.

"No idea," said Porter, studying his phone for a moment before holding it out again. "And there's another person MIA. Justin Hope. Says he's an account manager."

Kett took the phone from him, scrolling up the list of employees. Ben Reed was at the top, then Millicent, both named Managing Directors. William Talion and Seraphina Newton were account managers too, and Gloria Easterman sat beneath them, listed as Secretary. Justin Hope was last, a man in his late twenties with dark eyes and no sign of a smile.

"Gloria and Sephie told me he worked here until last week," said Kett. "Ben fired him. We need to find him."

"Oi!"

Clare's voice boomed across the street. They all turned to see him marching towards them, his shirt collar pulled up and his hair looking more like a nest than ever. He had an ugly scratch across his forehead.

"What happened to you, sir?" asked Kett as he closed in. "Nothing."

"Why were you chasing a seagull, sir?" asked Porter.

"I was doing no such thing, Detective," Clare spat.

"I literally watched you fighting a seagull, sir," said Savage.

"You need your eyeballs checked," he replied, straightening his collar and smoothing a hand over his hair. "What have you got?"

"Got a lead on the delivery guy who dropped off the packages," said Savage. "I sent you the photo."

"And there was another man, used to be on the staff," said Kett. "Got fired. Justin Hope."

"Good," said Clare. "Kett, Porter, I want you on the driver. Savage, check up on this Hope guy."

"We're missing somebody else from the office," said Kett. "Asif Nasir. He was here when the bomb went off, but nobody has seen him since."

"He's done a runner?" asked Clare, and Kett shrugged. "Savage, forget Hope. Find Nasir. But we need that driver, and we need him now. He's our priority."

"Anything else we can do here?" asked Kett, and Clare shook his head.

"They're locking it down until the EOD arrives," he said. "They think there's another bomb."

"What do you think, sir?" asked Savage.

They all watched as Ben Reed was loaded onto a stretcher, one paramedic holding the ventilator to his mouth while the other wheeled him to the ambulance—both of them throwing nervous glances at the burnt-out building. They pulled off at speed, the siren echoing back down the hill.

"I don't know," Clare said when they'd gone. "But whatever this is, it hasn't tossed its last toss yet."

CHAPTER SIX

"GET ME EVERYTHING YOU CAN ON THEM," SAID KETT, holding the phone to his ear. "Reed, Barnham and Crabbe. Reed's the only one of the founders left, but I think we should find out what happened to the other two. If there's some kind of grudge involved it might explain the attack."

"Yes, sir," said DS Alison Spalding, her voice fading in and out. "I'll get right to it, sir. Anything for you, sir."

"And can you get me an address for a Justin Hope?" he said, ignoring her tone. "In his twenties. He was employed by the same company but he got fired last week."

"I'll literally jump to it right now, sir. I'll drop everything else and hurl myself into action to get you what you need."

"You do realise sarcasm is the lowest form of wit, Alison?" Kett said.

"Is it, sir?" said Spalding. "Thank you so much for explaining that to me, sir. I can't tell you how grateful I am, sir."

"Right," said Kett. He hesitated for a moment. "But you are going to do it?"

Spalding hung up, and Kett slipped the phone into his pocket. He could hear the thump of an approaching helicopter, a big one, and he wondered if it was the army's bomb disposal squad. He had no idea where they were going to set down if it was, this part of the city was rammed. He turned to Porter, shocked to see the DI unwrapping a Snickers.

"Where the hell did that come from?" he said.

"The shop, sir," Porter replied, nodding across the street.

"I was on the phone for like thirty seconds. How did you even get over there?"

"I can move fast when I need to," he said, lifting the chocolate bar to his mouth. Kett raised one eyebrow, giving him *the look*—the one he used on his kids when they were about to do something naughty.

Porter hesitated, his tongue darting over his lips.

"It's a stressful case, sir. I need some sugar to get me through it, and it's peanuts, which basically makes it a vegetable."

Kett lifted his eyebrow a little higher.

"Just the one," Porter said. "Just a taste. I can't go cold turkey, sir, it will kill me."

His eyebrow crept higher still.

"Fine," Porter said. "I won't bloody eat it."

Kett held out his hand and Porter plopped the Snickers into it, folding his arms over his big chest and pouting. Kett wrapped the Snickers up and put it into his jacket pocket.

"You can have it later, if you've been good," he said, and Porter looked like he was about to reply when a constable clattered around the corner, stopping outside the little phone shop where Savage had found the security footage. She was out of breath.

"Sirs," she called. "You should come and check this out."

She turned and sprinted out of sight, the sound of her shoes echoing off the buildings. Kett followed, Porter lumbering along beside him.

"We should probably run," Kett said.

"Probably," said Porter.

They managed a brisk walk, rounding the corner onto Rose Lane, where the constable had stopped outside a petrol station. Kett was relieved to see that it was positively bristling with CCTV cameras. She held the door open for them as they wheezed their way through.

"You okay, sirs?" she asked.

"It's the smoke," said Kett.

"Gets in your lungs," added Porter. "That's the only reason we're out of breath."

"This way," she said as she led them to the office at the back. "Loads of white vans this morning, but only one that matches the footage that DC Savage found."

Kett nodded to the man behind the Plexiglas counter and stepped into the small, ordered room. There was a desk against the far wall, a flatscreen monitor waiting for them. The constable had paused the footage right where they needed it, the forecourt taking up most of the screen but the road visible beyond. A white van was stuck at the traffic lights just outside the garage, caught from behind. The registration plate was perfectly visible in the crystal-clear footage.

"Is that him?" asked the constable, craning past Porter.

"It's a Vauxhall," said Kett. "You're right, timing is perfect."

He scrubbed the security feed backwards a minute or so, then played it. The van stopped for the lights, a handful of people crossing the road, then it lurched forwards and out of sight. Kett kept watching, seeing one more white van—a Citroen—but nothing else that matched what Savage had found. He counted down the minutes until he saw a faint flash.

"That's our explosion," he said, rewinding the footage until the van came back into view. "It has to be him."

He made a note of the van's registration on his phone, texting it to the Superintendent.

"There was something else, sir," said the constable, squeezing past. "I don't know if it's relevant, but the cashier was a little alarmed. Hang on."

She scanned the footage until she found what she was looking for.

"This is from twenty minutes ago," she said.

Kett and Porter both leaned in, staring past the forecourt and the street to see a gangly shape running up the road, chasing what could only be a seagull.

"The cashier said there was a man acting oddly, said it might be important."

"It's not," said Kett, watching Superintendent Clare launch himself to an impressive height as he tried to grab hold of the bird.

"Wait," said the constable. "Isn't that the—"

"Good work," said Kett, closing the browser. "Really good work. Keep looking. If we can find some more footage of the driver, it will help."

"Yes, sir," said the constable.

Kett walked out of the room, making it halfway to the exit before he realised Porter wasn't with him. The DI was hovering by the bags of sweets, his fists clenching and unclenching, his jaw set. He looked pale and sweaty, the way addicts often did when they were due a hit.

"Pete," said Kett.

"Just one?" Porter said. "Bag of Fruit Pastilles? I'll share them."

Kett walked back and took his arm, giving him a gentle tug.

"Come on, mate," he said. "One step at a time."

Porter huffed his way out of the garage. Only when the door had closed behind them did Kett let go of his arm. He pulled out his phone only to see that it was already ringing, Spalding's name on the screen.

"Hi, Alison," he said as he answered.

"I've got an address for Justin Ian Hope, sir," said Spalding. "I've texted it. He's over in Sprowston. It's not a house, looks like a warehouse or something, but it's the only one I could find for him. According to Companies House, Reed, Barnham and Crabbe was founded in 1997 by Ben Reed, Patrick Barnham and Raoul Crabbe. It got into trouble when Crabbe went bankrupt in 2009. He died the year after."

"How?" asked Kett.

"Haven't got that far yet, sir, because you only asked me ten minutes ago."

"Right, sorry."

"Barnham is still going. Looks like Reed bought him out in 2013. Lives out near Brundall. I'll send you his address too."

"Thanks," said Kett.

"Is that it, sir? Am I allowed to go back to my own cases now?"

"Almost," said Kett. "Sorry. I have a plate number, can you run it for me?"

He read out the van's registration number and heard

Spalding typing. He could feel the force of her annoyance radiating from the phone.

"Registered to a man called Brian Beaney, but it's listed as SORN, shouldn't be on the road. It's not taxed or insured. You want his address too?"

"Yes, please."

"I'll text it over. He's local as well, Lakenham."

"Thanks, Alison," said Kett.

"I live to serve, sir," she replied, hanging up. Within seconds, Kett's phone buzzed three times, three addresses appearing on the screen. He called Clare, the Super picking up after a single ring.

"I think we have an ID on the driver, sir," he said. "Brian Beaney. Spalding found his address: Lakenham."

"Where are you?" Clare barked.

"Rose Lane, sir, the garage."

"I'll send Savage to pick you up. Find the house but do not make entry, you hear me? If this is our bomber then who knows what he's left for us. I'll need to speak to Gorski, and the 11th."

"Yes, sir," said Kett. "Any luck with Asif?"

"No," said Clare, ending the call.

"Brian Beaney?" said Porter, his phone out. "B-E-A-N-E-Y?"

"Yeah," said Kett.

He heard a siren and looked down the street to see an IRV rounding the corner. Savage's serious face was visible behind the wheel, Duke in the passenger seat. The car reached them in seconds and Kett opened the door, letting Porter slide across the back seat before climbing in next to him. Savage floored it before he was all the way in, the door almost taking his foot off as it slammed shut.

"Jesus, Kate," he said, fighting to get his belt on as Savage accelerated to what felt like the speed of sound.

"Sorry, sir," she replied. "Lakenham?"

"Yeah, Cavell Road."

"Brian Beaney," said Porter, holding out his phone. "Got to be this one, right?"

Kett fumbled for his glasses, almost dropping them as the IRV whipped past the Castle Mall. He slipped them on, seeing a Facebook profile picture of a shirtless man. He was in good shape, his muscular torso almost entirely covered with tattoos—including a Virgin Mary that started on his chest and ended halfway up his neck. There was also what looked like an Iron Cross right in the middle of his stomach. His head was shaved, his eyes fierce. His nose had been broken at some point in the past and badly reset—a boxer's nose.

"Boobs," said Porter.

"What?"

"There, on his neck."

The DI pointed to the photo, and Kett had to zoom in to see the tattoo on the other side of the man's throat. It was, as Porter had said, a pair of breasts.

"Who has a pair of boobs tattooed on them?" the DI said.

"Well you wouldn't have just one, would you, sir?" said Duke, looking back. "One boob would look weird. You need a pair."

"You really don't," said Porter. He took his phone back. "Says here he works for a company called Nordelex. Deliveries."

"Call them," said Kett. "Find out."

Kett closed his eyes as Savage accelerated, the force of it pushing him into his seat. She took the next turn so fast that if he hadn't been wearing his belt he would have ended up on Porter's lap.

"You didn't find Asif, then?" he asked.

"No sign of him," Savage said. "Searched the whole street, he's vanished. He was definitely there this morning?"

"According to Gloria and Sephie, yeah," said Kett.

"Who disappears after an explosion?" asked Duke.

"Could have been in shock," said Savage. "Might not have known what he was doing."

"Or he might have something to hide," said Kett.

"Hi," Porter said, speaking into his phone. "Yeah, this is DI Peter Porter, Norfolk Constabulary. Can I... Yeah, no, I can't wait... No, you put me on hold and you'll be in serious... Hello?"

He looked up.

"Bastard put me on hold."

"We're nearly there," said Savage, the IRV screaming past stationary traffic.

"We just look," said Kett. "Clare doesn't want us to breach in case Beaney's our bomber."

"Just look," said Duke. "Sounds like a good plan."

And it did, until Savage swung the IRV onto Cavell Road and stopped halfway up the hill; until Kett opened his door and heard the screams that tore their way from Brian Beaney's house.

CHAPTER SEVEN

"Shit," said Kett, hauling himself out of the back of the IRV.

Brian Beaney's house was in the middle of a terrace of smart-looking properties, all of which had neat, well-tended gardens. It was a quiet neighbourhood, and for a second Kett thought he'd imagined the scream.

Then it came again, even louder than before—a shriek that dropped out of an open upstairs window and seemed to fill the entire street.

"What do you want to do, sir?" asked Savage, out of the car. Duke was there too, one hand on his Taser. Porter was last, his phone still to his ear.

Savage was answered by another scream, followed by a muffled crash from inside the house.

"Shit," Kett said again. "Come on. Aaron, take the lead."

Duke kicked open the gate and cleared the path in three bounds. He thumped on the door with every ounce of strength—his knock almost as loud as Savage's.

"Police! Open up!"

"Round the back, Kate," said Kett, pointing to the low

hedge that separated this house from the end of the terrace. "Be careful."

"Sir," she said, moving off.

"Here," said Duke, unholstering his baton and throwing it to her. "Just in case."

She caught it, vaulting the hedge easily. Inside Beaney's house the screams were getting louder, full of anger. Kett checked the street—no sign of Beaney's white delivery van —and made up his mind.

"Get us inside," he said to Duke. "Now."

"Yes sir."

The big PC took a step back, braced himself, then drove his boot into the door. The wood splintered like it was polystyrene, and when he kicked the door again it ripped itself out of its frame, crashing into the wall and rebounding. Duke shouldered his way through it, vanishing into the dark interior.

"Police!" he roared. "Make yourself known!"

Kett jogged after him, his pulse drumming at the back of his throat, the adrenaline making him feel lightheaded. He was standing in a narrow front hall, a staircase right in front of him and three doors leading off into dark rooms. Duke grabbed the bannister so hard he bent it out of shape, hauling himself up to the landing. He was greeted by another scream.

"Stay where you are!" he yelled. "I mean it."

There was a thud as Duke lost his footing, sliding back down the stairs on his stomach. His hat came down after him, then something else—a hardback book that smacked him in the head.

"Oi!" yelled Kett, running for the stairs.

Somebody stepped out of the door on the right. Kett twisted around, lifting his hands just in time as the person swung an object. It struck him on the fingers, the pain like he'd plunged them into a fire. He fell onto his back, a woman launching herself at him—a meat tenderiser gripped in her white-knuckled hands.

Shit, he thought, the word lost as he snatched in a breath.

"What the fuck are you doing?" the woman screamed, swinging the weapon down like an executioner's axe.

Kett lifted a foot and the tenderiser bounced off his boot, spinning out of her hand. She threw herself onto him, long nails going for his eyes, her face contorted with fury.

"Police!" Kett said, or *tried* to say—the woman's knee was right in his solar plexus.

He rolled to the side and she toppled off him, sprawling onto the hallway tiles. Kett pushed himself onto his hands and knees, ready to call to Duke for a little help before seeing that the PC had his hands full. He was back on his feet and halfway up the stairs, wrestling with another woman. She was practically hanging off him, her legs wrapped around his waist, pinning his arms.

"Christ," said Kett, managing to get to his feet. He turned to see the first woman charging towards him, and he put his hands up again only to feel her drive her knee into his crotch.

He dropped harder this time, the world burning white, the pain unfathomably bad. He heard the woman's hoarse breaths as she closed in, then—mercifully—Savage's shouts as she entered through the back door. He looked up through watering eyes to see the DC hurl herself at the woman, both of them bouncing off the wall before tumbling to the floor. Savage landed on top, the baton over her head.

"This is your last warning, stay still," she said, glancing at Kett. "You okay, sir?"

"No," he whispered, on the verge of throwing up.

There was a sound like the house was falling in—Duke rolling down the stairs, the second woman still attached to him. She was a teenage girl, Kett saw, dressed in grey trousers and a blue blazer and looking like a sapling next to the enormous PC. Still, she was winning the fight, launching a bare-footed kick that glanced off Duke's chin.

"Hey," Kett yelled.

He couldn't make it to his feet so he crawled towards them. Duke was trying to get back up but the girl kicked again, this one connecting with the soft flesh of his neck. He croaked, reaching out and grabbing her foot as she tried to kick him a third time. She fell onto the bottom step, thrashing wildly as she fought to get free.

"Hey!" Kett shouted again. "Enough!"

The girl looked at him, and there was more fear in her expression than anger.

"Duke, let go of her."

Duke did as he was told and the girl shuffled up the steps on her backside. She couldn't be any older than fifteen, Kett thought. The badge on her blazer read Hewett, which was the high school right around the corner from here.

"It's okay," he wheezed, the pain still radiating from his crotch, filling every single cell. "We're police, we're not here for you."

The first woman had stopped struggling, Savage sitting on her back as she tried to fish a pair of cuffs from her jacket pocket. The woman glared at Kett with a hatred that had more to it than the events of this morning—it seemed ingrained in her, something primitive.

"It's okay," he said again. "Let's all calm down."

"You shouldn't be in here," the woman said. "You've got no right to be in my house."

"Let's start again," said Kett, leaning against the wall and doubling up. There was still a fairly good chance that he would chuck his guts. "We heard screaming, that's all."

"You never heard of kids before?" the woman spat. "Get the fuck off me."

Kett nodded to Savage and she stood up, backing away, the baton still gripped in her hand. The woman struggled to her feet, limping to the kitchen door and never taking her eyes off Kett.

"Got no right," she hissed.

"Like I said, we heard screaming," said Kett.

"Get out," she said. "Not taking no responsibility for what'll happen to you if you don't fuck off."

"We really need to talk," said Kett. "About Brian. Brian Beaney. You know him?"

"Never heard of him," said the woman. "So fuck off."

Duke had managed to get to his knees, one hand on the floor and the other holding his throat where the girl had kicked him. Kett looked out of the open front door to see Porter standing next to the car, his phone still to his ear, completely oblivious.

He turned back to the woman.

"This is important," he said. "There was a—"

Somebody flew out of the kitchen like a bullet, a little girl who rushed at Duke with an ear-piercing scream of defiance. The PC was too slow to react, the girl swinging a cast-iron frying pan that was almost as big as she was. It struck Duke on the head with a sound like a gong being hammered and he rolled onto his side. The kid looked like she was going in for a second strike, but luckily the teenage girl on the stairs scooped her up.

"Stop it, Blessed," she said as the girl tried to kick her way free. "Stop it."

"Told you," said the woman, folding her arms over her chest and firing a smug smile at Kett. "You don't fucking mess with us. You don't ever fucking mess with us like that."

Savage ran to Duke's side. There was an ugly bruise forming beneath his right eye, and when he got to his feet he wobbled.

"Okay," said Kett. "This has gone far enough. We're not going anywhere until we find Brian Beaney."

"Never heard of him," said the woman, still wearing that shit-eating grin.

"Because we think he detonated a bomb in the city this morning," said Kett. "We think he killed a woman."

And just like that, the smile was gone.

THEY SAT IN THE BEANEYS' small garden, in the shade of an enormous conifer tree that grew on the other side of the fence. After they'd managed to calm themselves down, the woman had asked them to leave. And when Kett had refused, the back garden had been a compromise. Even though she hadn't looked too happy about it, the mention of the morning's events seemed to have cowed her.

A bomb would do that.

Kett was perched on one half of a wooden picnic bench that looked like it was five seconds away from collapsing, ready to catapult Savage from where she sat on the opposite side. He wouldn't have bothered taking a seat, but the sickening pain still radiated through him from where the woman had kneed him in the crotch.

Duke leaned against the back wall of the house, pressing his fingers to the bruise on his face and wincing.

Off to the side, the little girl who'd almost knocked him out played in a small sandbox that was made up of more dirt than sand. She was five, her mother had told them, but she swung a pan like a fully grown man. She didn't seem concerned at all that her garden was full of coppers, and Kett suspected it wasn't the first time it had happened.

"Can't reach him," said the woman as she stepped out of the back door. She was wiry, her face knotted into such a fist of annoyance that it couldn't have seen a proper smile for months, maybe years. Her hair was bleached blonde, but it had been a while since she'd touched up the roots, and giant gold hoops hung from her ears. There were tattoos on her stringy arms, old ones—a Tweety Bird and a Tasmanian Devil and what might have been Betty Boop's lower half jutting from the sleeve of her T-shirt. She was clutching her phone so hard it might have shattered.

"He's not answering?" asked Kett.

"Phone's off," she said.

"So you are Mrs Beaney?" he asked.

She leaned against the wall on the other side of the back door, a mirror image of Duke. The sun was in her eyes and she scrunched her face up even more. She pulled a packet of cigarettes from the pocket of her jeans and lit one. The smell of it hit Kett instantly, and he inhaled it, still craving them after all these years—even with his smoke-punched lungs.

"Roisin," she said after she'd taken a drag. "Beaney. Yeah."

"Brian's your husband?"

"Well, he ain't my fucking brother," she said, blowing

out a cloud of smoke that seemed to settle on the little girl in the sandpit. "Even though we're in Norfolk."

"I'm Blessed," said the girl, looking at Kett.

"You're blessed?" he echoed.

"It's her name," said Roisin. "Blessed. After my grandmother."

"It's a beautiful name," Kett told the girl. "You should play tennis with an arm like that, you know."

She studied him without emotion, then went back to her game.

"She thinks coppers are no good," said Roisin. "All bent, all trying to get us for this or that. She thinks you lot are nothing but trouble."

"And did that come from you or Brian?" Kett asked.

She shrugged, taking another pull on her cigarette. There was a clatter of feet and the teenage girl appeared in the back door, a rucksack slung over her shoulder.

"I'm gonna go, Mum," she said. "Unless you need me to stay?"

Roisin shook her cigarette, motioning for her to leave. The girl turned to Duke.

"Sorry for kicking you an' everything."

Duke nodded his thanks and the girl bolted. Kett heard the sound of the front door slamming as she left. He checked his watch to see that it was past ten.

"She's doing her GCSEs," said Roisin, before he could comment. "Doesn't have to be in for her study periods."

"Was that what all the screaming was about?" he asked, adjusting his position on the uncomfortable bench and making the whole thing squeak. Savage rocked unsteadily on the other side.

"Kind of," said Roisin. "She didn't want to go in, but I told her she had to. We spend half our lives screaming at each other at the moment. Not like when they're little, is it?"

She looked at her younger daughter, who had managed to make a reasonably good sandcastle in the wet sand.

"Don't know what happens to them," she said.

"Roisin, can you think of any reason Brian might want to hurt somebody?" asked Kett. "Any reason he might deliver a bomb to an office in the city?"

She took another drag, held it, then blew out more smoke as she shook her head.

"He didn't do it," she said. "No way. Brian wouldn't hurt somebody, not like that. A fight, yeah. In his nature to fight. But a bomb? He wouldn't even know how to make one."

"How long has he been working as a delivery driver?" asked Savage.

"Only a few months," Roisin answered. "Six, maybe. Since just before Christmas. They were taking on extra drivers, and he just stayed on."

"Nordelex?"

"Yeah, Norfolk Deliveries something, I can't remember."

"Was he aware his van wasn't taxed? No insurance?"

"Fuck does he care? Still goes, doesn't it? Government'll try to screw your money each and every way, not a crime to try'n hang onto it. Look, they're a legitimate company, he just does drops, he doesn't do nothing bad anymore."

The last word was out of her mouth before she could stop it. Kett could almost see her trying to suck it back in.

"Anymore?" he said, and she rolled her eyes.

"Like I said, it's in his nature."

"Fighting?"

"Yeah, it's part of who we are, isn't it? It's part of the

culture. We have a problem, somebody's got a beef, we fight it out. Nothing wrong with it. We can't be persecuted for it."

"So who does your husband like to fight?" said Kett.

"Nobody," she replied, her cigarette forgotten. "I didn't mean to say it. He don't fight no more. He used to work the Carny circuit, the fairgrounds, used to have to defend himself from all the punters, that kind of stuff. Drunk men wheeling off the Dodgems, trying to look hard in front of their sweethearts. Pricks who think the games are rigged and want their money back. Nothing serious, he ain't never been arrested. Not for anything proper."

"What about the tattoo on his stomach?" Kett said. "The Iron Cross."

"What about it?"

"Does Brian have a thing about the Nazis?"

She spluttered a laugh.

"Doesn't have nothing to do with *them*," she spat. "It's a biker thing; about rebellion and shit."

Kett pushed himself up. The bench squeaked alarmingly, and so did Savage as her side dropped. She leapt nimbly to her feet before it could tip over.

"Can you try him again?" Kett asked.

Roisin rolled her eyes and slunk back into the house. She was replaced by Porter, who threw up a hand to shield his eyes from the sun as he walked into the back garden.

"Nice of you to join us," muttered Duke.

"What?" said Porter.

"You missed a fight, sir," said Savage.

"A *fight*?" Porter said.

"Did you not hear the shouting?" Kett asked.

"I was on the phone, sir," he said. He turned to Duke,

seeing the bruise on his face. "Jesus, who were you fighting?"

"The mum," said Savage. "And her teenage daughter."

A smile crept onto Porter's face.

"Wait, which one gave you the shiner, Duke? Please tell me it was the teenage girl."

"It wasn't her," said Duke.

"The mum?"

Duke sighed, turning his attention to the little girl who was still playing in the sand.

"*That* kid gave you a black eye?"

Duke didn't say anything.

"That tiny girl?" said Porter, smiling like it was Christmas Day. "What is she? Three?"

"Five," mumbled Duke.

Porter looked like he was about to emit one of his cannon-shot laughs, but Kett cleared his throat.

"What did you get, Pete?"

"Oh, right." He held up his phone. "Was talking to Nordelex, Norfolk Deliveries Expedited. They use local, self-employed drivers who have their own vans. They say Brian Beaney's been on their books for just over six months now. Works three days a week doing early deliveries. They're going to email a list of his addresses, but get this: Reed, Barnham and Crabbe wasn't on his call sheet this morning."

"It wasn't?" said Kett.

"No, there were no scheduled deliveries there or anywhere else nearby. They've got an automated file system. Beaney had just delivered a parcel to a wholesaler on Barrack Road, it had been checked off. His next delivery was supposed to be out in Horsford and he wouldn't have needed to come back into Norwich until he'd ended his shift."

"So he did the wholesaler job then headed into the city," said Kett. "Went straight to Reed's office."

"Nordelex doesn't know where the six packages came from, the ones with the bombs in them," said Porter. "But they didn't come through them."

"We don't know for sure the bomb was in one of those packages," said Savage.

"True," admitted Kett. "They say anything else?"

"Yeah, they said he hasn't made his Horsford delivery yet, or any of the others."

"Horsford's twenty minutes out of town, maximum," said Savage. "He'd have got there by now."

"So where—"

Porter stopped as Roisin stepped out of the door, squeezing past him.

"Phone's still off," she said, the first glimmer of worry on her face. "Not like him."

"Can you think of any reason Brian would stop delivering?" Kett asked. "Anything else he might be doing?"

"No, he needs the work, he needs the money, we all do. He's good at his job, never has any trouble. Why?"

The little girl was listening into the conversation again, her face strangely blank. Roisin walked to her and picked her up with no small effort, stroking her sand-spattered hair with yellow fingers.

"Why?" she said again.

"Because he hasn't made any deliveries since the one he made this morning," said Kett. "We don't know where he is."

Roisin turned her attention to the heavens, her eyes red raw. Her face held a lifetime of suffering, of turmoil, of disappointment, and Kett wished he could promise her that no more would come her way.

"His van's got a tracker," she said eventually. "Got stolen a few weeks back when he was on the job. He had to fork out for a couple of lost parcels. He put a tracker in it when he got it back, in case it happened again."

"Seriously?" said Kett. "Can you access it?"

"The thing's on his phone, he looks at it from there. No idea how to get on it."

She shrugged hard enough to jolt the little girl, who grinned at the sudden movement.

"But if it helps, I've still got the box?"

CHAPTER EIGHT

"You're sure?" asked Kett. "That's what it says?"

The IRV idled at the end of Cavell Road, Savage lightly gunning the engine as she waited for her orders. Kett held the phone to his ear, listening to the wet breaths of the woman who worked for the tracking company.

"I'm sure," she said. "I'm just double-checking now. Yeah, the last location of the tracker is on Gurney Road. Looks to me like a car park. Unless the tracker has been removed, you should find your vehicle there."

"Thanks," said Kett, hanging up. "Gurney Road, a car park."

"Mousehold Heath, maybe?" said Savage.

She floored it, turning right and accelerating hard—the tyres whistling as she took the next left. Kett felt himself being sucked back into his seat, his stomach protesting and the dull ache returning. He doubled over with a groan.

"You okay, sir?" Savage asked.

"Not really," he said. "She had really bony knees."

Savage winced, the world thumping past as she tore around the city's inner ring road. To the left, County Hall rose above the roofs of the houses, bringing nothing but bad memories.

"At least we're not chasing bones," said Porter from the back seat.

"I'd pick bones over bombs any day," Kett told him. "Can one of you call it in?"

"I'll do it," said Duke, the side of his face swollen, one eye half shut.

"Maybe get some backup out there," said Porter. "You know, in case there are more three-year-olds with frying pans."

"She was *five!*" protested Duke, as if that made any difference in the world.

He started talking into his radio and Kett tuned him out, wondering if he should ask Savage to stop for a bag of ice. He closed his eyes for a moment, thinking about the explosion, about the carnage it had caused. Shooting somebody was one thing, stabbing them was something else. But a bomb? It was indiscriminate; it was devastating. You set off a bomb to cause maximum damage. You set it off to annihilate somebody.

Or to send a message.

"Sir," said Savage, and he realised his phone was ringing. He saw Clare's name on the screen and put it on speaker so they could all listen in.

"Millicent Reed is dead," the Super said, without waiting for a hello. "There's barely a body. The 11th says she was inside her office on the first floor and the package must have been in her hands when it detonated."

"Jesus," said Kett.

"She wouldn't have known anything about it, if that's any consolation. They're telling me it's an Improvised Explosive Devise with homemade components. Probably urea nitrate or ammonia nitrate. The switch was victim operated, designed to detonate when the box was opened. They don't know for sure, but they're pretty certain there was no remote trigger."

"So the bomber didn't set it off, sir?" said Kett.

"That's what they're telling me."

Savage took a roundabout like they were riding a roller-coaster. Kett grimaced at what felt like twelve Gs.

"There are no other bombs," Clare went on. "Two of the packages were obliterated in the blast—including the one with the bomb, obviously—but the other four have been found. Each one contains a variation of the same message."

"Lucky Number One," said Kett.

"We've found Lucky Number One, Three, Four and Five. Each had stones in it, taken from a beach, most likely."

Why? Kett almost asked, before realising nobody could give him the answer.

"This doesn't make sense," he said instead. "There were six people in the office, six packages, one bomb. It was a powerful charge, it did some serious damage to the building. It could have been designed to kill everyone."

"Maybe not. The 11th tells me the charge was powerful but very short range. Unless you were standing right next to it, it wouldn't have killed you. The shockwave sent Ben Reed through the window, and it took out the floor joists, but according to the disposal team the building was close to falling apart anyway. It's old, a lot of dry rot."

"So the bomb was designed to take out Millicent Reed and nobody else," said Kett.

"Except it wasn't," said Savage.

"Huh?" said Kett and Clare at the same time.

"There were no labels on the packages, right?" she went on, the car slowing as they climbed the steep hill that led towards Mousehold. The city had vanished behind the acres of trees that made up the forested heath, an ocean of green. "You told me that they were given out randomly. If there were no names on them, then the bomber wasn't specifically targeting Millicent."

"You're right," said Kett. "Six packages without names, six members of staff, one bomb. It was random."

"It was *luck*," said Savage. "That's the message, right, sir?"

"But why?" said Clare.

They turned a corner and a car park appeared in the woodland, a smattering of vehicles parked on the dirt.

"That's it," said Porter, craning between the front seats and pointing.

There was a white van towards the back of the car park, its driver's door open. The engine was still running, the lights on and a cloud of exhaust forming a halo overhead. Savage slowed down and pulled through the narrow gate, switching off the siren. The IRV crawled halfway across the car park before Kett put his hand on her arm.

"Stop here."

She did as she was asked, switching off the engine. It was so quiet they might have fallen off the edge of the world.

"That's what?" said Clare through Kett's phone. "Where are you?"

"Mousehold Heath, sir," said Kett. "The top car park."

"Already?"

"Savage was driving. Beaney's van is here, no sign of him, but the engine's running."

"I don't want you anywhere near that van," Clare spat. "I mean it. Stay well clear. I will not lose an officer to this arsehole. Hang back, I'll tell the 11th where you are."

"Yes, sir," said Kett.

"Bollocks," Clare added. "I know that tone of voice, Kett. *Yes, sir*, you say, but what you're really saying is *Don't mind me, I'm just going to drag my knuckles over there and have a quick look, just a peek, maybe sit in the driver's seat and push a few buttons, have a quick toss all over the back.*"

"I—"

"I mean it. Whoever this is, they are serious about hurting people. And you may think you're immortal, Robert, but I can assure you that's far from the truth. Do *not* approach the van."

"I hear you, sir," Kett said. "Loud and clear."

"Loud and clear my hairy tosspocket," Clare muttered, hanging up.

"Hairy tosspocket?" said Savage, horrified.

"Try not to visualise it," said Kett.

"Too late. I'm never going to be able to unsee it."

Kett cranked his door open, the warmth of the morning creeping into the car.

"Sir?" said Savage. "The Boss said to stay in the car."

He grinned at her.

"Just a peek."

Although it would have to be at a distance, he thought, because Clare was right.

There were some things you just didn't mess with.

"Savage, Duke, can you seal off the car park, make sure nobody comes back to these cars until we know what we're dealing with?"

"Sir," they said together.

The van was thirty yards away and Kett walked in a wide circle around it, as far as the car park would let him. It wasn't just the front door that was open, the back doors were too. There was no sign of anyone, but Kett could make out a pile of brown cardboard boxes in the back—all different sizes. A pigeon sat on one of them, puffing out its chest and cooing like a pirate that had seized a treasure ship.

"Anything?" asked Porter as he walked after him.

Kett didn't know, so he didn't answer. He retraced his steps, taking one of the footpaths that led into the trees and following it until the other side of the van came into sight. Porter moved with him, pointing.

"That's blood," said the DI.

There was an arc of red on the panel of the van, maybe three feet across and two feet high, the shape of it so perfect that it looked like somebody had drawn the first layer of a rainbow.

"Maybe," said Kett.

"It's blood, sir," Porter said again.

He was right. Kett just didn't want to admit it.

"More on the ground," Porter said, pointing through the thick bushes. "What is that?"

Kett followed his finger away from the back of the van, past a puddle of crimson-coloured mud, to a sheet of white paper that was tangled in a bush. This, too, looked as if it had a streak of blood on it. The gentle wind tugged at it, trying to tease it free of the branches that had snared it.

Kett swore, pulling out his phone and calling Clare.

"Sir," he said when the Super answered. "You got an ETA on the bomb squad? We've got blood here, still no sign of Beaney."

"They're on the move," said Clare. "Just hold tight."

Clare hung up. Kett watched the sheet of paper dance in the breeze, trying to lift itself like a trapped bird.

"We can't lose it," he said. "You got gloves?"

"Not if it means you're going over there, sir," said Porter.

Kett held out his hand and Porter reluctantly pulled a set of gloves from his pocket, handing them over.

"You have no idea what's inside that van, sir."

"I'm not going anywhere near it, Pete."

It was a lie, but only a little one. The sheet of paper was a dozen yards away from the vehicle—close enough for him to be blown to smithereens, of course, if there was a bomb and it happened to detonate. He moved fast, before he could change his mind, the pigeon startling as he crashed through the trees and onto the dirt of the car park. He stuffed his hand into the glove as he went, not a single finger in the right place, and snatched the sheet of paper from the bush. Then he bolted back the way he'd come.

A horn blasted from the direction of the van, a klaxon so loud that it cut the legs right out from underneath him. He hurled himself into the bushes, landing hard in a cluster of nettles—waiting for the flash, for the thunder, for the concussive blast that would end him.

It didn't come. There was only Porter, leaning over and offering him a hand.

"You alright down there, sir?" he said. "Fancied a nap?"

"Something like that," said Kett, grabbing Porter and hauling himself up.

The sound of the horn came again, from deeper in the car park.

"Think somebody's trying to get out," Porter said.

"Do me a favour and arrest them," said Kett, brushing himself down with his free hand. His face was burning from the nettle stings, and when he looked at his leg he saw that he'd torn his trousers. "For fuck's sake," he said. "I've only just bought this suit."

"Good news is you can buy about five of them for a

tenner, sir," Porter said, looking at Kett's clothes with disapproval. "From the Salvation Army. What did you get?"

It took Kett a moment to remember the note in his hand, and he lifted it so they could both take a look. It was a sheet of A4 folded in half, nothing on the outer side. Kett opened it up.

"Shit," he said.

Written on the paper in small, neat capital letters were four words.

ARE YOU FEELING LUCKY?

CHAPTER NINE

"Van's clear."

The soldier from the 11th removed his helmet, his face dripping with sweat—although, whether it was from the job or the rising heat of the day, Kett couldn't be sure. He was kitted out in black armoured clothing, a thick neck plate concealing the bottom part of his face. Behind him stood two more soldiers, these in standard camouflage, and a robot that looked like a grown-up version of WALL-E.

The van sat in the same place they'd first found it an hour ago, the doors still open but the engine now off. The robot—called Harris, apparently—had done a good job of opening the boxes inside, and the bomb disposal technician had boarded the van afterwards to make sure.

"No sign of explosives in the packages and the van isn't rigged," he went on, wiping his brow with a gloved hand. "No residue, from what I can see. If this is our bomber's van then he's cleaned up, covered his tracks."

"But that is blood?" asked Superintendent Clare.

He and Kett were leaning against an IRV by the entrance to the car park while more coppers stood further back. It was shady there, but the day was warming fast, as if the heat from the explosion was creeping up the hill. Gurney Road had been closed off completely, the loudest sound the chatter of the birds in the trees as they watched.

The technician glanced at the side of the van.

"Not my purview, to be honest," he said. "But yeah, that's blood."

"We okay to take a look in the van?" Kett asked.

The man nodded.

"You're sure?"

"Sure as I can ever be," he replied. He turned and lumbered off in his heavy gear.

"How sure is that?" Kett asked Clare.

"Toss knows. Take a look but make it quick. Cara's on her way up with the forensic team."

"Yes, sir," Kett grumbled.

He walked past the robot and the soldiers, all of whom were watching him with severe expressions, then hauled himself into the back of the van. The parcels inside—maybe a dozen of them—had been opened, their contents unpacked by the robot's extendable arm. Kett used his foot to go through them, seeing packs of A4 paper, plumbing fittings, video games and what must have been thirty packets of edible underwear.

"Good job Pete's not here," he said to himself, as much to distract him from the idea of explosives as tell a joke. It was like a furnace in there, his shirt damp with sweat.

Somebody thumped the wall of the van, a hollow boom, and he ducked instinctively. He turned to see Clare outside the doors, ogling ferociously.

"Christ, sir," he said, one hand to his chest, his heart thrashing. "What did you do that for?"

"Because you weren't answering me," said Clare, gurning over the tailgate. "Anything interesting?"

"Well, I almost shit myself, if that counts," he muttered. "Nothing I can see, just looks like Beaney's deliveries. I'll cross-reference them with the list we got from Nordelex."

"Try the cab," said Clare.

Kett hopped down, the pain jarring his knees as he landed. He limped to the open driver's door and climbed inside. It was tidy, the smell of leather polish mixing with the strawberry scent of the air freshener. Mounted on the dashboard was a silver frame, a photograph of the two girls they'd met earlier grinning out of it. Lying on the passenger seat was a printout of the morning's deliveries and Kett scanned it.

"Anything?" blurted Clare in a voice that was far too loud, his face looming through the door like an angry turtle emerging from its shell.

"You are really testing my nerves today, sir," said Kett, whose heart was doing a jig against his ribs.

He reached for the glove compartment.

"Try the glove compartment," said Clare.

"I'm literally doing it, sir," Kett told him, popping the clasp.

"Then do it."

Kett bit back on his reply, craning over to get a look at what was inside. He could see the logbook and the manual, and on top of that was a white envelope and a black Sharpie. He took the envelope in his gloved hand and pulled it out.

"What's that?" barked Clare.

"I'm just about to tell you, sir," Kett said, turning it over in his hands. It was sealed, but when he held it up to the sunlight that streamed through the windscreen he could see the silhouette of what was inside. "Money. Notes." He tested the weight. "Not much."

"It's not money, it's an envelope," said Clare. He was sweating heavily, and he kept tugging the collar of his shirt.

"The money's in the envelope," said Kett, frowning. "Are you okay, sir?"

"Of course I'm okay," Clare snapped back. "Low blood sugar."

"You could eat Duke's cake?"

"I'd rather pass out," said Clare. "Is anything written on it?"

"No," said Kett, checking the envelope again just in case. "There's a black pen in here too, a Sharpie. He might have used it to write the letter we found. *Are you feeling lucky?* Black ink was used on the parcels at Reed's office, too."

Clare nodded.

"Nothing else?"

Kett pulled both sun visors down, then flipped them back up. He checked the cup holders and then ran his hand beneath the seat.

"Nothing, sir. It's clean."

Clare mumbled something beneath his breath as he sloped away. Kett hopped down from the van, counting twenty hurried steps in the direction of the parked IRV before he took a breath of relief. He slipped off his jacket and draped it over the bonnet, scrubbing his face.

"Don't know how they can do that for a living," he said, watching the bomb disposal technicians pack up their equipment. "Terrifying."

"Balls of steel," Clare said, nodding. "They're heading over to Beaney's house now, just in case."

"I don't think they'll find anything, sir. His wife and

kids were there, and we had a look around. There was no sign of bomb-making equipment, no place to do it. No garage, no shed, attic's clear."

Clare sighed, scratching his nose.

"What are your thoughts, Kett?"

"I don't know yet, sir," he replied. "Let's say Beaney's our man. He has a grudge against Reed, Barnham and Crabbe. He—"

"Why?" asked Clare. "Why a grudge against them? They sell insurance."

"Maybe they turned him down," said Kett. "Maybe he applied for something and they said no."

"I've been turned down for car insurance before. I didn't bomb Aviva."

"I don't know, sir, but—"

"I did send them a very angry letter," Clare went on.

"Right," said Kett, fighting to keep his train of thought. "They—"

"And a photograph of my angry face," Clare said. "Because it's hard to convey your true fury in a letter, and it's important to show them exactly how you're feeling."

"You sent them a photo of your angry face?" said Kett.

"I did."

"Did it make them change their mind?"

"No," said Clare. "But I like to think some young upstart still has the image of my rage in his little head. I hope that every now and again he wakes up from a nightmare of it."

"Okay..." said Kett. "Uh, where was I?"

"Grudges."

"Right, yes. So let's say Beaney has a grudge, for whatever reason. He makes a bomb, hides it in one of six identical packages, then uses his work as cover to deliver it. The notes on the boxes look like the same handwriting as the note we found here, did you notice that, sir?"

"I notice everything," said Clare.

"So maybe that was a trial, or maybe he was supposed to put that note inside the box with the bomb, I don't know. He drops the packages off knowing that somebody from Reed's office will be killed."

Kett sighed, shaking his head.

"That's what doesn't make sense, though. Why a random attack like this? Why not target the person who turned you down, the person you have a grudge against?"

"Because he's not angry at the person, he's angry with the company," said Clare. "He just wants to damage it."

"Okay. So he leaves the bomb. But if he wanted to convince us he wasn't responsible, that he was just a delivery driver, then why didn't he carry on with his route? He could have continued on his way and then pleaded innocence. Instead, he comes up here, leaves his van running, leaves the doors open, and vanishes."

"Not to mention the blood," said Clare.

"Right. And it's a fair amount of blood. So either he's injured, or he's hurt somebody else."

They both watched as the IRV that was blocking the entrance to the car park moved back, letting a forensic van in. Kett could see Cara Hay in the passenger seat and he waved to her.

"So maybe he's got another grudge," said Kett. "Maybe he met somebody here and attacked them. He could have had a second vehicle. Whatever this is, he might not be finished yet. But..."

He hesitated, staring at the bright sky and its smattering of clouds until it became painful. Clare waited for him, showing uncharacteristic patience.

"What if this isn't Beaney?" Kett went on, blinking spots of sunlight from his vision. "What if he was just the delivery driver? Somebody asks him to drop off six packages on his route, they say they'll pay cash. It's a nice bonus and it will only take half an hour to run into the city and back. He does it, and he drives up here to meet whoever was supposed to pay him."

"The envelope," said Clare.

"Right, but whoever this is doesn't want to leave any loose ends, so they attack Beaney. They knock him out, or whatever, load him into a car, and bolt."

"Why the note, then?" said Clare.

"I don't know, sir. Maybe he used it to distract him. Attacked him while he was reading it."

Clare nodded, his face bright red from the sun. A bead of sweat rolled past his nose and he scrubbed at it with both hands like a bear trying to defend itself from a wasp.

"I bloody hate the summer," he said. "Nothing worse than a sweaty tosspocket."

"You have to stop saying tosspocket, sir," said Kett.

"We need to work both angles," the Super went on. "For now, Beaney's our man, but what you're saying makes sense. Either way, we need to find him."

"On it, sir. Where are the others?"

"I've sent Savage to talk to Justin Hope, the man who was fired from Reed's office. I don't know where Porter is."

"Oh no," said Kett, studying the car park.

"If I catch him eating a Twix, I'm going to ram it up his tosshole," Clare said, walking towards Cara's van. "Both sticks. See how much he likes chocolate after that."

"Ouch," said Kett. He pulled his phone from his pocket and found Porter's number, counting the rings until the DI answered.

"Hello," said Porter.

"Hello?" Kett echoed. "Since when have you started saying hello when you answer the phone?"

"It's what you're supposed to say, sir," said Porter. His voice sounded thick, like he was eating something. "Hello."

"Where are you?"

"Just went for a walk in the woods, sir. See if I could find some witnesses," he said, followed by a gulp.

"Pete..."

"I'm not eating!" he said.

Kett breathed out a laugh that almost covered the sound of Porter furiously chewing.

"I need you back here," he said. "Van's clear."

"On my way, sir," said Porter.

Kett hung up, taking a moment to close his eyes and let the sun rest on his face. Despite the muted chatter that filled the car park, the day was perfectly still. The birds rejoiced, their chorus spectacular. And why wouldn't they sing? Theirs was a world without bombs, without murder. Death was nothing to them. He breathed deeply, the air warm and honey-scented with the gorse that grew here. It was almost calm.

Make the most of it, he told himself. *Because it won't be calm for long.*

He had a funny feeling there was a storm coming.

CHAPTER TEN

Savage steered the IRV down the narrow street, her attention fixed on the run-down buildings that squatted on the right-hand side of the road—almost hidden behind a metal panel fence and a cloak of scrubby greenery. Duke sat next to her, humming something with intense enthusiasm. His eye had almost completely closed now, but he refused to get it looked at.

"What is that?" she asked him.

"Hmm?"

"The song you're humming."

He frowned at her.

"I wasn't humming anything, was I?"

She returned his frown, then glanced at the map on the screen and took the next turn. Ahead was an industrial estate, a small one. Half of the businesses were long gone and boarded up, the other half barely scraping by selling scrap, doing bodywork and one—a beauty parlour that looked decidedly out of place—offering massages for £15.

"Could do with one of them," said Duke, flexing his neck. "Think I pulled something in that fight."

"Trust me, you do *not* want one of those." She looked at the map again. "This is weird. This is the address Spalding gave us for Justin Hope. But there are no houses."

She drove slowly, the road dented with potholes. There were a handful of cars and vans, most of them clustered around a tyre repair shop, but other than that the place was weirdly deserted.

"Where are you?" she said, talking to herself.

She turned a corner into a cul-de-sac, seeing a window-fitting warehouse that had gone bust, its windows—somewhat ironically—smashed out of their frames. Past that was a smaller building with a triangular roof, most of the white paint on its walls peeled away to reveal the worn bricks beneath. It had to have been a garage at some point, the door into the small porch closed but the wide shutter open. A sporty-looking VW Golf was parked outside, two wheels on the verge. She parked right in front of it, their bumpers almost touching, and opened her door.

"You want me?" Duke asked.

"Can you check in with Spalding, see if this is definitely right?"

"Sure," he said, relaxing into his chair. He started humming again almost immediately.

The day was fast becoming a scorcher, the heat fierce even though it wasn't even twelve yet, making the short walk to the building uncomfortable. Savage stared through the shutters, sun-blind, seeing only darkness. She could hear voices, though, and what sounded like something getting punched.

She stepped over the threshold, her eyes adjusting to the shadows and making out a large, open space that had definitely been a garage in the past. Now it was a gym, sparsely kitted out with equipment that looked like it badly needed upgrading.

In the middle of the space were two men, both in their twenties. One held a heavy bag that was suspended on a chain from the metal roof. The other was attacking the bag in a frenzy of punches and kicks and knees and headbutts. Both were dressed in shorts and nothing else, and they were drenched in sweat. Neither saw her as she crossed the room.

"Hey," she called out when she was close enough.

Still nothing. The man who was doing the punching grabbed the bag and bit it like a dog. She thought she could hear him growling as he tugged at the fabric.

"Hey!" she said again.

The man holding the bag turned to face her, his forehead creasing into a frown. But the second guy was lost in his assault, his eyes wild as he bit and gouged the heavy bag. It danced on its chain, the roof groaning.

"Juss," said the first man, and he nodded to Savage.

Justin Hope—she recognised him from his company photograph—swivelled those same dark eyes in her direction, his arms still wrapped around the bag, his teeth locked in the leather. He looked wild, and she had to force herself not to take a step back, mentally clearing the path between her and the exit in case they came for her.

Hope let go of the bag. He wiped his face with his swollen knuckles, never taking his eyes off her. He wasn't a big guy but he was strong, barely an ounce of fat to hide his muscles.

"Aye?" he said, his Scottish accent soft, a Fifer maybe. "Who're you then?"

Savage pulled out her warrant card and held it up, although neither man took the time to look at it. She guessed they'd both seen one before.

"DCI Savage," she said. "Norfolk Constabulary."

"Savage, eh?" said Hope, grinning at his friend. "We'll see about that, hen."

"Justin Hope?"

Hope shrugged.

"I could be, if you like."

"And who are you?" Savage asked the other man.

"Phil," he said. "Phil You-up."

They both laughed and the atmosphere seemed to thicken. There was a *lot* of testosterone in the room, it wouldn't take much to ignite it. She wondered if she should call for Duke, but she didn't want to look weak, and Duke had already been beaten up once today.

Besides, she'd never been one not to fight her own battles.

"Anyone else here?" Savage asked.

She saw the way Hope's eyes darted to the stairs that sat against the far wall, and the office that took up half of the raised platform there. There was a window in it, but the blinds were closed.

"Nah," he said, returning his attention to her. "Just us. What do you want, Savage?"

"Are you aware that a bomb went off this morning at the offices of Reed, Barnham and Crabbe?" she said.

Incredibly, Hope laughed again, a high-pitched giggle that echoed off the walls.

"You think that's funny?" said Savage.

"A bomb?" he said when he'd choked back the laughter. "Aye, that's fuckin' hilarious. The bastard dead?"

"Ben Reed?" said Savage. "No, he's alive. But his wife died, and several others were injured."

There was no denying the smug look of victory on the man's face. He lightly tapped the bag with his knuckles, gloating at Savage. *Goading* her. There was something about his straight-backed stance that made her think of the military—his close-cropped hair, too, come to think of it.

"You know anything about it?" she asked him.

"Know they probably fucking deserve it," he said. "Pricks, all of them. Millie's the worst. She's the one who got me canned. Hope she felt it."

"That's all you have to say?" Savage asked.

There was an air of cold indifference coming off Hope that was worse than the fury he'd shown when he was punching the bag. It gave her chills.

"Aye," he said, shrugging again. "Good fuckin' riddance."

"Where were you this morning, between eight and now?" Savage said.

"Right here. Never anywhere else."

"You live here?"

"Aye," he said, and once more his gaze swung up those steps, lingering there.

"Can anyone verify that?"

He shook his head.

"Fuck would I know about making a bomb?" he said.

At this, his friend laughed, and a flicker of annoyance crossed Hope's face.

"I don't know," said Savage. "What *do* you know about it?"

He didn't reply, he just kept tapping his knuckles against the bag, a pulse of dull thumps. Sweat ran down his naked chest. Once again she noticed that unmistakeable, rod-straight posture.

"What did you do before you started at Reed's place?" she asked. "Military?"

Hope gave his friend a long, unfriendly stare, as if he'd spilled the secret.

"Aye," he said. "For a while. The 6th. Those cunts threw me out as well."

"What for?" Savage asked.

"None of your fuckin' business."

"Let me guess," Savage said, taking a step towards the men. "Aggression, violence, insubordination, assault. One of those? Maybe all of them?"

"Piss off," he said, his voice quiet, *dangerous*.

"Maybe something to do with weapons?" she went on, advancing even further. "Explosives?"

"You've got nothing on me," he said, pivoting his body so that those swollen knuckles were aimed right at Savage. "So leave. You're not the only one here who can go savage, you hear me?"

"I hear you," she said. "Sounds like you're threatening a police officer. Sounds like I might have to arrest you."

"Then you'd better get a few more boabs out here, pal, because you don't stand a fuckin' chance."

"Juss," said the other man. "Enough, mate."

"You can piss off too, Sam," said Hope.

He had a short fuse, and it was almost burnt out. As much as Savage didn't want to show fear, she'd seen the way he attacked the bag, and she had no intention of being his next target. She slid a hand into her jacket and felt the cuffs there, wishing there was a baton to go alongside them.

"This is my fault," said the other man, Sam. "I'm sorry. It's what we do here. The aggression. It's the way we train."

He stepped in front of Hope.

"We go full feral," he said. "Life or death. Juss has just come off a session, he's amped."

"I'm no—"

Sam put his hand on Hope's chest and gave him a look that shut him up.

"He's amped," he told Savage again. "He's buzzing. He doesn't mean it."

His words worked. Hope deflated a little as he took a couple of steps back. He went back to lightly punching the bag, feinting and striking like a boxer.

"See, he's fine," said Sam. "You don't have to worry about him. You can go."

"You know as well as I do I'm not going anywhere," said Savage, talking to Hope. "You going to come nicely, or in cuffs?"

He pretended not to hear her, battering the bag with increasing force.

"He hasn't done anything wrong," said Sam. "He's not like that."

This time it was Sam's turn to look at the office door, licking his lips.

"He's not a bad guy."

"Then you don't have anything to worry about," Savage said, still talking to Hope. "Let's get your statement, take it from there."

"I'll do it," Hope said, still punching. "I'll come down to the station or whatever. Let me finish here and I'll come this afternoon, nae trouble, I promise."

"I wish it was that easy," said Savage.

Something flickered in the corner of her vision and she looked at the office—just in time to see the blind snap back into place.

"Who's up there?" she asked.

"Nobody," said Sam, the lie written over every inch of his face.

Savage started towards the stairs, hearing the punches

stop.

"Dinnae," said Hope. "There's no one up there."

She took the steps two at a time, but she only had to make it halfway to the top before she spotted the padlock on the outside of the office door.

"Shit," she said.

She turned to see Hope at the bottom of the stairs, the same look of fury on his face that he'd worn when he was training.

"Shouldn't've done that," he said.

He took the first step and Savage braced herself.

"You think you'll win," she said, keeping her voice as steady as she could. "But you won't."

Hope took another step.

Then he turned and bolted, slipping on the warehouse floor as he legged it towards the back of the building.

"Shit," Savage said again, watching him go, his arms cartwheeling as he tried to keep his balance.

Sam stayed where he was for a heartbeat, then he ran as well, heading for the open shutter.

"Shit!" she said. "Duke!"

She dropped down the stairs, pulling her phone out as she went. She dialled Kett's number as she rounded the raised platform, seeing an open fire door in the back wall. As she reached it, she slowed, checking that Hope wasn't outside waiting for her. But he was still on the run, impressively fast as he cut down the back of the derelict window shop.

"Kate," said Kett when the call connected. "Any luck?"

"Hope's running," she said. "I'm in pursuit. Need backup. I'm in Sprowston, the Manor Estate, an industrial place. He's heading for the main road."

Hope cut out of sight down the side of the building next

door. Savage upped her speed, a full sprint that narrowed the distance between them in seconds. She slowed as she reached the corner of the building, peeking around it to see that he'd vanished. There was a fence at the far end of the alley, topped with barbed wire.

"You okay?" said Kett. "Be careful, Kate."

There were three windows on the side of the building, all of them like open mouths with teeth of glass jutting from their gums. He could have climbed into any one of them.

"Justin?" she called out. "This is your last chance, mate. Get out here or we'll hunt you down."

Nothing. She reached the first window, peering through it into a void of darkness. Hope could have been right there, armed with anything.

Or he could have rigged the place to blow.

"Yeah, not happening," she said quietly, backing away.

"Kate?" said Kett. "What's going on?"

"Can you get some people out here, sir?" she said. "I think he's got somebody locked up. I need to get them out."

"Backup's on its way. Don't take any chances, okay?"

"I won't, sir," she said.

She hung up, retreating from the building. She could hear shouts as Duke pursued Sam, but she jogged back towards the gym, plunging into the darkness, the shift in light so extreme that she almost missed the first step. Grabbing the handrail, she hauled herself to the top, reaching the office door.

"Hello?" she said. "It's the police."

Nothing.

She scanned the raised area, seeing more weight benches and a couple of exercise bikes. A rack of dumbbells sat against the side of the office. There was no sign of a key anywhere.

"Hello?" she called out again, trying the door even though she knew it couldn't open. "You're safe, I'm police."

Something moved inside the room, making the blinds tremble.

"I promise, you're safe," Savage said. "Justin's gone, Sam too. It's just me."

More movement, then the blinds parted and something steamed up the inside of the window. Savage caught a glimpse of a wide eye, a hairy nose, a big tongue. The dog pushed its head through the blinds and barked at her—a friendly bark—its foot padding at the glass.

"You have got to be kidding me," she said. She put her hands in her hair and breathed out a long sigh. The dog barked again, then it jumped down and started scratching at the door, whining loudly.

"Kate?"

She turned to see Duke framed in the open shutter, just a silhouette.

"Tell me he didn't get away," she said.

"He was like greased lightning, sorry," Duke told her. "Yours?"

"Lost him, but he hasn't gone far. He's in the building next door. At least, I hope he is. Can you go take a look?"

"Sure," said Duke, moving off.

"Aaron," she called out after him. "Don't go inside, just keep an eye on the place, make sure he doesn't scarper. I'm coming too."

He waited for her as she dropped down the stairs.

"I thought there was somebody in there," she said. "It's a dog."

She'd messed up, she knew. She'd come back inside. She'd taken her eyes off the building where Hope was hiding and he could have legged it. He could have gone anywhere. The frustration boiled inside her, and as she passed the heavy bag she let loose a solid punch, one that made it rock on its chain, swinging wide like a pendulum.

"Don't beat yourself up," said Duke. "You weren't to... Oh."

He was looking over her shoulder at the office window, and she followed his line of sight. There was still a face there but this one definitely didn't belong to a dog. A pair of sad, dark eyes stared through the blinds, then a hand pressed against the glass.

"Shit," Savage said.

CHAPTER ELEVEN

"So let me get this right," said Kett, as Porter drove them up the hill into Sprowston. The traffic was heavy, but the IRV in front of them cut through it with ease, letting them ride in its wake. "You managed to find a shop in the middle of Mousehold Heath. Which, as far as I can remember, is two hundred acres of trees and grassland and nothing else."

Porter hung his head—as much as he could when he was driving, anyway.

"It wasn't a shop, as such," he muttered.

"But you managed to buy a chocolate bar somewhere? In the handful of minutes you were in the woods? *How*?"

Porter sighed.

"I saw a kid eating a Fudge," he said.

"Hang on, you stole chocolate from a child? Pete, please tell me—"

"I didn't steal it," he said. "I bought it."

The IRV was turning right and Porter followed, steering the Mondeo into a small industrial estate that was already rammed with police cars. Coppers beetled about the place, one of them pointing down the street. Porter followed the direction of her finger.

"You *bought* a Fudge from a kid?"

"Yeah," he said. "And I didn't have any change, so I had to give him a twenty. His mum didn't want to let me have it, but twenty quid's twenty quid."

"You paid twenty pounds for a Fudge?"

"And he'd already eaten half of it."

"Jesus, Pete," said Kett. "You really need to get on top of this, mate."

Porter nodded, slowing to a halt behind an ambulance and gripping the wheel with both hands. He was doing everything he could not to meet Kett's eye. Kett dropped a hand on the DI's shoulder and gave it a squeeze.

"Small steps," he said. "We'll get there."

Kett felt him shrug.

"You need me in there, sir?"

"No. Can you head up to the hospital and check on the staff from the Reeds' office? See if you can get some official statements."

"Sir."

Kett spotted Savage through the window and got out of the car, offering her a nod. She didn't return it. Her face was carved from stone, her eyes full of worry.

"You okay?" he asked her. They both waved Porter off as he steered the car back onto the road.

"Hope's gone," she said. "Sorry, sir."

She pointed to a large building that had manufactured windows once upon a time but which now stood empty. Somebody had forced the front door open and he could see Uniforms moving about inside.

"He ran in there, but he must have got out when I... when I went back to the gym."

She nodded to a smaller building next door, and her face fell even further.

"There was somebody there, but I should have kept my eyes on Justin. I shouldn't have let him out of my sight, sir."

"Don't worry," Kett said. "You did the right thing. Tell me what you found."

"I'll show you," she said, leading the way down the side of the ambulance. The back doors were open and a young woman lay on the stretcher, a paramedic examining her. It was pretty clear what was wrong with her—half of her face was lost beneath a mask of mottled bruises, her cheek swollen and her right eye bloodshot. She was as skinny as a rake, and young—not even out of her teens. Kett felt a familiar rush of anger, but he did his best to bite down on it.

"This is Zoe," said Savage, quietly enough that only Kett could hear her. "She won't give me her surname and she doesn't have ID. Spalding's trying to work out who she is. She's sixteen. She told me that much. I found her padlocked inside the gym, in an office. She was shut in there with a dog."

Savage pointed over her shoulder to the gym. A slim, black Doberman had been chained to a metal railing beside the open shutters. It lay on the tarmac with its front legs folded and its head resting on them. It looked up when it spotted Kett, its rear end wagging.

"The dog do that to her?" Kett asked quietly.

"No, the dog's a teddy bear," she said. "Justin did that, I think."

"Is she talking?"

"A little. Paramedics said they'd hold her here until you arrived, but she really needs a hospital. Hope's a nasty piece of work. Violent. He was beating the hell out of that heavy bag when I got here. Biting it, all sorts. He looked like an animal. She told me she's his girlfriend, that's about all I got."

"How old's Justin again?"

"Twenty-eight, sir."

Kett nodded, ready to step into the ambulance.

"That's not all, sir," said Savage. "We found something in the office."

"Yeah?"

"Yeah. I'll show you in a minute. You want me in there with you?"

"Yeah," said Kett.

He climbed into the back of the ambulance and Savage bounded up after him. The paramedic, a woman in her late fifties, gave them a withering look.

"Five minutes," she said. "I'm not waiting any longer."

"Thanks," said Kett, as the woman struggled down onto the road. He turned to the girl on the stretcher, wincing at the mess of her face. He tried to keep his voice as calm as he could, but he could hear the way the anger made it tremble. "Hi, Zoe?"

She nodded, her eyes darting to him and then away again, as nervous as a hummingbird. One was so bloodshot that she looked like she was wearing a crimson contact lens.

"My name is Robbie Kett, I'm with the police. You're not in any trouble, okay? You're safe. You've met Kate."

A shadow of a smile appeared on the girl's face as she looked at Savage.

"You're doing great," Savage said. "How are you feeling?"

The girl shrugged, kneading the blanket in her skinny hands, scratching it with dirt-caked nails. Something in the way she moved reminded Kett of Alice—his oldest daughter was only six years younger than this girl—and once again the fury clenched inside him like a fist.

"Can you go through it once more?" Savage asked. "Tell us what happened."

Zoe continued to work the blanket, as if she was searching for meaning in the crumples and folds. She shrugged again.

"Justin locked you in the room?" Kett asked, and after a few seconds, she nodded. "Is he your friend? Boyfriend?"

She shrugged a third time, her bony shoulders like mountain peaks beneath her black T-shirt.

"Boyfriend," Kett said. "How long have you been together?"

"You're really not in any trouble," Savage said when the girl didn't answer. "I promise. We're going to get you to the hospital, then get you home."

There was no mistaking the way the girl flinched.

"How long have you been dating?" asked Kett. "You and Justin."

She glanced at him quizzically.

"Dating?" Her voice made her sound even younger, and Kett had to lean in to hear it..

"Going out," he explained. "You know, how long have you been boyfriend and girlfriend?"

"Since April," she said. "Since my birthday."

"Can I ask where you met?"

"School."

"Zoe, did Justin do this to you?" asked Kett.

The way she shook her head was almost wild, her hair falling in front of her face. She used her fingers to brush it back behind her ears.

"He can't hurt you anymore," said Savage. "He can't get to you now."

Zoe looked between them, out of the ambulance.

"Where is he?" she asked.

Kett and Savage exchanged a glance.

"He can't touch you," Kett said. "I won't let him."

She must have heard something in his voice because she seemed to relax, her hands falling still.

"He didn't do it," she said. "He didn't touch me."

"But he locked you in the room?" said Savage.

"For my own good," she said. "He was only trying to help me. He's only ever trying to help me. He says it's the only way, that I have to learn."

"By locking you up?" Savage went on. "With the dog? Like an animal? How long were you in there?"

"Just since last night," she said. "It was fine. He's not a bad guy."

"You're the second person to say that about him today," said Savage. "I don't think I believe it."

"Did he say why?" said Kett.

She shook her head but answered anyway.

"To help me," she said, studying her hands. "He only ever does it to help me."

"That isn't how you—" Savage started, but Kett shook his head. She stood back, rocking on her heels.

"The important thing is you're safe now," said Kett, looking at the paramedic who waited by the doors, catching sight of the name on her badge. "Julie's going to take you to the hospital, make sure you're okay. We won't call anyone until you tell us to, okay?"

Zoe nodded, the relief evident even beneath the bruises.

"Can I just ask you one more thing before you go?" he went on. "Did Justin ever talk about his former employer, Ben Reed? Or the company?"

She nodded.

"Bad things?" said Kett. "Did he ever say he wanted to hurt them?"

A hesitation this time, but the nod came again after a few seconds.

"Did you ever see him making something, Zoe? A weapon? Or a bomb?"

She opened her mouth wide enough for him to see that one of her teeth was missing, then she snapped it shut again.

"Zoe?" Kett pressed.

"Time to go," said Julie, the paramedic. "You two, off you hop."

"You want me to come with you?" Savage asked the girl.

"No," said Zoe, with zero hesitation.

Kett climbed out of the ambulance, taking Savage's hand as she hopped down. The doors closed, the girl's dark eyes watching them go. The engine started and it trundled down the road, its lights on but the siren quiet.

"What did you make of that, sir?" asked Savage.

"I have no idea," said Kett. "But what if he locked her in the room because she knew what he was about to do? She said he'd spoken about hurting Ben Reed, threatened violence."

"He was furious with them for firing him," said Savage. "Told me he hoped Millicent had felt it when the bomb went off. No remorse at all."

"So Zoe found out what he was planning to do, or he told her. She threatened to tell, so he beat her and locked her up."

Something about it didn't click, but he couldn't figure out what.

"There are still too many missing pieces," he said.

"I've got something that might help with that," said Savage. "This way."

She set off towards the gym, the dog getting to its feet as it watched them approach. Its tail was still beating from side to side, its tongue hanging out. It whined gently and Kett let it sniff his hand. He scratched the back of its neck—no tag on its collar—and when it jumped up and planted its front paws on his stomach he let it.

"Who are you, then?" he said, the dog doing its best to lick his face. "You're a good lad, aren't you?"

"Zoe didn't know its name," said Savage.

"Doesn't know the name of her boyfriend's dog?" said Kett.

He stood back and the dog whined again, pulling on its chain and looking at Kett with big, friendly eyes. Kett spotted a couple of constables idling inside the open shutters and called to them.

"Can one of you get the dog some water? It's baking out here."

He ducked into the welcome shade of the building, finding a sparsely populated gym, the heavy bag still swinging gently on its chain. A small office sat on a raised platform at the back, the door open.

"Cara's still down with the delivery van, sir," said Savage, leading the way up the steps. "But we can look. Duke opened the office door, padlock's been bagged. It was a big one."

Kett stepped into the doorway, the office even smaller than it looked from outside. Taking up almost all the space was a double mattress covered in crumpled bedclothes, and the smell that came off them—half human, half dog, and utterly unwashed—made Kett's head reel. A duffel bag lay open and empty next to the bed. There were a couple of carrier bags as well, stuffed with clothes and toiletries, and an orange bucket that was, thankfully, empty. Two posters hung limply from the walls, a Celtic Football Club team photo from six years ago and a fading portrait of Cheryl Cole from her Girls Aloud days.

There was only one other thing in the room, and it sat in the gap between the mattress and the wall. It took Kett a moment to identify it, because the dog had practically shredded it—scraps of brown paper everywhere, and a scattering of stones. But there was no mistaking what it had once been.

"That's another package," said Kett.

"Like the ones delivered to the Reed office," said Savage with a nod. "It's exactly the same, identical paper, and the stones match the ones that we found inside the other boxes —the ones without the bomb, obviously. Look, there's handwriting visible there."

She was pointing to a sliver of paper close to the door, and Kett had to duck down to make sense of what had been written there.

UCK.

"Lucky," said Savage. "Lucky Number something."

"Did Zoe say where it had come from?" asked Kett.

"She told me Justin left it in the office this morning. She doesn't know what time because she didn't have her phone. She opened it because she was hungry. She was hoping there was food inside. The dog ate most of the packaging."

"You think it's a prototype?" asked Kett.

"I can't figure it out, sir. But yeah, it could be a prototype, or maybe Justin made one in case we came by, so he could protest his innocence, claim somebody was targeting him as well. Or, and I hate to say it, because he seems like a genuine fudging winker, but maybe somebody delivered it to him this morning."

"Beaney," said Kett.

"Yes, sir. But there's no way of telling because there are no cameras anywhere around here. Half the businesses are bust and the buildings are empty. Closest one's all the way back on the main road."

"We can check the tracking data on Beaney's van," said Kett. "But if this was him, it means he knew that Justin had been fired, he knew he wasn't working in the office anymore, and he knew where to find him."

"Justin's been living here, sir," said Savage, grimacing at the bed. "If you can call it living. Spalding couldn't find a home address for him, but he's been paying the bills for this place for a while."

"It's registered in his name?"

"No, sir. That's the weird thing. You'd have to dig pretty deep to find out Justin was staying here."

"Christ," said Kett, locking his hands in his hair. "What the hell is going on?"

"I have no idea, sir," said Savage, looking through the shutters to where the Doberman was once again sprawled in the sun. "Right now the only person who knows is the dog, and he isn't saying anything."

CHAPTER TWELVE

THE HOSPITAL WAS BUSIER THAN PORTER HAD EVER seen it. Every single car park was rammed with vehicles and the queues stretched halfway back to the main road. He waited for an ambulance to trundle past, heading into the city, before pulling into the opposite lane and overtaking the line of angry drivers—half of which leaned on their horns, serenading him all the way to the main building.

"Keep your knickers on," he grumbled.

There was nowhere to park, so he left the Mondeo in the empty taxi bay with its hazards on. Getting out was like walking into a sauna, the heat radiating off the central wing of the hospital and making his skin bristle with sweat. The sun bounced off every single car, blinding him so much that he didn't see the guy sitting outside the main door until he heard his name being called.

"DCI Porter?"

Porter shielded his face with his hand, blinking fire. Will Talion, one of the employees from Reed's office, sat in his wheelchair beneath a sign that said No Smoking, a cigarette in one hand. There were a couple of scratches on his cheek, and a bruise that crept down from his hairline, but he looked reasonably okay, all things considered.

Talion breathed out a cloud of smoke and offered a wave.

"It is you, isn't it?" he said, squinting. "I still can't see straight."

"It is," Porter said. "DI, not DCI."

"Sorry, I don't know the difference."

"DI's cooler," Porter said with a smile. "Will, right? How're you doing?"

Talion shrugged, taking another drag from his cigarette.

"Been better," he croaked, exhaling. He looked at his legs, hidden beneath a hospital blanket. His wheelchair was covered in stickers—pretty much everything in the geek spectrum from Star Wars to Star Trek. "Been worse, too."

Porter nodded.

"You got your chair back?"

"One of the firemen brought it up," he said. "They fished it out of the office, cleaned it up. Was good of them."

"Mind if I ask what happened?"

"Yeah," said Talion. "I do."

He saw Porter's expression and broke into a hoarse laugh.

"Kidding, mate. Just shitty luck. Motorbike accident, six years ago. Was bombing down the A11 way too fast and a car switched lanes, nothing I could do about it. Flew for about four miles before I hit the barrier, or it felt that way at least. Honestly, I'm lucky I didn't pop my clogs right there."

"Sorry to hear it," said Porter.

"My own fault." Talion put the cigarette in his mouth, pincering it between his lips and turning his next words into a mumble. "You worked out why somebody tried to bomb us yet?"

"We're following some leads," said Porter. The sun was beating on him like a hammer on an anvil, a headache brewing above his left ear. "You sound pretty calm about the whole thing."

"Yeah," said Talion, sucking one last lungful of smoke and then scuffing the cigarette out on the wall. Porter could see that his hand was trembling. "I'm freaking out more than you know, just trying not to think about it. Hence the fags. I haven't smoked in years."

He studied Porter, his face serious.

"Why would somebody do that? I don't get it. Why us? Why..." He shook his head. "They told me about Millie. They said she's dead. That true?"

"Yes," said Porter. "I'm sorry. She was a friend?"

"No. I couldn't stand her. Nobody could, not even her own husband. *Especially* her husband. But nobody deserves that."

He stared at the ground for a moment like it might be about to disappear from under him.

"She's dead?"

"How long have you been working at Reed's, Will?"

"Five years," he said, pulling a packet of cigarettes from his pocket and tapping it on his thigh. "Since I recovered from the accident, pretty much."

"You're an account manager, right?"

"Yeah. Pretty dull, but at least I get to sit down all day."

He forced a smile.

"That was a joke. Sorry."

"I got it," said Porter. "Did you ever hear of any arguments between the Reeds, or between them and their clients? Any grudges?"

"I heard plenty of arguments between Ben and Millie," said Talion. "They never stopped. Gloria had to tell them off at one point because clients started complaining. They could hear them on the phones."

"Do you know what they were arguing about?"

Talion opened his mouth, then closed it again.

"I don't think it's my place to say, sorry. I mean, I will if you really want me to, but... I don't know. I don't want to speak ill of anyone, especially when they're... when they're not here anymore."

"Fair enough," said Porter. "But if there's something that might help explain what happened this morning, it's important you let us know. Do you know what happened to Asif today, after the explosion?"

"No," he said, frowning. "That's so weird. Asif's a bit of, you know, a dick, but I don't know why he bolted like that. Hope he's okay."

"What about Justin Hope?"

"Justin?" said Talion. "What's that arsehole got to..."

Porter saw the exact moment the thought hit him.

"Wait, shit, did *he* do this?"

"What happened with him?" asked Porter. He felt the tickle of sweat as it ran past his nose and he scrubbed at it. "He got fired last week, didn't he?"

"Couple of weeks now," said Talion, still bouncing the cigarette packet off his leg. "But he must have known it was coming. He was just an arsehole, the worst kind of person. Big mouth, never had any control over what came out of it. Never stopped swearing, even when he was on the phone with a client. Talk about unprofessional. I said something to him. Everyone said something to him, but he was..."

He paused, searching for the right word. He tapped his temple.

"He's got something missing, up here. You can tell. The

way he looks at you sometimes, it's like a... You know those dinosaurs in Jurassic Park, the raptors."

Porter nodded.

"He has that look, like he could quite happily kill you. Like he wouldn't even feel a shred of remorse. Wouldn't even think twice about it."

"Why would Ben and Millicent employ somebody like that?" asked Porter.

"He can switch on the charm when he wants to," said Talion, clicking the fingers of his free hand. "It's the accent. When he first started, I thought he was great. Good laugh, great banter on the phones. He got more leads in his first week than I do in three. It was Ben who hired him. I think Millie saw through the bullshit straight-away. She wasn't a nice person, but she was straight, and she has this way of seeing what's going on even when nobody else can. Had, sorry. Shit. She hated Justin, and she hated Ben for hiring him. She tried to fire him first, and that's when the *real* Justin came out. He made that place hell for three months before Ben finally let him go. But there..."

Again, he petered out.

"What?" coaxed Porter.

"Nothing," said Talion. "You'll have to ask Ben. I don't want to spread rumours."

"But..."

"They hung out together a *lot*. Ben and Justin. You'd come into the office and they'd already be there, chatting away. And they'd be the last to leave. I don't know what Ben saw in him, with thirty-odd years between them, but they were tight. Probably the military thing, right?"

"They were in the military?"

"Ben was, for sure," said Talion. "When he was

younger. Justin talked about it a lot, but he was full of shit, so I have no idea really."

"This is really helpful, thank you," said Porter. "If you could make an official statement at some point, that would be appreciated. We have a lot more questions. When you feel up to it, obviously."

"Any time," said Talion, putting his fingers to one of the scratches on his cheek. "I'm okay, couple of cuts on my head. They say I can probably go home today. I was..."

He tailed off, his face falling.

"Lucky," said Porter. "Yeah. You coming in?"

"Just going to have another one of these," he said, pulling a cigarette from the packet.

"You do know you're not allowed to smoke here, right?"

The man smiled, then winced.

"Then you should probably arrest me," he said.

Porter laughed as he made his way through the doors. He stopped for long enough to write a summary of Talion's words in a text message, sending it to Kett, then he scanned the map and headed for the lifts. He held the door for an old couple who chattered quietly as they rode upwards. They talked about their daughter, about their grandchildren, and he wondered if he and Allie would ever be the old folks who still held hands in a lift.

He had to take a moment, because he wasn't sure he'd ever thought of him and Allie growing old together. Not that he didn't want to, it had just never crossed his mind. He'd barely got used to the idea of them being parents, let alone grandparents. It made him feel guilty, and he couldn't work out why.

He let the couple off first then overtook them, following the signs to the ward where the victims of the bombing were being treated. It was quiet inside, the lunch trolley parked outside an open door and a sister on duty behind the desk. He held up his warrant card as he approached, even though he recognised the woman from one of the million other times he'd been up here. She must have recognised him too, because she offered a big smile as she studied him over her pink, half-moon glasses.

"Can't keep you lot away," she said, dropping some paperwork onto the desk. "Let me guess, the explosion."

Porter nodded.

"Can't believe it, can you? A bomb, in *Norwich*? Doesn't make any sense."

"Nothing really does anymore," said Porter. "World's gone nuts."

"The two women are that way," said the sister, nodding to her right. "Bloke's round the corner."

"He's awake?"

"Came in awake. Bit banged up, but he's well enough to never stop bloody moaning. He got lucky."

"I keep hearing that word," said Porter. "Round the corner? This way?"

"Yeah, he's in with his solicitor, I think."

"Thanks," Porter called over his shoulder.

He passed the first room, peering through the door to see Gloria in one of the beds and the younger woman, Sephie, in another. Sephie was asleep, her head bandaged, and Gloria put her finger to her lips when she saw Porter. He nodded to her and carried on around the corner, hearing voices raised in anger. He stopped, cocking his head as he listened in.

"... won't hear it, Giles, it's done. It's over. Sort it."

"Ben, listen to me, if you push it now then I can't guarantee it won't come back to bite you. You were this close to dying this morning. Millie's gone, we can be patient."

"I know she's gone," spat the first voice. "Christ, Giles, I was in the same fucking room. It was almost me. This isn't what I—"

There was a clatter of wheels and the lunch trolley appeared, the caterer popping her head into Gloria's room. The voices in Reed's room dried up and Porter heard footsteps approaching. Seconds later, a tall man in his early sixties stepped through the door, dressed in an expensive suit and boasting a fluffy white beard that would have made Santa green with envy. All semblance to Father Christmas ended there, though, his face taut beneath its balding scalp, his body wiry and his blue eyes like those of a hawk. He fixed them on Porter, his mouth a grim line beneath his beard.

"What are you doing?" he asked, his voice so like a headmaster's that Porter felt the smallest shudder of fear pass through him—quickly buried. He pulled out his warrant card again.

"DI Peter Porter, Norfolk Police," he said.

"How long have you been loitering out here?" barked the man.

"Long enough," Porter said, returning the card to his pocket. "You are?"

"Giles Morton," the man said, his voice so loud that Porter half expected the sister to appear and shush him. "I'm representing my client, Benjamin Reed. I don't take kindly to eavesdropping, DI Porter. We have a right to our privacy."

"Well maybe don't talk like you're using a bullhorn," said Porter. "I could hear you from the car park, near enough."

Giles swallowed, his Adam's apple like a blade beneath

the skin of his throat. He never took those almost supernaturally bright blue eyes off Porter.

"Why are you here, Mr Morton?" asked Porter, taking a step towards the other man. "As far as I know, Mr Reed hasn't been accused of anything."

"No, but his business was targeted in a vicious attack. His life was threatened, his colleagues were injured, and his wife was murdered. I am not just Mr Reed's counsel, I am his friend, and it is important that we establish the motivation behind today's assault so that we can keep Mr Reed and his interests safe."

"Sounds good," said Porter. "I'm just going to need a quick word with him."

"Impossible," said Morton, blocking the door. "Mr Reed suffered horrendous injuries, he needs his rest. I will contact you when he is in a position to talk."

"Sounds like he's talking just fine," Porter said, walking so close to the solicitor that they were almost touching. Morton showed no sign of moving, opening his mouth to reply. From inside, Reed beat him to it.

"It's fine, Giles. Let him in, for God's sake."

Morton gave a classic *harrumph* as he sidestepped out of the way, revealing a small room with a single bed. For somebody who had been standing next to a bomb when it had detonated, Ben Reed looked exceedingly well. He had a number of lacerations on his face, all held together with tape —including a large one that stretched from his left ear almost all the way to his eye—and he, too, had a bandage around the top of his head. Patches of skin looked burnt, some covered in a mesh. One arm was held tight in a sling, his bruised fingers protruding from the end like sausages. Other than that, though, he seemed relatively untouched.

Lucky, thought Porter. *Word of the day*.

"Mr Reed," he said as he entered the room. Morton walked in behind him, standing close enough to make Porter feel uncomfortable. He didn't let it show. "How are you feeling?"

"How do you think?" Reed shot back, making a great show of adjusting his position in the bed without actually shifting himself an inch. "It was a *bomb*. In my *office*. I'm *hurt*."

He pronounced every last word like he was auditioning for something.

"I'm sorry about your wife," said Porter, noticing her absence from his reply.

"And I lost my *wife*," Ben went on, shooting Porter a look. "There wasn't even enough of her left to identify. My poor Millie. She's gone."

Porter had trouble identifying the noise that came out of Reed's mouth, although it was making a pretty good attempt at being a sob.

"How do you know that?" Porter asked. "About your wife's body?"

"He told me," Reed said, nodding over Porter's shoulder to Morton. "Which is more than you lot had the courtesy of doing."

"I am sorry," Porter said.

"It's horrific," Reed went on, although it wasn't clear whether he was talking about what had happened to his wife, or the lack of contact with the police. He turned his attention to the window, staring at it even though the curtains had been drawn. Sunlight leaked through them, pooling on the floor.

"I have to ask, Mr Reed," said Porter. "Do you have any idea of who might have done this?"

Morton cleared his throat with enough force that Porter

could feel his breath on the back of his neck. He walked to the foot of the bed to get away from the coffee and pipe tobacco smell of him.

"Because this was a bomb," he went on. "And as far as I know, there hasn't been one of those in Norwich since the Second World War. Why would somebody want to set off an IED in your office?"

"I don't know," Reed said, still staring at the window.

There was a knock at the door and everyone turned to see the lunch trolley there, the caterer offering a friendly smile.

"Can I interest you in something to eat?" she said. "We've got beef stew, but if it's a little hot then I can get you a sandwich."

"No," barked Reed.

"Got brownie and custard for dessert," she went on, rubbing her tummy as if she was serving lunch in the children's ward. "It's my favourite."

"No, thank you," said Morton.

"Well, I'm just going to plop it down here," said the woman, carrying a tray into the room. "No pressure to eat it, but you should keep your strength up."

They all waited as she placed the tray on the bedside table and walked out of the room.

"Have you—" started Porter, only for the woman to reappear with a plastic cup in her hand.

"A little squash," she said. "Stay hydrated, love."

She put it down on the tray, then left.

"Have you upset anyone recently?" Porter asked. "Have you had any dealings with criminal groups?"

"No," said Morton. "He hasn't. It sounds almost like you're accusing my client of—"

"We sell insurance," Reed said. "Bloody public liability

insurance, to companies. It's the most boring job in the world. It's impossible to offend anyone in this business because we don't do anything. We don't offer the policies, we're just a broker. Nobody's ever sent so much as an email of complaint, let alone *this*."

"What about you personally, then?" Porter went on. "Have you fallen out with anybody recently?"

"No," gasped Reed, a little too enthusiastically.

"And Millicent? Could she have been the victim of a grudge?"

"No," he said, firmer this time.

"There's nobody you can think of who would want to hurt your wife?"

"No," he said for a third time.

"You heard him," added Morton.

The sweet smell from the tray was filling the room, and Porter's stomach grumbled like an angry dog.

"You recently let a member of staff go," he said. "Justin Hope."

"What's that got to do with anything?" Reed said. Porter could almost see the anger rising in him, it seemed to make every part of him bristle.

"Did he threaten you after you fired him?"

"No," Reed said. He took a heaving breath. "Well, yes, but—"

Morton cleared his throat again, and Ben stopped talking. Porter turned to the solicitor.

"Do you need to get yourself a glass of water, mate?"

Morton didn't reply, those eyes boring into Porter's skull.

"Just the usual empty promises of violence," Reed said quietly. "He wouldn't have done anything."

"He wouldn't have done *this*?" asked Porter. "He was ex-army, wasn't he?"

"How do you—" Reed started, looking at Porter. "I don't know. Possibly."

"My client needs to rest," said Morton, but Porter spoke over him.

"As are you, Mr Reed? Is that right?"

For the first time, Reed's expression showed fear—only for a fraction of a second before he recovered.

"This is outrageous," said Morton, stepping up to the bed. "I must insist that this grotesque line of questioning—"

"It's fine," said Reed, shooting a look at his solicitor. "Christ, Giles, it's not like they can't bloody find out. Yes, I was army. A long time ago. Served in the Gulf. Logistics, not combat."

There were a dozen more questions Porter wanted to ask, but he held his tongue. Something was telling him this wasn't the right time. He took a deep breath of custard-scented air and changed tack.

"You were there at the time of the delivery this morning, weren't you?"

Reed nodded.

"I was in the kitchen, trying to get the damned coffee machine to work. I heard the van, but Gloria took the delivery. I didn't see the driver. Then I went upstairs to my office."

"Millicent was in the office already?" asked Porter. "Sorry, I know this must be hard."

"She was," he said, clearing his throat. He turned his attention back to the window, his eyes glassy. "I sat at my desk and a few minutes later Seraphina brought two parcels to us. There were no labels, so she gave one to me and one to... one to Millie."

A flurry of emotion crumpled his face, ironed out in a handful of seconds.

"That's definitely how it happened?" Porter asked. "Seraphina handed you each a parcel. She didn't hand them both to you, or both to Millie?"

"No, she handed one to Millie, and she took it. She placed mine on my desk."

"Did you open it?"

"God no," he said with an expression of distaste. "We get sent all sorts of shit from the companies we do business with. I never open them. This looked like cheap wine."

"Can you walk me through what happened?" Porter asked. "What you remember?"

Reed sighed, shrugged, winced. For a few seconds, the only sound in the room was Morton's heavy breathing.

"I remember I left the room," Ben said. "I needed to ask Gloria something about an Aviva account."

"Do you know if Millie had opened her box by then?"

"She was opening it as I left," he said. "I remember thinking... I remember thinking that if she spent less time opening gifts and more time..."

He faltered, and once again Morton cleared his throat. Porter ignored it.

"Last thing I ever thought about her," he said. "Can't even remember the last thing I actually said. Something about her squeaky bloody chair, I think."

Porter waited for Reed to find his way back.

"I walked to Gloria's office; it's on the other side of the landing. I... I think I spoke to her, or was about to speak. Then..."

He gasped like a fish out of water.

"I remember being outside, on the kitchen roof. I remember the firemen. The pain, it was..."

"Please," said Morton, softer now. "He really has been through a lot. I know you think we're arseholes, but I just want him to get some rest. He has nothing to hide, DI Porter. He will talk to you as much as you like, another time."

Porter nodded, then opened his wallet and pulled out a business card. He set it down on the foot of the bed.

"Thanks for your time, Mr Reed. If anything else occurs to you, let me know."

Reed nodded, staring at the window like he could see right through the curtains to the world that burned quietly outside.

"Just one more thing," said Porter, and Morton sighed like an irritated parent. "When I was outside, I heard you asking your solicitor to 'sort it.' Do you mind if I ask what you were talking about?"

"Yes, he does," said Morton, the same cold hostility returning. "It's a private matter, and nothing to do with what happened this morning."

"Yeah?" Porter said, directing the question to Reed.

"Yeah," Reed replied, not meeting Porter's eye.

"Fair enough," he said, waiting a moment more before heading for the door. He stopped on the way, looking at the tray of food that had been left. A square brownie sat in a puddle of custard in a plastic bowl, looking more than a little sorry for itself. "You going to eat this?" he asked.

"No," said Ben. "Wouldn't touch that shit with a barge-pole. Help yourself."

"Don't mind if I do," said Porter, picking up the bowl and the spoon and heading for the door. "We'll be in touch."

CHAPTER THIRTEEN

KETT STEPPED OUT OF THE KITCHEN, THE MUG OF TEA he'd just made burning his fingers. He shifted it to his other hand as he walked back into the offices of the Major Investigation Team. The bullpen was still deserted, so he made his way along the corridor towards the Incident Room. There was a noise like thundering feet from inside, as if a herd of elephants was stampeding from wall to wall, and he peeked cautiously through the door.

Four people were doing star jumps in the middle of the room, although some were finding it easier than others. Savage was bouncing like a gymnast, clapping her hands above her head each time she effortlessly launched herself into the air. Next to her, Duke looked like a bear who'd had its arse stung by a bee, performing clumsy half-jumps that more often than not collided with the desk next to him, shunting it across the floor.

DS Spalding was there too, clapping her hands without really jumping, and across the room a nervous, sweaty-faced PC Felicity Niven was doing her best to keep up with everyone.

At the head of the pack, watching the events with a glare that would have impressed even the most hardened drill instructor, was Superintendent Clare.

"That's not good enough," he roared. "Duke, those size-twelve boots have to leave the floor or it doesn't count. You're still on four."

"Four, sir?" panted Duke. "I've done, like, fifteen."

Kett pulled back into the corridor, but he was too slow. Clare whirled around and saw him.

"In here, Kett," he said. "You're not getting off that easily."

With a sigh, Kett entered the room, giving Savage a wide berth as she did her best to star jump through the ceiling. He set the tea down on an empty desk only for the Super to click his fingers at him.

"What, sir?" he asked.

"The tea," said Clare. "I can't reach it over there, can I?"

"*This* tea?" said Kett.

"Unless you've got another one stuffed up your hairy tosspocket? Of course that one."

"I, uh... I made this for me, sir."

"Tough titties, Kett," Clare said, practically gnashing his teeth. "You can't drink tea when you're doing star jumps. Hand it over."

Kett picked up the mug and deposited it on the desk closest to the Superintendent, staring lovingly at it for a moment before sloping back to where he'd started.

"Right, Kate, as you were saying."

"Can I stop, sir?" Savage asked, out of breath. "It's hard to talk and bounce at the same time."

"Blood flow is good for the brain," said Clare. "Keep jumping."

"Still no sign of Justin Hope," she said, struggling with

each word. "He's not in the window warehouse next to the gym, and PCs have searched every... building.. on the estate."

She stopped, one hand to her heart.

"That's a hundred, sir. I'm going to have to stop."

Clare grunted at her. She collapsed into a chair.

"We picked up his friend," she continued. "He's—"

"Hang on," said Clare, eyeballing Kett. "What do you think you're doing?"

"Me, sir?" Kett asked. "Nothing."

"Precisely. You do know what a star jump is, don't you, Kett? You did cover that in basic training, I presume? You do know how to operate your arms and legs in a sequence of rudimentary movements that will propel your sagging body off the floor and your arms into the air?"

"Sagging, sir?" said Kett, sucking in his stomach. "That's a little harsh, isn't—"

"Start jumping!" Clare roared, the shock of it launching Kett into his first leap before he even realised it. It was hard going, his legs protesting immediately and a stitch worming its way beneath his ribs after the first four jumps. Porter wasn't the only one who'd packed on a little weight in the last year or so, Kett could feel his gut wobbling a little every time he landed.

As much as he hated to admit it, maybe Clare had a point.

"Like I said, we picked up his friend from the gym," Savage continued. "Samuel Novak. He's a personal trainer, met Hope a couple of years ago and they've been tight ever since. He's under arrest but he's clammed up, doesn't know where Hope is and won't say anything about the girl. Hope must have some hold on him because Novak's looking at a kidnapping charge."

"He'll tell us what we need to know when I start shouting at him," said Clare.

"You can always make him do star jumps until he confesses," muttered Kett.

"We're hunting everywhere we can for Hope," said Savage. "There's a lot of heat pointing his way. He's ex-army, and earned himself a dishonourable discharge five years ago for threatening an officer with a loaded weapon. He has a big temper and a short fuse, and get this: before—"

She was cut off by the sound of a felled oak crashing earthwards as Duke tripped on his own feet. The giant PC took a table with him as he hit the floor, scattering two more chairs—including one that almost took out PC Niven on the other side of the room. Everybody turned to look at him as he struggled back up.

"Sorry," he muttered, his face slick with sweat. "I... I'm not really... designed for... cardio. I'm more of a... weights guy."

"You need to chase the bad guys, Duke," said Clare. "Not bench press them. Keep going."

"But I made you a cake, sir," Duke pleaded. "Remember?"

"How could I forget?" said Clare.

"Have you eaten it?"

"Yes," said Clare, his face too tight. He put his hand to his pocket, where the bulge of the cake was still visible. "It was... cakey. Now get jumping, Mary Berry."

Duke groaned at the ceiling, then started performing what looked more like a sulking hop.

"Uh, so yeah, Justin Hope," said Savage, obviously fighting to keep her train of thought. "He wasn't just discharged for the threat, he was also found in possession of some illegal reading material. Namely, how to make home-made weapons."

"Bombs?" asked Clare. The Super took a sip of the tea and Kett did his best to shoot daggers out of his eyes. He'd reached twenty star jumps and he felt like his spine was about to fold in on itself like a badly constructed house of cards.

"No," said Savage. "Guns. But there's not much between them, really. He was investigated internally, and by us, but I spoke with his CO, who told me they didn't actually think he was going to use the weapons. 'All mouth and no balls' is how she put it. We didn't prosecute, in the end. But it's the start of a pattern, right?"

"One... hundred..." said Spalding, collapsing into her chair.

"Are you sure?" Clare asked, eyeing her suspiciously. The look she gave him made it clear she was *very* sure.

"I've lost count," wheezed Duke, panic setting into his face.

"Then start again," said Clare. "For now, Hope's our number one suspect. There's too much pointing at him and he ran from the police. Any word on the girl he was found with?"

"Zoe Pankhurst," said Spalding, doing her best to catch her breath. "She's sixteen, lives with her dad about four roads over from Hope's gym. One of her friends posted on Facebook this morning asking if anybody had seen her, said she'd been missing for a couple of days. She told me Zoe's been dating Hope for a few months, and she didn't have many good things to say about him."

"You haven't... managed to talk... to her parents?" Kett said, struggling to get the words out.

"Her mum's out of the picture, left home years ago,"

Spalding continued. "Zoe lives with her dad. He's a builder of some kind, wasn't in when I knocked. I put a note through the door."

"Keep those legs up, Detective," said Clare, jabbing a finger at Kett. "Your feet have to leave the ground for it to be a jump. Higher."

"I can't jump… any higher… sir," he said, and it wasn't a lie.

"The profile on Hope is pretty damning," said Savage.

"Agreed," said Kett, whose jumps were now little more than painful stretches. "Aggressive, violent. That's got to be a hundred, sir."

"You're on 42," Clare said. "I'm counting."

"Christ," Kett muttered. "He made plenty of… threats against… Ben and Millie Reed, didn't he?"

The centre of his vision was going very bright, and a weird darkness was creeping in at the edges.

"He did," said Spalding. "They actually reported it to us weeks ago."

"They *what*?" said Clare.

"They sent four emails with screenshots, messages that Hope had sent to them. First was all the way back in April."

She shuffled through her papers until she found what she was looking for. Clare walked to her side and studied them for a moment, then he started to read them out loud. Kett took advantage of the fact that the Superintendent's back was turned, bracing his hands on his knees and sucking in air.

"'*You'll pay for this, you pair of raggedy cunts. I'll fucking end you and your shitty business. You don't treat a fucking alpha this way.*'"

"Alpha," said Savage, making a puking noise. "Why are

the men who call themselves Alphas always the ones who whine the most?"

"It goes on like this for some time," said Clare, without looking up. "But the gist is clear. This is a threat to life letter. Kett, why aren't you moving?"

"I am, sir," Kett said, everything aching as he did another star jump. "I did like thirty just now when you weren't looking."

"Likely story," said Clare.

"Why aren't *you* doing star jumps, sir?" Kett asked. "What happened to leading by example?"

"If I do a star jump, my entire undercarriage will fall into my trousers," Clare replied, still studying the papers in his hand. "You'll be mopping my haemorrhoids off the floor for a week. Do you want that, Kett?"

"God no," Kett said, pulling a face.

"Okay," said Clare, returning to the front of the room. "Okay, everyone stop."

Kett dropped into a chair so hard he shunted it backwards. The room pulsed white with every thrashing beat of his heart and he was drenched in sweat. Duke stopped as well, sitting on the edge of the table. He looked like he was about to cry. Only PC Niven was still going, resembling a wind-up toy as she leapt up and down. She'd been jumping non-stop since Kett had entered the room and must have been up to 200 by now, but she looked too frightened to say anything.

"I said stop, Felicity," said Clare. "No need to show off."

Niven looked insanely grateful—and a little nauseated— as she took her seat. Clare tapped the photograph of Justin Hope that had been pinned to the wall.

"Hope is our number one suspect. He's trained, he's dangerous, and he's evading arrest. It is essential that we find him, and I want everybody on it. What about our other man, Asif, any sign of him?"

"He's vanished off the face of the earth, sir," said Savage.

"But I did some digging," added Spalding. "Asif Nasir graduated top of his class at Oxford four years ago. Mathematics."

"What's he doing selling corporate insurance in Norwich, then?" asked Kett.

"He's been here since he graduated," Spalding went on. "Grew up in Manchester but came here because of a boyfriend. They're not together anymore, but he never moved away. His parents haven't heard from him since the bomb went off, and neither have any of the friends I've managed to speak to."

"We need to find him too," said Clare. "Any chance Nasir and Hope are in on this together?"

"Unlikely, sir," said Kett. "Asif was in the building when the bomb went off. He was lucky he wasn't killed in the explosion or buried alive. But it's weird, because people saw him on the street after the explosion, then he just vanished."

"Like Beaney," said Savage. "Anyone caught wind of him yet?"

"Nothing," said Clare. "No witnesses, no sign of him. The tracking data from his van put him at Hope's gym just before he drove to the Reed office."

"He made the delivery," said Kett.

"This case is five hours old, and it's already a mess," said Clare. "Our top three suspects are AWOL. I want everything we have up on the board now. And..."

He stopped, turning his attention to the door and sniffing like a lion that's caught the scent of a gazelle. Everybody looked with him, although there was nobody in sight.

"Porter, I know you're there," said Clare. "Get your roly-poly arse in here."

Nothing.

"In all my years as a father, I never once spanked my children," Clare went on, still talking to the empty door. "But I swear to the heavenly father, if you don't haul your panda-shaped body in here, I am going to bend you over my knee and give your arse the greatest fisting of its life."

"Oh God no," muttered Kett. "That doesn't mean what you think it—"

"Now!"

There was a shuffling sound from the hallway, and a second or two later Porter appeared in the door. He looked terrified, more so when he took in the sweaty, exhausted crew that sat inside the Incident Room.

"What's going on, sir?" he asked.

"It's called exercise, Pete," said Clare. "Get over here. I want a hundred star jumps while you debrief us."

"A *hundred*, sir?" Porter said, walking reluctantly into the room. There was a stain on his shirt, Kett saw, a hand-sized splodge of yellow. He decided not to mention it, but he wasn't the only one who'd spotted it.

"What's on your shirt, sir?" asked Duke.

Porter tried to cover it up with his jacket.

"Nothing."

"No, right there," Duke went on. "Looks like food."

"It's not bloody food, Duke, it's..." Everybody waited for him to finish. "It's bird shit."

"Bird shit?" yelled Clare. "What kind of bird shits bright yellow?"

"Uh..." said Porter, struggling. "An albatross?"

"It's custard," growled Clare. "I can smell it from here.

Who the hell has custard for lunch, especially when they're supposed to be on a diet?"

Porter hung his head.

"Start jumping, Detective. I want *two hundred* star jumps from you, and if you stop for any reason, you start again at zero. Understood?"

Porter nodded, doing something that was part jump and all jiggle.

"Go on, then," Clare barked. "What are you waiting for? What's your report?"

"Uh, I've just been to the hospital," he said, jumping again—so hard this time that his phone fell out of his pocket. He bent down and scooped it up, clutching it in his hand as he jumped again. "I spoke with Will Talion. He told me Justin Hope had made a lot of threats against the company after he was fired."

"Old news," said Clare. "Faster."

"Seraphina Newton was asleep, and I didn't get much of a chance to speak with Gloria Estefan."

"Easterman," corrected Kett.

"Right, yeah. But I did have an interesting conversation with Ben Reed, even though his brief didn't want me to."

"His solicitor was there?" said Kett.

"Yeah, and he's a bulldog. Claimed he wanted his client to be left in peace, but I could tell he was worried about Ben saying something he shouldn't. Before I went in the room..."

He had to pause to collect his breath.

"Are we starting at zero?" Clare asked, tapping his foot. Porter started moving again.

"I heard them talking, Reed and his solicitor. Giles Morton's his name."

"I know Morton," said Clare. "Pain in the arsehole, that

one. He's a criminal lawyer, too. What's he speaking to Reed about?"

"I didn't overhear much, just a couple of lines. I'd be able to think straight if I could sit down, sir."

"You can sit down when you're dead, Porter."

"Which probably won't be long," said Duke, who actually looked worried.

"I heard them talking about Morton sorting something for Reed, but he didn't want to do it because it would look suspicious. That isn't word for word, but it was the rough idea. Neither of them wanted to talk about it, and Morton made it very clear that if I kept asking questions he'd make life difficult."

"What are you thinking?"

Porter did his best to shrug mid-leap.

"I don't know, sir, but something's going on. I think we should look into Reed a little closer. Will, the guy in the wheelchair, said that Reed and Justin were tight, that they were up to something. They're both ex-army, so it might just be that, but I don't know, it felt off."

Clare nodded, deep in thought. Porter struggled on, almost to twenty star jumps and clearly suffering. He looked to Kett for help and Kett shrugged.

Sorry, Pete, he mouthed.

"Okay," Clare said eventually. "Porter, if your gut's telling you to follow Reed, then follow him. It's hard to ignore your gut."

"Especially *your* gut," said Duke.

"But be careful, because Morton's a vampire. Kett, Cara wants to talk. The rest of you, get after Justin Hope. I want him in custody by the end of the day."

"That's custody, sir," Duke said, aiming the words at Porter. "Not *custardy*."

Despite himself, Kett snorted a laugh through his nose, doing his best to cover it with a cough. Clare strode out of the room, looking back from the door with a gleam in his eye and a torturer's smile.

"But before you go, I want another hundred star jumps from all of you."

CHAPTER FOURTEEN

As soon as Kett opened the door, the smell of the sea hit him.

He walked into Cara Hay's office to find that the furniture had been rearranged, five tables positioned in a wonky pentagon. On each one was a cardboard box, some brown wrapping paper and a little collection of stones. In the space between the tables, Hay—Norfolk Constabulary's lead forensic technician—solemnly studied the exhibits. As always, she was dressed in a pair of white overalls and matching gloves. Her shaved head was so smooth that Kett could see the bright lights reflected on her dark scalp. She didn't even look up as he closed the door behind him.

"DCI Kett," she said in her strong Trinidadian accent. "How's the family?"

"Same as always, thanks Cara," he replied as he crossed to the nearest table. "The kids are feral, we're exhausted, and the house looks like King Kong has been using it as a nest. Alice is convinced I'm buying her a horse, and that it's going to live in the garden. Evie thinks the toilet is haunted. Moira's Moira."

Hay laughed, finally glancing up.

"You look flushed," she said. "Are you coming down with something?"

"Yeah, a bad case of Clareitis," he said. "He's been making us exercise."

"Exercise is good for the body and the soul," said Hay.

"Tell that to my poor knees," he said, and it wasn't a joke —his legs felt like there was glass in the joints. "What have we got?"

The door opened again before she could answer, Savage skipping quietly inside.

"Sorry, sir," she said. "I can go?"

"Stay," said Kett. "We need as many eyes as we can get. Can you make any sense out of this, Cara?"

She took a deep breath, studying the stones that sat on the table before her. Kett ducked down for a better look. There were over a hundred pebbles in each collection, and they all looked strikingly different. Some still carried traces of sand and seaweed, and up close the smell of them was stronger than ever. It wasn't a good sea smell, it was pungent and salty and it made him feel sick to his stomach.

"We have five boxes," said Cara. "These are the ones we were able to recover, four from the Reed office, that one from the gym where you found Justin Hope. There were two more boxes in the office, and we know one of those had the bomb in it. Both were destroyed in the explosion."

"Definitely just one bomb?" asked Kett.

"Yes. We haven't had the official report back from the bomb disposal team, they're still clearing the site. But I spoke with them and they are certain there was only one explosion, from a single point of detonation— upstairs, in the front room, closer to the door than to the window. The blast destroyed the other box that was in the same room, although we have recovered a number of charred stones that tell us that box was just like the others."

"Is there any way of differentiating them?" asked Savage. "Any names or details we might have missed?"

"No," said Hay.

She pointed to the table to her left and then the two behind her. Brown wrapping paper lay neatly to the side of each pile of stones, the cardboard boxes in the middle.

"I have studied them comprehensively, and there is nothing at all on the external wrapping—no invisible ink, no infrared ink, nothing. The paper was wrapped and folded in the same way, secured with glue—a Pritt Stick, or something of that ilk. Beneath the paper was a box, as you can see. It's a standard folding wine box, you can order them online for pennies. There is writing on every box that we have recovered."

"Lucky Number whatever," said Kett, reading the lines of text he could see.

"Indeed," said Hay. "We have recovered the boxes numbered one, three, four, five and six. Presumably, boxes two and seven were lost in the explosion."

"The text was written by hand," said Savage. "That's one thing, at least."

"They're written in Sharpie or the equivalent," said Hay. "Very neat, but not neat enough to be a stencil or a stamp of any kind. Your bomber has a very steady hand, not so much as a tremor. I've sent it to my handwriting friend, but there isn't much to go on."

"What about the stones?" asked Kett. "They're from the beach, right?"

"They are. We have a good assortment of rocks, all of which you could find on Norfolk shores. We have these flat ones, smaller pebbles, and the rounded shingles. We even have some quartz."

She pointed to the table on her right, at two marble-white stones flecked with blue markings.

"There are all kinds of different rocks here, all shapes and sizes—plus the leg of a crab, if that interests you?"

She pointed again to the table behind her.

"It tells me that whoever filled these boxes did so either quickly or carelessly. They weren't interested in a specific type of stone, they just wanted to pack the boxes as tightly as they could, filling the gaps with sand."

"Why stones, though?" asked Kett. "What's the significance?"

"Maybe there isn't one, sir," said Savage. "Maybe the bomber just lives near the beach. They knew one box was going to have a bomb in it. It was going to be heavy. They needed to make the other boxes weigh and feel the same."

Kett nodded.

"You're right, I think," said Hay. "These boxes were designed to be indistinguishable from one another. They looked the same, they weighed the same, they rattled the same if you happened to shake them. The only difference I can think of is that they would have smelled different."

"How so?"

"The explosives used in IEDs smell sweet. They often have a kind of almondy aroma. Marzipan. It can be subtle, but it's there."

"Any prints?" asked Kett. "Hairs? Anything we can use to track these back?"

Hay shook her head.

"I am afraid not, Robbie," she said. "The bomber was careful. They must have covered up—not a single hair, even in the glue, no prints on any of the stones. The paper is the kind that can be bought anywhere, and like I say, the boxes can be found in any wine shop, or online. I've asked a friend of mine to have a look at the stones, she's on her way. But just from the photograph I sent her, there's no possible way of pinpointing which beach. She thinks somewhere on the North Norfolk Coast, because of the crab leg, but..."

She petered out, her words becoming a sigh.

"I'm sorry, but we're dealing with somebody who knows what they're doing. It is no simple thing to make a bomb. And from my experience—which is almost entirely fictional when it comes to weapons such as this—bomb makers tend to be meticulous, organised and extremely careful. I don't think we will find anything helpful here, because I don't think we were meant to."

"Meant to?" asked Kett, frowning.

"Yes," said Hay. "Because your killer is sending a message, are they not? This was not a simple murder, this took time, it was planned out, and strangest of all, it was random. Six people would open a box and find stones, and one would set off an IED. There was no telling for sure who the victim would be."

"The hell kind of message is that?" asked Kett.

"That is what *you* need to find out, Detectives."

Kett studied the stones a little longer, trying to find some kind of meaning in those scattered pebbles, in those puddles of sand. The stench of them pushed its way deeper into his sinuses, so rich it could have been sewage. He retreated to the door, opening it.

"Thanks, Cara. Call me if something else shows up."

Hay nodded sadly before turning back to her work. Kett held the door open for Savage, closing it behind them. For a moment he stood in the too-bright light of the corridor, rubbing his face with his hands. Every part of him was aching, and he was a little disappointed in himself. There was a time he could have done a couple of hundred star jumps and barely broke a sweat.

"You okay, sir?" Savage asked.

"Getting old, Kate," he said.

"You're barely mid-forties, sir," Savage replied. "Age isn't the problem."

Kett lifted an eyebrow.

"What's that supposed to mean?"

"Nothing, sir," she said, setting off. Kett followed as she led the way back towards the bullpen. "The thing that gets me about this is the random part. The killer wasn't targeting a particular person. So this isn't a grudge, it isn't something personal."

"Unless when Beaney delivered them he left some kind of instructions," said Kett. "Some way to ensure the right package got into the right hands."

"Except he didn't," said Savage. "According to Gloria, he didn't say anything. Gloria brought the packages in and left them on Seraphina's desk. Beaney left without a word. Seraphina is the one who dished them out, as far as I know."

"What do we know about her?" Kett asked.

"Spalding's made a file, sir. I've skimmed through it. She's twenty-two, been working there a year or so. Fun, everyone likes her, no criminal record, and nobody in her family has one either. If she's come out of university—local uni, I should add—and switched from drama to murder, I'd be very surprised."

Kett walked through the door into the MIT's offices, feeling the familiar slow boil of frustration in his skull as he struggled to arrange the broken pieces of this case.

"And even if this was Sephie, sir," said Savage, "why risk it? Why deliver a bomb to an office and hand it out, knowing that at some point that person's going to open it and blow the place to smithereens? If everyone had been in the same room when that thing had gone off, they'd all be dead."

"True," said Kett. "Why go to the trouble of creating a bomb only to risk being taken out alongside it? Hay's right, bomb makers are meticulous, and the whole point of a bomb is being able to kill somebody—or a lot of people—from a distance. You don't want to be anywhere near it, unless you're making a political point, I guess. Has anyone looked into Reed, Barnham and Crabbe yet? A proper look?"

"I have, sir," said Spalding as she crossed the room, collapsing into her chair. She winced. "Anyone else's legs feel like jelly?"

"Yeah," said Kett. "He's a cruel taskmaster, for sure. What did you find?"

"Nothing," said Spalding. "They're an insurance broker, they deal with corporate insurance. They've never been in trouble, no fraud, no investigations. But..."

She left it hanging and Kett leaned in, Savage too.

"They weren't doing very well," she said eventually. "According to Companies House, they dropped into the red last year, income of less than £100,000 and seven salaries to pay out. Reed was leveraged up to the hilt. There aren't a lot of assets, either, and there was a pretty big director's loan taken out by Ben Reed earlier this year, which drained the company. They're treading water, and they're sinking pretty fast. One of the ex-partners is dead, the other's abroad and doesn't seem to bear enough ill will against Reed to want to kill him."

"Good work," said Kett.

"Not really, sir," Spalding replied. "I just went on a

website and clicked a few links. Anyone could have done it."

"Right," said Kett. "Well, thanks for—"

"Anyone except you, apparently," she muttered.

"What?"

"What?"

Kett cleared his throat.

"So we've got an insurance company going down the drain," he said. "Porter overheard Ben Reed and his lawyer talking about sorting something out, something that sounds dodgy. Then a bomb goes off."

"Ben Reed's wife died, sir," said Savage, reading his mind. "I don't think this is a scam to get money by destroying the business. Ben was in the room when the bomb went off, or just outside it, anyway. He's lucky he survived."

"They didn't even own the building," said Spalding. "It's leased. He'd have had nothing to gain by blowing the place up."

"So what is this, then?" Kett said, talking as much to himself as to the others. "What's going on?"

"Luck," said Savage. "That's what this comes down to, doesn't it? The boxes had Lucky Number something on them. Numbers one to seven, probably. None of the ones in Cara's lab carried the bomb. So that's numbers one, three, four, five and six. I'm guessing the dummy box that didn't blow up, the one given to Reed, was Lucky Number Two, and the seventh—the one with the bomb—was Lucky Number Seven."

"Unlucky Number Seven," said Kett, and she nodded.

"It's random," she went on. "It's like a game of roulette or something. There's no way of telling where the ball will land until it happens. It's pure chance. It's…"

She stopped, and Kett waited for her to find the words she wanted.

"It's a game, sir," she said. "The killer's playing a game."

"That's insane, Kate," he said, but she shook her head.

"It's not insane, sir. It's *extreme*."

There was no time to reply. The door to Clare's office swung inwards and he lurched out of it like a greyhound at the track.

"Drop your toss," he yelled as he stormed towards them, doing his best to put his jacket on as he went. "We've found our delivery man, Brian Beaney."

"Thank God for that," said Kett, following the Superintendent to the door. "Maybe he can clear this mess up."

"I doubt it." Clare wrenched open the door and looked back, his eyes red. "Beaney's dead."

CHAPTER FIFTEEN

SAVAGE DROVE THE IRV, BARRELLING THROUGH THE city with expert grace, cutting smoothly through traffic and taking the turns like a professional.

Sadly for Kett, he was riding up front one car back in Clare's hulking Mercedes. The Superintendent handled the wheel like he was wrestling a tiger, his big feet stamping the pedals like a possessed Morris dancer as he fought to keep up with the IRV in front. The fug in the Mercedes was worse than Kett had ever known it, the stink of unwashed teenagers rising from the boot as if Clare had a whole school football team hidden there. At least six air fresheners swung pointlessly from the rear-view mirror, plus two more slotted into the air vents, but they'd lost this battle a long time ago. Five rolls of toilet paper bounced around in the footwell, unravelling a little more with every turn.

"How much longer?" Kett asked, shifting his feet as one of the rolls tried to mount his boot.

Clare grunted, leaning over the wheel and attempting to defog the windscreen with his hand. There was a sharp crack as they overtook a stationary car, clipping its wing mirror.

"Oh, sir," said Kett, looking back to see the driver's shocked face. "I think you—"

"I didn't," said Clare, yanking the wheel so hard Kett thought it was going to come off in his hands. Kett's stomach pitched as they took the bend, Clare's tyres losing half their tread on the kerb.

There were more IRVs up ahead, a sea of blue lights, and the Super pulled up behind them. He honked his horn repeatedly until one of them took the hint and pulled over.

"Tosspots expect me to walk to the bloody crime scene?" he growled, honking his horn again to unblock the road. He wound down his window. "You're bloody fired, you hear me? All of you."

Finally, after a gruelling few minutes of shunting the car a further twenty metres up the road, Clare killed the engine. Kett climbed into the fresh summer air like a man who'd learned to breathe again, finally seeing clearly enough to figure out where they were. It was another industrial estate to the south of the city, this one bigger and newer than the one where Savage had found Justin Hope and Zoe. Giant warehouses straddled both sides of the road, a Screwfix to the left and what looked like a delivery warehouse to the right, its enormous roller door wide open.

It was around the delivery warehouse that the IRVs had arranged themselves, the area already thick with uniformed coppers. There were other people there too, Kett saw, a young woman who was pacing fast and screaming—*actually* screaming, the noise of it cutting through the warm air and leaving its cold touch on Kett's skin. Two constables were trying to console her, but she pushed them away hard enough to drop one onto her backside.

"Jesus," he said.

Clare was already marching towards the crowd. Kett spotted Savage, Porter and Duke getting out of the IRV and he met them on the way over the road. They didn't speak, there just wasn't room for their voices as the woman continued to scream and scream and scream.

"What the hell is going on?" Clare yelled, directing the question at a group of PCs standing by the open doors of the building. More coppers were visible in the shadows inside.

"We've got three more people in here," said one of the Uniforms, her eyes wide, her voice trembling. "And two... two bodies, sir. One is Brian Beaney. I recognise him from the alert."

"The other one?" asked Clare.

"I don't know, sir," she said. "He didn't have a... he didn't..."

"Another bomb?" asked Kett, and the PC shook her head.

"It's worse, sir," she said.

"What could be worse than a bomb?" said Savage.

Kett couldn't answer her, but when they stepped through the door and into the warehouse, he realised that the PC was right.

This was worse.

It was obvious that the warehouse wasn't being used, because it had been almost completely cleared out. It looked too big inside, a Tardis-like illusion that made the space between the walls seem gargantuan. There was a damp smell in the air, and the floors and the walls were badly stained, as if the building had recently flooded. Horizontal slit windows in all four walls let in shafts of light that hung like a giant's fingers, revealing the only structure in the otherwise empty room.

It was a scaffold of metal poles, professionally made and topped with a platform of rough timber boards. Blood dripped freely through the cracks between the wood, pooling on the floor beneath. The whole thing was maybe twelve-foot tall and twice again as wide, with a metal ladder leading from the floor to the top of the platform. Kett would have struggled to work out what it had been created for if it hadn't been for the seven lengths of rope that dangled from the ceiling.

Five of the ropes were limp. The sixth was an empty noose.

The seventh was a noose too, but this one wasn't empty.

"Christ," said Clare.

A man had been hanged there, his body swaying gently in the breeze from the open door, as if the day was trying to shake him awake. That was the only gentle thing about it, though. The man's death had been anything but. His eyes were open and still full of horror, his tongue a grotesque black snake that reached past his chin. His face looked like it had been beaten, his neck covered in scratches, the blood dripping past two tattoos—a Virgin Mary, a pair of bare breasts—and into the collar of his shirt. His fingers, too, were bloodied, and even from where Kett stood he could see that some of the man's nails had been torn free.

He looked away, staring through the doors at the blue sky, at the scudding clouds, at the birds who wheeled overhead, oblivious.

Only when he was sure he wasn't going to keel over did he turn back.

"The second body is up there," said the same PC who'd followed them in. She was pointing up the scaffold, although Kett couldn't see a thing other than the dripping blood. "Those three were here when we arrived. And the woman outside, obviously."

Kett followed her finger to the far wall of the warehouse, where two men and a woman were almost lost behind a wall of black uniforms. Most of those uniforms belonged to PCs, but three or four were young men in black T-shirts, the Screwfix logo plastered over them.

"They came to help," said the PC when she saw his puzzled expression. "The woman over there, she ran to Screwfix and used their phone, called it in."

"I'll speak with her," said Clare, walking over. "Kett, get up there and find out who our second dead man is."

Kett looked at the platform, at those fat drops of blood that fell through the cracks and spattered to the floor, and puffed out a long sigh.

"I can do it, sir," said Savage.

"It's okay," he said. "But I could do with some gloves, if you've got any?"

"I carry extra for exactly this reason," she said, pulling a pack out of her pocket.

"Thanks," he said. "You know me too well."

He offered her a smile, but it was like holding a fluttering match up against the night. The air was thick with the smell of blood, and he knew that nothing good waited for him on top of that scaffold.

Still, he planted his gloved hands on the ladder and climbed.

What else could he do?

It seemed higher than it had from the ground, higher than it had any right to be. The ladder must have been growing even as he was climbing, the platform stretching away from him with every step until—out of nowhere—he found himself level with it.

"Fuck me," he whispered. He couldn't have spoken any louder even if he'd wanted to, the air punched from his lungs.

Lying right in front of him, his limbs splayed in impossible directions, was a man.

At least, Kett *thought* it was a man. He was wearing black jeans and a grey hoodie, white trainers on his feet. His knuckles were tattooed, although Kett couldn't work out the letters beneath the crust of blood. There was a tuft of hair on his throat, the bottom half of a beard, but past that, there was nothing at all.

The man didn't have a face.

"Fuck me," Kett said again, his stomach clenching powerfully enough to make him groan. He shut his eyes, but he couldn't shift the sight of that glistening mess attached to the man's shoulders. The butcher-shop smell was overpowering, the sound of the blood dripping to the floor below surely louder than gunshots.

"Sir?" called Savage from a hundred miles below.

"I'm okay," he said. "Just give me a second, Kate."

She did as he asked, maintaining a respectful silence that was lost in the cacophony of noise that filled the warehouse. Kett reached for the man's leg, working his way up and then pushing into the pocket of his jeans. He was still warm, and for a terrible second—one that sent an electric jolt of adrenaline through his system—Kett thought he felt him move.

Hold it together, he told himself.

There was nothing in his left pocket, but when he tried his right he found the little leather square of a wallet. It seemed to take forever to tug it free, the entire platform wobbling, and he clung onto it as he descended the ladder. Even with solid ground beneath him, he felt like he was swinging wildly, as if it was he who dangled from the end of a rope. He had to force himself to suck in a breath as he opened the wallet, fishing out a driving licence.

"Stefan Kucharek," he read aloud, seeing a young, friendly man with a neat goatee looking back at him. He felt another sudden wheel of vertigo as he tried to match this man with the corpse that lay above him.

What happened to his face?

He leant his shoulder against the scaffolding bars that made up the platform, grounding himself there.

"He's twenty-nine," said Savage, leaning past his arm. "Definitely him?"

"I'm not sure," said Kett. "I don't know. He didn't have a face."

Savage put a hand to her mouth, glancing upwards.

"Kett!" yelled Clare from the back of the room.

Kett hurried over, his footsteps echoing. He passed the back of the platform, where a couple of wide-eyed constables stood guard over a spray of blood and matter on the floor. It didn't take a genius to work out that the mess had once been part of the man who lay on the platform, and Kett had to fight an almost overwhelming urge to turn tail and run.

Clare was standing in the middle of the crowd, the five uniformed officers and the Screwfix employees standing back to give the two men and the woman some space.

The men were like chalk and cheese, one tall and slim with shoulder-length hair who had to be in his late twenties, the other stockier with a closely shaved head and a beard who was maybe two decades older. His skin was a tapestry of old, faded tattoos, and he had too many piercings to count. The tall one had been crying, his eyes red raw. The stockier one had the look of somebody who'd just walked off a battlefield, his gaze locked on something in the middle distance. He was sitting with his back against the wall, and there was blood on his biker boots.

There was blood all over him, Kett realised.

The woman had the same build as the shorter man, a rugby player's physique. She had wide shoulders and a heavy stomach, her hair cropped short. She was covered in tattoos as well, including what looked like a knuckle duster on her elbow. She was dressed in a grey tracksuit and black trainers, and she paced back and forth like a caged pit bull. Her face was full of emotion, but there were no tears here, just fury.

All three of them, Kett saw, had swelling around their throats. The woman's was the worst, a ring of bruises that looked like a choker.

"Can you say all of that again?" Clare asked the woman.

"No," she said, her voice a hag-like croak. She put her hand to her throat, punching out words like they were causing her pain. "You fucking tell him."

"I will," said the taller man. His voice was surprisingly high, almost like a child's.

"Fuck off," croaked the woman, rounding on him. "How do I know you're not in on it? Eh? How do I know you're not part of this? Prick."

She spat on the floor by his feet, her saliva pink. The tall man looked for a moment like he was going to throw himself at her, but Clare got in the way, planting a big hand on his chest.

"You two, over there," he said. "Nobody says another word unless it's about what happened here."

A couple of constables moved in and the taller of the men stepped back, muttering darkly. The stockier one got to his feet like he'd just run a marathon, needing the support of one of the PCs just to make it to the door.

"I've got paramedics on the way," Clare said to Kett. "But they're going to be a while. Bloody ambulance service has been shredded." He looked back at the woman. "This is Linda Mayweather, she—"

"What the fuck are you going to do about it?" she said, still pacing. Her eyes were like two blisters, ready to burst. "You need to find this fucker, you need to make him... you need to find him."

"Can you tell me what happened?" Kett said, as calmly as he could. "From the start."

She looked as though she was going to punch him. Instead, she turned around and smacked both of her fists against the wall, resting her head between them.

"Fuck," she said. "I already told you, told *him*, I came here for a job, a security gig."

"Today?" asked Kett.

"Fucking yesterday," she said. "Walked through the door and some cunt started waving a shotgun at me, made me fucking chain myself up."

"There's chains over there," said Savage, walking over. "In the back room. Fixed to the wall. Seven of them."

"Yeah, I fucking know," said the woman, nodding across the room. "I weren't the only one, dickhead with the ink was already here, and the other man."

Kett saw her body coil into itself like she wanted to shrink away to nothing.

"The one who got shot," she went on, her voice softer.

"The man who threatened you, did you see his face?" asked Kett.

"No, fucker was wearing a mask, proper terrorist one,

black. Locked me up with the others. Christ, you'd better not let them go. If I find out they were in on this, I'll—"

"They're outside," said Kett, although he couldn't hear her screams anymore. "What happened next?"

"Nothing," said the woman. "We spent the whole fucking night here."

"Just the four of you?" asked Savage.

"Yeah. Lanky prick came in the night."

"You know the time?"

"Course I fucking don't, Columbo, he took my phone."

"Why didn't you call for help?" Kett asked. "Start shouting?"

"Because he was here half the time," she replied, her face still pressed to the wall. "And when he left he told us he'd be watching, told us if we said a word or tried to get our chains off we'd be dead, he'd come back and fucking shoot us, then he'd find the people we cared about and shoot them too."

"Do you remember anything about his voice?" said Clare.

"Yeah, fucker had an accent, something from up north. Don't know which fucking one. But he fucking meant it, didn't he? He fucking shot that man. He wasn't fucking around."

"Hang on," said Kett. "Back up a bit. You stayed here overnight, chained up. What happened next?"

"Nothing," she said, finally pushing herself away from the wall. Some of her fury had gone, but something else had rushed in to fill the void, something that made her tremble from head to toe. "Not until just now. I don't... I can't get my head..."

"One step at a time," said Kett. "Go slow. But get there, because this is important."

She shot him a cold look.

"Fucker came to get us about half an hour ago," she said. "An hour maybe, lost track because this doesn't feel… it's not *real*. He had another man with him, the one who hanged himself up there with the tits on his neck. He'd been beaten bad, face all split open. Fucker still had the gun. And that's the really stupid thing, isn't it?"

She looked at Kett like he might have an answer, then she turned away and spat on the floor again.

"We could have taken him, we should have taken him. He only had two shots, right? If we'd all rushed him, we could have fucking killed that prick. But we didn't, we just did what he said."

"What did he tell you to do, Linda?"

"Told us to climb the ladder, told us each to pick a rope."

She hesitated, and even with the noise of the crowd outside, the warehouse felt deathly silent.

"Told us all to pick a rope," she said again. "One each. He said only one was real, the rest were fake. He said we'd fall right through, all but one of us."

"Six of you, right? But seven nooses?"

She nodded.

"Did he tell you which rope to pick?" asked Kett. "Any clues? Anything like that?"

She shook her head and spat again, only this time it clung to her chin, hanging there.

"He just said to pick, but that one man didn't want to."

"Stefan?"

"Fuck do I know his name?" she said, wiping her chin on her sleeve. "Don't know him. Stupid prick called his bluff, told him he wasn't going to do it. Started yelling at him and…"

"And the man shot him," said Kett when she didn't finish.

"Yeah," she said, wiping her chin again. "Fucking shot him. Just once. He was standing on the ground and that other man was up there, about to come down the ladder, but it didn't matter. Just once, he shot him, and his fucking..."

She finished the sentence with her hands, an explosion of fingers.

"Just fucking *gone*."

The smell of blood had reached Kett again, gradually filling the entire warehouse. It sat on his tongue, in his throat, like he was drowning in it. He glanced at the door just to reassure himself that it was still there, that the world still existed outside this pocket of hell.

"Then what?" he said.

She didn't answer, staring at the wall like she was watching a replay of the last hour. She was, Kett realised. She'd be watching that same replay for as long as she lived.

"Linda, what happened next?"

"We did it, didn't we?" she said. "We fucking did it."

"You picked a rope?"

"Yeah. Put it round my neck. Didn't have a choice, did I? We all did it, him sobbing like a bitch."

She nodded to the taller man, who was out of earshot. She looked at Brian Beaney as he swung from the ceiling.

"Him too, wouldn't stop crying. We all put those fucking ropes around our necks and..."

The look on her face was something new; a pure, unfathomable horror. Her lips worked at silent words, froth appearing in the corners of her mouth.

"Did it," she said quietly. "He told us to step off the plat-form, and I did it. I did it. I did it."

"The noose wasn't real?" Kett asked, hating himself for

pushing the woman but desperate to know. Linda shook her head slowly, her eyes still locked on something only she could see.

"I fell," she said. "We all did. Rope undone itself. I hit the floor hard, too. But fuck…"

She looked at Brian Beaney again.

"We all hit the floor apart from him. Tried to save him but he was too high, couldn't fucking grab his feet or anything, and there was no time to get up the ladder. Had to watch him… had to watch him as he…"

"Linda, where was the man who did this to you?"

She looked at Kett like he was a ghost.

"Gone. By the time he'd stopped… he'd stopped choking…" Her brow furrowed into ridges, her eyes scrolling the floor. "Didn't even fucking stay to watch it. Just fucked off. We never saw him leave."

Kett caught Clare's eye.

"Just fucked off like we didn't even matter," said Linda.

"Can you think of anything else that might help us find this man?" asked Kett. "Anything at all?"

She shook her head, back and forth, back and forth, far longer than she needed to.

Then she stopped.

"But I don't need to tell you, do I?" she said. "You can watch it yourself."

"What?" asked Kett.

"Because he filmed it, didn't he?" Linda said. "He filmed the whole fucking thing."

CHAPTER SIXTEEN

The camera was an old Panasonic, with a tape rather than a memory card. It had been positioned on the floor in the corner of the warehouse, no attempt at all to hide it. Incredibly, when Kett walked up to it, he saw that it was still running, the whirr of the tape almost lost in the noise of people, in the growl of engines from outside the door. A little red light blinked on and off.

"It's recording," said Savage from his side.

Kett picked it up as gently as he could, turning it in his gloved hands until he found the stop button. He hesitated for a moment, thinking about the bomb and wondering if this, too, had been rigged to blow. But the camera was tiny and light, and he could see the little wheels of the tape rolling behind the transparent plastic door. He pressed stop and flipped out the viewing screen, but nothing happened.

"Not working," he said, tipping the camera upside down, then right way up again as if that might help.

"It's not a ketchup bottle, sir," said Savage. "Pass it here."

He did as she asked, fishing his reading glasses from the

pocket of his jacket. Savage clicked a button to stop the tape, then another one to rewind it. When it stopped whining she pressed play and the little screen fizzed into life, the picture dull and grainy. A black-gloved hand hovered in front of the lens, nudging the camera to the left until the scaffold came into view, too fuzzy from this distance to really make sense of.

"Hush," Kett said, leaning in. He could hear wet breaths, and past that the panicked shouts of a man.

The hand disappeared, and Kett saw a pair of shoes walking away. The rest of the man gradually came into shot. He was wearing a balaclava and a large coat, despite the weather, and in his right hand he held a shotgun.

"That's him?" came a voice in his ear, far too close, and Kett almost leapt out of his shoes. Superintendent Clare was standing beside him, his own breaths heavy and wet as he watched.

"I'm guessing so, sir," he replied. "Since he's the one holding the gun."

The man disappeared off-screen and a few seconds later, another round of screams rose, several voices crying out in a hellish chorus. The voices grew louder as, one by one, their owners stepped into the frame, some clinging to each other, some with their hands clenched in their hair, some looking like they might have been about to make a run for it before the man with the gun appeared again, this time swinging it wildly. Kett could hear him shouting—a definite accent there—but the camera's cheap speakers turned the words into static.

"We need a proper screen," said Clare, his words tickling Kett's ear. "I can't see a thing."

They craned in a little closer, watching as the man's victims climbed the ladder, forcing each other further down the gallows. The woman he'd been speaking to, Linda, almost fell off—or she'd thought about jumping, maybe. She'd been right, of course. There were six of them and one killer with, at most, two shots in his gun. If they'd rushed him, they might have got the upper hand.

Or they might have all ended up dead.

Kett wasn't sure what he'd have done if he'd been in their place. It was an impossible decision.

He wasn't sure he could have done *that*, though; he wasn't sure he could have reached out for that dangling rope and noosed it around his own neck. The squat man did it without hesitation, so did the woman outside. Only then did the other man, Stefan Kucharek, start shouting. Kett saw him gesticulating wildly, saw him lean over the platform, one hand on the ladder as he readied himself to climb down.

The man with the gun didn't give him so much as a second to change his mind. The screen flashed—thankfully, because Kett didn't want to see the moment Kucharek's face had been taken from him—and in the next frame he was slumped on the platform.

"No," said Savage, as if she hadn't already known the man's fate.

After that, there was only obedience. The three remaining victims looped the ropes around their necks and, in almost perfect succession, like synchronised divers, they stepped off the platform. Four of the nooses snapped immediately, a fifth—Linda's—took a few seconds.

Brian Beaney's didn't break at all.

Kett didn't watch him. He *couldn't* watch, because the horror of it was making his scalp fizz, making it feel like something was coming undone inside him, something that might never be fixed. Instead, he watched as the man with the gun bolted—literally the second the fifth rope snapped.

He ran from left to right, vanishing off the screen towards the back of the building.

"That's..." Savage started, but she couldn't find the words to finish. None of them could. Clare stepped back, his face ashen, his Adam's apple bouncing up and down in his throat as he swallowed. He met Kett's eye for a second before looking away, as if by acknowledging what they'd watched they would somehow make it worse.

"Time stamp is less than an hour ago," said Savage, squinting at the screen.

"He ran this way," Kett said.

He broke away, striding across the enormous space towards the only other door in the cavernous warehouse. It was open, leading into a narrow corridor with a toilet on one side and a cupboard on the other, and past that a small, windowless break room that was largely empty. A fire door stood open to the left, a welcome breeze feeling its way inside.

Somebody had secured seven bolt plates to the far wall, each three foot off the ground and spaced maybe twice that from its neighbour. Thick chains sprouted from each one, ending with a set of handcuffs—older ones, like the police used back in the 80s. The room reeked of human waste, puddles of yellow urine everywhere, and two mounds of shit against the wall.

"He didn't even give them a bucket," Kett said to Savage, who had walked in after him.

"That's weird though, sir," she replied, her voice quiet. "Because everything else has been planned out immaculately."

She walked to the wall and studied the nearest bolt plate, giving the chain a tug.

"Nobody's ever going to get these out. Must have taken

a while to get those bolts in. And the platform through there is professional, he must have had a scaffolder build it. Or maybe he is one."

"Maybe," said Kett.

"Either way, this is a lot of setting up, a lot of planning. You'd think somewhere down the line he'd remember they'd need to use the toilet."

"I don't think he forgot," said Kett, making his way across the room. "I don't think he cares. These aren't people to him. They're a game. Some kind of sport."

"Seven nooses," said Savage. "It's just like back at the Reed office. Seven packages, one bomb. Seven nooses, six rigged to fail and one rigged to kill."

"Lucky Number Seven," said Kett, stepping out of the fire door into the ferocious sun. There was nothing back there but an alleyway, the warehouse on one side and a weed-caked chain-link fence on the other. It was wide enough for a car, the alley emptying onto the main road that ran along the side of the building.

"*Unlucky* Number Seven, sir," said Savage. "Except there were only six victims here, right? Why? Where was the seventh?"

"There were only six people in the Reed office," said Kett, turning around and trying to make sense of the dark room through his sun-bleached eyes. "Justin Hope wasn't there."

"But Beaney delivered a box to Hope, sir," Savage said. "He was the seventh victim, but one of the lucky ones."

"Maybe," said Kett.

"Or maybe Hope made his own luck. Maybe he told Beaney to deliver the first box to him because he knew it was a dud, and it meant he could claim to be a victim too."

She checked her watch.

"Hope could have been here, couldn't he, sir? I went to his gym at twelve, or just after. He bolted. He could have come straight here. Maybe that's why he only had six victims instead of seven, because we found him. He might not have had time to find another one. We forced his hand."

"Beaney was taken before you met Hope," said Kett. "That would mean Hope kidnapped Beaney and took him somewhere, then went back to his gym, then went to get him again and brought him here. Seems like a lot."

"Except Linda told us the killer arrived *with* Beaney, sir," said Savage. "So Hope could have gone to collect him from wherever he was hiding him and driven back here."

"Why not bring him right here from Mousehold, though?" asked Kett. "He had the chains ready, it's isolated. Why wouldn't he bring him straight here with the others?"

Savage didn't answer immediately, studying the chains as if there were letters hidden in their endless loops.

"Linda said he had a Northern accent," she said after a moment. "Maybe she got it wrong. Maybe it was Scottish she was hearing."

This time, it was Kett who remained silent. He used the back of his gloved hand to scratch an itch on the bridge of his nose, and he suddenly found himself thinking about Billie, about the basement where the Pig Man had kept her for all those months. She hadn't been chained, not like this. Her binds had been emotional, and so much worse for it.

Why? he asked himself. *Why is this happening again?*

And he wondered, briefly, if this was *his* fault. If somehow he carried the curse of the Pig Man with him wherever he went. Because it just kept happening, again and again, these little flashes of hell that had crept through the cracks into the real world. It would never stop, he knew.

These monsters would just keep coming until the sun grew so big it swallowed the world.

"Sir?" asked Savage, studying him from the shadows.

"Sorry," he said. "Come on."

He made his way back through the corridor into the warehouse, seeing that it had been emptied of anyone who wasn't a copper. Colin Clare stood by the open main door speaking with a handful of uniforms, while other PCs scoured the corners of the room, their faces grave. The two dead men held their positions in the centre—one faceless, the other still swinging from his noose in the breeze from outside, both held up like trophies. Kett made himself look this time, out of respect. Because whoever these men were, whoever they had been, they deserved to be seen.

He couldn't look for long, though, because in his imagination he saw the hanged man open his eyes. He saw the faceless dead lift himself from the scaffold. His skin cold with sweat, Kett walked out of the warehouse into the heat of the day. There were still no ambulances, but it looked like Porter had corralled everybody into the shade on the right-hand side of the large door.

Thankfully, the woman had stopped screaming, and she sat against the wall next to the stocky man, her head in her hands. Porter was handing out bottles of water to the victims and he turned around as Kett walked over, offering one. Kett shook his head and Porter passed the bottle to the taller man, who took it like he'd been stranded in the desert for the last six weeks. He practically ripped off the cap, spilling more down his shirt than into his mouth.

"Okay," said Kett. "We're still waiting for the ambulances, and I know you've all been through a lot, but I need to ask a couple of questions. Would that be okay?"

The tone of his voice made it perfectly clear this wasn't

really a question, and they all heard it. Linda Mayweather grumbled into her bottle, kicking at stones, but everyone else turned their attention to him. He took a moment to study the two men and two women, using the back of his hand to scratch his nose again.

"I need to understand how you all ended up here," he said. "Linda, you told me you were here for a job?"

She grunted an affirmative.

"How'd you find out about it?" Kett asked. "An advert? Did somebody tell you?"

"Somebody texted me," she said, and both men nodded.

"You got texts too?" Kett asked them.

"Yeah, yesterday," said the shorter, older man with the tattoos. He sat back against the wall, rubbing the welts on his neck with both hands.

"What time?"

"Like, dinnertime," he said. "Didn't know the number, but they said they needed some security for a gig that night. Wasn't going to bother, but it was like thirty quid an hour, needed it."

He shrugged, blinking wet eyes.

"Did you all get texts?" Kett asked, and slowly everyone nodded. "You're all security guards?"

A less enthusiastic response this time, but nobody denied it.

"You know each other?" Kett pressed.

The stocky guy looked at the woman sitting next to him, the one who had been screaming, and Kett saw an answer there. They could have been brother and sister, Kett thought, both squat and broad, with matching scowls.

"You two? What are your names?"

"Bill Carroll," said the man.

"Roz," said the woman, nervously. "Carroll."

"You're related?"

Their scowls deepened.

"Married?" Kett tried again.

"Were," said Roz. "Long time ago."

"You're still in contact?"

They both denied it with an abrupt shake of their heads.

"Since when?"

"Why does it matter?" asked Bill.

"It just does," said Kett.

"Been three years now," he said. "Right?"

"Little longer," said Roz. "He ended it at Christmas. Slept with my sister."

"Didn't fucking sleep with her," said Bill, like he'd argued it a million times. "Wasn't like that."

"He's right, they weren't sleeping," said Roz, ramming a finger through the loop of her other hand. "Hard to sleep when your newt's crawling up somebody else's skanky drainpipe."

Linda Mayweather roared with laughter, but only for a second before her face fell again. She carried on kicking stones. Bill looked furious, but he kept his eyes locked on the ground.

"You were all texted around dinnertime yesterday?" Kett asked, trying to bring them back on track.

"I got mine later," said Roz. "After nine, it was."

"What did it say?"

"Exactly the same. Needed some last-minute security, only mine wasn't a gig. They wanted it for a few hours in the night. Gave this address."

Her puffy face seemed to deflate.

"He was waiting, had the gun, made me go into the back room and chain myself up." She nodded at the others. "Bill was there, him too, and Linda. I thought he wanted to... you know, I thought he wanted..."

"You really don't have to worry about anyone wanting to do that to *you*, sweetheart," said Bill, grimacing at her.

"Hey," said Kett, pointing a finger at him. "Any more of that and you'll be in the back of a car, in cuffs. Hear me?"

Bill sniffed, shrugging his beefy shoulders.

"Ignore him," Kett told Roz. "What happened? What time did you get here?"

"After ten. Drove. That's my car over there."

She nodded through the crowd to a Fiesta that had seen better days.

"You mean that's *my* car," said Bill. "Bitch took it when—"

"Last warning," Kett told him. He turned to the taller man. "You were next, right? What's your name?"

"Tommy," said Bill, the stocky guy.

"I know my fucking name, Bill," he shot back. "Tom."

"Lester," said Bill, and Tommy looked like he was going to try to kick the older man's head in.

"Tommy Lester," said Kett.

He heard the grumble of an engine, seeing the sun-washed side of a vehicle trundling down the road. He thought it was an ambulance until it moved into the shade and he saw that it was a forensic van. He didn't recognise the driver.

"You got a text, Tommy?"

"Yeah," he said, leaning against the wall. "Mine said the same as hers. An overnighter. Wasn't gonna come, but it's not payday for another week and I'm skint."

"That'll be all the weed," muttered Bill.

"Go fuck yourself," he shot back, turning to Kett. "I don't smoke weed, honest."

"I couldn't care less about the weed," said Kett. "What happened?"

"Walked over, only live up the way there. Prick with the gun was waiting for me."

"What time?"

"Fuck knows," he said. "Midnight, maybe?"

"Bit late to be going to work, isn't it?"

"Get all my jobs like that," said Tommy. "Last minute and shit. People know they can count on me."

"Fuck they do," said Bill.

"Enough," said Kett. "The guy who got shot, Stefan, what can you tell me about him?"

"Seen him on a couple of jobs," said Tommy. "Years back, mind. Thought he'd quit security to be a plumber or something."

The others nodded.

"You all seem to know each other," said Kett, "so I need you all to think, okay? Who would do this to you? A former employer? Somebody who has a grudge against security guards? What's the link?"

"I thought it was a joke," said Bill. "Saw the missus walking through that door and thought she was winding me up, thought it was one of those internet pranks. Nearly walked right out the door."

"Wish you had," said Roz. "Wish he'd shot you instead of that lad."

"Fucking charming, isn't she?" Bill said. "Cunt."

"You know what," said Kett, turning to Porter. "Get this arsehole in a car, he can finish this in an interview room. And not one of the air-conditioned ones."

"What?" spluttered Bill, watching Porter as he moved towards him. "Fuck you talking about? I'm answering your questions."

"You go nicely, or you go in cuffs," said Kett, glaring at him.

Bill held his hands up in surrender as Porter grabbed the front of his shirt, hauling him towards the nearest IRV.

"I'm the victim here," he bellowed, his voice cracking. "Fucking pigs, always the same, never treat us with anything but contempt."

Kett waited until Bill was inside the car, his shouts trapped behind the closed window, before continuing.

"What's he mean by *us*?" he asked Roz.

"Travellers," she replied. "He's part of the community, me too."

"And me," said Linda. "And he's right, you do always treat us like shit."

"Anyone else?" Kett asked, but nobody replied. He peeled off his glove and wiped the sweat from his brow. His eyes were stinging with it. "Do any of you know where your phones are? Or remember the number you were texted from?"

A sea of shaking heads.

"And the man himself. Did any of you see his face? Did you see any tattoos, or distinguishing features anywhere on his body?"

Nothing.

"His accent, then," said Kett. "Linda, you told me it sounded northern. Is that right?"

"Yeah," she said, but this time she sounded unsure.

"I can't even remember what he sounded like," said Roz, staring at the ground.

"I do," said Tommy. "It wasn't northern, or it was, but it was like it was fake, like he was putting it on."

"Putting it on how?" asked Kett.

"I don't know, it was like he was a northern person trying to hide it, trying to sound Scottish or something."

"Or a Scottish person trying to sound northern," added Linda.

"Yeah," said Tommy. "Maybe."

"Do any of you know a man called Justin Hope?" said Kett. He found a photo on his phone and held it up. Everybody but Roz shook their head.

"Roz?"

"I think I know him," she said, leaning closer. "Not sure. He's Scottish, right?"

Kett nodded.

"I worked a security gig with him last year. I'm not bad with faces, especially when they're young and cute. Although he was a nasty piece of work, punched a punter in the face when they started an argument with him. A girl. Knocked her out, got booted, never saw him again."

"Could it have been him? The man with the gun?"

Roz followed his gaze to the warehouse, her eyes serious.

"I don't know. I never spoke to him. But..."

She left it unfinished. Kett heard a familiar clomping of feet and turned to see Superintendent Clare marching towards him.

"Anything?" he grunted.

"Nothing concrete, sir," he said quietly. "But what they're saying doesn't stray too far from what we're already thinking. There's a link to Hope. Roz knows him."

Clare's eyes bulged.

"Then it's a good job his girlfriend has started talking," said Clare. "She's given us a list of possible addresses, so get your fat arse out there and find him."

CHAPTER SEVENTEEN

"I don't have a fat arse, do I, Kate?"

Kett hung onto the strap over the door as Savage drove the IRV. They were heading back through the city, the roads shimmering in the late afternoon heat. The sun hung right in front of the windscreen like it was trying to interrogate them, the force of it enough to blow out the back of his head. Another IRV rode in their shadow, packed with Uniforms.

"Uh, I'm not sure that's a question you can ask at work, sir," Savage said after a moment's consideration. "Not these days."

"You're probably right," he said. "Sorry."

"But exercise isn't anything to be afraid of, sir," she went on. "You know? I enjoy it."

Kett frowned at her.

"What's that supposed to mean? I'm not afraid of it."

"I'm just saying, sir, it's good for you. Not just your body, but your mind too."

"I *do* exercise, Kate," he said, although he was struggling to think of a recent example other than the Superintendent's forced labour. Luckily, Savage didn't press him.

"You should come running with me and the dog in the mornings," she suggested. "Just a quick 5k, half an hour at dawn. You'll be amazed how good you feel afterwards."

"Kate, you would wipe the floor with me," he said. "I wouldn't be able to keep up."

"I could go a little slower, sir," she said with a smile. "I could just walk. Backwards. On one leg. With my eyes shut. You could probably keep up with me then."

Kett made what he hoped was a sound of deep disapproval. He checked his phone to see Clare's text, a list of addresses provided by the young woman who Savage had rescued from Hope's gym. Kett didn't want to refer to Zoe as Hope's girlfriend, whether they were in a relationship or not. Anyone who did that to another human being didn't deserve a friend of any kind.

He felt the familiar itch of frustration, the need to catch their prime suspect stronger than ever.

"You okay, sir?" Savage asked, and he realised his fist was clenched on his knee, his knuckles blanched. He forced himself to relax it, flexing his fingers.

"Yeah. Portland Close, it's right there."

She was already indicating, pulling the IRV off the main road. The car felt a hundred degrees cooler now that the sun had shifted and Kett blinked the fire from his eyes to see a narrow street lined with bungalows. He checked Clare's notes again, no house number, just a handful of words: *vet, Reed, company, renovate, Hope / Zoe broke.*

"Where, sir?" Savage asked.

"I have no idea," he said. "Vet?"

"That'll be it," said Savage.

Kett followed her line of sight to a large building that occupied the end of the cul-de-sac. Past a large car park was a squat brick building with big windows that had been boarded up. A sloping white roof topped it off, like a badly designed birthday cake. All the letters on the woodwork had either fallen off or been removed, but their dirty shadows remained.

"Thorpe Veterinary Surgery," Savage said. "Vet."

She pulled into the car park and turned the engine off, the second IRV sliding into place beside them. Kett steeled himself, enjoying the last few seconds of air con before opening the door. The heat gathered him in a bear hug, the sweat oozing from him immediately. He slammed his door shut and joined Savage on the other side of the car. Five sizeable constables were pulling themselves out of their IRV —including Duke—reminding Kett of clowns clambering out of a Mini. He was relieved to see that all but one had Tasers strapped to their bodies.

"Right," he told them, checking his notes again. "*Reed, company, renovate, Hope / Zoe broke.* Your guess is as good as mine, but I'm thinking Reed's company owns this place and they were planning a renovation. Justin Hope and his girlfriend broke in, maybe?"

He looked at Savage, and she shrugged.

"Looks abandoned, but be careful. Our suspect knows how to make a bomb and he isn't afraid to use them. Oh, and he's almost certainly armed. If you see anything—and I mean *anything*—that doesn't look right, step away and let me know."

"We can't get the bomb squad out here, sir?" Savage asked. "Tactical team?"

"There's not enough of them to check every location," he replied. "There are fourteen places on Zoe's list. Just be careful."

Nobody looked reassured, but the coppers spilled out,

two heading for the main doors and two clattering around the side. Only Duke remained, and he looked troubled.

"Try not to let the case get to you, Aaron," said Kett. "This is a bad one."

"Oh, it's not that, sir," he replied. "It's the cake."

"Cake?" said Kett.

"See, nobody cares," Duke said. "Nobody even remembers. The cake I made Superintendent Clare."

"Oh, *that* cake," said Kett. "He said he'd eaten it."

"He was lying, sir," said Duke, pouting like a child. "I saw him pull it out of his pocket back at HQ. I think he was going to put it in the bin. I stopped him."

"Maybe he was just... admiring it?" Kett suggested, checking his watch. "But either way, Aaron, can it wait?"

"Oh, right, yes sir," said Duke, running off.

Kett and Savage followed him, rounding the corner to see that nature had done its best to reclaim the building, trees resting their branches on the guttering and fat, happy bushes nestling against the walls. The PCs were struggling to get through, looking like they were being eaten alive. There was absolutely no chance in hell that Duke would fit.

"Maybe we'll wait for them to open the door," said Kett, doubling back.

That wasn't going to take long. One of the PCs had managed to pry the board off the main door and the glass beneath had shattered, forming a puddle on the floor. Through the jagged-toothed frame was a throat of darkness, and a current of warm breath that felt even hotter than the day.

"You want me to go first, sir?" asked the PC.

"Yes, obviously," Kett replied, but with a sigh he walked past the man and sidestepped through the broken door. Glass crunched beneath his boots, the heat mummifying him. The air in here was like a sauna, so hot he could barely breathe. There was another smell, too, something sweet.

"Can I borrow a torch?" he asked, and the PC handed him one. He clicked it on to see a small waiting area, the chairs gone but the reception desk still in place. He sniffed the air again. That same sweet, chemical smell—like poisoned almonds. "Kate, can you tell those coppers outside to hang back?"

"Yes, sir," she said, and he heard the scuff of her feet as she ran off. It was only a second or two before she scurried back. "You're not going in there, are you, sir?"

"Just a peek."

He swung the torch to the left to see a toilet, then to the bare wall on the right. The only passage out of the room was behind the desk and he made his way towards it, the glass stuck in the tread of his boots carving trenches into the floor.

"Police," he called, the shadows gulping his words down almost instantly. "Justin, if you're here, let me know. I don't want anyone else to get hurt."

Especially me, he thought as he made his way around the desk. The door wasn't shut, thankfully, and he gave it a nudge with the torch so that it squealed open. Beyond was an ink-drenched corridor, two doors on either side and a fifth dead ahead, an emergency exit sticker on it. That sweet stench was stronger than ever.

"Justin?" he said, his voice breaking. "If you turn yourself in now, we can help you. Trust me, you don't want this to get any worse."

But he was speaking to dead air, he knew. The building was empty, not even a hint of a current.

It didn't make it any less dangerous, though.

He reached the first door and gently opened it, seeing a small room with an examination table in the middle of it.

Cupboards lined the walls, the doors were open, and a couple of damp-ravaged posters clung stubbornly to the damp plaster. One showed a sad, overweight dog staring at an outstretched hand that held a chocolate muffin. The slogan read: '*It's not a treat when it's killing them.*' He half thought about stealing it as a gift for Porter.

"Sir, you okay?" came Savage's voice, as if from a hundred miles away.

"Yeah," he said. "Don't come in."

He made his way to the next room, which was just as empty. The first door across the way led to another examination room, and the fourth led into a much larger space which was kitted out with a dining table and an ancient brown sofa. A kitchenette took up the far wall, the counter littered with empty wrappers and bottles. A stack of magazines sat on the table, and when Kett approached them he saw that most were fitness rags, well-thumbed. He didn't have gloves so he used his knuckles to spread them out, checking the dates.

The latest, a *Men's Health*, was from this month.

He scanned the rest of the room with the torch, seeing dozens of sweet wrappers but nothing that would explain that sickeningly sweet stench that filled the building.

"Sir?" came Savage's voice, much closer now. He glanced back to see her at the door, her own torch on.

"I thought I told you to wait outside," he said.

"Got lonely. Have you found anything?"

"Somebody's been hanging out here," he said, turning his torch back to the magazines. "Recent reading material, plus a lot of snacks."

"Cigarettes too," said Savage, nodding to the kitchen counter where a teacup was overflowing with butts.

"Although from the smell of it, they were smoking something else."

"I don't think it's weed we're smelling," he said, sniffing again. "It's like marzipan, isn't it?"

He saw Savage tense.

"That's what Hay told us to look out for, sir," she said. "IEDs have a sweet smell. We should go, get the bomb squad out."

"We should," he said, but he stepped cautiously the other way, heading deeper into the room. There was a wastepaper basket next to the sofa, full to the brim with tissues. He could see condoms as well, a lot of them. "Somebody's been busy."

"Poor girl," Savage said. "Zoe, I mean. If this is her. What a place to bring somebody. Hardly romantic, is it?"

"We already know romance isn't his strong suit," Kett said, running the beam of the torch along the counter. More magazines sat there, along with a portable LED lantern, a half-empty pack of toilet roll and a stack of unopened protein bars. "But this stuff fits what we know about him, right?"

"The fitness stuff for sure," said Savage. "And if this is him, he's left plenty of DNA."

"Grim," said Kett. "None of it explains where the smell is coming from, though."

He felt the shift in light as Savage lifted her torch.

"How about there, sir?"

He looked at the ceiling, which was made up of square panels. One, picked out by Savage's unwavering torchlight, wasn't flush, an angular grin of darkness around two of its sides.

"Good spot," he said.

He grabbed one of the chairs that sat around the table and hauled it across the floor, clambering unsteadily onto it.

"You want me to look, sir?" asked Savage.

"Kate, you may well be fitter than me, but I will always be taller."

"Unless you fall off, sir," she shot back.

He ignored her, using his torch to press the ceiling tile up and slide it back. Even with the chair, he wasn't quite tall enough to look inside, but when he gave the frame of the ceiling a solid tug, it didn't budge. He pocketed his torch, grabbed the frame with both hands and jumped up, every muscle quivering as he tried to haul himself into the gap.

"Let me give you a foot-up at least," said Savage, her voice quiet past the roar of blood in his ears.

Kett managed to hook an elbow over the frame, his legs kicking as he tried to haul the rest of his body upwards. His head was through the gap, but without his torch he couldn't see a thing. He tried again and his back threatened to cramp, but he clung on with everything he had—purely to show Savage that he was capable. The metal frame rattled and creaked.

"You're going to bring the ceiling down, sir," Savage said. "Be careful."

"I'm fine," he croaked, realising that he was going to have to let go with one hand to fetch his torch.

"It's not you I'm worried about, it's the building," she said. "Stand on me."

"I'm not going to stand on you, Kate."

"On my shoulders," she said. "I'm right here."

"I'm fine," he said, every muscle burning. "Just give me a sec."

Through sheer stubbornness of will, he snatched the torch from his pocket and clamped it between his teeth.

Then he hooked his other elbow through the gap and let himself hang there for a moment while he caught his breath.

Not such a fat arse now, eh? he thought, although he couldn't say it with the torch between his teeth.

He angled his head, seeing a large, high-ceilinged attic space beneath the sloped roof. Boxes were piled high on the far side, but there was another collection of packages closer, these ones smaller. The sweat rolled into his eyes, mixing with the dust and doing its best to blind him, but there was no denying that he'd seen those packages before.

"Shit," he said, or tried to say.

"Sir?"

There were three boxes there, all the same size and shape as the ones that had been delivered to Ben Reed's office that morning. Next to them was a large black suitcase. The sweet smell was stronger than ever, but it was mixed with something else, something much worse. Kett could smell the dead up here.

The *long* dead.

The stench of it, infinitely worse in the unbearable heat, made him heave, his stomach clenching into a fist. He barely kept hold of the torch, drool running over his chin and dropping onto his shirt.

"Sir, it's really fine if you want to stand on my shoulders. I'm stronger than I look."

He garbled a reply, sweeping the torch as best he could. The shadows parted reluctantly, revealing more boxes, and lumps of a deeper darkness that could have been hunched figures.

Then, out of nowhere, a set of glowing eyes stared back at him.

Shit.

Just an illusion, he thought. A pair of holes in the roof, maybe, or glass beads, or—

The eyes blinked in perfect unison, then started to move. He heard a thump as whatever it was accelerated towards him, a shriek of fury that seemed deafening in the dark.

"Shit!" he said, spitting the torch out of his mouth.

He shifted his weight, ready to drop, but he'd wedged his arms on the frame and he couldn't free them. The thumping noise drummed his way, that same awful high-pitched shriek rising even further. He tugged his arm, desperate now, the entire building seeming to tremble with his efforts.

It was too much, the frame snapping and a section of the ceiling collapsing. Kett fell with it, his top half still wedged through the gap, the sound like being caught inside a clap of thunder.

He hit the floor hard, too much dust to see anything— anything except the enormous ball of feathers that flapped its wings, the owl shrieking again as it hurricaned its way out of the room.

"Jesus, sir? Are you okay?"

Savage emerged from the chaos, sweeping a hand in front of her face as she ducked down beside him. Past her, Kett could see that half of the ceiling had come away, scattering the contents of the attic over the room. Dust was still raining down, decades worth. There were bones too, he saw —partially wrapped in thick, dark pellets and too delicate to belong to anything other than birds and mice. The frame of the ceiling was wrapped around his chest like a whalebone corset.

"Sir?" she asked again.

"That had nothing to do with my weight," he croaked.

Savage managed a smile. There were more footsteps now as the PCs from the car park ventured into the building, nervous shouts echoing through the dark. Duke was the first of them, his eyes widening as he entered the break room.

"Noted," said Savage. "You need help getting yourself free, sir?"

"No," he told her, coughing the dust from his lungs. "I'll be fine. You call it in."

CHAPTER EIGHTEEN

"Let me get this straight, Savage," said Clare.

The Superintendent was outside the derelict veterinary surgery, pacing back and forth in the caged-tiger way he did when he was extremely agitated. He'd taken off his jacket and unbuttoned his ill-fitting shirt to reveal a yellowing vest beneath, sprouts of dark hair peering over the top of it like they were pleading to be rescued. Savage didn't think she'd ever seen anyone so completely drenched in sweat. It was like the Super had gone for a swim in a tub of Vaseline.

"You didn't just disturb a crime scene," Clare went on. "You demolished it."

"To be fair, it wasn't—"

"You set about it with what appears to be a demolition ball, raining toss onto anything that we might have been able to use as evidence. Is that right?"

"Uh..." Savage glanced past the Super to the door, where half a dozen coppers could be seen milling around in the reception area, lit by halogen lights. Kett had managed to get himself out of his self-made restraint fifteen minutes ago, but there was no sign of him now. "I mean, the evidence is still there, sir. It's just... dusty."

Clare's brow knitted together like the clenched jaw of a Venus flytrap.

"And all because absolutely nobody in this tossing team can fit into their trousers anymore," he raged, spit flying from his mouth and glittering in the sun. "How do people know the Extreme Crime Task Force has been on the job? Because they walk into a building and the bloody thing collapses, that's how! What's next? They get into a car and the bloody wheels fall off? They go for a walk and end up rolling down a hill like some great big bloody wheel of tossing cheese? I've had enough! No more food for any of you, ever again!"

"It was an owl, sir," said Savage. "It had been roosting up there. It startled DCI Kett and when he tried to move out of its way, the ceiling—"

"I don't give a toss!" Clare said, apoplectic now. "Please, at least tell me we've got something we can use against Hope."

"I think so, sir," said Savage, relieved at the subject change. "Hope's been hanging out here, no doubt. After the, uh, ceiling incident, I went through some of the stuff from the break room. I found a bank statement with his name on it and a utility bill from the gym folded up and tucked into the sofa. There are a lot of receipts too. I'm sure we'll be able to pin the card number to Hope. If that fails, we've got prints everywhere and other DNA too. He's been bringing somebody here, probably Zoe."

"It's definitely her," said Clare. "She told us so, reluctantly. She said she and Justin came here every now and again when the gym was in use, so they had time together. Building's registered to a separate Limited Company with both Ben and Millicent listed as Directors. Reed Cutter Developments. It's one of three properties on their books and all are abandoned. I've spoken to Ben. They wanted to do them up, sell them, but they didn't have the cash to do it. They're broke, although he won't admit it. He had no idea Justin was using the place."

"Justin would have known about it from work," said Savage. "We know he was close to Ben, he would have found out it was empty. It was a good place to hook up, but it was a good place to work from as well. We found a roof space, accessed through a loose panel in the ceiling."

"The ceiling that isn't there anymore," grumbled Clare.

"Yes, sir. There were boxes in it, the same kind that were used for the delivery to Reed's office. There's a suitcase too. It was open, looks like a bunch of tools inside. The smell in there, it's sweet. Cara told us to look out for it. We left it well alone."

"As relieved as I am that you're not touching explosives, Detective, I'm still aware that you let said suitcase drop from a great height. You're lucky you didn't both get your hairy tosspockets blown inside out."

"Sir, what *is* a hairy—"

"I want to know everything I can about what Hope used this place for," Clare interrupted. "I need you to go and talk to Zoe. She trusted you, she'll open up more than she did to the Uniform who interviewed her."

"Sure, sir," she said. "Now?"

"No, next week when it won't tossing matter," said Clare, his eyeballs bulging further than ever. "Yes, of course now. Go!"

Savage didn't need to be told twice, escaping the Super like he was a house fire. Duke was nowhere to be seen either, so she patted her pockets to make sure the keys were still there then spent a good minute trying to find her IRV in the sea of police cars that had arrived after they'd called it in.

Clare's Mercedes had blocked off the entrance to the car park, but she had no intention of asking him to move. Instead, she eased the car over the barren flowerbed, ignoring the bone-shaking clunk as she dropped over the high kerb onto the road. The engine protested as she gunned it, then settled as she headed back towards the hospital.

She'd only been driving for a couple of minutes before her phone rang, and she pulled over to see that it was Porter. She put it on speaker as she pulled back into traffic again.

"Everything okay, sir?"

"Yeah. Just tried Kett, but he isn't answering."

"He lost a fight with an owl," Savage said.

"An owl?"

"Long story, sir. No sign of Justin Hope, but we think we've found one of his hideouts, maybe even the place where he made the bomb."

"Nice," said Porter. She could hear him walking, then the clatter of a door. "I'm still at HQ. Interviewed Bill Carroll, one of the group forced to hang themselves. Turns out he knows Hope as well."

"Yeah?"

"Yeah. He didn't have anything good to say about him. Looks like Hope did some security work after he left the army, a few years ago. Long before he joined Ben Reed's firm. Nothing serious, mainly gigs, but some festival work too, carnivals, that kind of thing."

"Bit of a coincidence, don't you think, sir?"

"That they know him? Yeah, and not just a bit. It's massive. Bill said he never worked with him, he just saw him on the circuit a few times. Hope was an outsider—not part of the travelling community, I mean—so nobody really opened up to him. But he got jobs because he was tough. Had a reputation for scaring people off. Had more than one fistfight, by the sound of it."

"Fits what we've heard already," said Savage, stopping at a red light and tapping the wheel impatiently. "He punched a woman on the job, and we know he assaulted Zoe."

"Yeah, scum," said Porter. "Eventually he pissed off so many people that nobody gave him work anymore. Hence the change in careers."

"Carroll didn't give us anything else, sir?"

"Nothing useful. Carroll is *not* a nice man. You still with Kett?"

"No, I'm heading to the hospital. Clare wants me to speak with Zoe again."

"Zoe..." said Porter.

"Pankhurst. Hope's girlfriend."

"There are way too many people in this case," said Porter.

And it's only going to get worse, Savage thought when he'd hung up. She threw the phone onto the passenger seat and bullied her way through the congested rush-hour streets until she pulled into the hospital car park. It was as busy as ever, people filling the corridors like bees in a hive, the buzz of chatter almost deafening. A nurse buzzed her into the ward when she flashed her warrant card, and frowned as she approached the desk.

"Please tell me you haven't brought us any more people," she said. "I think today's a record for you lot."

"Just me," said Savage. "For the moment, anyway. I'm looking for Zoe Pankhurst."

"She's here," said the nurse, hooking a thumb at the wall behind her. "Right at the back."

"She okay?"

"If you ignore the bruises, then yeah. She's good to go, actually. You know who's been taking chunks out of her?"

"Yeah," said Savage.

"Do us all a favour and throw him off a cliff, yeah?"

Savage nodded as she walked away, rounding the corner of the ward and catching sight of a handful of familiar faces through an open door. Gloria Easterman and Sephie Newton lay in twin beds, Will Talion in his chair between them. They all looked around when they heard her footsteps. Apart from the exhaustion, they seemed reasonably healthy—incredible, really, considering what they'd been through.

"Hi," said Gloria. "Any news?"

"Not yet, sorry," said Savage. "We're working on it, though."

"Was it really Justin?" asked Sephie, and Will's cheeks blazed.

"Sorry," he said. "I didn't say it was definitely him, I just... It's just your colleague, the chunky one, said you were looking for Justin. I didn't mean to accuse him or anything."

"It's fine," said Savage. "It's one line of enquiry we're looking into. You guys here for the night?"

"We're waiting to be discharged," said Gloria. "Been waiting for hours, I think they've forgotten about us."

"Unlike Ben," muttered Will.

"Ben?"

"Saw him leave ages ago," Sephie said. "One rule for the boss, one rule for the workers. Nothing ever changes."

"What time was that?" asked Savage.

"About two, I think," said Will. "He left with another man; tall, kind of like a scary Father Christmas."

"Thanks," said Savage. "It won't be long, I think. Don't leave the city, okay? We may need to speak to you again."

"But I live in Blofield," said Sephie, her face falling. "Where am I going to sleep tonight?"

"No, I mean don't go too far," Savage explained. "You can go home."

Nobody looked too happy, but Savage didn't wait for questions, making her way around the circular ward until she found Zoe's room. The girl was sitting on the edge of her bed, her expression vacant, her legs swinging, looking about five years younger than she actually was. With the sun-drenched window behind her, it was almost impossible to see the bruises on her face. Then Savage walked through the door and Zoe's face emerged from its silhouette, wide-eyed and frightened. The bruises were darker than ever, a veil that stretched from her right ear all the way down to her neck, creeping into the collar of her T-shirt.

"Hey," Savage said, as gently as she could. "How are you doing?"

The girl replied with a soft nod.

"I'm Kate. Do you remember me from earlier?"

Another nod.

"The nurse just told me they've discharged you. I'm happy to take you home."

The girl's body grew tense, as if every single muscle had locked tight. She was biting her top lip hard enough to draw blood, her teeth crimson.

"You're okay to go home?" Savage asked.

Another nod, so small it was barely there. Zoe swallowed, cocked her head.

"Can I see Justin?" Her voice was a croak. "Can you take me back to him?"

There were so many things Savage wanted to say, but she locked them deep inside.

"I can't, Zoe," she said instead. "He's not family. I can only release you to a parent or guardian."

The girl's eyes dropped to her swinging feet, her teeth nibbling at that same dark scab on her lip. Savage wondered if the girl was neurodiverse, or if her behaviour hinted at a much deeper trauma than the one they'd uncovered today.

"If there's anything you want to tell me, anything important, then it's safe to talk," said Savage. "If there's a reason you can't go home, I can help. Are you worried about getting in trouble?"

She shrugged, those feet still swinging.

"I'll talk to your dad, Zoe. I'll make sure he understands that none of this is your fault. Okay?"

Savage waited a moment for the girl to answer, but she just sat there, staring at the floor, biting her lip like she was trying to eat herself whole. It hurt Savage's heart to see somebody so broken, and it occurred to her that the nurse was right. It would be better for everyone if Justin Hope simply fell off a cliff.

They had to catch him first, though.

"I'm ready if you're ready," Savage said, trying to infuse some excitement into her voice. "My car's right outside. Have you got any stuff?"

The girl shook her head as she hopped down from the bed, her eyes still locked on the floor—or on something else, something a long way away. There were no flowers, no cards, no balloons. Zoe had only been in the hospital for a few hours, and just for a check-up, but it was weird that nobody had been in to see her, especially as her father had been notified.

"You mind if we chat a little on the way?" Savage asked as they walked out of the room.

The girl shook her head again, following with all the enthusiasm of a train carriage being pulled after the engine. Her feet scuffed the floor, her shoulders slumped.

"I mean it," Savage said. "You can talk to me about anything. I'm a friend."

The girl's head shook from side to side like she was trying to scare away a fly.

"Do you like dogs?" Savage persisted as they walked to the desk. "That was a cute dog you were with when I found you."

Nothing. Savage spoke briefly to the nurse, signing the release paperwork, then gently steered the girl towards the doors.

"I've got a dog. She's mad. Her name's Colin."

This, at least, got the merest glimmer of a smile.

"Yeah, it's a daft name. I called her that after somebody I know. Somebody even hairier."

They walked into the corridor, Zoe moving like an automaton. Savage thought about taking the girl's arm, but something in the wiry tension of Zoe's body made her sure she wouldn't like it.

"Thanks for telling us about the vet's," she said. "That was really helpful. Did you hang out there much, you and Justin?"

Zoe sniffed, then nodded.

"Every week?" Savage pressed. "Every day?"

"No."

Savage walked in silence for a moment, letting the question hang.

"Like, maybe twice a week," Zoe said eventually, her quiet voice almost lost beneath their footsteps. "After school."

"He'd pick you up?"

A nod. Savage almost asked what they got up to when she remembered what they'd found in the wastebasket.

"You haven't done anything wrong, Zoe, I promise," she said, using her elbow to hit the button for the lift. "Did Justin ever talk about taking other people there? Did you ever see anyone else?"

Zoe shook her head again as they walked inside, and they rode down to the next level in silence.

"Last question," Savage said as they crossed the lobby. "I'm sorry, but it's important. Did you ever see Justin doing anything unusual when you were at the vet's?"

"Unusual?" Zoe asked, squinting up at Savage.

"Working on anything, or building something. It might have looked like a package, or a box, or a... I don't know, like a science project or something. Wires, or putty, or stones, like the kind you get at the beach."

Zoe was looking at her like she was mad, and she didn't blame her. She wasn't doing a great job of explaining.

"Anything at all," Savage said. "It doesn't matter how crazy it sounds."

"We just..."

They stepped into the sun and Zoe flinched, the bruises on her face such a deep shade of purple in the light that they didn't look real. She stopped for a moment, as if she was afraid of the day.

"It's okay," said Savage. "The car's right here. I'll put the air con on."

Zoe shuffled reluctantly forwards, the heat radiating off the pavement like they were stepping onto a grill. Savage knew full well that Zoe should ride in the back, but she opened the passenger door of the IRV for her.

"Don't touch anything," she said. "There's an ejector seat button in here somewhere, we had to fetch the last passenger down from a roof."

Another smile, gone before it ever truly landed. Savage closed the girl's door, then climbed behind the wheel, starting the engine.

"So, did you ever see Justin doing anything weird while you were there together?" she asked as she reversed. "You were about to say something."

"No," said Zoe. "Sorry."

"You don't ever have to say sorry to me."

"We just, you know..."

"Had time together," said Savage, and the girl nodded.

Savage waited for a bus to pull onto the road, then followed it down to the roundabout, breathing in the fumes that blasted through the vents.

"And he didn't take you anywhere else? Other than the vet and the gym?"

Zoe gave a quick shake of her head. There seemed to be a whole world of secrets in there, and Savage knew it would take more than a quick car journey to get them out.

"I know I'm asking a lot of questions. It's my job, you never get out of the habit of it. We just want to keep you safe, that's all. We want to make sure he never locks you in a room again, never hurts you again."

"He didn't hurt me," Zoe said. "He does it to *help* me."

"I know he says that, but I don't think it's true."

Zoe rested her head against the glass.

"You wouldn't understand."

"You'd be surprised," Savage said.

But she'd lost her. Zoe's dark eyes watched the world fly

past, her teeth working relentlessly at that scrap of bloody lip. Savage felt a rush of love for the girl that made her scalp shrivel up, an unexpected wave of emotion. She'd have happily taken her home right now and kept her there, kept her safe in her own little flat, if that had been an option.

Instead, she pulled off the main road onto a quiet residential street, marking off the numbers until she spotted the one she wanted. It was a pale-bricked, semi-detached house that seemed to have sunk into the jungle of its front garden. A caravan that looked just as dejected as the house occupied most of the driveway, and behind that a scaffold had been erected up the side of the building, leading to a platform that leaned awkwardly against the chimney. Savage studied it, feeling a sudden chill.

"Is this the one?" she asked. "This is your house?"

Zoe nodded, but she seemed to have hunched her body even tighter around an invisible pillow. Savage cut the engine, the quiet of the street bleeding into the car.

"Please, Zoe," she said, her voice soft. She reached for the girl but once again hung back, fearful that if she so much as rested her fingers on her shoulders, she might shatter into a thousand pieces. "I'm right here. I can keep you safe from Justin. If you want, I can make sure there's a car here tonight, until we find him. Would that help?"

It probably wasn't even something she could arrange, although she knew for a fact that Duke would happily do it —even on his own time, if she asked him. It was one of the reasons she loved him.

Oh, she thought, another shockwave running through her, this one not entirely welcome. She hadn't meant to think *that*, she hadn't meant to say it, not even inside her head.

Pull yourself together, Kate.

Zoe was looking at her, her eyes a vibrant shade of hazel.

"Sorry," she told the girl. "Zoned out for a minute. You ready?"

"You don't have to come in," Zoe said, and there was an edge of panic in her voice. She pulled the handle and the car door opened. "I'll be fine."

"Hold your horses," Savage said, climbing out. "I have to make sure you get in, have to hand you off to a parent. Your dad's home?"

Zoe nodded, her face growing tight. She looked up at the house like Savage had driven her right back to the gym where they'd found her, right back to that locked room.

"Come on," said Savage. "Lead the way."

The girl did as she was told, taking those same small, shuffling steps through a gateless fence and along the damaged paving slabs that made up the path. Green shoots stretched up from the cracks, trampled effortlessly, and Savage couldn't help but see the resemblance to the skinny, bent-backed girl in front of her.

"I've got a key," Zoe said. "I can let myself in. You don't have to be here, please."

That rising panic laced every word, the girl's hands working reflexively in the air as she reached the door— clenching and unclenching, clenching and unclenching. It was leaching into the air, making the hot day feel cold, making Savage feel like she was underwater.

"I'm right here," she told her. "I'm not going anywhere. I'll talk to him, I promise."

"Please," Zoe said again, not looking back.

In the end, the decision was taken out of her hands. The door clicked and slowly opened, revealing a short, over-weight man draped in long shorts, an England football shirt and a cape of shadow. He was holding a beer in his hand,

and judging by the way he swayed it wasn't his first. He regarded Zoe with big, wet eyes that were so yellow he might have been a lizard. Then his gaze crawled over to Savage, lingering on her chest for a second or two before rising to her face.

"Mr Pankhurst?" she asked, her stomach sinking.

He responded with a belch, wiping the back of his free hand over his sagging, stubbled jaw. He had a scab on his lip in the exact same place that Zoe did.

"You're aware of what happened to your daughter today?" Savage went on. "Where we found her?"

The man turned his attention—if you could call it that, he seemed barely able to keep his eyes open—to Zoe. The smell coming off him was enough to get drunk on. Savage's eyes were actually watering.

"Yeah," he grunted, or something to that effect. "You found him yet?"

"Justin? No. Not yet. I'm happy to stay, and we can arrange to have a car—"

"No," the man said, wiping his mouth again. "Don't need it. Inside."

Zoe flinched at the order, scuttling through the door and twisting past her father, who refused to move an inch to let her by. He wasn't a tall man, standing barely an inch over Savage, but there was bulk visible beneath his football shirt, and his arms were wiry with muscle. His hands were covered in scabs, Savage noticed, the knuckles swollen.

"She's been attacked," Savage said, only because her dad hadn't seemed to notice.

"Doesn't look too bad to me," he said.

Her stomach sank even further. Pankhurst started to close the door.

"You're a builder?" she asked. "You make that scaffold outside?"

"Fuck does that have to do with anything?" he said, his words slurred. "Thanks for bringing her back."

"This isn't her fault," Savage said as he pushed the door again. "Zoe's a child, Mr Pankhurst, and Justin Hope is an adult with a track record of violence and abuse. I need to know you're not going to blame her for this."

He ignored her, pushing the door almost all the way closed. Savage had to move fast to stop it from clicking shut, using a hand to shunt it open. Beyond was a dark corridor, smoke-stained walls and a filthy carpet. Zoe had already vanished, like the house had eaten her alive.

Pankhurst glared back, his loose face tightening into a knot of anger.

"We're fine," he slurred. "You can go."

"I need to know you're not going to blame her," Savage repeated, firmer this time. "I need to hear you say it."

The man's face grew soft again, those yellow eyes blinking. He took a deep breath and coughed it back out again.

"She's my little girl," he said after a moment. "I'm just glad you got her away from that prick before he killed her."

He belched again.

"Or worse. Got her pregnant."

Savage studied him for a moment, unsure. She thought again about calling Zoe back, about driving her to the flat. But if she did that to every beaten and broken girl and young woman she met on the job then her home would be crammed with dozens of people, hundreds, even. There wouldn't be room for her anymore. The thought cast a dark cloud over her, made her feel like she'd stepped out of the sun into the shade of a vast, forgotten forest.

"I'm going to swing by and check on her tomorrow, okay," she said, and it wasn't really a question.

Zoe's father shrugged, taking a swig from his beer can as he walked off.

"Whatever you want," he said. "Just close the door behind you."

And after another small eternity of wondering, she did.

CHAPTER NINETEEN

Kett was standing in the corridor of the veterinary surgery, replying to a text from Billie, when he heard the shout. It rose over the general hubbub of the busy building, over the hum of chatter and the scuff of feet as a swarm of officers searched for evidence.

"Sir, over here!"

He sent the text—*Sorry, going to be a late one, give everyone a kick from me*—cursing autocorrect as he slid the phone into his pocket. He squeezed between two PCs who were loitering in the doorway to the break room, seeing a third standing by the boiler against the far wall. The front panel had been removed, and the constable was holding a jiffy bag in her gloved hand.

"It was inside the boiler, sir," she said as Kett crossed the room, his boots crunching on the carpet of shattered ceiling tiles. "Right inside, hard to find. Looks like a passport, documents. I haven't opened it."

Kett took it from her, holding it up to the light that blazed from the closest halogen lamp. His arm ached from his fall. In fact, his entire body ached, his ribs bruised from where he'd been stuck in the framework. It had been bad, but it could have been a whole lot worse. The suitcase that had fallen next to him still lay there, the lid open. Inside were plenty of tools, but thankfully no explosives. If Hope had been storing something else inside then the entire building might have been blown to kingdom come—him, Savage and the bloody owl right alongside it.

He pulled his glasses from his pocket and slid them on, the room becoming a blur but the contents of the envelope taking shape. Opening it, he pulled out the passport and flicked to the ID page, seeing Justin's dead-eyed expression staring back.

"What's all the shouting?" came Clare's voice from the corridor. The Super pushed between the two Uniforms, flapping his arms at them. "What am I? A twig? Move out of the way, you great pair of tossbollocks."

"It's Hope's passport," said Kett. "He stashed it here, in the boiler."

He passed it to Clare then pulled out the collection of papers, spreading them on the dusty counter.

"Birth certificate too. And this, it's the V5C for his Golf, insurance documents, and..."

He studied the last document, checking it against the rest.

"It's a separate logbook, this one for a SEAT Ibiza, 2011 model, registered to a Craig Mallet, Norwich address."

"Why does he have that?" asked Clare.

"Not sure. I'll put out an alert, see if we can find it."

"Do it," Clare barked.

"I literally just said I was going to do it, sir," Kett muttered, too quietly for Clare to hear him. He pulled out his phone again to see a text from Billie.

I take it that was a typo, or was it a Freudian slip?

He laughed, texting back.

I meant kick, not kick.

He'd sent the text before he realised the bloody thing had corrected him again.

"For fuck's sake," he said, ignoring Clare's bug-eyed fury as he called DI Spalding. He gave her the car's registration, adding a 'please' before realising she'd already hung up.

"Why not keep this stuff inside the gym?" asked Clare. "Why risk storing it here? For all he knew, Ben and Millicent could have demolished this place at any given moment."

"If he knew them well enough to find this place, he probably knew they were broke," said Kett. "People were coming in and out of the gym all the time. This is as safe a place as any. Do we know why he doesn't have a residential address?"

"Never had one," said Clare. "Not since he came out of the army seven years ago. Been sofa surfing, far as we can see. Gym's owned by a woman called Marie Goodson, but she's been overseas for a decade. Can't reach her, don't even know if she knows Hope's been using it."

Kett sighed, dropping the last of the documents onto the table and massaging his temples. The sun had given him a brutal headache. Or maybe it was the case, the pieces like broken glass in the flesh of his brain.

"So we know Hope's been here," he said, thinking aloud. "We know this is where he was keeping his equipment. This is his stash house, right? He keeps everything here in case he needs to bolt. So the question is..."

"Why hasn't he been here to collect his stuff?" Clare finished, checking his watch. "He's had nearly six hours since Savage busted him. He could have come here, grabbed his documents and tossed off."

"Probably wasn't time for the last one, sir," said Kett. "So maybe he panicked. He might have thought if we'd known about the gym, we'd know about this place. He didn't want to risk it."

"And he had more important things to do," added Clare. "Because he had a warehouse full of people he wanted to force onto a gallows and hang."

"Right," said Kett, trying to get his head around it only for those broken-glass pieces to cut deeper. "Porter around? Savage?"

"I've sent Savage to take Zoe Pankhurst home, try to press her for more information," said Clare. "Porter's probably chins-deep in a bowl of custard. Call him, tell him to check out Craig Mallet's address, see if we can find out why Hope's driving his car."

Kett pulled out his phone, only for it to start ringing.

"Spalding," he said when he answered it. "You've got something?"

"No, sir," came her reply, as dry as ever. "Thought I'd just call for a chat. You and I don't speak as much as we should. How's the family? Found a horse yet?"

He blew out a sigh.

"We got lucky with the Ibiza. Uniforms pulled it over two hours ago when they saw it speeding in Heartsease. Didn't ticket the driver because he admitted it, apologised. Said he seemed like a nice guy. They tailed him up Woodside Road until he turned off onto Greenborough."

"It was definitely Hope? Why didn't they bring him in?"

"Scottish, fit. Gave a false ID, and they never asked."

"Christ. Greenborough? And this was when, exactly?"

"Just after four," said Spalding.

"Thanks," he said, hanging up.

"Uniforms pulled Hope over in Heartsease two hours ago, but cut him loose because they didn't know who he was. That was right after the hangings, he would have had time to get across town. He might still be there."

Clare wheeled around like a drunkard, marching towards the door.

"I'll call tactical," he boomed back. "But let's get over there. Now."

Kett rushed after him, almost tripping on the discarded frame of the ceiling. In the time they'd been inside the old veterinary surgery the sun had slipped earthwards, the air cooling, and it was a blessed relief to be outside—only, that was, until Clare beckoned Kett towards his Mercedes.

"I'll ride in an IRV, sir," he said. "It's fine."

"You'll ride with me, Detective," Clare bellowed back. "Get in the car."

He jabbed a hairy finger at the crowd of PCs.

"Heartsease, now! We're looking for a silver SEAT Ibiza, parked in a driveway or on the street, if we're lucky. Kett's got the registration."

Kett shouted it out, then he took a deep breath and clambered into the car. With the windows closed it had become a furnace, the smell like somebody was burning a heap of soiled underwear.

"Oh God," said Kett, choking. "It's so bad."

He started to wind down his window as Clare reversed.

"Do *not* touch that, Kett," Clare yelled. "I've put the air con on."

He had, but the air that vomited from the vents was *hot*, the smell infinitely worse.

"I think something might have died in there, sir," Kett croaked. "Let me open the window."

"You open it, I'm tossing you out of it."

It would almost be worth it.

Clare waited for an IRV to pull onto the street, its lights on and its siren keening down the road ahead of it. He floored it, the Mercedes' monstrous engine as loud as a jumbo jet. Kett fanned his face with a hand, mentally working out how far away Heartsease was and wondering if he could hold his breath until they got there. He spluttered it out after thirty-four seconds when his phone rang again, Savage's name on the screen.

"Kate," he said. "You okay?"

"Yes, sir," she said. "I've just heard, you found Hope?"

"No, but we've got a good lead. Heartsease, can you meet us over there?"

"I will, sir," she said, and he could sense the hesitation in her voice.

"What's up?"

"Probably nothing," Savage said. "I've just dropped Zoe at home. Something doesn't feel right."

"No?"

They'd reached a junction and Clare seemed to stamp both feet on all three pedals at once, the car lurching through like a bucking mule. Kett had to brace his free hand on the dashboard to stop himself from going through the windscreen.

"Zoe's dad was drunk," Savage went on. "There's something about him. He's a scaffolder."

"A scaffolder? He told you that?"

"Not exactly, but there's a scaffold up the side of the house. I know scaffolds all look the same, but it wasn't too far away from the one we found in the warehouse."

Her sigh rattled the line.

"I'm overthinking it, sir," she said. "It's probably nothing. But..."

He didn't interrupt, partly because he wanted to give her time to say what was on her mind, and partly because Clare was fumbling with his phone with both hands, the car skimming the kerb at fifty miles an hour. The Super recovered, wedging the phone between his ear and his shoulder while Kett's heart danced the tarantella in his chest.

"I'm just going to wait here for a little while," she said, oblivious to his near-death experience. "Half an hour, just to make sure she's okay. Is that alright, sir?"

"Do what you have to do, Kate," he said. "Keep me updated."

He hung up, tuning into Clare's conversation, which wasn't hard because the Super was bellowing like a moose that had woken up during dental surgery.

"Surround it, but do not enter. Do you hear me? Stay out of that house."

He hung up, throwing his phone at Kett like he was trying to knock him out.

"I had a unit close by, they've found the car. Hammond Close. Tell Gorski."

Kett did as he was told, calling the head of the tactical unit and relaying the information.

"We're ten minutes out," she replied, the thunder of an engine almost drowning out her words.

Kett was closer, Clare following the IRV as it bouldered around the corner onto Greenborough Road, its tyres smoking. He accelerated with such urgency that Kett would have lost his lunch if he'd remembered to eat any. The Super was practically hunched over the wheel, the muscles of his neck like steel wires.

"AR is ten minutes away," said Kett.

They turned again, then again, and this time Kett saw the police car up ahead. A single constable flagged them down and Clare mounted the kerb hard and fast enough to ring Kett's head off the ceiling.

"Ow," Kett said, opening his door.

Clare unfolded himself from the car as the constable ran over.

"It's that one, sir," he said, pointing down the street to a bungalow that barely looked bigger than the double garage of the house next to it. Sure enough, a silver SEAT Ibiza sat in the driveway, tucked away so neatly behind the conifer hedge it was almost invisible. From where he stood, Kett couldn't see the registration plate.

"You're sure?" he asked.

"Sure, sir. Plates match. No sign of life and we pulled back so he wouldn't see us. PC Butler's round the back in case he legs it. If the suspect is inside, I don't think he knows we're here."

He'd know soon enough. More cars were pouring onto the street, some with their sirens on. Kett took a few steps towards the house, seeing that the curtains were drawn. They weren't so much as twitching.

"Hope's armed and very dangerous," Clare was shouting as the PCs got out of their vehicles. "Tactical's on the way. Our job is to contain him, but I don't want anyone taking any risks, you hear me? I'm not losing any of you to this tossrag. Hang back, and turn those sirens off."

The constables scattered, the street falling silent, or as silent as it was possible to be with so many people. Kett spotted Duke extracting his enormous frame from an IRV, Porter appearing a second later from a different car. They ran over together, Duke sprinting, Porter doing some kind of addled jog.

"He in there, sir?" Porter asked when he was close enough.

"Not sure yet," Kett replied.

"Get around the back," Clare boomed, sweeping his arm through the air. "Don't intercept him if he tries to run. I just want a perimeter."

Kett wasn't sure who the Super had given the order to, and when he started to run across the street he found Porter and Duke moving alongside him. The houses were densely packed, but there was a pedestrian path that curved around the back of the buildings and through a small park. He took it, happy for the cool embrace of the trees.

"Which one is it?" Porter asked, already out of breath.

Kett didn't know, but there was a constable up ahead doing his best to hide behind a tree that was far too skinny to provide any sort of cover. He peeked out when he heard their footsteps, visibly relieved to see them. Kett slowed to a walk, studying the fenced gardens to his left.

"It's that one," the constable—PC Frank Butler, Kett realised, recognising him—said, nodding at the back of a house. The ground-floor windows were hidden behind a fence and the top ones had their curtains drawn. Somebody was home, though, because a cloud of exhaust billowed from the boiler vent.

"Surely he can't have the heating on," said Porter, noticing the same thing.

"If we're lucky, he's in the shower," said Kett. He checked his watch. "Tactical will be here any minute."

Duke grunted his disappointment, his big hand resting on his Taser. Porter leaned against the tree, wiping the sweat from his brow.

"Hope so," the DI said. "Happy to sit this one out. It is way too hot for running."

The only reply was a thud from the back of the house,

the sound of footsteps, and the scrabble of somebody throwing themselves onto a fence.

Kett threw Porter a scowl.

"What, sir?" Porter asked.

"You bloody jinxed it, didn't you, Pete?"

A face appeared, Justin Hope hauling himself over the rickety fence panels and dropping onto the path. He glanced over his shoulder at them, his eyes dark. He was dressed in camouflage combats and a green T-shirt, and on his back he had a canvas rucksack.

"Oi!" Kett yelled, moving towards him. "Stay right where you are."

Hope tensed his muscular body, flashing them a dangerous smile.

"You follow me, you fucking die," he said.

Then he started running.

CHAPTER TWENTY

THE PANKHURST HOUSE WAS STILL AND QUIET, BUT Savage had the funny feeling it was lying to her.

She'd been sitting in the IRV for twenty minutes now, watching the building through the window. For the first ten of those, the engine had been running, her hand on the wheel and her foot tapping the accelerator as she prepared to leave. Then, for a reason she still couldn't quite identify, she'd turned the engine off and sat there in the deafening silence of the street, waiting.

Waiting for what, though?

For this feeling to pass, she knew. It was like something was kicking her in the spleen, and she'd been on the job long enough now to know that it was trying to tell her something. Something important. It's what her grandfather—Big Jeff Savage, a uniformed police officer all his life—had told her. It was the first lesson he'd passed on, even before Savage had any inkling that she might become a copper.

Everybody has a secret, you just have to learn to see it.

And whatever else you do, always trust your gut. In this line of work, it's the best friend you've got.

She could hear his voice like he was sitting next to her, as if the whorls of dust that circled the hot car were the fragrant contrails of pipe smoke he'd left in his wake everywhere he went. She could see the brightness of his smile, that flash of mischief in his eyes, and she put her hand to her chest where the lucky police whistle he'd given her hung on its chain, covering her heart.

Trust your gut, Kate.

Her gut was telling her that something was wrong, that they'd missed something important, and that the answer lay right here.

She opened the door, rising out of the hothouse of the IRV and into the cooling day. The curtains on this side of the house had been drawn against the sun, so she made her way down the narrow, weed-strewn path that sat between the house and the caravan. A glance through the window told her the caravan was deserted, the interior stripped bare of everything, including its doors. The scaffold towered up the side of the house, its joints rusted and its boards caked in old paint and grime. Past that was a brick shed, the window covered with a sheet of plywood. She tried the door as she passed, only to find it locked.

The back garden was neater than the front, a square of browning grass fringed by flowering bushes. A concrete birdbath sat in the middle, hosting a pair of hedge sparrows. They took flight as soon as they saw her and she hesitated, wondering if she'd got this wrong, if she'd misread it.

Something crunched inside the house, the sound of a heavy object being shifted. Savage stepped closer to the dark windows, peering through the first to see a small kitchen. Nobody was there, but she could hear a man's voice —raised, but not enough for her to make out what he was saying.

The next room along had a set of French doors and she walked to them, her feet crunching on the gravel path. They were slightly ajar, and the voice was clearer now.

"... say for yourself, eh? I want to hear you say it. I want you to tell me."

It was Zoe's dad, for sure, that same drunken slur. He didn't sound angry, but there was an edge to it that made Savage's skin crawl. She paused for a moment more, locking her breath in her lungs as Zoe answered in a tremulous whisper.

"I'm useless. I'm a disappointment. I'm a failure."

"Again," said her father. "Louder."

The teenage girl repeated the words at the same volume and Savage could hear the tears that accompanied them. She crept towards the door and found Zoe and her dad standing on the far side of a dining table.

"And?" asked Pankhurst.

"I don't want to."

"You'll fucking say it, because it's what you are." The words were fat and wet and full of the promise of violence. "You'll say it or you know what'll happen."

"I'm a slut," said Zoe, sobbing freely now. The sight of it set a fire in Savage that burned through her so fast and so bright that for a moment she couldn't see anything at all.

"Again," said her dad. "Louder."

"I'm a slut," she said.

"And what do sluts get?"

Zoe turned her head away, her eyes screwed shut, her shoulders hunched in anticipation of what she knew was coming. Pankhurst's body was rigid, too, his right hand flattening into a blade, moving back like a gun being cocked.

Savage grabbed the door and wrenched it all the way

open, the adrenaline blazing like rocket fuel as she lunged into the room.

"Oi!" she yelled. "Don't you dare!"

Zoe's eyes snapped open, her mouth dropping into an expression of horror.

"No!" the girl shouted.

Her dad was either too drunk to have noticed Savage's appearance, or he just didn't care. He twisted his whole body, his arm wheeling around, the flat of his hand catching the side of Zoe's head like a shovel. The sound of it filled the room like a gunshot, louder than Savage's cry, louder than the hammer of her feet as she ran around the table.

Zoe fell like a snapped sapling, sprawling to the floor. Her father turned, his hand raised again, and only now did he seem to see Savage hurtling towards him.

She threw herself at him only to feel a hand locked around her ankle—Zoe, her swollen face warped with pain and with something else, something that might have been fear. Savage tripped over the girl, her arms cartwheeling as she struggled to regain her balance.

Pankhurst loosed the missile of his hand at her instead. Not a slap, this time, but a punch.

It struck her in the cheek hard enough to set off a cathedral bell inside her skull. Her own momentum threw her into the man and she bounced off his sturdy frame, spinning through the door into the hallway beyond.

"No!" Zoe was screaming now. "Dad, don't!"

Savage shook her head to try and clear her double vision, leaning against the wall, *two* Pankhursts striding towards her now. He was yelling something but she couldn't hear it over the ringing in her ears. She backed away, reaching for the panic button on her radio out of habit—

even though it had been years since she'd been in uniform—
her head filled with so much static it almost blinded her.

How hard had he hit her?

"Stop," she ordered as Pankhurst stepped out of the
room. Her voice was like toffee, caught in her throat. "Back
off, now."

The squat man didn't reply, upping his pace and
snorting like a bull. Zoe had appeared in the doorway
behind him, still sobbing. She looked at Savage, desperate
now. She wasn't speaking, but her message was clear
enough.

He'll kill you.

"Call the police," Savage said, hearing the panic in her
voice. "Zoe, do it now."

The girl shook her head.

Savage backed into the front door, scrabbling for the
handle.

Locked.

Shit.

Pankhurst was halfway down the hallway now, both
fists bunched. His scaffolder's shoulders seemed to fill the
entire width of the hall, wall to wall. His eyes were yellow—
not a scrap of emotion anywhere on his puffy face.

Savage braced her right foot against the door, twisted
her body side-on.

"Last chance," she said.

He was too gone to care, throwing another punch as he
charged towards her. Savage ducked underneath it, feeling
his fist skim the top of her head and thump into the door.
She tried to step out of the way of his trailing body but
wasn't quick enough, the sheer bulk of him knocking her
onto her backside.

She kicked herself backwards—too slow, his hand in her hair, his face looming, his fist raised like a club.

She kicked out, her shoe catching him in the knee; then again, this time finding his crotch. He grunted, his fingers still locked in her hair, his fist dropping. She jerked her head down, felt his knuckles crack against the top of her skull. Then she leaned back and kicked out again.

This one hit gold, Pankhurst doubling up with a sound like a braying donkey. Savage scrabbled clear of him, using the wall to get to her feet. She took a moment to shoot Zoe a cast-iron glare.

"999, now!"

The girl seemed to snap out of whatever trance she'd been snared in, disappearing into the dining room. Savage turned back to the girl's father, still doubled up, one hand splayed on the wall as he fought to get his breath back. He was grunting, his face screwed up with pain and with fury.

"Stay down," Savage said, no conviction in her voice. "Stay where you are, or this gets a lot worse."

Pankhurst spat out an ugly laugh, pushing himself back up. He stood as straight as he was able, his shorts hanging so low that they were ready to slide right off. He took a step towards her and stopped, making another braying sound deep in his throat.

Then he opened his mouth and unleashed a torrent of yellow puke.

"Shit," Savage said, leaping back.

The vomit struck her trousers, splashing onto the walls and the floor, the awful, acidic smell of it filling the house from top to bottom in an instant. She gagged, her eyes watering, as Pankhurst hurled again, stumbling towards her even as the sick dripped from his lips.

"Last warning," she said again, well aware he couldn't have cared less.

He broke into a clumsy run, his hands out to claim her.

This time, she was ready for him.

She stepped to the side at the last minute, almost slipping on the wet floor, and launched a powerful uppercut. It caught Pankhurst in the soft meat of his chin, snapping his jaw shut with a clack. He stumbled, falling, and she let him go, watching him tumble through the dining room door and ram the table with his forehead—shunting it almost all the way to the French doors. His lights were out before he hit the floor.

Savage ducked onto her haunches, swallowing hard to stop the contents of her own stomach from making a swift exit.

"Zoe?" she said, her voice broken into a million pieces.

No reply. Savage took another few seconds to catch her breath then pushed herself up, walking into the dining room. Zoe had pressed herself into the corner like she was trying to hide in the shadows, shrunken by fear. She shook her head at Savage.

"It's okay," Savage said, crouching down and resting her hand on Pankhurst's back just to make sure she hadn't killed him. It was painfully obvious that Zoe hadn't called the police, so she used her other hand to pull her mobile from her vomit-damp pocket, dialling 999. She tried to smile at Zoe but her face wouldn't let her. "You're okay, and your dad's okay. Everything's going to be okay, I promise."

Zoe continued to shake her head, like she could will the last few minutes into oblivion. She wasn't sobbing anymore. Her face had taken on that same distant look it had when Savage had first met her—wide-eyed but unseeing.

"Yeah, hi, my name's DC Kate Savage, Norfolk Police,"

she said when the call connected. "I'm on Frere Road, I need immediate police backup and an ambulance."

She hung up, calling Kett. It rang for a moment before going to voicemail, and when she tried Clare it did the same. She was about to call Porter when Pankhurst's body gave a sudden lurch, the man drawing a gasping breath.

"Stay down," Savage told him as he stirred.

She wasn't sure whether it was because he was listening to her, or because he simply didn't have the strength, but he lay there quietly, blowing bubbles of snot and vomit out of his nose. She thought about running back to the car and grabbing a set of cuffs, but she didn't want to risk leaving him and she was pretty sure Zoe wouldn't do it. She checked her watch, hoping backup would arrive before Pankhurst came around fully, and wondering whether she should just sit on him.

"You okay?" she asked Zoe, nodding to her face where a fresh bruise was spreading. Her cheek was swollen, her eye bloodshot.

Zoe nodded, her mouth dancing into an attempt at a smile—something that had been programmed into her by her father, Savage understood. How many times had she been made to say it? *I'm okay, it was an accident, I walked into a door*. And that fury was back, so powerful that—if Savage had been alone, if she could be sure she would get away with it—she would have dug a grave in the garden and buried Pankhurst alive in it.

"Your dad's the one who's been beating you?" Savage asked.

Zoe shook her head, still smiling, her eyes dead.

"He'll never touch you again," Savage told her. "I prom-ise. He'll never even get near you again. But you have to be brave, you have to tell me. Was it him doing this to you?"

She'd seen it herself, of course, but if Zoe wanted out of this she had to let people know what he'd done. She had to make the world listen to her.

"Zoe?"

A siren in the air, as welcome as birdsong after a long night. Savage forced herself to take a long breath, using it to ask the question again.

"Zoe, please, just one word. Did your father beat you?"

Zoe turned those dead eyes to Savage, that rictus grin still warping her face. Then they dropped to the man who lay on the ground and the smile dropped away, replaced by an expression of fury that was so powerful it didn't look real.

"Yes," she hissed, her little fists clenched. "Yes, he did this. I hate him, I hate him."

"Nobody else hurt you?" Savage asked. "Not Justin?"

She shook her head violently from side to side.

"Just him," she said.

She took a step towards her father and for a second Savage thought she was going to attack him. Instead, she walked to the table and sat down on one of its scattered chairs, putting her head in her hands. Pankhurst was groaning, his hands groping the air, his feet scuffing the floor as he tried to push himself forward. But the siren was louder, possibly already on the street.

"You're absolutely positive that Justin never hurt you?" Savage asked. "Because we're going to keep you safe, Zoe. Safe from your dad, safe from anyone else who ever laid a finger on you."

"Justin never touched me," she said from the cocoon of her hands. "I told you, he never wanted to hurt me. He loves me. He did it to keep me safe."

"That's why he locked you up?" Savage asked. "To stop you coming home?"

Zoe nodded.

"Because I can't stay away from Dad," the girl went on, her voice muffled. "I can't stay away because it just makes it worse."

Savage heard an engine from the front of the house. Seconds later, somebody hammered at the front door.

"Round the back," she yelled, and the footsteps rose in volume, the room growing dark as two uniformed constables crowded the French doors. Zoe looked up in alarm, wincing as if expecting a fist to come crashing down on her.

"Easy," Savage told the two men as they crammed their way inside. "He's down, I just want him cuffed before he gets back up."

"Blimey," said one of the constables as he pulled his handcuffs free. He sniffed the air, pulling a face. "What did you hit him with?"

"The table," said Savage. The constable whistled, and she moved out of their way as they went to work. Taking Zoe's arm, she led her out of the house into the fresh air and muted sunlight. They both took a breath together, perfectly in sync.

"You mean it?" Zoe asked, looking back. "I don't have to see him again?"

"I'll make sure of it," said Savage.

Zoe swept a hair from her face with a trembling hand, wincing as her fingertips brushed against the fresh bruise. Savage touched the one that was forming on her own cheek, wincing.

"Can you take me to Justin?" Zoe asked.

"Not yet," Savage told her.

The girl sighed, staring at the big, blue sky.

"He would never hurt me," she said. "He'd never hurt

anyone. I know he comes across as... as this tough guy. But he's not. He's sweet. He wouldn't hurt a fly."

"You're sure about that?" asked Savage, reaching for her phone again.

"I'm sure," said Zoe. "Whatever you think he's done, it's not him."

Savage swore, trying Clare's number again.

Please answer.

CHAPTER TWENTY-ONE

"Stop fucking running!"

Kett bellowed the words at Justin Hope as he sprinted down the path. Beside him, Porter struggled to keep up. They'd been running for a handful of seconds before Duke roared past, as fast and as loud as a freight train.

"Careful, Duke!" Kett yelled. "He could be armed."

If Duke heard him, he didn't slow down. Hope was twenty yards ahead of them, his head down, his arms pistoning. He ran like he was still in the military, like his life depended on it, and he was gaining ground with every step.

Kett pulled out his phone, almost dropping it. He had to slow down in order to find the Super's number, Porter pulling ahead and wheezing like he'd swallowed an accordion.

"He's on the run, sir," he said as soon as Clare had answered. "Heading east on foot."

"Well catch him then!" Clare yelled. "I'll send somebody to intercept. Stay on the line."

Kett forced himself to run faster, following the bend in the track as it cut to the left and narrowed between two gardens. Hope was already out of sight, Duke too, although he could hear the big PC bellowing from the next street. Porter was slowing, his cheeks so red they could probably be seen from space.

"Come on, Pete," said Kett as he overtook him.

The path spat them out into a square courtyard and he followed the echoing footsteps to his right, clocking the street sign.

"Harrisons Drive," he panted as he reached the junction. Duke was scrambling over a hedge into the gardens of the houses opposite and Kett called out to him. "Aaron, be careful."

The big PC didn't reply, dropping out of sight.

"Fuck," said Kett, still on the phone. "He's hopped over into the next street, still heading east." He looked back, Porter running like a man with too-small shoes. "Go left," he told him, pointing. "Cut round the back. And hurry up."

Kett went right, running as fast as his aching joints would let him. The hedge went on forever, no sign of a road, so he found a break in the foliage and cut through, branches scratching at his face and neck. He stumbled on a root, jarring his back, every step agony as he changed gear into a run again. He checked the name of the street, surprised to see it was the same.

"Still on Harrisons Drive, sir," he said. "I've lost him."

"Find him, Kett," Clare hissed.

He skirted past three houses before the road turned back in on itself, a handful of people loitering in their doorways as Duke's voice echoed from somewhere close by.

"Where did they go?" Kett shouted to them, and as one they pointed towards the driveway of a bungalow.

Kett snatched in a breath and jogged down it, cutting across a small garden before vaulting a fence which was, thankfully, about three feet tall. There were no more houses ahead, just a building site which stretched all the way to Salhouse Road in the distance. The ground had been levelled like there had been an explosion, and he could see Duke and Hope a hundred yards away, still running.

"They're on the building site past Hawthorne, sir," he told Clare. "Still going east, east, east."

"Tactical is *en route* from the south," the Super replied. "You should see them."

Kett could barely see anything past the sweat that dripped into his eyes. He scrubbed his sleeve over his face, blinking. Porter was waddling this way—less a run than a fast walk—and Kett pointed across the street.

"Go," he shouted, and Porter shot him a look.

"I am... bloody... going," he said.

The site was guarded by a wire fence but the gate was open, a handful of workers in hi-vis jackets watching as Kett and Porter thundered over the rough ground. Duke was slowing, but it didn't matter. Hope was burning out fast, struggling on the terrain.

"Duke!" Kett yelled. "Fall back!"

A wave of black uniforms was running their way from the right-hand side of the site, seven armed officers moving fast. There was nowhere to hide, nowhere to run, and Hope knew it. He staggered to a halt, wrestling his backpack off his shoulders as he spun around to face Duke.

"Aaron, stop!" Kett roared.

Duke saw the danger, skidding to a standstill a stone's throw from Hope. Kett slowed too, closing in—thirty yards away now.

"You got him?" said Clare, and Kett returned the phone to his ear.

"We've caught up to him, sir," he said. "But we don't have him yet."

"No closer," Hope shouted, breathless. He opened his backpack, reaching inside and leaving his hand there. He hadn't noticed the tactical team yet, his attention squarely on Duke. "I fucking mean it, pal. You take one step closer and I'll fucking gut you."

Duke rested one hand on his Taser, keeping his distance.

"Justin," said Kett, walking now. "Put the bag down, mate. There's nowhere to go."

Hope looked at him, sniffing. He still had his hand in the rucksack. He wouldn't have been able to fit a shotgun in there, unless he'd sawn off the barrels, but he could have a pistol.

Or a bomb.

"Drop the bag," Kett said again. "There are armed police right there, Justin. You're not going to get another chance."

Hope glanced over his shoulder, finally seeing the tactical unit. They'd closed the gap, circling him from a dozen yards away, their rifles up.

"Armed police!" shouted Sergeant Julia Gorski from the middle of the pack, curls of red hair visible below her ballistic helmet. "Drop the bag and get down on the ground. Now."

Kett felt his phone buzz, glancing at it to see Savage's name on the screen. He ignored it, keeping the line open to Clare.

"Justin, just do as they say," said Kett. "Whatever you've done, there's a better way than this."

"Whatever I've done?" he shouted, shaking his head. "I

fucking did it to help her. I did it to keep her away from *him*."

"Drop the bag!" Gorski ordered, taking another few steps.

"Do it," said Kett. "Come on, mate. The bomb, the nooses, none of that matters right now. Turn yourself in and we can help you."

Hope frowned at him, the bag dipping.

"What the fuck are you on about?" he said.

"Drop the bag!" Gorski yelled. "Final warning."

"I never wanted to hurt her," Hope said, shaking his head. "I only wanted to keep her safe. I—"

He pulled his hand out of the bag—too fast. A gunshot cut through the day and Hope spun like he was on a string, an almost perfect helix of blood spiralling from his shoulder.

"Cease fire!" Gorski screamed. "Cease fire, goddammit!"

She was running towards Hope, her rifle still braced against her shoulder. The other officers swept their guns earthwards, one with smoke rising from the barrel.

"We need an ambulance, now," Gorski said, ducking down onto her haunches beside Hope. He wasn't moving, his body sprawled across the dirt like a rag doll.

"Hope's down," Kett said into his phone as he ran to join them. "We need paramedics, sir."

We're going to need more than that, he thought as he reached Hope. Gorski had her gloved hands over the young man's shoulder, but blood was jetting through her fingers.

"Gloves on," she commanded Duke. "Press here."

The PC fumbled on a pair of gloves and took over, pushing down with all his weight as Gorski adjusted Hope's head. She put her ear to his lips.

"Fuck, fuck, fuck."

Another officer had reached them, this one holding a first aid kit. Gorski ripped it open, finding a bandage inside.

"Move," she said, and Duke fell back, his hands crimson.

She pressed the pad to Hope's shoulder, her expression grim beneath her visor.

"Come on," she said.

It was a losing battle, and she knew it.

Kett couldn't bear to watch, so he turned his attention to the rucksack that lay at his feet, open like a dead man's mouth. There was a laptop inside, a silver HP, plus what looked like a bundle of clothes. There was a knife too, he saw, the handle black, the blade short but lethal.

No gun, though. No bomb.

"Shit," he said.

"Chest compressions," Gorski shouted, and the other officer did as he was told.

But Hope just lay there, his body an empty vessel.

Kett heard a shout and looked back to see Clare climbing out of his Mercedes. IRVs were pouring onto the street, and in less than a minute the building site was flooded with black uniforms. He went to hang up on Clare and saw that Savage was trying to call him again. He answered it this time.

"Sir," she said before he could squeeze in a word. "Justin Hope didn't give Zoe those bruises. Her dad did."

"What?" said Kett.

"He was beating her. Justin was trying to keep her safe. That's why he locked her up. He knew she'd go home, she was too scared of her dad to stay away from him. That's why he was running. I don't think he's got anything to do with the bomb."

The day was still hot, but Kett felt every scrap of

warmth drain out of him. He watched as Gorski and her officer tried to magic some life back into the young man beneath them, but it was too late.

"Hope's dead," Kett said. "Tactical took him out. You're sure about the dad?"

Savage's sigh roared down the line.

"I saw it myself. He came at me, too. He's under arrest."

Clare had reached them, the sweat rolling down his face. He gurned at Hope, then at Kett.

"Threat to life?" he barked.

"Not exactly, sir," Kett replied. "He had his hand in the bag. We didn't know what was in there. Tactical made the call."

"What did he have?"

"A knife," said Kett.

Gorski was still doing her best to work a miracle, but Hope now lay in a puddle of blood that was far too big. She sat back, rocking, then she pulled off her gloves and threw them to the ground, unclipping her helmet and cradling it in her lap. Taking his cue from her, Duke pushed himself to his feet, staring at his bloody hands with wide-eyed horror.

"Savage just called," said Kett. "Zoe Pankhurst's dad is under arrest for beating his daughter. It wasn't Hope. She thinks he ran from us because he'd locked her in the room, not because of the bomb."

Clare grunted, his shoulders heaving as he recovered his breath.

"So this might not be our guy?" said Porter.

"It's him," said Clare. "We've got motive. He hated Ben and Millicent, and he talked about doing something to hurt them. We've got means, too. Ex-army, and we found his place of work. We have a witness who puts him at the vet's, another witness who claims their attacker was Scottish. I don't give a toss about his girlfriend, everything tells me this is him."

But even he looked doubtful, the ridge of his Adam's apple bobbing relentlessly as he swallowed. Gorski stood up, one hand on her rifle, the other shielding her eyes from the low sun.

"That shouldn't have happened," she said.

She glanced across the building site to the officer who had taken the shot. He still had his helmet on, his face unreadable beneath the visor.

"No, it shouldn't," said Clare. "But better him than one of us. Hope made his choice."

He had made his choice, but Kett felt a sickening wave of guilt at the sight of the young guy in the dirt. If this wasn't the man who'd bombed the Reeds' office, who'd forced six people to climb onto a gallows and hang themselves, who'd shot one of those men point blank in the face with a shotgun, then they'd made an awful mistake, and Hope had paid for it with his life.

"It's him," said Clare. "Get him out of here. I want a full report from you immediately, Sergeant Gorski."

She nodded, taking one more look at Hope before trudging back to her team.

"What about us, sir?" asked Kett. "We can help."

Clare checked his watch.

"No," he said after a moment. "It's been a day from hell. Go home, take a breath. We'll meet first thing and try to figure this mess out. Hope's our man, I'm sure of it. We'll find enough to make it stick."

"And if we don't, sir?"

"Then we're all fucked," said the Super.

He glanced at Duke, who was still staring at his gloved

hands, the blood such a brilliant shade of red that it could have been paint.

"Aaron, go and get cleaned up," said Clare. "I know it won't feel like it now, but you did good work catching Hope."

"We all caught him, sir," grumbled Porter.

Clare gave Porter a once over, his eyebrow climbing towards his hairline.

"The only thing you caught, Porter, was a stitch. I want you in extra early tomorrow morning for some callisthenics, you hear?"

Porter's bottom lip jutted out, but he didn't argue.

"Right, you lot, off you go," said Clare.

"Come on, mate," said Porter, taking hold of Duke's arm. "Let's get these gloves off and find a tap."

Kett watched them walk away, the sun turning them into silhouettes. Then he turned back to the dead man. One of Hope's eyes was closed, the other peeking up as if waiting for them all to leave, as if this was some kind of trick. All Kett wanted to do was cover him up so that he could begin his long rest, but he knew nobody could touch him until the forensic team arrived, until photographs were taken. Whoever had taken the shot had done so far too rashly, but Clare was right. Better him than any of them.

Right?

He heard a tinny voice and realised he was still holding his phone, Savage on the line.

"Sorry," he said. "You okay? You said Zoe's dad attacked you?"

"Gave me a proper shiner," she said. "Could have been a lot worse. Don't know how Zoe survived as long as she did, getting beaten like that. Social has her. They're going to find a place for her tonight."

"Good," said Kett, although there was nothing good about any of this.

"You heading back to HQ, sir?" asked Savage.

"No," said Kett, glancing at Clare, who was listening in like a hawk. "Boss is sending us home. You should go too."

"Okay, sir," she said. "I'll see you in the morning. Call me if you need me, I can't see myself getting much sleep tonight."

She hung up and Kett slid the phone into his pocket. He felt exhausted, and it wasn't just the run.

"My car's back at HQ," he said. "But I can walk home from here."

"I'll give you a lift," replied Clare.

"Oh, God no, sir. Please. It's fine, it's just down the road."

"I said I'll give you a lift, Detective," growled Clare. "So get in the bloody car."

CHAPTER TWENTY-TWO

It was a short enough journey, thankfully; just nine minutes from the building site to Kett's house on Wroxham Road. Clare parked the Mercedes half on and half off the kerb, leaving the engine idling.

Kett's three daughters were all on the driveway, enjoying the evening sun. They had dragged out the kitchen chairs and arranged them in pairs, using various mops and brooms to form jumps. Alice was galloping around like she was riding an imaginary pony, her little 'neighs' audible even through the closed windows of the car and over the thumps of passing traffic. Her sisters were trailing her, Evie doing her best to clamber over the jumps and Moira using common sense to duck underneath them. They all laughing their heads off, and the sight of it made Kett take in a long, welcome breath.

Billie sat on the front step, the door open behind her and a cuppa cradled against her chest. She looked up and smiled at him.

"They look happy," said Clare. "I remember when mine

were that age, sweet as anything. Make the most of it, Robbie, because they change in the blink of an eye."

"I thought your kids were all good'uns, sir?" said Kett.

"They are, most of the time," Clare said. "But the triplets are teenagers now and... how do I say this without offending anyone? They're all in sync. The whole bloody lot of them are in sync. It's a minefield."

"Oh, right, sir," said Kett.

"You'll find out for yourself soon enough. Why do you think I'm giving you a lift? I don't want to go home."

Kett laughed, but Clare's face was deadly serious. The Super watched as Alice took a jump and missed it, sending the broom clattering over the driveway.

"She really wants a horse, eh?"

"Yeah," said Kett. "And she deserves one, you know? She's really struggling at the moment. Hasn't been to school in weeks."

He and Billie had been talking with the head of Alice's primary school about moving her somewhere more suited to her abilities and her moods, but the process was so complicated he didn't even know where to start. On top of that, the council fought you every single step of the way—taking you to court, if you put up too much of a fight—because they didn't want to have to pay for it. It said a lot about a country, he thought, that it would attack a parent for trying to give their child the best possible shot at being happy.

"Her sisters are doing okay," he went on. "I think they'll always be okay. But Alice just can't settle, she can't seem to make friends. Breaks my heart, sir."

As if to prove his point, Alice had switched from fun to fury in a heartbeat, screaming something at her sisters. She picked up a broom, brandishing it like a weapon. Kett had his hand on the door, but Clare was speaking again.

"Clarissa was the same. Not exactly, but she had real difficulty managing her emotions."

"Clarissa?" said Kett with a frown. "She's like the nicest young person I've ever met."

"We took her riding one weekend when she was about nine," Clare went on. "It did her a world of good. Something about the horses calmed her. She never looked back."

"Right, sir?" said Kett. "I mean, we've only taken Alice a couple of times, but she's a different person around horses. That's why we were talking about getting one, but where are we supposed to keep it? The shed? I don't know a thing about them."

Clare seemed to consider something, clucking his tongue.

"What are you doing now?"

"Now, sir?" Kett said. "Sitting here with you—"

"Not right now, you great bellend. I mean what are your plans for the evening?"

"Nothing, sir," said Kett, checking his watch to see that it was already coming up for seven. "Dinner then bed. Same as always."

Clare leaned over Kett and wound down the passenger window, bellowing out of the car.

"Alice, get in here."

"What, sir?" Kett said. "Where—"

"In fact, you can all get in," the Super barked. "And get a bloody move on."

Alice stomped over, the broom still in her hands. Evie and Moira trotted after her, both of them whinnying like Shetlands.

"Do you want to go and look at some horses?" Clare asked them.

"Wait, sir, it's really late—"

Kett's protests were drowned out by a round of cheers, Alice's face opening in disbelief.

"Really, Dad?" she said. "Are we going to buy a horse?"

"Yes," said Clare before Kett could answer. "But only if you get in the bloody car."

Alice opened the door, trying to get inside while still holding the broom. Her little sisters managed to squeeze past her, scrabbling into the backseat of the Mercedes with squeals of excitement.

"Put the broom down, Alice," said Kett. "No, don't throw it onto the street, give it to Mum."

Billie had strolled over, the cup of tea still in her hands.

"What's going on?" she asked.

"We're buying a horse," said Clare.

"A horse?"

"A horse," said Kett, shrugging. "Apparently."

"A horse!" squeaked Moira.

"Get in," ordered Clare.

"There aren't enough seats," said Billie. "And I've got food on, and I think this is something we should probably talk about before—"

"I've talked about it plenty," said Clare. "It's what's happening."

Alice had managed to get into the car and she slammed the door shut.

"A horse? Really?"

"It smells in here," moaned Evie, holding her nose. "And there are no car seats."

"That's a good point," said Kett. "We should probably get the spare ones out of the garage, sir."

Clare wasn't listening, hunching over the wheel as he punched the accelerator. The car lurched forwards, Evie and Moira practically rolling across the back seat as the Super accelerated.

"Christ, Alice, plug them in!" said Kett, leaning over and trying to reach the seatbelts. The two little girls were laughing hysterically.

"They're fine," said Clare. "It's just up the road."

Alice clipped in Moira, although there was hardly any point because she was far too short, the seatbelt covering her face. Evie managed to buckle herself in, beaming with excitement.

"Are we really getting a horse, Dad?" asked Alice, bracing her hands on the back of Clare's seat, her face full of an excitement that Kett hadn't seen in days—weeks, maybe. He glanced at the Super.

"Do I have a say in this at all, sir?" he asked.

"No," said Clare. "So shut your tosspocket and roll with it."

IT WAS a little over twenty minutes later that Clare pulled off the road onto a rough track. It had felt like hours, though, because the girls had been singing the same song for the entire journey—a high-pitched serenade of *Horsey Horsey Don't You Stop* that had driven Kett right to the brink of madness.

"Look! Horses!" screeched Alice, the volume of her voice high enough to shatter glass.

On either side of the track, past low hawthorn hedges, were several large paddocks. Most were empty, but three horses paraded in the closest field on the left, two stately brown ones and a little grey pony that was rolling happily on the short grass. They all looked over at the sound of the approaching Mercedes, their eyes full of curiosity, their tails swishing.

"That one's doing a roly poly," said Evie, laughing.

"It's not a roly poly," said Alice. "They do that because of the flies, and to help them shed their hair. I saw it on YouTube."

"No, it's doing a roly poly," said Evie, defiant.

They trundled down the lane, joggling in every pothole until Clare turned the corner into a large courtyard. Ahead, behind more hedging, was a small cottage, its roof thatched. Surrounding it like the walls of a castle were a dozen or so stables, a couple of horses peering over their doors like gossiping neighbours.

Another horse stood in the far corner of the courtyard, and even though Kett knew next to nothing about them, he understood that this creature was magnificent. Its coat was such a dark shade of brown that it was almost black, its mane worked into several short, neat braids. Its shoulders had to have been taller than him, its muscular body standing perfectly still as a man ran a brush over its flank. Both the horse and the man looked over as Clare hammered the brakes and cut the engine, and Kett saw that he was tall as well, and remarkably handsome.

"Quite something, eh?" said Clare, although Kett wasn't sure exactly which of them he was talking about.

The girls were positively apoplectic with excitement in the back, all of them out of their seatbelts and crowding through the gap between the front seats. Kett couldn't make out a single word in their cacophony of screams and squeals, and he held up a hand to try to silence them. In the end, it was Clare's booming voice that made them fall quiet.

"Horses are not to be trifled with," he said. "They are gentle creatures with kind souls, like me. But they, like me, will not tolerate bad behaviour. So I need quiet voices and calm bodies. Is that clear?"

All three of them nodded, falling silent. Alice was almost drooling as she studied the horse through the windscreen.

"Good," said Clare, opening his door and extricating his gangly body like a stork.

Kett followed him out, all three girls fighting quietly as they clambered out of the back door. The air was full of that unmistakeable smell of horses—manure and sweat and mud and dirt—but somehow not a bad smell at all. Kett took a lungful, feeling instantly like he was at home even though he'd never ridden a horse in his life. The girls, too, had levelled out, Alice too awed to say anything at all and the two younger ones clinging to each other as they took it all in. Swallows darted in and out of the stables, belting out their summer song. There were hollyhocks everywhere, reaching for the heavens.

"Erik," said Clare, waving. "Busy?"

The man threw his brush into a bucket and rested his hand on the neck of the horse for a moment, as if to reassure it. He was wearing faded jeans and brown motorcycle boots, and a T-shirt that was tight enough to outline the muscles of his chest and arms. He hadn't shaved for a few days, his hair tousled into wild patterns, but his smile, when he offered it, was broad and genuine and contagious.

"Colin," he said. His voice bore a slight accent that sounded vaguely Scandinavian.

He turned that smile to Kett, and then to his daughters.

"Hello, everybody, what brings you all out here?"

"We've come to buy a horse!" Alice said, her voice far too loud.

The horse nickered, tapping a hoof on the hard ground with a musical *clop*.

"Quiet, Alice," said Kett. "Remember, they don't like loud noises."

"You can be as loud as you like," said Erik, walking towards them. He had a distinct limp in his left leg, one that seemed to cause him a lot of pain. "Southpaw here is used to the noise. Nothing will faze her."

"Erik North, this is DCI Robbie Kett," said Clare. "And his kids. Alice, the tall one, Evie and Moira."

Erik brushed his hand down his filthy jeans and offered it to Kett, who shook it.

"Sorry," said Erik. "Doesn't matter how many times I wash them. I've seen you on the news, haven't I?"

"Probably," said Kett. "But don't believe everything you hear. This place is amazing."

"We're working on it."

"Erik's ex-Met, like you," said Clare. "Mounted Branch. The horse, too."

"Wow," said Kett. "I've seen you guys at work, it's impressive."

"They're the impressive ones," said Erik, looking back at the horse. Southpaw snorted as if in agreement, clopping her hoof again. "We just have to not fall off."

He laughed gently.

"He's just moved up to Norfolk," Clare said. "What, three months now?"

"Nearly," said Erik. He braced a hand on his thigh. "We needed a change, me and Southpaw. So we bought this place."

From somewhere on the far side of the stables, a horse whinnied, and Southpaw returned the call.

"So, you're here to buy a horse, is that right?" asked Erik.

"Uh, yeah, kind of," said Kett, glancing at Clare. "I mean, we really don't know what we're doing, and we don't have anywhere to keep it. We live in the city, but..."

He looked at Alice, his oldest daughter so full of nervous excitement that her body seemed to vibrate with it. The look on her face was so desperate, so full of hope, that it broke his heart and mended it again, all within a single breath. Erik saw it too, studying Alice with eyes that seemed far too bright, seeming to really *see* her in a way that most adults didn't.

"That's why I'm here," said Erik. "That's why I bought this place. I've got a stable full of horses and nobody but me to love them. Do you want to look around?"

Alice made a noise like an old fashioned kettle coming to the boil, her hands clenched into fists in front of her face.

"I think that's a yes," said Kett, feeling the smile on his own face. "But really, I don't know if we can—"

"You can," said Erik. "Pick a horse. They can live right here and you can come and see it whenever you like, all of you. I can show you the ropes and you can do as little or as much as you want." He nodded to Alice. "Let me introduce you to the herd. I've got a pony called Twinkle I think you're going to fall in love with. She's fourteen hands, and she's desperate for a haircut."

"Twinkle!" exclaimed Moira with a giggle.

The girls wandered to the nearest stable, Clare walking with them, all of them cooing and clucking at the scruffy-headed pony who was leaning over the door. Kett hung back, waiting for them to be out of earshot.

"Are you sure about this?" he asked. "I don't even know if we can afford one."

Erik waved his words away.

"Forget the money. I don't need it. I bought this place from a breeder, they couldn't have cared less about the animals. It was all sport to them, business."

He sighed, scuffing his boot on the ground to kick a stone from the treads.

"They didn't see them as living things," he said. "They didn't even see them as animals. They were goods to be bought and sold, to be bet on and then discarded. They played the odds, but it's a rigged game if you're a horse. Nobody wins."

"Huh," said Kett, and for a second something flashed inside his head, a jigsaw piece of the case clicking into place —but only one, the picture still a mystery. "Nobody wins," he echoed.

"That's right," said Erik. "But these horses are safe enough now. They need friends above anything. They need family. And I know a family when I see one. I know a good heart, and a safe place."

There were so many things Kett could have said to that, so many arguments he could have offered, so much evidence against the idea that he was a good man. But Erik planted a strong hand on his shoulder and chased them away.

"Come on," he said. "Let's find your girls a new friend."

CHAPTER TWENTY-THREE

Tuesday

"You'd better bloody make it up to me, Lee."

Lee Holland pulled his truck over to the side of the road, trying to ignore the voice that screeched from the speakers. Outside, the world was pitch black, the quiet street drenched in the fierce glow of the Nissan's headlights. The clock on the dash read 2:23 am, which was an hour off because it hardly seemed worth changing when you had to do it again in six months.

"Lee?" said Ashley, her voice crackling as the connection threatened to drop. "If you've hung up on me, I swear to God I'm packing—"

"I'm still here," he said, twisting the key to kill the engine. "It's one job, Ash, and we need the money."

"We don't need the money, Lee, we need time," said Ashley, and Lee repeated her whining words beneath his breath. "This is the first time we haven't got the kids in months and you had to go and answer the fucking phone at three in the morning? I wanted breakfast, I wanted to go out with you."

Yeah, well I wanted a shag, and that didn't happen, did it? he thought.

"Just go back to sleep," he said. "I'll be an hour, tops."

If I come home at all.

Except of course he would, because he was thirty-nine now and pot-bellied and balding and he couldn't even remember the last time he'd changed his underwear. Ashley, on the other hand, was eight years younger than him and he saw the way men at his work ogled her when she brought him his lunch. She'd replace him in a day or two, but who else would have him now? The thought of it sent a ripple of cold panic through him.

"I'm sorry," he said. "I love you. I'll bring you breakfast."

Ashley mumbled something he couldn't make sense of, then she hung up. Lee blew out a long sigh, the panic turning to a loathing that he felt deep inside him—loathing for her, loathing for his job, loathing for whoever was desperate enough to call him out in the arse end of the night to fix a fucking freezer.

He picked up his phone from the passenger seat and checked his messages again. The caller had sent him the information after Lee had agreed to come out—for double his regular fee, of course, because when it was the middle of the night he could charge whatever he liked. This was definitely the place, a small unit on an industrial estate on the outskirts of the city. The sign over the door read Watson's, but other than that there was no clue at all what the building was used for. There were lights on inside, and five cars occupied the small car park. It must have been some emergency.

His door creaked like the trumpets of Armageddon as he got out, and he made a mental note to oil it—another job to add to the endless list. He walked to the open truck bed and hauled out his tool chest. It seemed to weigh more every time he picked it up, and he struggled, banging his knee twice on his way through the car park. By the time he reached the door there was a rage inside him that he was having trouble keeping a lid on, and he hammered his free fist on the uPVC hard enough to make it rattle, huffing and puffing as he waited for an answer.

He didn't get one.

"You'd better fucking be in there," he said, dropping the tool chest and banging again. "Hello? It's Lee. I'm here for the freezer."

Still nothing, and he wondered if they'd got somebody else to fix it, if he was only one of several numbers they'd called. People sometimes did that when they needed a job done quick. '*Oh, yeah, sorry about that, it's sorted, off you trot.*' There wasn't much in the world that made him madder.

He went to knock again, then changed his mind, pushing the handle of the door instead. For a moment he thought it was locked, but it was just stiff, and after a little persuasion it surrendered. Hefting up his tool chest again, he made his way into a small waiting room with a deserted desk and an empty sofa. Strip lights sucked the colour out of everything, the hum of them making his head feel weird. Several posters clung to the walls, their corners peeling, all displaying the Watson's logo.

"All your industrial freezer needs met," he read aloud from a poster with a goggle-eyed chicken on it. "Fast, cheap and reliable."

Not so reliable now, are you?

The place had a weird vibe, the furniture caked in dust like it hadn't been used for a while. There was a door to his left and a door straight ahead, behind the desk. This one was ajar, and he thought he could hear soft voices spilling out of it. Were they whispering? The thought of it drew a cold finger up his back, the goosebumps breaking out on his arms. Why the hell would anyone be whispering?

"Hello?" he said, his voice quieter than he'd wanted it to be, like a bird that didn't want to leave the safety of his mouth. He cleared his throat, tried again. "Hello? I'm here for the freezer."

More sounds from the room, only this time there was something wild about them, something inhuman. Were there animals in there? Had they defrosted and come back to life? Was that how freezers worked? He had a sudden image of walking through the door and seeing a farmyard of frosted beasts, their knees knocking, their teeth chattering, as whoever ran this place tried to pack them back inside.

Mad, he thought, although he wasn't sure if he was referring to the idea or to himself.

The sound shifted again, a soft cry that was definitely human. Lee held his breath, wondering whether he should leave right now, climb back into his truck and drive home, throw himself into bed with Ashley and hold her tight—so tight that when he woke again, they'd still be in each other's arms.

Then he thought about his bank statement, how far in the red he was because he'd bought that shitty truck on tick, how he'd already missed two payments and for those arse-holes your third warning was your last. He'd get three notes for this, maybe more. It would be enough to keep him above water.

He cleared his throat again, clutching the tool chest and pushing through the door.

"Oi," he called out as he went, his patience worn thin. "I'm here—"

He choked on the last few words, coughing hard to expel the spit from his windpipe. He stopped dead, the heavy tool chest sliding from his sweaty hand and hitting the floor with a world-ending crash.

In front of him was an open space surrounded by enormous silver freezer units. Seven small tables had been arranged in a line from left to right, and behind five of those tables were five people, all kneeling, as if in prayer. Only none of them had found any kind of peace here. Their faces were warped with fear as they stared up at him.

He took an instinctive step back, every single alarm bell his body had clamouring for him to get the fuck away from this whimpering congregation of penitent terror.

Then he stopped, because as he scanned their faces he realised that he *recognised* these people—three of them, anyway. And he knew one of them well. He'd known one of them all his life.

"Shit," he said. "*James*?"

His uncle stared back at him, so familiar and yet so alien, because in all his nearly four decades on Earth Lee had never once seen his Uncle James look like this—so full of desperation, so full of horror. Even now, as James' eyes filled with tears, as he lowered his head, Lee couldn't be sure it was him. It looked like somebody who was wearing his uncle's face as a mask.

"What's going on?" Lee asked, his voice a husk. "What's—"

Something jutted into his back, something hard, and he staggered forward with a choked scream, spinning around.

A man stood in the doorway, dressed all in black, his face hidden by a balaclava—like a terrorist, or an SAS soldier.

He held a shotgun, an enormous double-barrelled beast of a weapon that was pointed right at Lee's chest. He'd seen a gun like this before, a Churchill. His dad had owned one once upon a time, and Lee had watched it cut a rabbit in half from twenty feet away.

He was a lot closer than that now.

The man used the gun as a prompt, gesturing towards the line of kneeling people.

"Move," he said.

"What?" Lee answered, his voice higher than it had any right to be. "What the fuck is going on?"

He turned to his uncle.

"James? What's going on?"

James didn't look at him. He didn't even lift his head.

"Move," the man with the gun said again, jabbing it at Lee with more force. He spoke with an accent, something Scottish, maybe. "I'm not going to say it a third time."

Lee felt the tears gather in his eyes, felt the burn of them. A thousand thoughts seemed to rush through his head at once, like a high-speed train—he could run, he could grab the gun, he could scream and scream and scream until he woke up from this bullshit nightmare—but they were gone before he could make sense of them, before he could work out what to do.

The barrel of the gun smacked him in the forehead. It felt like a hammer, making his skull ring, and he retreated towards one of the two empty tables. The tears were flowing freely now. The gun had made him a child again, and he wanted James to pick him up the way he'd done when he'd fallen over and skinned his knee, or all those times Marty from down the street had thrown stones at him. James was his dad's brother, and he was only a handful of years older than Lee—more of a sibling to him than an uncle. He glanced at him as he went but James still didn't look up.

"Pick a table," said the man with the gun.

Lee staggered to the closest empty one.

"On your knees."

He found his body obeying without his permission. He crashed down hard enough to send a bolt of agony into his lower back, and he grabbed hold of the table to stop himself from collapsing completely.

The table. He hadn't noticed it before, but something was lying on it: a length of copper attached to a thick, black wire. Every table had one, and Lee followed the wires across the floor like he was solving one of the maps his kids got in Pizza Hut, seeing the place where they merged into one. That single, snaking cable vanished behind one of the freezers. He realised that he could hear something over the roar of his heart—a deep, bone-rattling hum that could only be one thing.

Electricity.

"What the fuck?" he said quietly, looking at the man next to him. He couldn't remember his name, but he'd met him before on a job somewhere. He was a mechanic too, like him, like James as well. The man turned his head and caught Lee's eye, only for a second, though, before looking away almost shamefully. "Hey, come on, this is bullshit, we—"

"Shut up," said the man with the gun. He spoke the words rather than shouting them, but there was no denying the danger there. "We're all here, so let's get this over with."

He took a step towards them, the gun lowered slightly but his gloved finger still tight on the trigger. His voice seemed to fall in and out of its accent, as if he was struggling to remember how to speak.

"I need you to listen very carefully because I'm only going to explain this once. If you break the rules, if you do it wrong, if you fuck it up, I'll shoot you in the face."

Somebody down the line was sobbing, the sound of it making Lee feel like he'd been hollowed out and filled with ice. He needed to piss, his bladder throbbing.

"You've all chosen a table, at random, as I asked you to," the man continued. "On the table is a metal rod. Six of these rods are connected to a dead wire. Nothing will happen to you when you touch them. One, however, is connected to a live wire carrying 15 amps of current. Death will be instant."

A swell of panic rose, a chorus of voices all saying the exact same thing.

"Please," said Lee, joining them. "You don't have to do this. Please don't."

The man lifted the gun, resting the barrel almost casually on his left forearm.

"Each of you has an 85% chance of survival," he said. "I'd call those good odds. You have five seconds."

The panic grew, and the guy to Lee's side started to get up—*Allan*, he suddenly remembered. That was his name.

The man with the gun moved fast, crossing the room with three powerful strides, the shotgun locked on Allan's head. Allan dropped back down onto his knees, his hands up, his breaths so hard he had to be hyperventilating.

"One," said the man with the gun. "Two."

He was counting too fast, he wasn't giving them enough time.

"Three."

Lee looked at James, and this time his uncle looked

back. The fear had gone, replaced with something else: resignation.

"Four."

James reached out and grabbed the copper bar on his table.

"No!" Lee screamed.

Nothing happened, his uncle releasing a groan of relief.

"Five," said the man with the gun.

Jesus Christ.

Lee was almost paralysed, he almost couldn't make his body work. But he forced his hand out, he wrapped his fingers around the copper bar—expecting a flash of pain and then nothing, nothing else for the rest of time.

The copper sat in his hand, cool against his skin.

There was a flurry of movement as everybody reached for their table. Allan, too, his eyes almost bursting from his face as he lifted his hand, as he dropped it into place.

The crack was so loud, the flash so bright, that for a moment Lee thought the man had been shot. His body flew back like it had been hit by a car, the lights in the warehouse snapping off before he hit the ground. The room was plunged into a darkness so profound that Lee immediately lost all sense of which way was up. He tried to stand but vertigo took hold of him and he staggered, reaching out for the table to stop himself before realising he didn't know which one was his and which one was Allan's—that copper pole still thrumming.

He pulled his hand back and fell, his elbow hitting the ground first and releasing such a powerful blast of agony that he could see it—a firework show against the night. He crawled forwards, smelling charred flesh and smoke, hearing the howls of the survivors as they hurled their grief up to the ceiling.

"Lee?"

It was his uncle's voice, and it came from a million miles away. He crawled towards it, a body thumping off his before retreating into the night, somebody else treading on his fingers. He didn't care, crawling towards his uncle like he was five years old again until he felt those strong arms wrap themselves around him, until he felt James' voice against his ear.

"You're okay, you're okay."

He curled into him, the static in his head too much, the screams too much, the knowledge that he could have died *just too much*. He lay there and sobbed into his uncle's chest, hearing—as if from a great distance—a door closing.

And a lock snapping shut.

CHAPTER TWENTY-FOUR

KETT ROSE FROM A DREAM OF WILD HORSES AS THE buzz of his phone cut through the thunder of their hooves. He rolled over in bed, rubbing his eyes, the room lit only by the ghostly glow of the screen.

"Don't," moaned Billie, her voice thick with sleep.

And for a second or two, he didn't, closing his eyes and trying to remember his dream. But the phone kept buzzing, nagging him until he slid it off the bedside table and answered the call. Clare's voice crowed like a rooster's.

"Kett."

"Sir," he said, wiping the drool from his lips. Without his glasses, he couldn't make out the digits in the corner of the screen. He had no idea what time it was. "What's happening?"

Billie groaned, pulling the covers over her head. Kett sat up, and as he did so he felt a heavy lump at the bottom of the bed. It took a few moments for him to realise it was Alice, lying across the covers like a dog and snoring gently. He couldn't remember the last time she'd come into their room like this, and it brought a smile to his face.

She was so grown up now that these odd little moments when she reverted to her younger self were more than welcome.

"So?" said Clare, and Kett realised he'd missed what the Super had been talking about.

"Sorry, sir, can you say that again?"

"Sure," said Clare, simmering. "It's not like I've got anything better to be doing. There's been another death, same killer."

"Shit," Kett said quietly. "So it wasn't Hope."

He saw the lad lying in the dirt, the blood draining out of him, and the dark night grew darker.

"Evidently not," said Clare, his voice laced with the same regret. "Or if it was, he wasn't working alone. I wish there was a way of finding out for sure. Oh, wait, there is."

"Sir?"

"Get your hairy tosspocket out of bed and get to work!"

Clare hung up, Kett's ear ringing. He checked the time —just after four—and dropped the phone back onto the bedside table. Scrubbing his face with his hands, he tried to summon the strength to stand up. His body was aching, probably from those bloody star jumps. But that was a sign, wasn't it? Maybe when he came home later he'd dig out his trainers and go for a run.

Yeah, right.

Billie peeked out of the blankets like a field mouse, frowning at him.

"You've got to go?" she asked.

"Yeah, sorry. You'll be okay?"

"We'll cope."

He dug his hand into the covers and stroked her hair.

"Did we really get a horse last night?" he said, and Billie laughed.

"Well, *you* did. Why do you think she's in here? She was too excited to go back to sleep."

"I never even heard her," he said.

"That's because you snore like a horse."

"I don't snore," said Kett, easing himself out of the bed as smoothly as possible so as not to wake their eldest daughter. "I play soothing night music. With my nose."

Billie laughed again, watching him as he pulled on his suit trousers.

"It's nice to see her happy though, isn't it?" she said.

"It's the best," he replied, buttoning up a fresh shirt.

And it was. The image of Alice, wide-eyed with wonder as she hugged the little pony called Twinkle—that sudden feeling of hope he'd had for her, the relief that she'd found something to love—would stay with him for the rest of his life.

His phone buzzed with an arriving text and he hunted for his glasses. It was from Clare.

Crime scene crowded, need you at HQ. Get out of bed.

"I am out of bed," he told the phone, slipping it into his pocket. "Go back to sleep, I'll try not to wake the girls."

Billie was already drifting off again, her eyes closed.

"Will you be late home again?" she asked.

"No," he said.

But he already knew that was a lie.

———

HE DIDN'T HAVE the Volvo, and by the time his taxi had dropped him off outside the main doors of Police HQ, the sun was up, peering over the low houses to the east as if curious about what had woken it. It was already hot, the morning haze burned away and the sky bright. It was going to be another corker.

Unfortunately.

He made his way to the Major Investigation Team's offices, relieved to see that somebody—probably the cleaning crew—had rearranged the desks and tables the way they were supposed to be. At least they wouldn't be doing any more bleep tests, unless Clare was heartless enough to make them run outside.

There was nobody here, and he made his way down to the Incident Room to find that deserted as well. A bunch of new photographs had been pinned to the wall, the six people that had been forced to climb the scaffold and pull a noose around their neck, and the two men who had never climbed down again. Brian Beaney's scowl emanated from one photograph. Stefan Kucharek, the man who'd been shot point blank in the face, grinned from another. There was no indication at all in that smile that he would die such a horrific death, just a wide-eyed innocence.

Justin Hope was there too, his glowering military portrait—head shaved, eyes sunken and somehow empty, the way they often were in young men who had seen combat. Kett wasn't sure if Hope had been a good man, but he wasn't their killer, and he hadn't deserved to bleed out in the muck the way he had.

Kett sighed and left the room, returning to the bullpen to find Savage dumping her bag on her desk. She looked at him, as exhausted as he was. Her face was swollen from where Zoe Pankhurst's gorilla of a father had thumped her.

"Where did you come from?" Kett asked.

"Just got here," she said, stifling a yawn with the back of her hand. "You've heard?"

"Another death?"

She nodded.

"Same MO as before. Call came in an hour ago, some bloke called 999 saying somebody had taken them at gunpoint, forced them to electrocute themselves."

"Shit," said Kett. "Electrocution?"

"Only one man died," said Savage. "Five lived. But it was the same killer. Shotgun, mask, and he made them play a game of chance."

"Who is this guy?" Kett asked. Savage shrugged.

"Three of the victims have been taken to the hospital," she said. "Two wouldn't go. They're here, apparently. Boss wants us to talk to them."

"Where are they?"

"Interview room," she said, and Kett frowned.

"They're suspects?"

"I don't think so," she said. "Duke put them there when he brought them in."

"Where is he now?"

"He's gone to meet Porter. They think they've found Asif, the missing guy from Ben Reed's office."

"Yeah? That's something, at least."

Savage pushed her chair back, leading the way across the bullpen.

"You said there were six victims?" Kett asked as they went. "Not seven?"

"That's what I've been told," she said. "Six victims, but seven electrical wires. Only one of them was live."

"Like the nooses," said Kett. "Seven nooses, six victims. Why?"

"Maybe he didn't have time to find his seventh," she said. "He must know we're onto him, maybe he's rushing."

"Maybe. Do we know the name of the man who died?"

"Allan Currier. He's 46 years old, local. No connection

at all to anyone at Reed's office, or to anyone from the hangings yesterday."

They pushed through the double doors into the corridor.

"This one, sir," said Savage, opening the door of the first room.

Two men sat behind the table, watching them as they walked inside. One was around fifty, tall and broad, his balding head covered with scraps of greying hair. He'd had a broken nose at some point in his life, and his mangled ears made Kett think it was probably more to do with rugby than boxing. The guy next to him was a little younger, smaller and neater in every way, but there was enough of a similarity between them for Kett to understand they were related.

Everything about them was taut, a spring that needed to be released. They carried their hands in fists, their teeth were gritted, and the nervous energy coming off them was enough to power a small town. Even if Kett hadn't been told what had happened to them, he would have known that they'd been through hell. Some traumas rewrote your entire body.

"Hi," he said, taking a seat. Savage remained standing, leaning against the back wall. The men switched their gazes back and forth between them like they were watching a tennis match. "My name's DCI Robert Kett, this is DC Kate Savage. I'd like to start by thanking you for coming in today."

Neither of them replied, the bigger of the two swallowing noisily.

"I'm just catching up on everything," said Kett. "Can you walk me through what happened last night?"

"This morning," said the smaller of the two men. "It

happened this morning."

"Sorry," said Kett. "You are?"

The man looked at the older guy as if asking for permission.

"Lee Holland?" he said, like it was a question.

"And you're brothers, right?" asked Kett. This, at last, cracked the stone façade of the bigger man's face.

"Uncle," he said.

"Pretty much brothers, though, ain't we?" said Lee.

The older man didn't reply.

"What's your name?"

"James," he said, reluctantly.

"Okay," said Kett. "So, who wants to go first?"

Again, Lee turned to his uncle, and when James didn't say anything the younger man cleared his throat and began in a soft, tremulous voice.

"I, uh, I got a call about an emergency repair. Some bloke asked me if I'd come and fix his freezer because he had a bunch of shit in there he didn't want to lose. I didn't want to, because... Well, you know, it was early."

"What time, exactly?"

"Like, three? Early, but the money would have come in handy." He frowned, as if just realising something. "He didn't even pay us."

"Who didn't?" asked Kett. "The man who tried to kill you?"

"Yeah," said Lee. James rolled his eyes.

"So you got an address?" Kett prompted.

"Yeah, he texted it to me after the call. Me bird wasn't too happy about me going because the kids are at her mum's, but like I said, a job's a job. Got there just after three, black as my arsehole outside, but there are lights on, cars and stuff."

He hesitated, his eyes growing distant as if he was losing himself in the memory.

"You want to go next?" Lee asked James. The bigger man sighed, lifting his hand to his face and studying his knuckles.

"Same," he grunted after a second or two.

"You got a call about a job?" Kett asked. "You're both, what? Mechanics? Engineers?"

"Mechanics," said Lee. "James did it first. I followed him. He's got most of the qualifications and shit, I just kind of taught myself. Dad was a mechanic n'all, I picked it up when I was a kid."

James rolled his eyes again.

"What time did you get there?" Kett asked him.

"Three," he said.

"You're sure?"

James grunted something that wasn't quite a word.

"There were people there when you arrived?"

A nod. Kett blew out a sigh of frustration.

"How many?"

"Four."

"Including the gunman?"

James thought about it.

"Five."

"He isn't famous for his long speeches, are you, James?" said Lee, attempting a smile. James shot him an impatient look, drumming his knuckles on the tabletop. Lee seemed to shrink even further.

"You were the last one to arrive?" Kett asked Lee.

"Yeah," he said. "Gunman was right behind me. Must have been in the room I walked in through, there was another door in there. He had that gun, couldn't have done anything, could I?"

"And you?" Kett asked James.

"Same."

"He made us kneel beside these tables," Lee said. "Wires and shit on them, made us each grab a metal thing and..."

He licked his lips, staring into the middle distance again.

"Could have been any of us," he said. "Could have been me."

"Did the killer tell you which table to kneel beside?" asked Kett. "Did he give you any clues at all?"

Lee shook his head.

"Was only two left when I got there, hardly a fucking choice, was it?"

"And you, James?"

"No."

"No, he didn't guide you, or no, you didn't get a choice?"

"First."

"He means the first one," translated Lee. "They were all talking about it while we waited for you lot. They all picked a table while the man with the gun watched. He didn't tell them which one to choose."

James offered a minuscule nod.

"Told us he'd shoot us if we didn't do what he said," Lee went on. "But he wouldn't have, would he? I think maybe we should have just got up and left, because he wouldn't have shot us, would he?"

"I think he would have," said Kett, trying not to see Stefan's faceless corpse and seeing it anyway.

He gulped air, looking back at Savage. She understood his silent request and opened the door, letting out a little of the stale, hot air.

"Uh," said Kett, trying to get his bearings. "The gunman. What can you tell me about him? James?"

"Scottish," said the older man.

"I don't know," Lee added. "I thought he was at first too, but there was something not right with his accent. It was like he was putting it on. He wasn't a tall guy, about my height, I think. He had a mask on, one of those terrorist ones, a..."

He struggled for the word.

"Balaclava," said James.

"That's it, one of them. Could see his eyes, though."

"Can you describe them?"

"They were... round," said Lee, struggling. "He had two of them. I couldn't see the colour cos he was too far away, but I want to say blue, or brown."

"Right, so your height? Five-eight?"

"I'm five-ten," said Lee, and James snorted a laugh through his nose. "I am," protested Lee, stretching up in his chair. "Five-ten, in the morning anyway."

"Slim build?" asked Kett.

"Lean," said Lee.

"I'm talking about the gunman, not you."

"Oh, right. No, he wasn't thin, wasn't fat neither. Had a little bulk to him. He was wearing boots, dark trousers, a dark jacket, gloves."

Kett made a note of it all in his pad.

"You can't tell me anything else about him?"

Lee shook his head. James didn't so much as twitch.

"Nothing?"

Twin blank stares.

"Okay, then what about—"

"Oh, wait," said Lee, brightening. "I can tell you about the gun. It was a Churchill side-by-side, twelve gauge. Dad used to have one back at the fair, for shooting pigeons and shit. Right, James?"

James shrugged.

"You're sure?" Kett asked, and Lee nodded.

He scribbled it down.

"That's good," he said. "That's helpful. What about the other victims? The dead man? Can you tell me anything about him?"

"Well, yeah," said Lee, as if it was the stupidest question in the world. "Allan, we know him. Knew him, didn't we, James?"

James didn't respond, but that didn't slow his nephew down.

"He worked with us on the circuit, friend of Dad's for a while, until they fell out. Allan borrowed a car once and never gave it back, Cavalier."

"What circuit?" asked Kett.

"The carnivals," said Lee. "The fairgrounds. He was a grease monkey like Dad and Uncle James, worked the machines, the rides. Well, he used to, haven't seen him in years. Wonder what he's…"

Kett saw him remember, saw him live out the man's death again the way he would over and over and over for the rest of his life.

"What about the others?" Kett asked. "Did you know them too?"

Lee nodded, coming back to the room.

"A couple, yeah."

"From the same circuit?"

Lee nodded.

"Mechanics?"

"Yeah," he said. "I mean, maybe not all. Some were ride operators, I think. They tinker, but they don't do the work.

You need to know what you're doing with those things, they're beasts. But this is from way back, I don't know what they're doing now. I haven't worked the circuit in five years, James neither, right?"

James made a noise in his throat.

"Is that a yes grunt or a no grunt?" Kett asked him.

"Yes," he said.

"I haven't even seen *him* for about two years," said Lee, hitching a thumb at his uncle. "Never answers my calls."

James rolled his eyes for a third time and Lee saw it, falling quiet.

"Can either of you think of any reason you'd be targeted like this?" Kett said. "Any reason this man would come after you? Because this isn't random, is it? You two are related, and you know the other victims. You're connected. There has to be a reason he'd go after you."

Lee shrugged dramatically.

"It's a game, isn't it?" he said. "Making us go against each other like that. It's like the ones we always used to offer to punters. The ducks, the horses, the hoops. You think you've got good odds, but you don't. It's all rigged."

"Nobody wins," said Kett, sighing again.

"That's right. Even when you think you have, you haven't."

Kett tapped his pen on the table and stood up.

"Thanks," he said. "You two okay to hang around here a little longer? I'm going to send somebody else to follow up."

"Yeah," said Lee, stifling a yawn with the back of his hand. "We'll be alright."

The bigger of the two men sat back in his chair and closed his eyes. He was shaking, Kett saw, although he was doing his best to control it. They were alive, these men.

They'd survived. But part of them had died in that room. They'd never be the same.

Kett left them to it, walking back into the corridor. He looked at Savage, who mirrored his miserable expression.

"Nobody wins," she said, and he nodded.

"Nobody wins."

CHAPTER TWENTY-FIVE

"Is he dead?"

Porter and Duke leaned over the metal railing that separated the footpath from the wide, murky river below. Roughly three feet beneath them was a narrow, shrubby embankment littered with beer bottles and takeaway wrappers. Lying face-down in the mess, utterly motionless, his fingers lapped by the gentle water, was a man. From the footpath, in the soft morning light, it was impossible to tell whether he was alive or not. Only one thing was painfully obvious.

He was completely naked.

"You should probably go and check, sir," said Duke, rubbing his face. The bruise had settled around his eye from where he'd been hit by the little girl, something that still brought Porter an enormous amount of joy. "He might need our help."

Porter raised an eyebrow.

"One of us definitely needs to check," he said. "But there's no way I'm climbing down there. This suit is a Tom Ford."

"Well, *this* suit is an Aaron Duke, sir," said Duke, tucking his thumbs into his belt like a cowboy. "They had to order it for me because I wouldn't fit in the standard uniform. I can't get it wet."

"Bullshit," said Porter.

"It's true. Ask the Guv. My chest is too big, and my arms."

"Is that why you got your arse kicked by a three-year-old?"

"Five," muttered Duke.

Porter flexed his own bicep. It had been so long since he'd got a good pump out of it that he'd forgotten what it felt like. He really needed to get back to the gym before it was too late.

"It's fine, sir," said Duke. "I'll go. I'm not sure you'd even get over the railing."

"What the hell is that supposed to mean, Constable?"

Duke gave Porter's sizeable gut a good once over.

"You cheeky git," said Porter. "I could get down there just fine."

"It's the getting up again I'm worried about, sir," said Duke, barely suppressing a smile.

"Right," said Porter, jabbing a finger at the PC. But he couldn't think of anything to follow it with, so he let his hand fall limply to his side.

For a few moments, they both stared at the body beneath them. A swan had paddled over, its beady eyes scanning them for treats. It had almost collided with the possibly dead man's floating arm before it noticed him, lowering its orange beak for a peck.

"We really should get him out of there before the ducks eat him," said Duke.

"That's a swan," Porter said in disbelief. Duke shrugged.

"Same thing."

"It's really not."

There was a groan from below them and the swan panicked, its enormous wings carrying it twenty yards up the river. The naked man pulled his arm out of the water and flailed it around in the air like he was trying to take off as well.

"Not dead, then," said Duke.

"You really are observant," said Porter. "I have no idea why you aren't going for detective."

"No fun in it," Duke said, missing Porter's sarcasm completely.

The man lifted his head, groaning again and sounding like a zombie from a cheap horror movie.

"Up here," Porter called down, and the man looked left and right in search of the voice. "Above you."

He figured it out, rolling onto his side and blinking at them like a landed fish. His entire body was caked in mud, but it was still easy enough to identify him.

"Asif Nasir, right?" said Porter. "Want to tell me why you're skinny dipping?"

"What?" said Nasir.

He looked down at himself in slow motion, taking in his naked chest, a nasty scratch on his stomach, and then his crown jewels, which were looking anything but royal. He turned his head back to Porter, a look of comedy shock on his face.

"Where am I?" he managed.

"About half a mile out of the city," Porter said. "You remember anything about what happened yesterday?"

Nasir answered with another groan, pushing his feet into the mud until he'd managed to get onto his hands and knees, his skinny arse pointing skyward. His back arched and he heaved out a jet of puke that would have put a fire-hose to shame.

"Oh Christ," said Porter, the smell of it reaching him—the pungent aroma of rum beneath. "Asif, you should really try and get up here, mate. I don't want you falling in."

"No," he croaked back. "Leave me alone."

"I would," said Porter, looking over his shoulder at the empty play park that sat next to a tired-looking block of flats. "But there are kids around here, and nobody wants to see your goldfish flapping around outside its bowl, if you get me. And there's the small matter of the bomb that went off yesterday. You remember that?"

Nasir hadn't remembered it. Porter could see the way the memory struck him like a hammer.

"Fuck," the young man said. "Fuck fuck fuck."

"He's going to run," said Duke.

"He's not going to run, he hasn't got anywhere to—"

Nasir pushed himself off like a sprinter on the blocks, one foot hitting the water and seeming to plant itself there, like somewhere in the night he'd discovered divine powers. Then his other foot followed and he bombed into the river, everything disappearing beneath the surface.

Porter waited for him to reappear, counting to seven before realising he wasn't going to.

"For fuck's sake," he said, stripping off his jacket.

He clambered onto the railing, Duke doing the same, both of them dropping onto the muddy bank. Nasir had managed to get a single bare foot up, but the rest of him was still down there, lost amongst the weeds. Porter took a step into the river and slipped on the steep slope, landing on his arse.

"Fuck!" he grunted, the water ice cold.

"Here, sir," said Duke, offering him a hand.

"Forget about me, get *him*!"

Duke waded into the river, up to his waist immediately. Porter got to his feet, taking another step and slipping again, this time sliding all the way in. The water gushed over his head and into his nose, doing its best to suffocate him. He scrambled for the ground but it was deep, his Cleverley's scuffing the rocks below.

He gargled, grabbing great fistfuls of weeds in order to secure himself to the bank.

Something grabbed his trousers, and he reached down with his free hand, knotting his fingers in Nasir's hair. He yanked hard, the young man's face bursting free from the water, eyes bulging. He sprayed a mouthful of river directly into Porter's face, then wrapped him in a choking hug.

"I can't swim," he said, or something to that effect.

"No shit," Porter said, trying to keep his footing to stop them both from being sucked back under. Nasir had locked his legs around him too, holding on like a squirming, naked barnacle. "Duke! Grab him!"

Duke was wading over, his face twisted into a grimace.

"He's got no clothes on, sir."

"I know," spat Porter. "I can feel his bloody jellied eel. Grab him!"

Duke hauled himself back onto the bank, staying on his hands and knees as he took Nasir under the arms. He hefted him up, falling back with a squawk. Nasir squirmed on top of him, wailing like a newborn baby.

"Oh, God!" Duke screeched. "Get him off!"

Porter tried to pull himself back onto the bank, but his arms were trembling and his shoes couldn't find purchase in the mud. He grabbed Nasir's leg and used it like a rope, climbing hand over hand until the river finally let him go. He rolled over onto his back, clawing in breaths and listening to Duke puffing and panting as he tried to extricate himself from Nasir's fleshy embrace.

After a couple of seconds, Porter struggled to his feet, his waterlogged clothes ridiculously heavy. The first thing he saw was a couple of teenage lads leaning over the railing, their phones out and their faces plastered with grins.

"Oi!" he yelled. "That's enough. Put them away."

"Sir!" hollered Duke. "Help!"

Porter took hold of Nasir beneath the arms and dragged him off Duke. The fight had been sucked out of the naked man and he lay there, his face in the mud, his chest rising and falling urgently. Porter offered Duke a hand and he took it, wobbling to his feet. He slipped, and for a second it looked like they were both going back in for a swim. Porter grabbed the ridge of the concrete walkway and steadied himself, while Duke turned his attention to the boys overhead.

"Oi!" he yelled, a lot louder than Porter had done. The boys scattered, laughing.

"See you on YouTube!" yelled one.

Porter grabbed the railing and planted his foot on the concrete wall, every muscle protesting as he tried to climb back up. Just when he thought he was about to fall, he felt a hand on his backside, a solid boost. He scrabbled over the top bar and onto solid ground.

"I didn't need any help," he told Duke. "I was getting over just fine."

"Course you were, sir," the PC replied.

Nasir was sitting in the mud, looking as miserable as anyone Porter had ever seen.

"Get him up here," Porter said. "And if he dives in again, let him drown."

Duke helped the naked man stand, lacing his fingers

together and allowing him to use them as a foot-up. There was a moment, when Nasir was halfway up, that he almost planted his bare arse on the PC's face. But between them they managed to ease him over the railing onto the path. Porter offered Duke a hand but the PC refused, scaling the wall and the railing like King Kong.

"That is *not* how I expected to spend my morning," he said, brushing a hand down his uniform. His trousers were caked in river weeds, his boots brown with mud. Porter checked his own lower half and saw that his suit and his shoes were ruined. He threw a glare at Nasir, who had dropped onto his haunches, his head in his hands.

"Want to tell me what that was all about?" he said.

"Sorry," the young man replied, peeking through his fingers. "I wasn't... I just thought..."

A woman was walking towards them along the track, a young girl riding her bike beside her. Porter pulled his jacket off the railing, looked at it mournfully, then handed it to Nasir.

"Put this on and get walking," he said. "Nobody wants to see your damp little ding-a-ling."

Nasir stood up and slipped into the thousand-pound, Italian-tailored cotton and silk-blended jacket, his shoulders slumped, his head hanging low. Porter took his arm and steered him in the direction of the IRV that was parked on the footpath up ahead. His shoes squelched with every step.

"If you try to run, Duke here will Taser you right in the nutsack," he said. "That's not a bluff. I've seen him do it before."

"By accident," protested Duke.

Nasir barely looked capable of walking, let alone running. He limped obediently to the car and ducked into the back when Duke opened the door for him. Porter took a breath, holding his face up to the sun to try and chase a little of the chill from his body.

"Right," he said. "I'm going to ask you again. Why did you run?"

"Swim," corrected Duke.

"Whatever," Porter said. "Why did you try to get away from us? You know what that tells me? You've done something wrong."

"I haven't," said Nasir, with a nasal Mancunian accent. He was shivering so hard that Porter thought he could hear his bones rattle as he rocked back and forth in the seat.

"You were stark naked and practically floating in the river, for a start."

"I don't..." Nasir started. "I'm sorry, I don't even remember why..."

"Start from what you do remember, okay? You were at work yesterday morning and a bomb went off. You got out—people saw you on the street after the fire crew had arrived—and then you decided to disappear. Why?"

Nasir's mouth worked silently, his voice taking a while to catch up.

"I... I don't know. I panicked, I was in shock."

He looked up, caught Porter's eye.

"That has to be it, doesn't it? I was in shock. I just started walking, ended up in a bar. A pub. Riverside. The Wetherspoons. I just wanted a drink, a quick one. I..."

He turned his gaze to the window, and the distant city beyond.

"I don't think I just had one."

"You reckon?"

"I remember another bar, a club. I think the bouncers tossed me out. I think I came up here and..."

He faltered, searching for memories that wouldn't come.

"I'm sorry," he said. "But shit, a *bomb*. That happened?"

Porter nodded.

"Is everyone okay?"

"Millicent Reed is dead," said Porter, and he saw the shock of it register on Nasir's face. "The others are okay, but they spent the rest of the day in hospital. Still there, for all I know."

"I didn't do it," Nasir said. "I would never..."

"So why run?" Porter asked again. "Yesterday and today, why did you run away?"

Nasir laughed bitterly, gesturing to himself.

"Because of this," he said. "You know what happens when bombs go off, don't you? They look for the nearest brown person to take the blame. I knew you'd come after me for it."

"First, I'm not coming after you for anything," said Porter. "Second, the colour of your skin has nothing to do with anything, as far as I'm concerned, except for the fact that you shouldn't be parading around *in* the skin. Can you tell me where you were yesterday at around three? And this morning, at three as well?"

"No," said Nasir. "But there will be CCTV, wherever I was. Why?"

"No reason," said Porter. "So that's it? That's the only reason you bolted?"

Nasir shrugged, staring at his bare feet.

"I don't know," he said quietly. "Like I said, I wasn't thinking clearly. I was in shock, it's a real thing. You try getting blown up, see how clearly you think."

Porter blew out a sigh, thinking about the tunnels beneath the city, thinking about the explosion that had almost killed him just six months ago, the one that had almost stopped him from meeting his son, from becoming a father.

"Yeah," he said. "I get it. But we're still going to need to bring you in and get a statement."

"Am I under arrest?"

Porter thought about it for a moment.

"Not yet," he said. "Although after the bullshit you just pulled, I'm sorely tempted."

He stamped his soggy shoes on the path, water spurting out of them.

"Duke here will get you back to the station and find you some clothes."

"Where are you going, sir?" Duke asked.

"On a pub crawl."

"Now?"

"To find some CCTV," he explained. "Make sure he's telling the truth."

He went to shut the door, but hesitated.

"Asif, before you go, if you know anything at all about what happened yesterday, about the bomb, about why somebody would want to do that, then now's your chance. Prove to us that you want to help."

Nasir blinked rapidly, his eyes bright in the darkness of the car.

"Millie died?" he said.

"Yeah."

"She didn't deserve that. I mean, she was a bitch, don't get me wrong. I hated her. Everyone did. You know she was the one who cancelled our bonuses last year? But gave herself an extra big one. Can you believe that? But... but she didn't deserve that."

He paused, and Porter gave him all the time he needed.

"It's just weird that she was the only one who died," he said. "Like, aren't bombs supposed to take out everybody?"

"What are you getting at, Asif?"

"Nothing," he said. "I mean, probably nothing. Ben was okay? He wasn't hurt?"

"A little beat up, but he walked out of the hospital on his own two feet."

"That's what's weird," said Nasir. "How the hell didn't he get blown to kingdom come? They work in the same office."

"Luck, I guess," said Porter. "Unless you're telling me otherwise?"

"I'm not saying that. I'm just saying that he had a lot to gain from it, you know?"

"From what? From the bomb?"

"No," said the young man. "From his wife dying."

Porter leaned in.

"How so?"

"Because of the insurance policy," said Nasir. "He'd just taken one out. I helped him. Life insurance, for Millie."

"Shit," said Porter. "Seriously?"

Nasir nodded.

"He's lost his wife, but he's a million quid richer. That'll take the sting out of anything, right?"

CHAPTER TWENTY-SIX

IN ALL HIS YEARS ON THE JOB—ALL THOSE CRIMES, ALL those victims, all those countless deaths—Kett couldn't remember a case as complex as this one. There were so many moving parts that it hurt his head to try to put them in any kind of order. Even standing in the Incident Room, with every photograph and document and timeline arranged in neat rows on the wall, he couldn't make any sense of it.

"Right, you tossbags," said Clare, walking through the door. "Let's get started."

"Just one tossbag here, sir," Kett said, looking around the empty room. "Sorry."

"Two," said Savage as she followed Clare through the door, a trio of teacups clutched in one hand. She managed to set them down on a desk without spilling a drop. "Not much milk left, sorry sirs. Little stronger than usual."

"As long as it's tea, I don't care," Kett said. "Thanks, Kate. Porter and Duke back yet?"

"Duke is. He brought Nasir in. Porter's still out. Apparently they all went for a swim."

"A swim?"

"In the river, sir. Nasir ran." She frowned. "Swam."

"Nearly drowned," added Clare, perching himself on a desk.

"So he's guilty?" asked Kett.

"Of being a stark-naked bollock who was trying to molest a swan, yes," Clare said. "Of the bombing, probably not. Porter just called to say he's got CCTV from The Queen of Iceni, down at Riverside. Nasir was in there yesterday from eleven until gone four, pissed as a fart."

"That puts him out of the running for the hangings," said Kett. "Doesn't mean he wasn't involved in the rest."

"We'll see," said Clare. "Porter thinks he's innocent. But Nasir did share an interesting titbit of information. Benjamin Reed took out a life insurance policy on his wife three weeks ago. Over a million pounds."

"What?" said Kett.

"What indeed. Spalding's been doing some digging, and... Why am I wasting my voice on this?"

He grumbled his way to the door and leaned out.

"Spalding!"

Kett waited patiently.

"Spalding!" Clare bellowed.

"You okay?" he asked Savage. "How's your face?"

"Still attached, sir," she said, touching her swollen cheek and wincing. "Just about. I still look better than Duke does."

"True."

"*Spalding!*" Clare screeched, loud enough to make Kett flinch. The Super's voice echoed down the corridor, and by the time it had faded, Kett heard footsteps. A second or two later, DS Spalding beetled into the room, her face flushed.

"Sorry, sir," she said. "I didn't hear you."

"Lies," Clare said as Spalding reached the front of the

room. "My grandmother heard that, and she's been dead for forty years. Tell them what you've found."

"I did some digging," Spalding started.

"I already told them that," snapped Clare.

"Uh, right, did you tell them about the accounts, sir?"

"No."

"Right, so I checked in with Companies House. Reed, Barnham and Crabbe is a failing company."

"It's on its last legs," said Clare.

"Yeah, uh, Reed spent a lot of money buying out one co-founder."

"A lot of money."

"Not only that, but he's been raining dividends on himself and Millicent like they're going out of fashion. They've pretty much drained the company of everything. It's broke."

"Facing bankruptcy," added Clare, earning a glare of frustration from Spalding.

"Do you want to tell them, sir?"

"No. I do not."

"Okay. So I did a quick check on Reed's personal finances. Couldn't get much, obviously, but I ran a credit check, and he's taken out over a hundred grand in loans this year."

"One hundred thousand pounds," parroted Clare, like he was a backing singer in a band.

"Ouch," said Kett. "What for?"

"Not sure, but one's a car loan for his Range Rover. They're long-term loans, and he's already missed repayments."

"So he's in trouble," said Kett. "Bit suspicious, then, that he takes out a massive life insurance policy on his wife."

"What's more suspicious is that he didn't take one out

on himself," said Spalding. "I mean, he's got life insurance. He took out a policy nearly two decades ago when his kids were born. It's worth a fraction of the one he arranged for Millicent. Hers is a million quid."

"A million pounds," echoed Clare.

"I just said that, sir," said Spalding.

"That's motive," said Clare, ignoring her. "A pretty decent one, if you ask me."

"He's got means, too," said Savage. "Ex-army, and get this: he worked with munitions, handling explosives."

"You have got to be shitting me," Kett said.

"No, sir. The report came in this morning. Reed served in the Royal Logistics Corps as an Ammunition Technician. That's how he started his career. He was never in the bomb squad, but he was responsible for disposing of ammunition."

"Wow," Kett said, trying not to get too excited. "It's not looking good for him."

"He discharged himself from hospital about two hours before the hangings," said Savage. "He would have had plenty of time to get to the warehouse, especially if he already had his victims chained up."

"We need to bring him in," said Spalding. "If nothing else, we need to know where he was yesterday afternoon and this morning."

Clare nodded.

"You're right. Now that Hope's out of the picture, Reed's looking like our man."

"And they might have been working on it together," said Kett. "We know they were close." He took a moment to study the photographs on the wall, popping his lips. "Have we considered the notion that these might be separate crimes?" he asked after a moment.

"How so?" asked Clare, picking up one of Savage's teas,

then dropping it back to the table, sucking his fingers. "Christ, Kate, where did you boil the water? In the sun's arsehole?"

"Sorry, sir."

"I mean, Reed looks like a good fit for the bombing," Kett continued. "Let's say he's broke, he's desperate, his business is going down the toilet and he's up to his neck in debt. He doesn't exactly get on with his wife, so he takes out an insurance policy on her, then builds a bomb. He knows that however his wife dies, it's going to look suspicious, right? So he goes all in. He builds a bomb and sets it off at work while he's in the same building. Nobody's going to suspect him if he's almost blown to smithereens himself."

"Except he's not in the same room when the bomb goes off," said Savage. "He waits until Millie's opening her package then he leaves the room. He somehow arranged for her to get the parcel with the bomb in it. A mark on the wrapper that only he can see, a subtle difference in the weight. He knows the charge is powerful but local, he'll miss the explosion and catch the shockwave. It'll hurt, but it won't kill him."

"Right," said Kett. "But maybe the bomb has nothing to do with the hangings. Maybe they're separate crimes."

"I hate to break it to you," came a tuneful voice from the corridor, "but they're not."

Cara Hay walked into the room, followed by PC Duke. Duke was soaked from the chest down, his shoes sucking wetly with every step. There were still strands of river weed stuck to his legs, and some in his beard, too. Kett heard a quiet laugh and turned to see Savage trying to hide it with her hand. Duke saw it too, throwing a deep frown her way.

"Sorry, Aaron," she said, still giggling. "But you look ridiculous."

"Thanks," he said, pouting.

"Why don't you change, mate?" said Kett.

"I can't, sir," said Duke, pulling out a chair and crashing down in it. "It's a custom uniform, I'm too big for the regular one."

"No you're not," said Kett.

"I am!" he protested, gesturing to his legs. "I'm too muscly, they don't make them in my size. Ask the Boss."

Everyone turned to Clare and he nodded.

"It's true. Quads like a bloody Italian ham. Hay, you were saying."

Hay had moved to the front of the room, where she perched on the corner of a desk. She held a collection of papers in one hand, but she didn't look at them.

"I'm almost certain your three incidents are connected. When the packages were delivered to the office yesterday morning, each one had a message written on it. *Lucky Number One* all the way through, we assume, to *Lucky Number Seven*. We know the bomb was either in box number two or box number seven, and I'm guessing it was the seventh."

"Why?" asked Kett, picking up a mug of tea and instantly regretting it as it burned his fingers. He didn't let go, though, in case somebody else stole it.

"Because I've just finished an examination of the ropes that were used for the hangings," Hay went on. "Seven of them, of course. As you know, six were rigged to fail, and five did just that—one wasn't used at all."

"Because Stefan Kucharek was shot before he could use it," said Kett, and Hay nodded.

"One was used, and it wasn't rigged to fail. As per Emily Franklin's autopsy, Brian Beaney died from asphyxiation. It was not a good death. Whoever rigged up the gallows from the scaffolding poles did so at a height of four metres, and that's important, I think."

"Because of the length of the drop?" said Savage.

"Exactly. If the gallows are high enough, then the neck will almost certainly break as soon as the victim drops. The spinal cord is severed, causing instant paralysis and unconsciousness. It's merciful, if nothing else." She sighed. "But Beaney did not die so easily. His hands were unbound, meaning that he was able to hold the rope and support his weight for some time. But he wouldn't have been able to remove the rope, and he was too high for the others to help him. Slowly, agonisingly, he would have suffocated."

"Jesus," said Kett. "So it was designed to make him suffer?"

"Not necessarily," said Savage. "The killer needed his victims to be able to use their arms so that they could climb the ladder, right? And so they could put the noose around their necks. He wouldn't have been able to do it himself because they could have overpowered him."

"That is correct," said Hay. "He had no choice, but it's not to say he didn't want his victim to suffer. I took a closer look at the ropes and found something very interesting."

She held up the top sheet of paper, but it was too far away for Kett to make any sense of.

"The nooses were shipping rope, each one constructed from individual strands of nylon and extremely strong. I think the killer made the ropes himself because something has been woven into them. A small scrap of cotton, each one with a phrase written on it."

"Numbers?" said Kett.

Hay nodded.

"Lucky Number One, all the way through to Lucky

Number Seven. You can guess which one I found in Brian Beaney's rope."

"One?" guessed Duke, with a shrug of his big shoulders.

"Seven," corrected Kett. "Right?"

"Right."

"Right," said Duke.

"The other ropes were numbered one through six, and like I say, the nooses were fake slipknots designed to unravel as soon as any force was applied to them. But the seventh was real."

"Is there any way the victims could have seen the numbers?" asked Kett.

"No. I didn't even know they were there myself until I started dissecting the rope."

"So it's the same killer," said Clare, frowning at the ceiling.

"Undoubtedly," said Hay. "Even their handwriting matches, they made no attempt to hide the similarities. And there's more."

"There's always more," Clare groaned.

"The copper rods used in the third incident, the electrocution, were each engraved with numbers. No words this time, presumably because it would have taken too much time. But the killer etched a single numerical digit into each rod, about a centimetre high and not deep enough to be seen easily. The one carrying the charge was also carrying the number seven."

"So he's obsessed," said Kett. "He's playing a game and these are his rules, these are the odds. Six live, one dies."

"But why?" asked Spalding. "If you want to kill somebody, why go to all this trouble? Kidnapping one person is difficult, surely taking seven hostages is nearly impossible, and attacking seven people *three times* is just insane."

"He is insane though, isn't he?" said Duke. "Someone with all their marbles wouldn't do this."

"It's not that easy, Aaron," said Kett. "Did you find anything else, Cara?"

"We've done a preliminary examination of the veterinary surgery," she said. "Hope's prints are there, and so are Ben Reed's. There are trace elements of some of the ingredients needed to make an IED, hence the sweet smell in the air."

"That's another nail in Reed's coffin," said Clare.

"And a shovelful of soil to boot," added Spalding. "I haven't got to the best bit yet. Reed has access to guns."

"Shit," said Kett. "He's got a firearms license?"

"No, but Millicent Reed did. That's why it took a while for me to find it. Millicent Reed grew up in the sticks, her parents are farmers. She got her license as soon as she was old enough and she's kept it active. According to our records, she owns two side-by-side shotguns."

"Please tell me one of them is a Churchill," said Kett.

"How did you know, sir?"

"It's him," he said, pushing himself off the table. "It's Reed, it has to be. One of the victims from this morning identified the gun, a Churchill."

"Hang on," said Clare. "Hold your horses, Kett. We have to be sure. Where are we on other suspects? Hope's out of the picture. What about the arsehole who took a swing at you, Kate?"

"Geoff Pankhurst," said Savage. "Arsehole is right. Zoe's opened up a little now that he's been arrested, told us he beat her regularly. He has done since she was ten or eleven."

A live current of anger passed through everyone in the room, electric and dangerous.

"Used to keep it to the torso, but more recently he's

been smacking her about the face and head. She was worried for her life, but more worried about what he'd do to her if she ran or talked. She's convinced Justin was trying to keep her safe, and I can't find anything that suggests he wasn't."

She shook her head.

"The bruises will heal, but her dad's done so much damage to her mind I can't see her ever getting over it. And now... Now her boyfriend's dead."

"Do we think Pankhurst had anything to do with the bomb?" asked Clare.

"No," said Savage and Spalding together, and Spalding continued.

"He was a scaffolder, sir, but he hasn't worked in a while. He's been signed off with a back injury."

"Didn't seem injured when he was throwing me around his house," said Savage.

"He's been questioned, and his alibi has come through. He was in the pub during the hangings, I've seen the CCTV."

"He doesn't match the description of the killer, either," said Kett. "Everyone we've spoken to said we're dealing with a well-built guy, five-ten or eleven, well built. Somewhere in his thirties or forties, judging by the voice."

"Reed is 51," said Savage.

"Could still fit," said Clare. "Bring him in. Does anyone have anything else before I let you go?"

"Nothing of any note," said Spalding. "A couple of the hanging victims have minor convictions—shoplifting and D and Ds. Nobody at Reed's office has any history with us, and neither do any of the mechanics. There's nothing to connect them."

"But there is," said Kett. "There has to be. The killer

picks seven people, right? Or six, if he doesn't have time to get the seventh. But it's not random. They're connected. The first attack happened in an office, everyone there worked in insurance. That's the connection."

"So?" said Clare.

"We found six people in the warehouse where the hangings took place. The four who were still alive told us they'd been called there for a security job."

"But Brian Beaney was a delivery driver," said Savage.

"A delivery driver who used to be a security guard," said Spalding. "Quit four years ago after he was attacked on the job. The other dead guy, Stefan Kucharek, worked security before he became a nightclub bouncer."

"And the electrocutions this morning," said Kett. "They were all mechanics or engineers."

"So our killer doesn't like insurance brokers, security guards or mechanical engineers?" said Clare. "Where the toss does that leave us?"

"It might not be that he doesn't like them," said Kett. "Maybe this is something else. Maybe he's... I don't know, *punishing* them."

"That doesn't fit, sir," said Savage. "Does it? I mean, if you're punishing somebody for something, you don't take six other people and throw them into the mix too. That doesn't make sense."

Kett puffed out a breath. Savage was right, none of this made any sense at all.

"I don't know," he said. "But there's something there. I just can't see it yet. If we're going to work out who the killer's next victim is, we need to understand why he's going after these specific groups. We need to find out what these people have in common."

"We'll find out soon enough, won't we?" said Duke, and

everybody looked at him. "I mean, it's not over yet, is it? He's not finished."

"No," said Kett. "I don't think he is. Whatever he's doing, he's been planning it for a long time. He'd have to, you can't wing something like this."

"You'd need to secure the premises," said Savage. "Get addresses, find out where people work, where they live."

"Exactly," said Kett. "He must have been planning this for months. And something this big draws a lot of heat. He knows he doesn't have long to finish. If he's going after another set of victims, he's going to do it today."

"I'll make sure any misper reports come straight to us," said Clare. "Kidnappings, everything. And we'll release a statement, let people know what to watch out for."

The Super finally managed a sip of his tea.

"But our first priority is Ben Reed. Go get him."

CHAPTER TWENTY-SEVEN

THE TACTICAL TEAM WAS PRIMED AND READY TO GO, and Gorski's van bulldozed its way along a tangle of country roads with half a dozen IRVs riding in its wake. Kett sat in the first of these, Savage at the wheel, Clare and Duke sliding around in the backseat every time she took a turn.

"If I wanted you to plant your damp arse on my lap, Constable," Clare said. "I'd take you out for dinner first! Move over!"

Duke clipped in his seatbelt to anchor himself in place, but it was hardly worth it. The drive wasn't a long one, less than five miles from HQ to a village on the outskirts of Wymondham. If Ben Reed had been having money worries, he hadn't told his house—an impressive mock-Tudor hall that sat behind a pair of wrought-iron gates and in the middle of a sprawling garden. Gorski pulled the van up to the gates and cut the engine, climbing out and checking her helmet and her rifle.

"Gates are automatic," she said when Kett got out of the car. "Won't be able to get the van through. But there's that."

She nodded to a pedestrian gate that sat alongside,

secured with a thick length of chain. A small security camera sat over it.

"Get it open," said Clare, walking over. He threw Gorski a look. "But don't bloody shoot him unless he's coming at you in a tank, okay? We can't afford another cockup like yesterday."

"Sir," she said with a tight-lipped nod.

"Should we just ask him to come out, sir?" said Savage as she joined them.

"Under ordinary circumstances, I would," Clare replied. "But these are far from ordinary. Bombs, guns and live wires. I can't risk it."

Besides, if Reed was home, he'd know they were there. One of the tactical team was using an angle grinder on the padlock, a fan of sparks bristling off her helmet. It lasted all of twenty seconds before snapping, the chain dropping limply to the ground. She stood back and another officer kicked the gate open, all six of them funnelling through into the garden, their rifles raised.

Kett followed at a safe distance, walking past a carport where a silver Range Rover sat in the shadows next to a black Mercedes.

"He's home," he said.

One of the team took down the door with an Enforcer ram, and Gorski entered the house with a volley of shouts. Kett locked the air in his lungs, waiting for the shots to start, waiting for the screams. All he could see was Justin Hope lying in the puddle of crimson mud, slowly bleeding out. The smell of his death, that metallic tang, was still in his nose.

As much as he didn't like Benjamin Reed, he didn't want to see anyone else meet the same fate.

Even if they deserved it.

A crash from inside, a shout.

"Come on," Kett said beneath his breath.

A dark shape appeared in the open door as Gorski stepped into the day. She pulled off her helmet to reveal that crown of red hair, and her expression was one of undeniable relief.

"We've got Reed and another man," she said. "Subdued."

"Did he try to run?" asked Kett, as he made his way to the house.

"He was too busy shitting himself," she said. "Other guy's a solicitor, going by the tirade of abuse that's coming out of his mouth."

Kett stepped into the cool interior, crossing a tiled entrance hall into a large, empty kitchen. He could hear two voices raised in anger coming from a door at the far end, and he followed them into a light-drenched living room. Three armed officers stood to attention, their weapons pointed at the floor but their bodies tense and ready. Benjamin Reed knelt on the cord carpet between two of them, his hands on his head. He was wearing salmon-pink shorts and a red T-shirt that almost perfectly matched the colour of his cheeks.

Kneeling in an identical position next to him was an older man with a hawkish face that was mostly hidden by a white beard. He was dressed—despite the heat—in a three-piece suit. Although they were doing a good job of talking over each other, it was the second man's voice that was winning.

"And you," he said, hurling the words at Kett like they were weapons, "are about to find out what it's like to have the book thrown at you. Not just thrown at you, mind. I'm going to make you eat it. Understand? You have made the biggest fucking mistake of your career coming here."

"Not sure about that," said Kett. "I've made some pretty enormous mistakes in my time. You are?"

"Giles Morton," came the reply, not from the man, but from Superintendent Clare as he walked into the room. "You do end up in some god-awful places, Giles. Perhaps it's time to rethink your career."

"Colin?" said Morton. "Christ, man, what the hell is going on?"

"Why don't you tell me?" said Clare, taking a seat on the sofa closest to the men. "You going to do anything stupid?"

"I'm sorely tempted," said Morton. "But no."

"And you?" asked Clare, looking at Reed. The man turned his sweaty face to his solicitor, who shook his head.

"No," said Reed, quietly.

"Then get up," said Clare. "Sit over there. And keep your tossholes shut until one of us asks you a question. Understood?"

Both men nodded as they got to their feet—Morton needing a little longer, his face creased with pain as he straightened up. Reed crashed into a chair opposite Clare, but the solicitor remained standing.

"Can't sit," he said. "My back."

"Then stay there where we can all see you," said Clare. "And no sudden movements."

"I heard about the young man you executed yesterday," said Morton, walking to the window. The curtains blew gently in the breeze, like they were caressing him. "That's going to cost you a lot, and I'm not just talking about money. Family's on the warpath, and they'll take legal action."

"Story of my life," said Clare. "But we're not here about that. We're here about you."

He pointed a long finger at Reed, who pushed himself back into his chair like he was trying to disappear.

"My client has already told you, he had nothing—"

"Shut it, Giles," said Clare. "It's too hot, and I'm not in the mood. Kett."

"It's not looking good, Ben," Kett said, walking into the middle of the room. "We know about the insurance policy you took out on Millicent."

Reed floundered, opening and closing his mouth like he was silently speaking. Once again he stared at Morton, who gave him a cold, hard look in return.

"How?" Reed started. "How do you know about that?"

"You took it out three weeks ago," said Kett. "A million pounds. Can you tell us why?"

"What?" Reed spluttered. "I... Giles!"

"This line of questioning is irrelevant," said Morton. "And, quite frankly, disgustingly insensitive, even for you. Ben's wife died yesterday, and you're coming after him because of an insurance policy? Why don't you come after me too? Eh? My wife has insurance. I'd wager yours does too, Colin. Probably even more than Millie's."

"Yes, but my wife wasn't blown up," said Clare.

"Is it true that you handled explosives when you were in the army, Mr Reed?" said Kett.

"Show me a man who didn't," said Reed, regaining some of his composure. "But my area was ammunition."

"But you'd know how to make a bomb?"

"Enough," snapped Morton. "This is unconscionable. Outrageous. Egregious."

"Oh, put your bloody thesaurus away, Giles," said Clare.

"Can you answer the question, Mr Reed?" said Kett.

"Am I under arrest?" Reed replied.

"Give me one good reason why you shouldn't be," Kett told him.

"Because I was in the fucking room when the bomb went off!" he snarled. "I could have *died*."

"Not good enough," said Kett. "Where were you yesterday, between two and four? And this morning at around three?"

Reed's cheeks were glowing again, and he used a hand to clear the sweat from his forehead.

"What's that got to do with anything?" he said.

"Because this isn't just about the bomb anymore," said Kett. "Where were you?"

Reed glanced at Morton again, but the solicitor had fallen quiet.

"I was... I was at the hospital yesterday, as you well know," he said.

"You discharged yourself from the hospital at one," said Kett. "Try again. Where did you go?"

Another look Morton's way, like a child seeking reassurance from a parent.

"Here," he said after a moment. "I was here, all day and all night. Just as my wi—"

Kett saw the moment he remembered that Millicent had died, the colour literally draining from him. He sagged back into the chair, his hands kneading his thighs.

"Shit," he said. "I... I forgot. But I was here, you have my word. Where else would I have gone?"

"How about to a warehouse in the city?" said Kett, pulling his notebook from his pocket. "Do any of these names mean anything to you? Bill Carroll, Roz Carroll, Brian Beaney, Linda Mayweather, Tom Lester or Stefan Kucharek."

"No," said Reed, and there was no hint of a lie there. "I was here. Giles can vouch for me, can't you Giles?"

"Sorry," said Morton, clearing his throat. "But no, I can't. I left the hospital at the same time you did, I didn't see where you went."

The hurt on Reed's face was painful to see.

"I know, but you... I mean, you know me, you know I'd never..." He turned to Kett. "What are you accusing me of? What do you think I did?"

Kett didn't reply, using the tension to make the man squirm. It was heating up fast, the room like an oven.

"I was here," Reed said. "I haven't left since yesterday afternoon, I swear."

"Tell them," said Morton, staring at the floor.

"I can't," said Reed. "You know I can't."

"Just fucking tell them, Ben."

"Tell us what?" asked Kett, taking a step closer, so that Reed had to crane his neck back to meet his eye.

"It's nothing," said Reed, speaking too quickly. "I don't have anything to hide, I don't need to talk to you anymore, I..."

"Arrest him," said Clare. "Now."

"No!" said Reed. "Wait, I..."

One final, pleading look at Morton, but the solicitor turned away.

"Christ," said Reed. "I didn't kill her. I didn't do anything."

He put his head in his hands and groaned like a man who finally realised he was in mourning.

"She was sick," he said. "She had cancer."

A moment of silence before Kett responded.

"Millie did?"

"She was diagnosed in the spring. She wasn't even... she

wasn't even ill, it was a fluke we even saw it. It was in her bones. They said she'd have a year, tops, but probably a lot less."

Kett stepped back, giving the man some space as he gasped for air.

"She wasn't insured, she didn't have anything. I always made sure I did, because of the kids. I always wanted them to be okay, but we never bothered getting her coverage because I thought..."

He seemed to choke on the words, breaking into a cough and taking a moment to recover.

"She was so fit, so healthy. She went on that stupid Peloton thing every day, ate fucking Ryvita and avocados. I thought she'd live forever, and it pissed me off because I never even... I didn't like her. I *hated* her sometimes."

The tears were flowing now, and no matter how hard he scrubbed at his face, he couldn't seem to stop them.

"But I loved her. I bloody loved her."

"Hang on," said Kett. "So you found out she was ill, and *then* you took out insurance?"

Reed nodded.

"She didn't want to leave me with nothing," he sobbed. "We're fucked. Me, the company, we've got nothing left. She wanted to bail me out, but we knew we'd never get it if they found out she was terminal. So we lied."

"Lied to the insurance company?" said Kett.

"Yeah, it was Giles' idea."

"I deny this in the strongest possible way," said Morton. "I have no idea what he's talking about."

"Oh fuck off, Giles," said Reed. "I bribed our GP not to add it to her record, but the consultant wouldn't—"

"Enough," said Morton.

"He wouldn't listen, so we threatened him, said we'd kill

him if he told anyone about her cancer. We did it together, we said we'd split it."

"Enough!" said Morton, a shout now.

"How did you threaten him?" asked Kett. "A gun?"

He could see the answer in the way Reed's head dropped, in the way the solicitor's shoulders slumped. Kett blew out a breath, tapping his boot on the carpet as he gathered his thoughts. It was almost impossible to think straight in the heat.

"I didn't want to hurt him," said Reed. "I wouldn't hurt anyone. I just had to do it. The report was omitted, we took out the policy. Then... then she died. Some arsehole didn't even give her the time she had left. He killed her. But it wasn't me, I swear."

There was nothing in Reed's actions to suggest it was a performance. He was just a man who had lost everything, and who sobbed his regret onto the floor. Kett turned to Clare and saw his own thoughts reflected in the Super's sweaty face.

It's not him.

But it didn't mean the killer wasn't in the room.

"Mr Morton," said Kett, turning back. "It seems like you might have had something to gain from this. A million pounds is a lot of money to split. Where were you yesterday afternoon and this morning?"

Morton gulped hard, his Adam's apple bobbing.

"I'm declining to answer," he said.

"You're sure that's where you want to take this, Giles?" said Clare.

"I'm declining to answer," Morton said again through clenched teeth.

"Then we're going to arrest you," said Kett. "Both of you."

"I'd like the honour of that," said Clare, wheezing his way up from the sofa. "I've had wet dreams about arresting you, Morton."

"Not sure that's what you mean, sir," said Kett, pulling a face. He turned to Reed. "I need to see those guns, right now."

Reed nodded, struggling out of the chair and walking to the door. Two of the armed officers tracked him, Kett following them into the large, airy kitchen.

"They're down in the cellar," said Reed. "They're locked away."

"How many?" Kett asked as the man opened another door, revealing a wooden staircase leading into darkness. A breath of cold air welcomed them as they stepped carefully down.

"Four," said Reed. "They're all Millie's, she's the gun nut."

His sigh echoed upwards.

"*Was*, I mean. You know, it was where we met. Her father opened their farm up to corporate events years ago, before he died. Clay pigeons. I found the whole thing ghastly, but there's something to be said about a beautiful woman with a gun, isn't there?"

Nobody answered him. He led them into a low room with earthen walls, a timber beam holding up the ceiling. Three of the four walls were lined with wine racks that stood almost empty, but in the opposite corner to the stairs was a wooden cupboard. Reed opened the door to reveal a large gun safe, but when he slid the key into the lock, the closest member of the firearms lifted his weapon.

"Nope," he said. "We do that."

Reed stood back, rubbing his swollen eyes and sniffing like a lost child.

"You're sure there are only guns in there?" Kett asked, thinking about the bomb and moving back a few feet.

Reed didn't have time to answer before the locker door swung quietly open. Even from where he stood, Kett could see that the maths didn't quite add up. Reed had noticed it too, his hands clutching at his hair.

"You told me Millicent owned four shotguns," said Kett. "You're positive?"

"I am," he replied, his eyes wide and white in the dark cellar. "Four of them, she's always owned four."

Kett walked to the locker to make sure, counting the guns again.

All three of them.

CHAPTER TWENTY-EIGHT

KETT WATCHED AS BEN REED WAS ESCORTED OUT OF the gates of his house to an IRV, a constable placing a hand on his head as he sank into the back seat. He'd been cuffed, although Kett didn't think the man was capable of resisting. He stared out of the window in a way that made him look almost catatonic, his eyes empty.

In contrast, Giles Morton was a seething ball of fury as he walked out of the house. He, too, wore a set of handcuffs. He fought them like a daredevil contortionist trying to escape his chains, shrugging his shoulders, twisting his arms and even kicking his feet for good measure. Two PCs kept their distance as he jigged his way down the driveway towards the gate. Morton threw a look at Kett as he passed, his face a knotted fist.

"You're finished," he snarled. "You hear me, you're finished."

"I wish," Kett replied, looking at his watch to see that it was only mid-morning. "Got the whole bloody day left."

Morton unleashed a flurry of choked swearwords that lasted all the way to the IRV.

"He's a real charmer, sir," said Kett when he saw Clare walking over.

"I told you he was a turd," the Super replied. "Whatever else happens today, I'm glad we've got him under lock and key. What kind of suppurating anal gland tries to intimidate a consultant with a gun?"

"The kind who wants his share of a million pounds," said Kett. "Pretty stupid alright. You think he's behind the bomb? The hangings?"

Clare thought about it, idly combing his nose hair with his fingers.

"What's your gut telling you, Kett?" he said.

"I don't think it was Reed," he answered. "I think he was trying to cash in on his wife's illness, but I can't see him blowing up his workplace like that, and I certainly don't think he was behind the other attacks. Morton, though, he's got an edge. I think he's got a hold over Reed, too. What if he coerced Reed into making the bomb, then he arranged for the delivery? Or maybe he made it himself. If they were in on this insurance scam together, then Morton would have won no matter who died in the bombing, because he'd have been the one doing the paperwork. He could have easily funnelled the money to himself."

"And he's the kind of man who holds a grudge," said Clare. "We need to find a connection between Morton and the other victims."

Kett realised he was shaking his head, a nagging feeling that this wasn't quite right, that they'd missed something.

"What does Morton have to gain by forcing people to hang themselves?" he asked. "Or by electrocuting them? I can't see the bigger picture with him. This feels like it's about more than money, right? More than a grudge, too."

"It's not Morton," said Savage as she walked out of the

house, her phone to her ear. "You're sure? Yeah? Okay." She hung up, crunching down the driveway. "He was drinking at the Norfolk Club after he left the hospital yesterday. Got there just after two and didn't leave until six. A dozen or so witnesses and they have CCTV in the car park."

"What about this morning?" said Clare, obviously disappointed.

"No alibi for this morning, sir, but we're looking at the same man, aren't we?" Savage replied. "The witness statements for the hangman and the electrocutioner are identical."

"Electrocutioner?" said Kett, and Savage laughed.

"I think I may have just made that word up, sir."

"It's a good one."

"We'll know more when we've searched this place," said Clare. "And I'm getting a warrant for Morton's house and office. If they're hiding something, we'll find it."

He reached into his pocket and pulled out a Bounty Bar, unwrapping it with his teeth. Holding it over his mouth, he squeezed the first half out, swallowing it whole. He had to slam a fist on his chest a few times as he worked it down.

"Bloody hell, sir," said Kett. "You're supposed to chew them."

"No time," wheezed Clare.

"You eaten Duke's cake yet, sir?" asked Savage.

"No," said Clare, patting his pocket. "I'm saving it."

"Oh, good."

"Until after I'm dead," he added. "Right. Let's assume, then, that this is another dead end. We've ruled out Hope, and Reed and Morton. It wasn't Zoe Pankhurst's father, or Asif Nasir. Who else have we got?"

While he waited for an answer, he dropped the last half

of the Bounty into his mouth, gurning as he sucked it down. Kett watched, wide-eyed.

"I was thinking," Savage said. "It's weird, right, that Beaney was the man who delivered the bomb, and then he ends up being the victim of the hanging."

"Kind of," said Kett. "I'm guessing the killer knew he was going to target Beaney, and he knew he was a delivery driver, so he killed two birds with one stone. So to speak."

"Asked him to make the delivery, then took him prisoner when he'd finished," said Clare. "I agree. What are you thinking, Kate?"

"I don't know, sir. I keep coming back to numbers. We had six people at the hangings, and seven nooses. And we had six people in the warehouse this morning, but seven electrical wires. What if one of the targets is being asked to carry on the mantle? What if that's the price you pay for surviving?"

"Interesting," Kett said.

"Doesn't work," said Clare. "Because none of our witnesses mentioned seeing another victim."

"True, sir," Savage said, rubbing her head. "This case is ridiculously confusing."

"Worth looking into, though," said Kett. "I think that's what we need to do, sir. Go back to the witnesses and try to figure out why our killer was targeting these specific groups. We need to find out what links them, and what it means to him. If we can figure out why, we can figure out who."

"Go on then, toss off," said Clare, pulling another Bounty from his jacket. "I need to head back to HQ. Take a car, and keep me informed."

"Sir," said Kett.

He hesitated for long enough to watch the Superintendent choke down another lump of Bounty, then made his way down the drive. Savage walked with him, laughing quietly.

"It's going to be on his headstone, isn't it, sir?" she said. "Devoted father, respected copper, killed by coconut."

Kett laughed too, letting Savage through the gate first and following her past the tactical team's van to an IRV.

"He put hundreds of criminals behind bars, but there was one foe he couldn't vanquish," Savage went on when they were inside. "The taste of paradise."

"Serves him right for eating Bounties," said Kett. "Back to HQ?"

"Yes, sir," she said, putting the car in gear. "How's the horse?"

"I have no idea," he said. "I literally don't know anything about them. They're a bit scary."

"Scary, sir?"

"Yeah, the size of them. If a horse wants to do something, you can't exactly stop it. I don't know, I'm probably worrying too much."

"What's her name, the horse?"

"Twinkle," said Kett.

"You're right, she sounds terrifying."

They settled into the journey as Savage picked up speed. It was blisteringly hot, but the IRV was a new one and the air con turned it into a fridge. Kett was almost disappointed when the radio mast of the police station rose over the rooftops. He could have happily sat there for a little while longer.

"Okay," he said, as Savage turned off the roundabout. "Can you take the victims from the hangings? See if we can work out how they're connected, other than their job. I'll take the ones from this morning."

"Yes, sir," she said.

She was reversing into a parking space when Kett's phone rang.

"Spalding," he said when he'd answered. "What's up?"

"Not sure if it's relevant, sir," she said. "But we've just had a 999 call into control. A suspected kidnapping."

"Where?" said Kett.

"The city."

Kett motioned for Savage to move and she pulled out of the parking space, heading for the road.

"A neighbour reported a woman getting into a red van," Spalding went on. "Trafford Road. Said she looked distressed. He actually went after them in his car, followed as far as Cringleford, then he lost them."

"Cringleford," said Kett, and Savage flicked on the siren. She navigated onto the roundabout and floored it onto the dual carriageway. Kett grabbed the strap over the door as his stomach tried to exit through his rear end.

"Like I said, it might not be connected," said Spalding. "But the Boss asked us to look out for missing people. Woman's name is Rebecca Leigh, she's thirty-seven. Caucasian, brown hair, her neighbour says she's, and I quote, 'On the shorter end of the tiny side.' Van's registered to a Chris Dingle, but he reported it stolen a couple of weeks ago. It's a red Vauxhall Vivaro. I'll text you the plates."

"Thanks, Alison," Kett said. "One more thing. Does the neighbour know what she does for a living?"

"I asked, said she worked for the council. I've put the word out."

"Can you let Gorski know where we're going?"

"Yeah."

Spalding hung up.

"Possible kidnapping," Kett said. "A woman, works for the council. We're looking for a red Vauxhall Vivaro."

"It's him?"

"Maybe," said Kett. "Maybe not. But the van was nicked a couple of weeks ago. Our guy has been planning this for a while now, I think. He's been putting everything in order."

"Because he has to move fast if he wants to finish," Savage said. "If he draws it out too long, he knows he's going to get caught."

Kett nodded.

"We know he's using warehouses. The one he used for the hangings was abandoned, right?"

"Yeah," said Savage. "The one this morning was too, I think. The company's not in business anymore."

"So he'll be using another disused place."

"There's an industrial lot in Cringleford," she said. "There's a Jewson's there, some other buildings. Can't think of another one off the top of my head."

"Worth a shot."

She bombed down the fast lane, the thump of the passing cars echoing the pounding of Kett's heart. The adrenaline roared through him, enough to make his ears whine. Savage sling-shotted them around the roundabout at what felt like nine Gs, only hitting the brakes as they hit the tangle of smaller roads that led into the suburb. From there, it was only a handful of minutes until she pulled into the car park of the industrial estate.

"Not sure how to get around the back, sir, hang on," she said, leaning over the wheel as she stared down the road towards Jewson's. The car park was mobbed, a dozen people wandering through the shimmering heat haze. There was no sign of a red van anywhere, but why would there be? If the killer had brought his victims there at gunpoint, they would have been spotted in seconds.

"This isn't it," said Kett. "Turn around."

She did as she was told, reversing onto the main road with the siren still blaring. She took off without waiting for an order, rolling through a red light before accelerating again.

"Where are you going?" he asked.

"There's another estate, round the back of that one," she said. "Or at least there was. I think they were building flats there or something."

She took the next right, keeping her speed low as she scanned the road signs. It was quieter down here, mostly residential. After a quarter of a mile, though, she pointed to a dense hedge that had grown up along the right-hand side of the street. Kett was about to ask her what she'd spotted when the sunlight flashed off a metal gate almost lost in the foliage.

"That's the estate?" he asked.

"I think so, sir," she said, pulling up beside it and keeping the engine running. She took out her phone and typed something into it, her face a mask of concentration. "Yeah, look."

She handed him her phone and he slipped on his glasses, seeing a satellite image of a small industrial site. He counted the roofs of three buildings, the central one bigger than the other two put together.

"Turn the siren off, Kate," he said, and she did. The only noise was the hammer of industrial machinery from nearby.

Kett opened his door, stepping out of the arctic chill into the heat of the day. The sound of building work was louder here, the revving of an engine and the clang of equipment from further down the street. The gate was made of wire mesh and sealed with a shiny padlock, thick strands of ivy clinging desperately to it. He found a gap in the ivy, but the track beyond was shaded by scrubby trees and he couldn't make much sense of the shifting shadows.

"You see a way in, sir?" asked Savage, and he shook his head.

"Doesn't look like anyone's been here recently," he said, giving the gate a rattle.

"That padlock's newer than the gate," said Savage. "A lot newer."

She walked a little way up the street and stopped.

"Sir."

He caught up to her, seeing that something had pulled down the top of the wire fence, causing it to sag. Beyond was a patch of unhealthy-looking woodland, the birds busying themselves in the branches.

"I can get over there, sir," she said. "If you give me a foot-up."

"Not sure that's a good idea, Kate," Kett replied.

"Just a look. If I see the van, I'll come back and call it in."

Kett studied the trees, and the dense undergrowth that clung to them. It was incredibly peaceful here, other than the distant building work and the faint growl of an engine—certainly no shouts or screams or gunshots.

"Okay," he said. "But I'm coming with you."

"All due respect, sir," Savage started, looking at the drooping fence and then back at him.

"What?"

"I mean, it's still five foot off the ground, sir."

"Are you saying I can't make it over a five-foot fence, Detective?"

"Uh... No?"

"No you're not saying it, or no you don't think I can?"

"Uh..."

Kett ducked down, cradling his hands and allowing Savage to plant her boot in them. He braced himself, his back threatening to cramp as he took her weight. It was only for a second, though, before she grabbed the top of the fence and vaulted over it, landing nimbly on the other side. She turned to face him, the shadows dancing over her face.

"Come on then, sir," she said with a little too much enthusiasm. She patted her thighs with both hands. "You can do it."

"I'm not a dog, Kate," he said, reaching up and grabbing the top of the fence for a second before letting go. "You know what, I'd better call the Boss, tell him where we are. You go."

Savage threw him a knowing smile that he chose to ignore, and set off into the slim trees.

"If you see anything, you come back here," he called after her. "Don't Kett this up."

"Wouldn't dream of it, sir," he heard her say.

Then she was gone.

CHAPTER TWENTY-NINE

PORTER STOOD SIDEWAYS IN FRONT OF THE MIRROR, staring forlornly at the bulge of his belly. He'd never, in his entire life, been this out of shape, and it broke his heart a little bit because he'd always taken such pride in his fitness. He'd never been obsessive—except for a brief spell in his early twenties when he'd first joined the force—but he'd always promised his body that he'd look after it because he knew that if he did, his body would always look after him.

"Sorry," he told it, prodding his stomach. It had gone past the 'whole barrel' stage, as Allie always called it, and had reached the point where it was drooping over his belt like a depressed sloth hanging from a branch. He sucked it in and it barely made a difference.

"Come on, Pete," he told his reflection.

It wasn't like he even had an excuse anymore. He'd piled on the pounds partly because of the pregnancy, because he'd wanted to encourage Allie to eat when she wasn't, and then make her feel better about eating when she was.

But Bobby was four months old now, and Allie had

shed most of her baby weight taking him for walks in the buggy and staying up all night with him—and by breastfeeding, of course, which she delighted in telling him burned hundreds of calories a day. Porter, meanwhile, had continued to consume calories like he was preparing for the end of days, and the fact that he was chained to his desk for most of the time at work didn't help.

He needed to find his passion again. He needed to rediscover his lust for life. He needed to set a good example for Bobby.

"You need to be better," he told his reflection. "You need to sort this out."

The words just made him feel hungry.

The bathroom door crashed open with immense force and Superintendent Clare walked in, stopping abruptly when he saw Porter standing there. Porter tried again to suck in his stomach, turning on the tap and washing his hands while Clare eyed him suspiciously.

"What are you doing in here, Pete?" he asked. "Who were you talking to?"

"Uh, nobody, sir," he replied. "Just talking to myself. I didn't think you'd be back so soon."

He dried his hands on his trousers and headed for the door, only for Clare to block his path.

"Sorry, sir, can I just—"

"No, you can't," Clare said, looking him up and down. His face softened, and when he spoke next his voice was quiet. "I heard what you were saying to yourself. Look, Pete, I know I give you a hard time about... about that."

He nodded at Porter's gut.

"And I'm sorry that I said you looked like a pregnant hippopotamus who's swallowed a family of whales."

"Oh, uh, I don't remember you saying that, sir," said Porter.

Clare frowned.

"Must have just been thinking it. Anyway, what I'm trying to say is that I don't want it to get you down. I'm all for a bit of podge. I like a fuller figure, more cushion for the pushin', as they say."

"Not sure they say that, sir," said Porter, feeling decidedly uncomfortable.

"I think a bit of fat is a good thing," the Super went on. "It's healthy. But what isn't healthy is this."

He tapped Porter's head.

"I think you've been piling it on because something isn't right up here."

"Oh, I mean, I don't think so, sir," stammered Porter. "I think it's just I like cake, you know?"

"So do I," said Clare, touching the pocket of his jacket. "Unless Duke made it, of course. But no, becoming a father is a hugely emotional time in a man's life. Not to mention stressful. It can do funny things to your mind. It's a chain reaction, because once you start to put the weight on you become depressed, and then you eat more, and then you become even more depressed. You have to break the cycle, Pete, and I don't mean getting your fat arse on a bike. I mean you have to change this." He tapped Porter's head again. "Before you can change this."

He prodded Porter's stomach with his finger, and Porter squealed.

"Because this is about more than me having officers who don't pass out after eight star jumps," Clare went on. "This is about me saying something to a friend before it goes past the point of no return."

To Porter's surprise, he felt himself welling up at the

Super's words. He sniffed, clearing his throat to try to hide it.

"Can I show you something?" Clare asked, looking back at the door before reaching for his trousers.

"Uh..."

"You probably all think I've always been fit and healthy," he went on, pulling his wallet from his pocket. "That I have the perfect fat-to-muscle ratio for a man."

"Uh," Porter said again, looking at the Super's gangly frame. "I mean, you do eat a *lot* of Bounties, sir."

"They're coconut, it's *fruit*. But believe it or not, Pete, I haven't always been this way."

He pulled something out of his wallet and held it up. It was a crinkled, faded photograph of a young man on stage, dressed in shorts and a shirt and holding a silver flute to his face. He was obviously midway through an energetic performance, his elbows up, his long, curly hair billowing behind him, his face contorted into a look of ecstatic concentration.

He was *enormous*.

Porter leant in, shaking his head as he studied the obese form of the man in the photograph, the folds of fat that threatened to burst from his clothes, the chins that seemed to prop up the flute.

"That can't be... it's not... is that *you*, sir?"

"The Islington Jazz Flute semi-finals, 1989," he said, looking at the photograph with immense pride. "I was nineteen, and in the prime of my musical ability. That was one of the greatest nights of my life, until Bertie Salamander beat me to the grand prize." He scoffed. "But only because his father was bribing the judges."

"Uh..."

"Just as well, though," said Clare. "Otherwise I may have taken a very different career path. Look at me, Pete."

Porter couldn't have taken his eyes away from the photograph if he'd tried.

"It was the morning after this that I knew I had to change my life. I weighed nearly twenty-four stone in that picture, can you believe that?"

"I mean, yes," said Porter. "I can."

"And it was making me miserable. I thought I was a failure, physically, mentally, flautally. I realised I'd been depressed for a long time. I'd written myself off. So I decided to do something about it. I changed everything, and slowly but surely the weight came off."

"That's... impressive, sir," said Porter. "Is there any chance I can take a photo of that?"

Clare pulled the photograph away, slipping it into his wallet.

"No," he snapped. "And if you so much as mention this to anyone else, then being a pie-faced chunker is going to be the least of your worries."

Porter let out a long sigh, and Clare clapped him awkwardly on the shoulder.

"You've got this, Pete," he said. "The important thing to remember is that your mind is a powerful thing, it is capable of anything. You can shift the weight. Just don't write yourself off."

He clapped him on the shoulder again, harder this time.

"Now toss off, or I'm going to piss myself."

Porter did as he was told, scuttling out of the bathroom. The image of a gigantic, sweaty Colin Clare playing the flute was stuck in his head like a fishbone in his throat, but the Super's words hadn't been unwelcome. He felt a renewed sense of purpose, enough to make him bypass the kitchen and head straight for the bullpen. He opened his drawer, pulled out the multi-pack of fudge he'd hidden beneath the files, and threw it into the wastepaper basket. Then, because he didn't trust himself not to eat out of the rubbish, he fished them out, carried them across the room and hurled them into the larger communal bin.

"New man," he told himself as he returned to his seat. He picked up his phone and looked at the photo of him holding Bobby. He booped the baby's nose. "For you, buddy. I'm not going to write myself off."

Something about those words was nagging him, something he couldn't quite put his finger on. He pushed the mouse to wake up his computer, typing in his password.

"Don't write yourself off," he said, drumming his fingers on the desk.

What was it? What was he missing?

"Don't write yourself off," he said again.

"What was that, sir?" asked Spalding as she snuck up behind him, a pile of papers clutched to her chest.

"Nothing," he said. "Just... Don't write yourself off, it's what the Boss said to me. I'm stuck on it and I can't figure out why."

"Write yourself off?" she asked. "Like a car?"

Shit, that was it, wasn't it?

"Write-offs," he said. "The buildings the killer has been using, they're all abandoned, right? They've been damaged in some way."

"Yeah," said Spalding. "What are you driving at, sir?"

"I don't know," Porter said, trying to collect his thoughts. "Have we got access to Benjamin Reed's files? From the company?"

"Some of them, sir." Spalding caught up. "Shit, hang on."

She ran to her desk, dumping the papers and logging

into her computer. It took her a moment to find what she was looking for.

"What was the address of the warehouse where the hangings took place?" she asked, then answered before Porter had the chance. "It's here. It was a delivery hub—we knew that much—but there was a flood six months ago, the main water pipe cracked. Everything was written off and the building was declared uninhabitable."

Porter leaned over her, seeing the details in black and white.

"The insurance company was Reed, Barnham and Crabbe," said Porter. "That can't be a coincidence."

Spalding flicked through some more files, stopping at a building they both recognised.

"This is where the man was electrocuted this morning," she said. "The refrigeration company. There was an electrical fire here just last month. Not enough to write off the building, but the company went into administration."

"Reed was the insurer?" Porter asked.

"Yeah," said Spalding, jabbing the screen hard enough to make it wobble. "It's right there, and Ben Reed was the account manager."

She flicked through some more pages.

"There are dozens of them," she said. "All these buildings, they've been written off. If the killer had access to these files, he'd have known they were empty."

She stopped.

"Oh."

"What?" asked Porter, staring at the building on-screen. It was another warehouse, this one lower, with a set of rolling doors along the front.

"The alert that just went out, it was somewhere in Cringleford, wasn't it?"

"Yeah," said Porter. "Or at least that's where they were heading."

"This place is in Cringleford," said Spalding, prodding the screen again. "There was a fire. The whole estate was written off years ago."

"That's where he is," Porter said. He pulled out his phone, heading for the door. "I'll let them know."

CHAPTER THIRTY

SAVAGE WEAVED HER WAY THROUGH THE TREES, THE heat making her feel like she was walking through a remote jungle and not a disused industrial estate a few miles outside of the city. She could hear the building work from further up the street, and distant sirens too, but the thick canopies were doing their best to mute it.

The birds weren't bothered by her, their song undisturbed as she crunched over empty drink cans and crisp packets, twigs snapping beneath her feet. She had to bypass bigger pieces of detritus—rusting scraps of metal and countless degraded tyres and an enormous rotting sign that had collapsed in on itself. It felt like the end of the world had happened here, the epicentre of the apocalypse.

Then the trees thinned out, and she saw the remains of a small car park up ahead. The asphalt was cracked and broken, weeds pushing up from the unforgiving terrain and straining towards the sun. On the other side of it were the buildings she'd seen on Google Maps, an enormous warehouse in the middle, and a lower satellite building on either side. The one to the right must have been a garage at one point, because there were four wide roller doors along its face. Three were closed, coated in graffiti.

One was open—just a crack at the bottom.

Another noise had peeled itself away from the hammer and clang of the builders, this one closer. An engine. Savage scanned the car park and the surrounding trees, but there was no sign of anybody.

Taking heart, she stepped into the sun, her skin prickling in the heat as she made her way along the front of the larger warehouse. There was only one door, boarded up and sealed with a rusted chain that was thicker than her arm. She put her ear to it anyway, holding her breath and trying to hear anything past the thump of her heart.

Nothing.

She pressed on, her shadow cutting a path in front of her before climbing the front of the lower building. She put her fingers to the weather-scabbed bricks, making her way past the first shuttered door.

There, she stopped.

The noise of an engine was louder now. It was a big one, or maybe there were several running at the same time. Could she hear voices, too? It was hard to tell over the call of the sirens as the police scoured the city.

Savage pulled out her phone, hesitating. She knew Kett was right there on the other side of the fence, but she felt completely alone.

She took a step, and then another, passing the second shuttered door. The sounds were louder now; it was definitely an engine she could hear, revving hard. She didn't want to risk her voice carrying, so she texted Kett.

Somebody here, can hear a car.

She kept walking, the heat a hammer that relentlessly beat the side of her head. She lifted a hand to shield herself from it as she passed the third shutter, the light bouncing off the side of the building with such force it literally blinded her. When her phone buzzed and she squinted at the screen, she couldn't see anything at all.

She paused, blinking until the words swam into focus.

Wait there, I'm on my way.

If you can get over that fence, she thought.

She was sliding her phone back into her pocket when she felt it vibrate, Porter's name on the screen.

It would have to wait.

The partially open door was five metres away and there were definitely sounds spilling out of it. Past the engine, she could hear that same clanking noise, almost regular now, like somebody trying to play the drum.

Drums, she realised as she closed in. It wasn't just one she was hearing, but several, all thumping out a different rhythm.

There was a smell too, the caustic aroma of exhaust fumes.

She stopped at the open shutter, got down on her knees, and peeked inside.

For a moment, she couldn't make sense of what she saw —a cavern of darkness filled with smoke, broken up by glowing beams of red and white light. It looked almost like a disco, a warehouse rave.

Then her eyes adjusted and she realised she was staring at a line of cars, all stationary, all facing away from her, and all with their engines running. She could make out people inside them, all in the front passenger seats, nothing but silhouettes as they hammered at the windows.

She could hear their screams, too, muffled by the engines, swallowed by the building.

She backed away, staring at the sky as she tried to work

out what to do. The sun was a spear that penetrated her skull. She pulled out her phone again, texting Kett.

It's him.

Somebody shouted, a voice full of rage that sounded louder, more immediate, than the screams.

She didn't want to, but what choice did she have?

She crawled forward, peering into the garage again, still sun blind. The engines roared, the people inside the cars screamed. The air was full of the choking stench of fumes, nowhere for them to go except out of the door she kneeled next to. They were coming from the cars, but when she looked at the tailpipes she saw that all seven were connected to hoses that looped back around, feeding into the rear windows.

It didn't make sense—until she worked her gaze along the line of vehicles, their occupants clearly visible, and landed on one whose interior was obscured by a cloud of poisonous gas.

Shit.

It was happening again. Six cars rigged to spew their exhaust into the air.

One car designed to kill.

Another shout. Savage stared past the cars to where their headlights splashed against the far wall. A collection of shadows had gathered there, all moving as one in time with the man who paced like a boxer, a shotgun braced against his shoulder. A black balaclava obscured his face but his eyes, full of the light from the cars, burned bright. His mouth twisted itself around words that she couldn't hear over the growl of the engines.

He was engrossed in his work. He hadn't seen her.

Yet.

"Kate!"

Kett's voice, and too loud. She looked back to see him charging across the car park, his boots scuffing the broken ground. She waved her arm frantically and he got the message, dropping into a crouch and crashing into the wall next to her.

"What's going on?" he asked in a whisper.

"Killer's right there, sir," she said. "He's got seven cars, one of them's full of fumes from the exhaust. Somebody's inside it."

"Shit," said Kett, checking his watch. "I called it in, tactical's on its way."

"They're going to be too late," said Savage. "I don't know how long they've been in there. It only takes minutes, sir."

Kett rubbed his eyes, thinking hard.

"He's armed, sir," Savage said. "The shotgun."

"We can't risk it," Kett said. "We know he'll use it, Kate. We can't go in."

But they didn't know who was in there. They didn't know who was dying *right now*. A mother, a father, a son, a daughter.

A kid.

The sirens had faded, just the birds cheering on the execution like spectators in the Colosseum, and that same angry shout.

"We don't have time," said Savage. "I'm sorry, sir."

She took a breath, feeling Kett's hand on her arm but shaking it free. She moved fast and low, crawling beneath the shutter and plunging into the poisonous darkness of the garage. The fumes punched into her lungs, made her gasp for air that just wasn't there. She stumbled on, her foot almost slipping into a mechanic's pit that was lost in the shadows.

The cry of shock was out of her mouth before she could stop it.

Ahead, the shadows turned together, and he saw her.

"Police!" screamed Savage, because she couldn't think of anything else to do.

She ran, keeping the line of cars between her and the killer.

"Drop the gun!"

He didn't. He levelled it, took a breath.

Pulled the trigger.

Savage dropped, sliding into the cover of the nearest car and hearing the shot tear its way over the roof. A roaring fist of adrenaline struck her in the stomach, her ears ringing from the fear, and from the volume of the gunshot.

"Police!" came Kett's voice from the door. "You're surrounded, drop the weapon!"

She couldn't hear anything else over the thunder of the engines and the screams from inside the cars. The killer could be right there, moving swiftly. Panicking, she crawled along the back of the car, ducking her head underneath it to try and find him.

Too many fumes, and she smudged her hands over her eyes, the nausea like a punch to the gut.

"Kate?" Kett called. "Where are you?"

"Stay back!" she shouted.

She sucked in vapours, the garage spinning wildly as she pushed herself up and peeked over the boot of the car.

The gun went off again, closer this time—the force of the shot shattering the rear window in a hail of glass. She dropped to the floor with a scream, her face burning. She put her fingers to her forehead and felt blood.

Fuckfuckfuck.

Crawling again, she smudged blood out of her eyes as

she rounded the side of the car. She heard a door open, somebody screaming, then footsteps pounding her way.

Savage wasn't going to go out on her hands and knees. Gritting her teeth, she used the car to haul herself up just as somebody ran into sight right in front of her. She threw herself at the shadow, her fists bunched, before realising it was a woman.

The woman screamed, her feet skidding on the floor as she abruptly changed direction—making it all of three feet before a car came roaring out of the smoke and thumped into her.

"No!" Savage said, the word caught in her throat.

The woman spun, airborne, skimming the bonnet of another car before sliding out of sight. The first car spun in a tight circle, its tyres screeching on the smooth floor, then the driver—it was him, Savage saw, a masked face turning her way for an instant—floored it towards the shutter. It crunched through with such force that the entire building seemed to tremble, the hose connected to its tailpipe dragging in its wake.

"Kate!" roared Kett, and a second later he ran from the shadows. He took in her face with a look of horror. "Jesus, are you shot?"

"No," she said. "I don't think so. There's a girl behind the car. She's hurt."

"Wait," he replied.

Savage ignored him, running to the car that had filled with fumes. She grabbed the handle and pulled hard, but it was locked.

"Come on!" she said, running to the passenger side.

Locked.

There was nothing inside but a cloud of poison, surely too much of it for anyone to be alive in there. She took a step back then rammed her foot into the passenger window. Then again. And again.

This time it shattered. Fumes poured out through the gap, as thick as water, and she held her breath as she reached in, fumbling for the lock. The world was spinning even faster, she couldn't get a breath in, she couldn't get air.

Come on, she said, or maybe didn't say. She gagged, inhaled, the darkness of the garage now nothing to do with the lack of light.

She found the lock and wrenched the door open, wrapped in a shroud of exhaust. Somebody rolled out of the car and she struggled to catch them, grabbing them under the arms and trying to haul them away. They wouldn't move, anchored in place somehow.

Handcuffs, she realised. The person was chained to the door.

She tugged hard, even though she couldn't see anything, even though her limbs were so numb they didn't even feel like hers anymore. She just pulled and kicked and wrestled the limp, lifeless body until the last of her strength left her and her legs buckled.

You're going to die, she told herself.

She tried to get up and realised she couldn't. Her body wasn't hers, it was a formless, cloudy thing that spiralled upwards like the exhaust fumes—already a ghost. She held tight to the other person just so neither of them would have to go alone.

At least there's no pain, she thought.

And there wasn't.

No pain. No fear.

Just a memory of Aaron, smiling at her.

Then nothing at all.

CHAPTER THIRTY-ONE

"Kate?"

Kett ran between the cars, trying to make sense of anything through the swirling clouds of exhaust, through the oil-thick dark of the garage. He held his jacket over his face but it did nothing to protect his eyes, which burned like somebody had thrown acid in them. The sound of the revving engines thrummed inside his skull, almost loud enough to drown out the screams that echoed from every direction.

"Kate! Where are you?"

He slipped down the side of a Ford and yanked on the handle, but it was locked. Inside was a man in his fifties, his face warped into an expression of horror when he saw Kett. He was cuffed to the passenger door, his wrists bleeding as he tried to tug his hands free. There were no fumes inside. He was safe, for now.

Kett tried the next one along—a Fiat—but this was locked too. He moved to the next and stopped.

Savage lay on the ground between the Fiat and a BMW, another woman lying next to her. The passenger door was open and clouds of poisonous gas rolled out of the BMW, settling on the two women like a morning mist.

"Jesus, Kate!"

Savage's mouth gaped. Her eyes were open, unseeing. He dropped down beside her, feeling for a pulse and not finding one over the thrash of his own heartbeat.

"Hang on," he said, grabbing the other woman and rolling her away. She looked dead, and even if she wasn't, there was nothing he could do for her now—she was chained to the car door.

He took hold of Savage's jacket lapels and began to drag her away from the car, inch by inch, his back screaming as he fought to pull her to safety. The room was filling fast as the engines roared, the air toxic, and he could feel his own thoughts swimming. He knew what they said about carbon monoxide poisoning: that you were unconscious before you even knew what was happening.

But he kept moving, hauling Savage towards the square of golden light where the shutter had been ripped away until, finally, they fell into the hot, fresh summer air. He pressed his fingers to her neck again and felt for a pulse —*please, God*—finding one.

"Kate?"

She groaned, her arms flailing, grabbing drunkenly for his face. She blinked up at the big, blue sky, searching for something and not finding it. Her lips shaped words that he couldn't hear.

"Just hang in there," he said. "You're okay. You're okay."

He looked across the shimmering, heat-soaked asphalt, no sign of the vehicle that had driven away. Then he pulled out his phone and called Clare. While he was waiting, he ran across the car park, finding a loose chunk of asphalt the size of a melon. It was heavier than it looked, and he cradled it against his chest as he stumbled back into the toxic darkness of the garage.

"What's going on?" said Clare when the call had connected.

"We almost had him, sir," said Kett. "He drove off, I didn't see the car. Intwood Road, I think. You've got units on the way?"

"They're seconds away," said Clare. "What happened?"

"Hang on, sir."

He reached the first car, a Volvo, lifted the rock, and smashed it against the driver's window. The glass cracked, didn't shatter, and he did it again. Reaching in, he turned off the ignition only to find that the vehicle was empty.

He retrieved his rock from the seat and hurried around to the Ford.

"He's using cars as gas chambers, sir," he said. "Well, one of them. The rest have hoses going into the back windows but the fumes are escaping somehow."

He rested the phone on the roof of the car so that he could lift the chunk of asphalt with two hands, striking the driver's window of the Ford. It disintegrated into chunks, and he switched off the engine, pulling the key out. The handcuffed man inside was sobbing, shaking his head like he thought Kett was the killer.

"Police," Kett said, more cough than word. "You're safe."

He didn't bother with the phone, exhaustion like a lead suit as he limped to the Fiat. It took three attempts to smash the window of the little car, and he turned the key with such force that it snapped off in his hands. The engine shuddered and fell quiet. There was a woman inside this one, in her sixties, her face streaked with tears as she fought against her handcuffs.

"Police," said Kett, although he wasn't sure if she heard him.

He switched off the BMW's engine and took care of the final two cars—one empty, one occupied—hurling the chunk of asphalt to the ground. The air had fallen so quiet that he wondered if it was a symptom of the carbon monoxide, if his senses were failing him. But the fumes were dissipating already, escaping through the ruined shutter.

He stopped for a moment to let his spinning head settle before walking back to the Ford—running his hand along the backs of the cars to stop himself from keeling over. He was so breathless that even after he picked the phone up he couldn't get a word out.

"Kett?"

"I'm... here, sir," he said, returning to the woman who Savage had pulled out of the BMW. She lay on her back, her eyes closed, her chest still. "We've got one down, three others, I think. They're handcuffed to their cars. It's a mess."

He pressed his fingers to the woman's neck, finding a pulse as weak as a butterfly's wings. He put the phone down again in order to turn her to the recovery position, then picked it up to find Clare halfway through a sentence.

"... no sign of him, are you sure he drove onto Intwood?"

"No, sir," he said. "I didn't see, sorry. He could have gone anywhere."

He walked to the front of the cars, and only then did he see the second body.

"Shit," he said, running over.

It was another woman, this one younger, slim and very short. She lay drenched in a blanket of darkness in front of the bonnet of the first car, and the wounds she bore hadn't been caused by exhaust fumes. Her arm was bent the wrong way, a shard of bone poking through the surface and a set of handcuffs locked around her wrist. She wore a mask of blood, a flash of broken teeth.

But she was alive.

She stared at Kett with one eye, the brightest thing in the room, kicking the ground gently as she tried to push herself away from him.

"We really need that ambulance, sir," Kett said, crouching beside her. "We've got another woman down. Hey."

He held up his hands.

"My name is Robbie, I'm a policeman, you're going to be okay but I need you to lie still, okay? There's an ambulance on the way."

He saw the words slowly penetrate her terror, watched her rest her head on the ground, her mouth searching for air. She reached for him and he held her hand for a moment, her skin as cold as a corpse's. Then he let go.

"I'll be right back, okay? I promise."

He ran to the roller doors, Savage still lying where he'd left her. She was moving, though, trying to roll over like somebody who'd drunk nine pints of cheap cider. He could hear sirens, close, and he forced himself to stop, to take a breath, and then another, and then as many as it took for his pulse to slow. He planted his hands on his knees and doubled up, his lungs so heavy from the fumes that he felt like a donkey had kicked him in the chest. And he stayed that way until the first IRV came bouncing down the weed-strewn path.

He gave the driver a wave before steering his broken body around and heading back inside to count the dying, and the dead.

IN THE END, though, they were lucky.

The headlights of the cars had all been switched off along with the engines, but there was enough daylight creeping through the open door to throw the scene into stark relief. Two constables sat with the woman who had been hit by a car, talking in gentle voices as they tried to stop her from falling asleep where she lay. One was working with a first aid kit, although it wasn't doing her much good. Despite the severity of her injuries, the woman clung onto the PC with her good hand like she was hanging from the top of a mountain, her knuckles white. She was a fighter. She was going to be okay.

Two other Uniforms had freed the woman who Savage had rescued from the deadly BMW, carrying her through the broken door into the safety of the car park. She lay in the shade of the trees—unconscious, not dead—the birds doing their best to wake her. A welcome breeze from outside had cleared the garage but Kett could still smell the fumes every time he breathed in. He felt sick to his stomach, but the poisoned air was only one reason for that.

What he'd found inside this building was the other.

Three people still sat inside their cars, handcuffed to the doors. Kett had asked one of the constables to find him a hacksaw, but that had been ten minutes ago and nobody had come back. He'd spoken to all three of the victims, but none of them had truly acknowledged him, and none of them had answered his questions.

He checked his phone, then resumed his rounds, walking to the Fiat first and to the older woman who sat in the passenger seat. Like the others, her thin wrists were red raw from where she'd tried to free herself, the handcuffs slick with blood. She was wearing a floral summer dress, Birkenstock sandals on her feet. Her long hair, almost entirely grey, had been tied up in a ponytail, but most of it had been shaken loose, sticking to the sweat on her face. She glared fearfully at Kett as he leaned down to look through the broken driver's window, and he held up his hands to show her he meant no harm.

"It won't be long," he said. "We'll cut you out of there, I promise."

The woman swallowed, nodded.

"He's gone?" she said, her voice a whisper. "You're sure?"

"He's gone," Kett told her. "You're safe."

She laughed at this, a harsh, brittle sound.

"Safe? You call *this* safe?"

"Can I ask your name?" Kett asked. He'd tried before but she hadn't responded. This time, though, she did.

"Matilda Sloan," she said, giving the cuffs another tug and wincing, her voice laced with hysteria. "Can you get these off me?"

Kett heard an engine, a big one, and he looked over his shoulder to see a fire engine squeeze into the sun-bleached car park. This, he thought, was infinitely better than a hacksaw.

"These guys will get you out in a heartbeat," he said. "Just hang in there, Matilda."

He could hear the man shouting in the next car over, thumping his head against the window to get his attention. Kett ignored him for the moment.

"I know this is the last thing you'll feel like doing," he said to Matilda. "But can you tell me how you ended up here?"

She scoffed, shaking her head like Kett had asked the stupidest question in the world. She didn't answer it, though, staring through the windscreen at the far wall of the garage as if the man with the gun was still there.

"Please, Matilda."

"I got a text," she said, quietly. "It was my daughter, but a number I didn't recognise. She told me she'd lost her phone and needed a lift. She told me she was here."

"Can I ask you what you do for a living, Matilda?" Kett said.

"What does that have to do with anything?" she replied.

"I need to know."

She chewed on it for a little while, the blood dripping from her savaged wrists.

"Nothing much," she said. "I'm retired. Or as retired as you can be when you've got a state pension and no savings."

"What did you do before?"

She squinted at him.

"Worked for the council," she said. "Thirty years of small-minded, bureaucratic bullshit and they didn't even give me a gold watch when I walked out the door."

"Which department did you work for?"

She blew out a breath, her attempt at a shrug limited by the handcuffs.

"Every one, pretty much. Mainly planning, though."

"Planning? For houses?"

"Mostly, yeah."

Kett heard voices and turned to see two firefighters enter the garage in their fluorescent overalls and bright yellow helmets. One was holding a big torch, the other a set of long-handled cutters. Kett stood straight, waving to them.

"We've got three people chained to the passenger-side doors," he said. "Looks like standard cuffs."

"This'll get through them, no trouble," said the fire-fighter holding the cutters. "Who's first?"

"Me," shouted Matilda from inside the Fiat.

Kett opened the driver's door for them, shattered glass falling out of the frame. He gave Matilda a nod of reassurance and made his way to the Ford, the man inside still knocking his forehead against the glass.

"Finally," the guy said, when Kett looked through the shattered driver's side window. "You getting me out of here or what?"

"They won't be a second," he said. "Mr..."

"Atterbury," he replied after a moment's consideration. He was in his fifties, stout and short. His hair was balding but two of the bushiest sideburns Kett had ever seen sprouted from his ruddy cheeks. He wore a green tweed jacket and chinos which were soaked at the crotch. He hunched himself over to try to hide it, the cuffs rattling. "What the hell is going on here? Who was that man?"

"That's what we're trying to figure out," said Kett. "What brought you here, Mr Atterbury?"

"A text."

"From your kid?"

"From my wife," he said. "Silly cow lost her phone and needed me to collect her. Got here and *he* was here, made me lock myself in the car. He had a gun."

"Was everybody here when you arrived?"

Atterbury looked around, confused.

"How would I know that? I think so, apart from the woman he brought with him, the little one. I saw him throw her out of the car when you lot showed up, then run her over."

Kett heard a snap from the Fiat as the cutters bit through the chain, then the sound of the door creaking open. One of the firefighters helped Matilda out, the woman struggling to hold herself up. The other hurried over with the cutters.

"This one?" he asked, and Kett nodded.

"Just one question, before I go," Kett asked Atterbury. "Do you work for the council?"

The man shook his head, and Kett was moving out of the way to let the firefighter through before Atterbury spoke again.

"Not anymore."

"But you did?"

"Until three years ago," Atterbury said. "But they're a nightmare. I quit, got a job over at May Gurney. Less pay but better hours. Why?"

"You worked in planning?" Kett asked, and he nodded. "You two know each other, then?"

Atterbury glanced through his window to see Matilda being escorted across the garage. He shrugged angrily.

"I recognise her," he said. "Don't know her name."

Kett moved out of the way to let the firefighter into the car, seeing two other people walk through the door. They were just silhouettes against the sun, but it was impossible to mistake the gangly outline of Clare and the portly shape of Porter. Porter was struggling with something enormous and obviously extremely heavy.

"Toss me off," boomed Clare, earning a cry of shock from Matilda as she passed him, "the top of a bridge, because I don't want to be here anymore."

"Sir," said Kett, welcoming him with a nod. "Did you see Savage?"

"She's lucky," Clare said.

"Yeah, another few minutes and she probably wouldn't have—"

"Lucky she didn't get my shoe up her arse," Clare said.

"Bloody idiot that she is, running in here by herself. I wonder where she got *that* from?"

"Uh..." Kett scratched his head, looking away to where Atterbury was being helped from the car. "I mean, it's good that she did, sir. The woman she pulled from the BMW wouldn't have survived if we'd waited. They *all* could have died."

"Was that his plan, do you think?" asked Porter. It was an angle grinder he was holding, Kett realised, an industrial one with a blade that had to be a foot in diameter.

"What have you got that for, Pete?" asked Kett.

"Because you said they were cuffed, sir," Porter replied.

"And you were going to cut them free with *that*?"

Porter frowned at the angle grinder, then nodded.

"Right," said Kett. "Uh, his plan? No, I don't think he wanted to kill them all. Have you seen the cars, sir?"

Clare was looking at them now, his expression gravely serious.

"Six cars? Not seven?"

"The killer took one," said Kett. "Engine was already running, he just jumped in and floored it through the shutter."

"With a victim inside?"

"No, he released her," said Kett. "A young woman, he uncuffed her, threw her out of the car, then ran her over on the way out. Not sure if it was deliberate or not, but my guess is it was an accident. She wasn't his victim, because she was one of the lucky ones."

"Who was the unlucky one, sir?" asked Porter.

Kett pointed to the BMW.

"Every car has a hose attached to its exhaust pipe, and the hose has been fed through a hole in the rear window on the driver's side and taped in place. When we got here all the cars were running in neutral. But there were fumes everywhere, the garage was full of it."

"So the hoses were duds?" said Clare.

"Six of them, sir, yeah," said Kett. "But the Beemer was a death trap. The car was full of exhaust. Savage broke the window, opened the door, got the woman out. It was a gas chamber, though. The killer meant for her to die."

"She still might," said Clare, checking his watch. "Where the hell are my ambulances?"

"We might be quicker driving them, sir," said Porter. "I'm happy to do it."

Clare nodded.

"Take an IRV, blues and twos."

Porter nodded, laying the angle grinder on the ground.

"I'll leave it here, in case either of you need it."

"We won't," said Kett.

"We found his van out back," said Clare as they watched Porter go. "Nothing in it."

Kett turned back to the cars, and for the first time he studied their license plates. He'd expected to find it somewhere, of course, but not so blatantly.

"51, sir," he said, pointing to the Ford. "It's the second digit. That plate's 02, that one 53, 65, 06."

They turned to the BMW together.

"07," said Clare. "Jesus Christ. At least we know the car he escaped in has an 04 plate."

The firefighters had cut the final woman free, but she must have still been unconscious because one of them called over.

"We got paramedics yet?"

Clare shook his head.

"Is she hurt?" asked Kett.

"She's alive, looks like she was knocked out," said the man. "Passed out, maybe."

"What do we know about them?" said Clare.

"I've only spoken to two, but they both worked at the council," Kett said. "Planning."

"Planning?" said Clare. "What's planning got to do with anything? Is he pissed off that he didn't get permission for his extension?"

"That's one theory, I guess," said Kett. "I don't get it, sir. We've got seven members of staff from an insurance firm targeted with a bomb, six security guards forced to hang themselves, six mechanics forced to touch a live wire, and now this. Five council workers sealed inside cars."

"Five?" said Clare.

"Two of the cars were empty," said Kett. "The Volvo there, o6, and the Prius, 53."

Clare nodded, and he looked like he was about to ask something else when they heard a voice howling across the car park, as loud as an air horn.

"Kate!"

Kett hurried out of the garage to see Duke sprinting across the car park towards Savage. Porter had helped her sit up, but she was swaying like a sunflower in a strong wind and her eyes were as wide as saucers. Duke called her name again, then skidded down beside her, wrapping her in his big arms.

Kett jogged over.

"Are you okay?" Duke asked, holding Savage's face and peering into her eyes. "Kate? Honey?"

"She's okay," Porter said. "She just breathed in a lot of fumes. She'll be—"

"Mr Peanut?" said Savage, frowning at Duke. She still looked drunk, her pupils huge.

"No, it's Aaron," said Duke, stroking her hair. "I came as soon as I heard."

Savage laughed like somebody had told a joke.

"Mr Peanut," she said. "You look funny."

She booped Duke on the nose and laughed again.

"Why is your face so hairy?"

Duke looked up, and Kett shrugged.

"Let's get her to A&E," he said. "Porter, can you—"

"I'll do it, sir," said Duke, standing up. "Which car?"

Before anyone could answer, Duke lifted Savage in his arms like he was carrying her over the threshold.

"You're so funny, Mr Peanut," she giggled, trying to boop him on the nose again but poking him in the eye instead. "I love you."

Duke almost choked.

"This way, Mr Peanut," said Porter, leading them both to an IRV. "Before this gets any more awkward."

Kett looked for the woman who'd been in the BMW but he couldn't see her—although another IRV was turning in a wide circle and heading for the exit. The two people who had been released from their cars sat in the shade of the trees on the other side of the car park, an audience of misery.

"Who the hell is doing this, Kett?" said Clare. "Who goes to this much trouble to kill four people?"

"I don't think it's about the murders, sir," said Kett. "You can walk up to somebody in the street and shoot them in the back of the head. That's murder. This is something else."

"You think he's sending a message?"

Kett thought about it for a moment, then shook his head.

"I don't think it's that, either," he said. "This feels different. This feels *new*."

"New?" said Clare.

They both watched as Porter and Duke helped Savage into the back seat of an IRV, the DC still laughing her head off.

"Seven chances," said Kett, thinking aloud. "Six chances to live, one to die. But why seven?"

"You tell me," said Clare.

"I think something happened, sir. I think something happened to the killer and this is... I think it's related to that number. Seven."

"Well, whatever it is, we're closing in," Clare said, scrubbing the sweat from his brow. "Porter found this place on a list of properties that had been written off by Reed's insurance firm. Ben Reed was the project manager for each of them, and Morton acted as the solicitor."

"Shit," said Kett. "Seriously?"

"The veterinary surgery was there too, and both warehouses, the one used for the hangings and the one used this morning for the electrocutions. It's how he's finding his locations."

"That's good work," said Kett. "We need to figure out which ones he hasn't used yet, and which ones fit his MO. Because this isn't over, sir. He hasn't finished."

"Spalding's made a list," said Clare. "I've dispatched teams to every single one of them. If he's going to use them, we'll find him there."

"Reed and Morton are still under arrest, sir?"

Clare nodded.

"It can't be either of them, unless they have an accomplice."

"Can we get a line of sight on the other members of staff at Reed's place?" Kett said.

"We can, but it won't do much good. Porter saw them all at the hospital yesterday."

"What about anyone else who would have access to that list?"

"Already on it," said Clare.

The engine of Duke's IRV roared, the car lurching across the car park. Savage's face was smooshed against the window like she was kissing the glass.

"You think he's going to kill again, Robbie?" Clare asked as they watched the car disappear into the trees.

Kett glanced into the dark garage. He thought about what he'd found there, and realised it was the easiest question he'd ever had to answer.

"Yes, sir. He is."

CHAPTER THIRTY-TWO

"Right, what have we got?"

Kett stripped off his jacket as he walked into the Incident Room, throwing it onto an empty desk and unbuttoning his cuffs. He rolled his sleeves up, grateful for the cold kiss of the air conditioning on his bare wrists. There had been so much to take care of at the garage that it was now late afternoon. The sun was on the warpath, Kett's skin burning from the force of it. It was so hot that he wasn't even sure he wanted tea.

"How's Kate, sir?" asked Spalding, the only other person there. She was pinning yet more photographs to the wall, even though there wasn't much room for them. The display of victims and evidence had spread around the corner of the room like some kind of fungus, creeping towards the door.

"Good, I think," said Kett, checking his watch. "Duke just called from the hospital. She's out for the count again, but they say she'll be fine."

"That's great," said Spalding, visibly relieved. "They found him yet?"

"No," said Kett, walking over. "He vanished. Nobody saw the car he was using so he probably slipped right past us. He could be anywhere."

"He could be long gone," said Spalding.

"No. He's still in the city, I'm sure of it. Whatever this is, I don't think he's finished yet. Have you dug up anything else on the victims from the garage?"

"A few bits and pieces, sir," she said. "But nothing much. There are a lot of connections between them, they all seem to know each other. Weird, right?"

Kett didn't answer, scanning the faces on the board. Spalding had been quick, adding the five victims they'd found in the garage. Kett recognised Atterbury and Sloan and the two women who had been unconscious when he'd arrived—one pulled from the BMW, the other out for the count inside the Prius. The woman who'd been run over was there too, looking younger than he'd thought she was without her mask of blood.

"Rebecca Leigh," said Spalding, pointing to her. "This is the woman whose neighbour reported her as kidnapped." She moved her pen along the line. "The woman Savage rescued is Laura Boyle, the other one is Amanda Long. They're all local and they all work in the city."

"The council?" asked Kett, and Spalding nodded. "That was his target this time around, council workers. Do you know if they worked in planning?"

"I can find out, sir," she said.

"What else? What connects them to the other incidents?"

"I've been on the phones all day, sir," said Spalding. "The connections between each group of victims are almost entirely work based. Even when there's another link, like

Lee and James Holland, the killer targeted them because of their jobs."

"You spoke to those two after I interviewed them, didn't you?" asked Kett. "Did you get anything interesting?"

"They haven't seen each other for years, but before that they worked together as mechanics. Did they tell you that?"

"Yeah, I think so," said Kett, struggling to put his memories in some kind of order. "With Lee's dad, right?"

"But they stopped working together in 2015, didn't speak much after that."

"They say why?"

"Not in so many words, but I get the impression something might have happened."

"You didn't press them?" said Kett.

"Nah, sir," she said, scowling at him. "I didn't want to upset them, so I kept the hard questions to myself. Of course I bloody pressed them. They clammed up. They're not under arrest, they walked. But get this."

Spalding moved to the board, using her pen to tap the photograph of Bill and Roz Carroll, the ex-husband and wife who had been victims of the hangings.

"These two worked together in 2015 too, doing security for an outfit called Rooster's."

"Rooster's?" said Kett.

"Don't ask, because I don't know. They recruited security for gigs, festivals, that kind of thing. Kept all their workers self-employed so they didn't have to pay benefits."

"Did you ask them where they worked in 2015?"

"Of course, and they couldn't remember. Don't keep records, apparently. But this guy."

She tapped the photograph of Brian Beaney.

"His wife told me that before he became a delivery driver he was a security guard. He started in 2015 and only worked four gigs over the summer. One was at Latitude, the festival, the second was the Sheringham Carnival, and the third was a fair somewhere, but she couldn't remember where. The last one was where he got badly assaulted, didn't want to do the job after that."

"Hang on, go back, a fair?" said Kett.

"Yeah. Rides and stuff, hook-a-duck, that kind of thing."

"The kind of rides you need a mechanic for," said Kett, looking at the photographs of Lee and James Holland. "That's a connection *between* the groups, not just in them."

"I was thinking the same thing, sir," said Spalding. "Something happened, something that connects them. I'm going through the archives now, but it could be anything, and we don't even know it definitely happened in 2015, not for sure."

"2015," said Kett, doing the maths. "Seven years ago. That's some coincidence."

"Or not."

"Keep looking," Kett said. "Can I do anything to help?"

Spalding shook her head, then nodded.

"Actually, yeah," she said. "I've got one of the victims from yesterday waiting in the lobby. Linda something."

"Linda Mayweather," said Kett. "I spoke to her already."

"Yeah, but I'm trying to get more out of her. You can talk to her again, sir, if you want to."

"Sure," said Kett.

"Might want to take a PC in with you," said Spalding. "She's scary, that one, and she's been waiting over an hour."

Kett crossed the bullpen, stopping in the kitchen to down a pint of water from the cooler. It hit his head like an ice pick and he winced, gritting his teeth until the pain passed. He was heading out again when his phone rang.

"Thank God, it's you," he said when he answered, and he heard Billie laugh.

"Is it that bad?"

"Worse," he said. "This case is... I can't even find the words. He's running absolute rings around us."

"Sorry," she said. "If it makes you feel any better the kids are running rings around me, too. They're being an absolute nightmare. Alice won't stop going on about the horse and she's recruited her little sisters to her cause. Can you hear them?"

She must have tilted the phone because he could suddenly make out a chant coming from another part of the house, the three girls yelling, "Horsey! Horsey! Horsey!" at the tops of their voices.

"It's been going on since they got back from school, Robbie, I can't cope. I can't believe you got them a horse."

"I mean, technically it wasn't me," he said, leaning against the wall. "It was Colin."

"Well, I'm blaming you," she said, and he could hear the smile in her voice. "Look, I'm calling because they want to go and see Twinkle, but I don't know what the deal is. Will your friend be okay if they go out?"

"Erik? He's not my friend, but he said they could visit anytime. The horses love company."

"Yeah, Robbie, but these are *our* girls," said Billie. "They're not ordinary children. They'll let all the horses loose or something, start a stampede. Moira will end up riding down the road as naked as Lady Godiva, terrifying the locals."

Kett laughed a little too loud at the thought of it.

"I think they'll be fine," he said. "Just don't let them ride or anything."

"You know what Alice is like, she'll insist."

"She's not ready," said Kett. "She needs a few lessons. If something happened I'd feel terrible."

"Me too," said Billie. "She's so vulnerable."

"I mean I'd feel terrible for *Erik*," Kett said. "After he's been so kind."

"Oh," said Billie, laughing. "Yeah, you're right. It's not his responsibility to keep her safe."

She said something else, but Kett had stopped listening. He'd felt that little *click* at the back of his head, the sound of something slotting into place. He dropped the phone for a moment and reached inside the storm of his thoughts.

It's not his responsibility to keep her safe.

"Robbie?" said Billie, and he put the phone to his ear again.

"You're okay for them to go?" she asked.

"Yeah," he said. "Yeah, it's fine. Have fun, give Twinkle a kiss from me."

"I will do no such thing," she said. "Love you."

"Love you," he replied, but she'd already gone.

He stayed where he was, running those words through his head.

It's not his responsibility to keep her safe.

But they continued to mean nothing, and after a moment he set off again, returning through the bullpen and traversing the warren of corridors back to the lobby. It was busy, but it wasn't hard to find Linda Mayweather. She held court in the corner of the room next to the coffee machine, broadcasting her views to an audience of overheated punters.

"... and we're paying for it, that's the real irony," she bellowed. "Me, you, you. Probably not you, because you don't look like you've paid taxes for a good long while, but definitely you. They're taking money from your pockets and what do they give you back? Absolutely fucking nothing."

"Oi!" yelled Shelley from the other side of the desk. "I warned you."

"What are you going to do?" Linda yelled back. "Arrest me? I have a God-given right to protest whenever and wherever I like. If you're not careful, I'll start a fucking riot right here in—"

"Hey," said Kett, walking over. "Linda, sorry, we're ready for you."

Linda huffed and puffed for a moment, then strutted over, her thumbs hooked into imaginary braces. Kett had forgotten how intimidating she was. She looked like she could have picked him up and thrown him headfirst in the bin without breaking a sweat. The bruise around her throat was darker than ever, but the swelling had gone down.

"About time," she said. "An hour I've been here, mate."

"Yeah, sorry, it's been a crazy couple of days." He held the door open for her and she walked through. "Were you really planning to start a riot in there?"

"Nah," she said. "Just bored."

"You doing okay?"

He saw her reach for her throat, her fingers stopping short before falling to her side.

"Fine," she said. "Barely a scratch. You caught him yet?"

"No," said Kett, as he took the turn that led to the interview rooms.

"He's done it again, though," she said. "I heard it on the radio on the way over here. Another man died."

"Yeah," Kett said, finding an empty room and ushering her in. "And then some."

"Feels like I'm under arrest," she said as she sat down at the desk.

"You're not," said Kett. "We're just a little short of space."

"You gonna record me?"

Kett shook his head.

"Shame. Used to a be singer. Punk band. We were called the Queefs." She laughed hoarsely. "I was quite good. Can give you a rendition if you like?"

"Thanks," said Kett. "Maybe later."

He pulled out his notepad and patted his pockets, realising he'd lost his pen.

"Right," he said. "Thanks for coming in, Miss Mayweather. We're just following up on what happened yesterday. I'd like to ask you some questions, if that's okay?"

"Linda," she said. "And yeah. Not like I've got anything better to be doing."

He wasn't sure if she was being sarcastic or not.

"As you know, the man who attacked you has been involved in another incident. *Three*, actually."

"Three?"

"One yesterday morning, before you were attacked. A bomb."

"In the city? That was him?"

Kett nodded.

"There was another attack this afternoon, it hasn't hit the news yet. But each incident followed a pattern. Six or seven victims, a game of chance. One died, the rest lived—unless they tried to fight back or run."

Linda jolted in her seat like she'd received an electric shock—the memory of Stefan Kucharek being shot, Kett thought. She recovered, scratching at the surface of the desk with her thumbnail.

"Each group of people is linked by their work," Kett

said. "The people you were with yesterday were all employed as security guards, is that right?"

Linda nodded.

"Roz and her dickhead husband couldn't fight their way out of a wet paper bag, but yeah, they call themselves security."

"Can you remind me the kinds of places you work?" Kett asked. "Specifically any place you might have all worked together, going back as far as 2015, if you can."

"I do everything," said Linda. "Starting to get myself a little team, too, so we can do bigger jobs. Proper business-woman, me. Wouldn't work with those tits from yesterday if you paid me double."

"But you *have* worked with them?"

"Here and there," she said. "Mostly on the carnival circuit, years ago."

"Fairgrounds?" said Kett.

"Yeah."

"Local?"

"All over, mate. Worked Hull for a while, that one's bloody huge. When I moved down here, I followed Parkin's around for a bit, they do a lot of the seasonal fairs. They used to use their own boys, but there's less trouble when they use us. Got a hell of a temper on them, some of those lads. We keep it cool."

Kett had known Linda for long enough now to know that probably wasn't true, but he didn't comment.

"Can you remember any particular incidents in the last few years?" he asked instead. "A grudge, maybe? Or an accident? Something that might have put you on the suspect's radar?"

Linda blew out a long breath, sitting back in her chair.

"That list would be longer than my arm," she said. "I

pissed off a lot of people, mostly drunk pricks who thought they'd win a fight against a woman. But no." She shook her head. "Nothing stands out."

"Can I read you some names?" Kett asked, pulling out his phone. "See if any of them ring a bell?"

"Sure," she said. "Good with names."

He started from the beginning, listing everyone who'd been in the Reeds' office when the bomb went off. Linda sat quietly, her face blank. He moved on to the electrocutions, reading out the first three names with no reaction.

"Allan Currier," he said, and Linda snapped to attention. She clicked her fingers like she was trying to remember.

"Currier. Currier. I know that name. Fuck, where... He was a driver, right? No..."

She gurned at the ceiling, grunting in frustration. Then she slapped a hand on the desk so hard it made Kett jump.

"He was a grease monkey. I knew I'd get there. Fixed up the rides."

"That's right," said Kett. "Where do you know him from?"

"I don't know him, not really. Worked with him two, maybe three times for a man called, uh... Dutch, was it? Something Dutch."

"Holland?"

"Oh, yeah. Isn't that weird? How the brain works. Holland, that's right."

"Lee or James?"

"Chris," she said. "Lee and James were his sons, I think. Or wait, one of them was his brother, but they were almost the same age. Pair of useless ballsacks, if you ask me. Chris ran a touring funfair over Lowestoft way, I think. Or was it King's Lynn? Could have been anywhere. I did a couple of gigs for him, but the bald prick always found an excuse to dock my pay. Wrong uniform, too many tattoos, punched a punter, stuff like that."

"When was this?" asked Kett, fishing for a pen again just in case he'd missed it the first time around.

"Years back," she said.

"2015?"

"Maybe."

"Would you have kept payslips? Anything like that?"

"Oh sure," she said with another laugh. "I get my accountant to keep 'em in his gold safe. Payslips, fuck would I do with them? Cash in hand, mate."

"Would you say Chris Holland had a grudge against you?"

"Fair to say he does," she said with a shrug. "Fat lot of good it'll do him, heard he was pushing up daisies."

"What about his brother, James, and his son, Lee?"

"What about 'em? Like I said, useless. James was alright, just kept his head down, but the kid's a dunce. That was another reason I fell out with his pa, because they didn't know what they were doing, those two. Dangerous."

A rush of static shivered over the back of Kett's skull.

"Dangerous how?"

"Because they didn't give a shit about those machines," she said with genuine anger. "Some of their kit was older than I am, cobbled together from stuff they found after the war when they tore down the factories. Hadn't been looked at since it came off the bench. They couldn't have cared less about the punters, just interested in this."

She rubbed her thumb over her fingers.

Money.

"Did something happen, Linda?" Kett asked, leaning in.

"Did something go wrong with the equipment back in 2015?"

Linda studied the table for a moment, frowning. Then she nodded.

"Yeah," she said. "Yeah, a kid, now that I'm thinking of it. I don't remember. It was years back, but yeah, I think something did happen."

It's not his responsibility to keep her safe. Billie's words rang through his skull like a cathedral bell.

"The kid got hurt? You were there?"

"No," she said. "I mean, no I wasn't there, but yeah, some kid got hurt. I don't remember, sorry. It was so long ago."

"And you're sure you weren't there?" he asked. "Think hard, because if this guy is out for some kind of revenge, if this has anything to do with what happened back then, then he thinks you're involved too."

Linda was scratching the desk again, looking uncomfortable.

"This is really, really important," Kett told her. "He's going to do it again, Linda. He's going to find seven people, and he's going to murder one of them. Think."

"Alright," she snapped. "Fucking fine. I weren't there, I swear. If it's the night I think it was I was out cold. Used to have a problem, but I don't no more. Sober for four years, near enough. Back then, I was a mess. I'd wake up on the street every other night, blitzed. Chris fired me for missing too many shifts. I weren't there."

"Would your name have been on the list?" Kett asked. "The work schedule?"

Linda shrugged.

"Maybe," she said. "Yeah, I guess."

"Can you tell me anything else about what happened?"

She shook her head, looking miserable.

"Different world, mate. You know, they say every single cell in your body changes over seven years or so. You ever hear that? You're completely different. I'm not *her* anymore."

"You're sure you can't remember what happened?"

"Nobody died," she said. "I remember that much. There would have been more of a fuss if somebody had died. Nothing changed, life just went on."

"Not for him," said Kett, getting up and heading for the door. "For him, everything changed."

CHAPTER THIRTY-THREE

KETT FLEW INTO THE BULLPEN SO FAST HE TRIPPED, HIS arms wheeling as he fought to stay upright. Porter was at his desk and he looked up in shock at the sudden clatter of feet.

"Oh no," said the DI. "He's not making us run laps, is he, sir?"

"No," said Kett, crashing into his chair, his heart hammering. "I think I've found something."

"Yeah?" said Porter, wheeling his chair over.

Kett impatiently clapped the mouse against the desk as he waited for the old PC to wake up. Then he opened Google.

"You remember an accident at a funfair seven years ago?" he asked. "Owned by a man called Chris Holland. King's Lynn, or maybe Lowestoft."

"Funfair," said Porter, rolling back to his desk. "Maybe. Hang on."

Kett waited for the search page to load, scrolling through adverts for carnivals and a handful of links to roller coaster accidents in the States. He narrowed the terms, still finding nothing.

"Oh, wait, no," said Porter. "I was thinking about the bouncy castle that took off in the wind. A kid died. It was awful. Can't find anything about a funfair."

Kett sat back in his chair.

"Linda Mayweather said she remembered an incident at a funfair owned by Chris Holland; his son Lee and his brother James were two of the people forced to grab the wires this morning. She said they neglected the rides and somebody got hurt. A kid."

"Encyclopaedia Jones would know," said Porter. "You can try her, see if she's awake?"

Kett pulled out his phone and called Savage, leaning back in his chair as he counted the rings. He was about to give up when she answered.

"You okay?" he asked, putting her on speaker so that Porter could listen in. "How's your head?"

"So, so bad, sir," she groaned. "I feel like somebody was let loose in there with a sledgehammer. Thanks for getting me out."

"It's no problem," he said. "You'd have done the same for me. For any of us."

"She would have struggled with Porter," came Duke's voice, followed by a soft slap. "Ow!"

"How's Mr Peanut?" asked Porter, and Savage laughed.

"I have literally no memory of that, sir. I don't even know a Mr Peanut."

"Sure," said Kett. "Listen, Kate, I know you're probably not up to doing much, but I need your help. Can you remember an incident on a funfair seven years ago? 2015. Somewhere in the county."

"Lowestoft," said Porter from his desk. "I just checked, Holland's fairs ran a circuit all along the coast, but they were based in Lowestoft. Pakefield, really."

"That's Suffolk," said Savage. "Out of our jurisdiction, and before my time. You should talk to Clare."

"I tried," said Kett. "He's not answering. Sorry, Kate, get some rest."

"Didn't go by the name Holland," said Porter. "Was called Barney's, after the mascot they used. I think it's a badger."

"Hang on, sir," said Savage, and he heard her sitting up in the bed. "Barney's? I do half remember something. Was it in the summer?"

"Yeah, I think so."

"Because Granddad always loved the fairs. He worked in them himself when he was younger, before he became a copper. That's how he ended up in Norfolk, fell off the back of a travelling show."

"Never knew that," said Kett.

"Why would you, sir? He didn't like to boast about it. But we always went to Barney's when it came up to Hemsby. Kept going even as late as 2015, even though I was a bit old for it by then, wouldn't have bothered if it hadn't been with him. Was it that year? I can't remember, I'd have to check. But there was one year when he wouldn't let me go. I can't even remember why. Sorry, sir, this isn't very helpful."

"No, it is. Keep thinking."

"That's all I remember, sir. But whatever it was, it would have happened wherever Barney's was before it came to Hemsby, because I think he changed our plans at the last minute, took me into the city instead. Try Yarmouth, or maybe California. Like I say, it was a long time ago, I may be completely wrong."

"Thanks, Kate," said Kett. "I'll keep you posted."

He hung up to see Porter staring at his computer.

"She's right," said the DI. "Look at this."

Kett got out of his seat, adjusting his glasses. On Porter's screen was a photograph of a funfair, the dodgems taking up most of the frame and the arcades flashing bright in the foreground. A Ferris wheel could be seen in the distance, towering over everything. There was nobody in the shot, just a couple of seagulls overhead. Past the rides, Kett could see a golden beach, a blue sky.

The headline read: *Summer Carnival Closed After Accident*.

"It was Yarmouth," said Porter, reading. "'*Barney's annual travelling funfair was closed until further notice after a teenage boy was injured on the big wheel. Sebastian Ballard, 15, had his leg trapped by a carriage door after it malfunctioned. He was taken to Norfolk and Norwich Hospital by paramedics, where he remains in a critical condition. Chris Holland, the owner of Barney's, was questioned by Norfolk Police and released without charge. He has not made himself available for comment.*'"

"Sebastian Ballard," said Kett. "Can we find him? He'll be 22 or 23."

"I'll try, sir," said Porter, drumming the name into the keyboard.

Kett called Clare's number again, the call going straight to voicemail.

"Here, sir," said Porter.

On-screen was a photo of a grinning teenage boy, his long, fair hair hanging over his face but doing little to hide his bright eyes. It was a school photo, Kett saw, although he didn't recognise the badge on the blazer. But it wasn't just a school photo.

It was an obituary photo, too.

"Sebastian Ballard," Porter said. "That's definitely him."

They scanned the text together, another newspaper article, this one dated July 2016. There was no mention of how the boy had died, but the phone number at the bottom was indication enough.

"They only usually put suicide prevention numbers when they've committed suicide," said Porter.

"Yeah," said Kett. "Keep digging."

He returned to his desk, trying the Superintendent's number again and this time leaving a message.

"Where are you, sir? I think we've found something."

He dropped his phone onto the desk and typed Barney's funfair into Google, clicking through the results. Whatever had happened in 2015, the fair had never recovered. It had closed down that year, the rides sold off or taken away for scrap. Kett found a couple of photographs of Chris Holland, a big man, his hand always up in front of his face as he fought off the reporters. Then came Holland's obituary in the local paper—one paragraph of faint praise followed by three paragraphs about the incident in Yarmouth. Kett grew cold as he read through it.

"Sebastian killed himself in 2016," he said. "Says here he never recovered from the accident. He lost his leg, couldn't handle the pain."

"I've got the same," said Porter. "Found a few quotes from his dad. Walter Ballard. Mean anything to you?"

"No," said Kett. "But that's one hell of a motive, right? Your kid's injured, has his leg amputated, kills himself a year later. This has to be it. This has to be the link."

"What link?" asked Spalding as she walked through the door. "You've got something, sir?"

"An accident in 2015," said Kett. "At a funfair owned by the father of two of the men who were at the electrocution. Allan Currier, the man who died, worked there too. Barney's, it was called."

"Barney's?" she said. "Hang on."

She bolted back through the door and Kett returned his attention to the screen.

"This is our connection," said Kett. "Linda Mayweather said she was supposed to be working the night of the accident, although her memory is a little fuzzy. She and the others were security. The Holland brothers and Alan Currier—the others too, I think—were mechanics, ride operators."

"That doesn't explain the bomb at the Reed office, though," said Porter.

"It does," said Spalding as she ran back into the room, a sheaf of papers clutched in her hand. "I knew I'd seen the name Barney's before. Reed, Barnham and Crabbe provided the insurance policy for Holland's funfair. Public liability. They gave them the go ahead to tour."

"No way," said Kett, his skin crinkling into goosebumps. "They bodged it?"

"Must have, sir," said Spalding, papers scattering over the floor as she tried to find the one she needed. "Here, says they did a full inspection of all equipment and found it to be operational and safe. This was December 2014."

"And they would have needed planning permission for the fair," said Porter. "They'd have needed a permit from the council."

"This is him," said Kett. "I need everything we can get on Walter Ballard, Sebastian's father. We need a photograph, *now*."

He tried Clare again, just to be sent to his voicemail.

"Where's the Boss?" he said.

"He got a call," answered Spalding, who had made her

way to her desk. "Somebody had some information about the case and he said"—She put on a pretty decent impression of the Super's accent—"'All of you tossers are too busy, too fat or too high on carbon tossing monoxide to bloody do it.'"

"Got him," said Porter, pounding his desk. "Found him. Walter Ballard."

Kett pushed himself off his chair and hurried over in time to hear Porter swear.

"What is it, Pete?"

But he saw the answer for himself. On-screen was a photograph of a man whose dark eyes held nothing but fury. Ballard's son, Sebastian, sat next to him in a wheelchair that was covered in stickers, a portrait of misery. His leg had been amputated from the knee down.

The father and son were so similar that there was no mistaking their relationship. So similar that Kett didn't know how he hadn't noticed it when he'd first seen the boy's face.

"That's not Walter Ballard," he said, pointing at the father. "That's Will Talion."

"Talion's in a wheelchair though, sir," said Porter.

"Yeah," said Kett, tapping the screen. "*That* wheelchair. His son's."

Porter looked at him, his face ashen.

"That's impossible, sir," he said. "I saw him at the hospital yesterday, he was there with the others after the explosion, he..."

"He went back," said Kett. "He left and went back. We never checked."

"He would have had access to the list of properties that Reed's company wrote off," said Spalding, logging into her computer.

"Including the vet's," added Kett. "And he'd have known about Millicent's guns, too. Where does he live?"

"He's got a flat down in Riverside," said Spalding, reading the document on screen.

"Call it in," said Kett. "Now."

"Hang on," said Porter, holding up a hand. "This doesn't make sense. Talion was in the office when the bomb went off, he could have died. Why would he risk it if he's out for revenge?"

"I don't know," said Kett. "We just have to find him."

He pulled out his phone again, but a shout from Spalding stopped him before he could call the Super's number.

"I've found the Barney's report," she said. "Completely missed it because the case ended up with Suffolk Constabulary. Looks like nobody in Norfolk gave a shit about what happened. It got passed around from detective to detective before getting dumped over the border. They didn't need to give a shit, because the fair got shut down after the accident. Holland admitted fault and Ballard got compensation. It was case closed as far as we were concerned. Sebastian didn't die until the following year, and there was nothing to link it to the accident. Nothing concrete, anyway. He took his own life."

"But Ballard blames us," said Kett. "Who was in charge of the case back in 2015? We know Ballard isn't finished yet. He's going after every single person involved in his son's death. If you're right, that includes the police. Who oversaw the case, Alison?"

But he already knew the answer. He could see the signature on the screen in front of him.

"It was the Guv, sir," said Spalding. "It was Superintendent Clare."

CHAPTER THIRTY-FOUR

THE LINE OF POLICE VEHICLES TORE THE CITY IN TWO, a dozen IRVs following the tactical van through the sweltering heat. Kett was behind the wheel of one of them, the siren howling out its panic as they thumped off the inner ring road and cut towards the river. People watched them from the pavements, their eyes wide and their jaws on the floor—it wasn't often that Norwich saw a parade of force like this one.

But it wasn't often that a Superintendent went missing.

"Still not answering," said Porter, his phone to his ear. "His phone's off."

"His phone's never off," said DS Spalding from the backseat. "He picks up in the middle of the night."

"He picks up when he's in the shower," said Kett. "Something's very wrong. He didn't say anything about where he was going?"

In the rearview mirror, Kett saw Spalding shake her head.

"Just that somebody wanted to talk to him, sir."

"That's how Talion—or Ballard, whatever his name is—

gets his victims," he said, seeing the lights of the car in front blaze red and hitting the brakes. "He calls them or texts them, tells them he has something they need. A security job, information, their kids need a lift, whatever."

"And when they arrive, he turns the gun on them," said Porter.

"But that's good," said Kett, easing the car around the public swimming pool and accelerating.

"Good, sir?" asked Spalding.

"Yeah, good. He doesn't kill them straight away. And he doesn't kill everyone he takes."

"Let's hope so," she said.

The brake lights of the IRV in front flared again, the convoy shuddering to a halt in the shadow of the residential apartment blocks that littered Riverside. Kett got out, hearing the thunder of a dozen car doors opening and closing, the roar of shouts as the coppers mobilised.

He ran through the crowd of Uniforms to find Gorski and her team organising themselves in front of a square, six-storey building that looked like a prison. People were scattering at the sight of so many police, and Porter charged towards the doors before they could close, wedging his foot in the gap.

"You got an address?" asked Gorski, checking her rifle.

"Fifty-eight," Spalding said as she ran over.

"He's armed," said Kett. "We know he uses a double-barrelled shotgun, but he could have other weapons, and we don't know for sure he isn't working with somebody else."

"That's fantastic," said Gorski, dryly. "Anything else?"

"Oh, yeah, he can make bombs."

"You really know how to make a girl happy."

"He has Clare," Kett said. "We're almost sure of it."

"I know." Gorski pulled her visor down over her face. "Nobody gets to do that."

She turned to her team.

"Move out."

They swept forward almost silently, sliding into single file as they passed Porter and entered the building. Kett started to follow, but stopped when he heard somebody call his name. He turned to see Savage jogging towards him, dressed in a black tracksuit and trainers. Keeping pace beside her was Duke, still in his uniform. The pair of them looked like they'd been in a boxing match.

"Kate?" said Kett. "Shouldn't you be in hospital?"

"That's what I've been trying to tell her, sir," said Duke.

"No way, sir," said Savage as she reached him. She doubled over, struggling for air. "Not when it's one of us. He's in there?"

They looked up at the building together.

"I hope so," said Kett. "Come on."

They ran into the lobby, which was packed with PCs trying to control the trickle of people evacuating the building. The lift was busy, so Kett found the stairwell and started up it. He took the steps two at a time until he reached the third floor, where he had to stop to catch his breath. Duke charged past, grunting like a bull. Porter was hauling himself up using the handrail, and even Savage was struggling.

"Do you think he's just pretending to be missing..." panted Porter, "to force us to do some exercise?"

Kett started climbing again, reaching the fifth floor. Duke was holding the door open for him and he walked through, finding himself in a long, narrow corridor. Gorski was bellowing, and he followed the sound of her voice around the corner to see that the tactical team had already breached the door. By the time he'd reached them, Gorski had appeared, her gun secured by her side.

"It's empty," she said, her face taut with anger.

Kett swore as he entered the apartment, crossing the hall into the living space. Gorski was right, the place was deserted, and it looked like it had always been that way. It was Spartan in design, the only furniture a sofa that was still wrapped in plastic, positioned next to a small TV. The kitchen, with its wheelchair-friendly counters, boasted a kettle and a toaster and nothing else.

He checked the two bedrooms—one empty, one with a low single bed with a pulley and a carefully folded stack of duvet covers—and the bathroom, with its single tooth-brush and accessible shower, then returned to the living room.

"We're sure this is right?" said Savage. "No pictures on the walls, no photos, no books, no mail."

"Pizzas in the fridge," said Porter from the kitchen. "Nothing else. Milk's in date."

"Sir?" came a voice from outside.

"Tear it apart," said Kett as he walked out.

The corridor was crammed, and it took him a moment to find out who had called for him. A PC was standing by the lift doors, his hat in his hands.

"The Superintendent's car is in the car park, right outside," he said. "Doors are locked. No sign of him."

Kett swore again, his hands in his hair as he made his way back to Talion's apartment. Savage was waiting for him there, her face etched with panic.

"We're running out of time," said Kett. "He's going to make Clare play the odds. He's going to make him hang himself, or electrocute himself, or worse."

"But he needs six other victims, sir," said Savage.

"Right? Lucky Number Seven, there have to be seven of them in all."

"Unless he's counting himself," said Kett. "And not always. There were only five in the cars. He's getting desperate. But you're right, if he's going after police, we need to find out if anyone else is missing."

"On it, sir," said Savage, pulling out her phone.

"DCI Kett."

The shout came from further up the corridor, and Kett followed it to the open door of another apartment. A woman in her late twenties stood there, wrapped in a leopard print dressing gown, a glass of white wine in her hand. A PC stood next to her and he nodded to Kett as he walked up.

"This is... Uh..."

"Patricia," said the woman. "You really looking for Will?"

"We are," said Kett. "Have you seen him?"

"About an hour ago," she said. "He was heading out. I sometimes help him into the lift, you know? If he's carrying stuff. Always told him he should have bought one of the flats on the ground floor."

"You helped him today?"

"Nah," she said. "He was sorted. Had somebody with him."

"Tall guy? Lanky? Suit?"

She nodded.

"Looked kind of angry, but they were chatting loud enough."

"Did you hear what they were talking about?"

"No," said Patricia. "I'm not like a stalker or anything. Seemed friendly, though. Got in the lift, didn't see them again."

"And this was an hour ago? You're sure?"

She shrugged, slopping wine over her arm.

"Thanks," said Kett. "If you think of anything else, and I mean anything, let us know. Even if it doesn't seem relevant. Somebody's life could depend on it."

He made it halfway back to Talion's apartment before he heard Patricia's voice above the clamour.

"You've checked both flats?"

"Both?" he asked, turning back.

"Will owns fifty-eight, but I see him going into fifty-nine all the time as well."

Kett spun on his heels, running back into the throng of officers.

"Gorski?"

There was no sign of her. Kett tried the handle of the next apartment along, finding it locked.

"Sir?" asked Savage.

"Move back," he shouted, clearing a space around the door.

He charged forward, slamming his boot into the door just beneath the handle. The building was new, and corners had been cut. The door almost folded in two, and a second kick sent it crashing inwards, the frame splintering.

"Sir?" Savage said again. "What—"

"It's his," said Kett, walking into the dark. "Will? Super-intendent, sir? Is anyone here?"

He flicked the switch, a dim light illuminating the entrance hall. There wasn't a single sound from inside, the air calm, undisturbed. Still, he gave it a second before advancing any further, just in case somebody hurled themselves out of one of the rooms, a shotgun in their hands.

"Christ, Kett, what are you doing?" Gorski asked, following him in.

"Neighbour said she saw Talion leave with the Superintendent," said Kett. "Said this is his place too."

"You didn't want to check the door for explosives?"

"Uh..." Kett swallowed hard. "Yeah, that might have been a good idea."

Gorski rolled her eyes beneath her visor.

The apartment was the complete opposite of the one next door. Every single scrap of wall was covered in framed photographs, and the same happy face stared out of all of them.

"Sebastian," said Kett. "Ballard's son."

Gorski wasn't listening, her rifle to her shoulder as she stalked towards the living room.

"Armed police," she roared. "Make yourself known."

Kett scanned the photos: Sebastian as a baby, in the arms of an exhausted woman; as a toddler, his father teaching him how to ride a bike and giving him a lift on his shoulder; older, sitting by a river holding a rod. The love radiated from those pictures, it seemed to give the whole building warmth. Here was a life, Kett saw, and it had been a good one.

Until it hadn't.

"Clear," said Gorski.

She walked into the first bedroom, then tried the door to the second room.

"Locked."

"Get it open," said Kett.

He made his way into the open plan living room and kitchen. Half of it was taken up by a weight bench and a litter of dumbbells, a heavy bag hanging motionless from the ceiling. Several bookcases seemed to groan under the weight of brightly coloured Lego models and action figures from TV shows. The walls were lost beneath a gallery of photos of Ballard and his son. The woman was there too, although noticeably absent when the boy was older.

"Do we know what happened to Sebastian's mother?" he asked as Savage, Duke and Porter entered the room.

"Flora Ballard," said Savage. "She died in 2009, cancer. Sebastian would have been nine."

Kett walked into the kitchen, finding cupboards full of crockery and a fridge laden with food.

"Why did he keep all his stuff in here but live next door?" asked Duke, giving the heavy bag a gentle prod that sent it swinging. The ceiling creaked, dust raining down.

"Because he was living two lives," said Kett. "Will Talion lived next door; unmarried, no kids. But when he came in here he was Walter Ballard again. He was a father."

"He didn't want anyone to know," said Savage. "Because he's been planning this for years, hasn't he?"

She was answered by a crunch as Gorski opened the bedroom door.

"Kett, you might want to get over here," she said.

He did as she asked, staring through the door of the second bedroom and finding himself face to face with an altar of vengeance. The walls here were covered too, but there were no smiling faces this time, no happy families. Straight ahead were the official staff photos of everyone who worked at Reed, Barnham and Crabbe, all fixed to the wall by a nail hammered through their forehead. Talion was there too, his smile not touching his eyes. There were documents taped next to the photographs and Kett had to move closer to read them.

"It's an insurance policy," he said when Savage appeared in the door. "Public liability, 2014. Barney's. Reed's company gave them permission to run their funfair. It's where it all started."

The next set of photos showed the six security workers who had been forced to hang themselves. Kett spotted Linda Mayweather amongst them—not an official photograph, but one taken discretely from a distance. More paperwork completed the collage, lists of shifts and staff, even contracts, all faded with age.

"How on earth did he get hold of all this?" Savage asked.

"Because he's had all the time in the world to do it," said Kett. "Years. He has money, too, the compensation from Holland. His position at Reed's firm was a cover, but it let him access a lot of files, a lot of documents. It let him put his plan together."

He scanned the photographs of the six mechanics, then the pictures of the men and women from the council who had been handcuffed inside their cars that afternoon.

"Six of them," he said. "There were only five people in the cars, but there are six photos here."

"Who was missing?" said Savage.

"This guy," said Kett, tapping a photograph of a young man. "Greg Partridge. Can you find out where he is?"

Savage disappeared, Porter taking her place.

"Bloody hell," he said. "Shit, sir, there he is."

Porter was pointing to a lower section of wall on the left, partially hidden by the open door. Superintendent Clare stared up at them, his official police photograph from the website. Five other dour faces formed an identity parade around him. Kett recognised two as top brass, but the other three were younger. He scanned the paperwork around them, case files that Ballard should never have been able to access.

"We need to find them," Kett said. "Before Ballard does."

"Something tells me we're way too late for that," said Porter.

Savage bustled back into the small room.

"Greg Partridge works for the council, sir. Planning. He's on holiday, left a couple of days ago."

"That's why there was an empty car," said Kett. "Ballard couldn't get hold of him."

"So who was the last car for, sir?" asked Savage, looking at the photos on the wall. "Seven cars, six people. Seven nooses, six victims. Seven exposed wires but we only found six people in the refrigeration warehouse. Who are we missing?"

"Ballard," Kett said. "It has to be. He was there in the office yesterday, when the bombs were delivered. He didn't hand them out, Sephie did, right? He had no idea which one he was going to get."

"That's insane, sir," said Porter. "He wouldn't have risked it, surely. Why go to all this trouble looking for revenge if you're going to die before you can finish it?"

"Because he doesn't care," Savage said. "He's happy to die. This is something else."

"He's playing the odds," said Kett. "It's all about that Lucky Number Seven. He's giving himself the same chance as everyone else."

"You're saying if none of his victims had picked the right noose, he'd have climbed that scaffold and hanged himself?" said Porter, frowning. "Or he'd have grabbed the live wire if nobody else did? I just can't see it, sir."

But Kett could. It was all in the numbers, all part of the game, and it made a horrible kind of sense.

He turned his attention to the far wall, which was dominated by a photograph of the same Ferris wheel he'd seen on the computer back at HQ. This shot had been taken at night, and from a different angle, the entrance to the fair marked by a flurry of brightly burning lightbulbs.

"Barney's," Kett read.

"Look at the big wheel, sir," said Savage.

He did, and he saw it. There were fourteen carriages in all, but some were shut up with chains and marked with 'Out of Order' signs.

"Seven," he said, counting the working carriages again just to make sure. "Shit. Seven of them. Ballard's giving himself the same odds that life gave his son."

"Sebastian chose a carriage to ride in and ended up losing his leg, and then his life," said Savage. "It was bad luck, pure and simple."

"Lucky Number Seven," said Kett. "Six chances to live, one chance to die."

He tapped the photo with his knuckles, turning to the others.

"Seven years ago this summer," he said. "I think I know where they are."

CHAPTER THIRTY-FIVE

EVEN WITH THE SIRENS ON, YARMOUTH WAS TWENTY minutes away.

It felt like the longest twenty minutes of Kett's life.

Savage drove east into the evening, the sky on fire behind their IRV as the sun dropped earthwards. There were fewer cars now than there had been on the way into the city because they didn't know where Ballard was hiding. Kett had been forced to split his resources until they knew for sure. But Gorski's van roared ahead of them, coming close to bulldozing smaller vehicles off the Acle Straight as it ploughed its way towards the sea.

"Come on," he said quietly, feeling his phone vibrate in his hand. It was an unknown number.

"Kett," he said as he answered.

"Sir, my name's PC Taiwo," came the reply, a woman's voice. "I'm in Yarmouth. We have eyes on Ballard. He's here, and so is the Super."

"Clare's alive?"

"He was when I saw him, sir."

"Where are you, exactly?" said Kett, leaning forward in his seat.

"Just off Freemantle Road, sir," she said. "It's fenced off, and Ballard is armed."

"Stay back," said Kett, bracing one arm on the dash as Savage accelerated. "We've got a firearms team inbound, five minutes. But don't let them out of your sight, okay?"

"Might be harder than you think, sir," said PC Taiwo, but she'd hung up before Kett could ask why.

"It's just north of town," said Spalding from the back, where she was wedged between Porter and Duke. She leaned between the seats, showing Kett her phone. "Up by the racecourse. You'll never believe it, sir, but Ballard owns the land."

"What?" said Kett.

"I'm looking at the deed now. He bought it the year after his son's death, same year he bought both flats. He doesn't have a mortgage, I checked. He paid cash. He got a payout."

"The compensation," said Kett as Savage roared over the roundabout, chasing Gorski's shadow.

"Yeah," said Spalding. "He cleaned Holland out in court."

They tore up Caister Road, the violent sun doing its best to blow Kett's head off through the window. Arcades and seasonal shops still packed with punters gradually gave way to houses, the traffic quiet enough for them to hit sixty.

It felt like they'd travelled for miles along the straight, wide road before Gorski's van suddenly slowed. She dashed through a red light, her tyres smoking as she pulled to the right. Savage followed, controlling the car with quick, tight movements before flooring the pedal. On one side were more houses, on the other nothing but allotments.

Then they passed a bank of bushes and Kett saw it.

"It's still there," he said.

The Ferris wheel rose above everything else, the tallest thing in the flat terrain even though it had to be half a mile away.

It looks like a monument, Kett thought, as Gorski's van thumped off the road onto a dirt track, kicking up a cloud of red dust.

Or a mausoleum.

"He left the wheel where it was," said Savage, the IRV bouncing wildly on the potholed track. "Why?"

"So people wouldn't forget," said Kett, clinging to the strap over the door. "He bought the land and left it so that nobody would forget his son."

Savage said something else but it was drowned out by the thunder of a helicopter as it flew low over their heads, the dust storm so thick that Kett couldn't see a thing through the windscreen. The IRV slowed, Savage flicking on the wipers and leaning over the wheel. She drove like this for another couple of minutes until Gorski's brake lights flared through the storm and the van came to a halt.

Kett opened his door before the car had fully stopped, almost tripping as he struggled out. Ahead, just a hundred yards or so now, was the Ferris wheel, hurling its enormous shadow over the marshy grasslands that led up towards the dunes and the sea. It had to be fifty foot high, its hulking, rusted frame creaking in the powerful breeze that blew in from the water. The sound of it was almost like screaming, as if this thing was still in mourning at what had happened.

Or like it was sounding an alarm.

"Get that gate open," yelled Gorski, as she climbed out of the van.

She was pointing to a heavy-duty steel gate that barricaded the track, connected to an eight-foot-high razor-topped fence that circled the entire site. Between the perimeter and the big wheel was a maze of long-forgotten buildings, their roofs missing and their contents spilled in the dirt. There were rides, too, the lurid caricatures of movie stars and horror icons bleached almost invisible by seven years of sun.

"We tried," said a PC who stood by the gate, her IRV parked next to the fence. Another officer sat in the passenger seat, speaking into his radio. "Chain's too big. We didn't have anything to cut it with."

"Just stand back," Gorski told her. "Bryant, get the cutter."

"You think he's in there, sir?" asked Savage, climbing out. Porter and Duke followed, Duke offering Spalding a hand as she extracted herself from the seat. Behind them, the track was a sea of blue lights as the cavalry arrived. The helicopter passed overhead, banking sharply, filling Kett's head with noise. He threw his hands up to cover his face, coughing dust from his lungs.

"He's in there," he said. "He has to be."

"Not going to get far though, is he?" said Duke.

It didn't matter. Ballard had nowhere to go, but he had a job to finish. This could only end one way, and for all Kett knew, it had already happened.

Superintendent Clare might already be dead.

A metallic shriek cut through the air, a wave of sparks coursing from the angle grinder as one of Gorski's officers attacked the chain. The PC who had been standing there moved back and Kett went to intercept her.

"You're Taiwo?" he shouted, his voice barely audible over the noise.

"Yes, sir," she said, a hand up to shield her eyes from the sun.

"Where are they?"

"I saw them between those two buildings," she said, pointing to a couple of corrugated iron shacks that looked like they might disintegrate at any moment. "There was a man in a balaclava with a shotgun, he was herding the Superintendent that way, towards the wheel. There was another man as well."

"Hostage or suspect?" asked Kett.

"Hostage," she said. "He was walking between Clare and the gunman. This was..." She checked her watch. "Nineteen minutes ago. Haven't seen them since, but heard some shouting about five minutes after that."

The helicopter had settled, hovering a hundred feet or so over the park. The thrum of its rotors reverberated in Kett's head, making it hard to think. The angle grinder sheared its way through the chain until, with a snap like a gunshot, it released its hold and dropped to the dirt. Two of the firearms team grabbed the gates and heaved them open, allowing Gorski to funnel through.

"Armed police!" she yelled, using two fingers to steer half of her team towards the buildings on the right. She went left, two officers following her lead.

"Where do you want us, sir?" asked Porter.

"Well back," he told him. "Until Ballard's secure."

"Come on," said Savage, chewing on a nail as she watched the firearms team evaporate between the ramshackle buildings. Duke stood next to her, his hand on his Taser, his body twitching like he wanted nothing more than to run in after the tactical team.

They waited, hearing the shouts echo off the buildings,

hearing the relentless scream of the big wheel as it rocked in the wind.

Then Gorski's voice.

"Kett! Get over here!"

We're too late, he thought as he broke into a run, Savage and Porter and Duke by his side. *He's dead.*

"Kett!" Gorski shouted again.

Her voice echoed between the structures that littered the park, bouncing off the shell of the dodgems track and the wooden skeleton of an ice cream stand; reverberating from the hollow cone of the helter skelter. It was impossible to tell where it was coming from.

Then a firearms officer skittered into sight, waving them on.

Kett ran past the helter skelter into a parcel of open land, throwing a hand up against the inferno of the dipping sun. The Ferris wheel sat right in front of him. Caught in its enormous shadow were Gorski and her team, their guns aimed at the base of the ride where two figures squirmed in the shimmering heat.

"Drop the gun!" Gorski yelled. "Drop it now, or we will shoot."

She ushered Kett on with a flick of her head. He jogged to her side, the sun disappearing for a moment behind one of the remaining carriages on the big wheel and letting the scene come into focus.

The base of the wheel was a platform, maybe six foot high and accessed by a set of steps. At the top of the steps was a small, metal ticket booth. Its windows were boarded up, although one panel had slipped free to reveal the dirt-streaked glass behind.

Colin Clare was on his knees by the side of the booth, his hands on his head. His suit was filthy, the buttons of his shirt torn to reveal the vest beneath. His face was streaked with sweat, but his eyes were calm, his expression set in stone. He glanced at Kett and shook his head.

Don't, was the message, loud and clear.

Don't Kett this up.

Kneeling to Clare's side was another man, and Kett recognised him from the photographs in Ballard's second apartment. He was in his fifties and on the large side, his belly spilling out beneath his untucked shirt. He had his hands laced in his thinning hair, his face contorted with the pain of having to maintain that position.

For a second, Kett couldn't see Ballard. Then he caught a shifting movement behind the filthy window of the ticket booth and the barrel of the shotgun slid through the door—pointing right at Clare's head.

"Drop the gun!" roared Gorski, taking a few steps forward. "We *will* open fire."

Kett wasn't sure it would matter. The booth was made of steel, and Ballard was well hidden inside it.

"Hold up," Kett said. The sun exploded from behind its carriage, blinding him, and he used both hands to shield his eyes. "Let me talk to him."

"Get him to show his face," said Gorski, quietly. "Get him to step out of that fucking booth and we can take the shot."

"Who's the other man?"

"Jim Stibbe," Gorski said. "He was a DCI, retired a few years ago, before you got here."

Kett moved towards the Ferris wheel, his hands up, his pace steady. Overhead, the helicopter roared, scattering the seagulls that had claimed this place as their own. The wheel creaked its song, the wind cutting between its spokes and rattling the buildings. He looked back once, seeing a line of police watching him go—Savage and Porter and Duke all wearing expressions that seemed to plead for him to come back.

He closed in on the Ferris wheel, twenty yards away now. Clare was still shaking his head.

He'd taken three more steps before a voice bellowed from inside the ticket booth.

"That's far enough. Stop there."

No Scottish accent this time, or even an attempt at one. Talion didn't have to hide anymore, he just had to finish what he'd started.

Kett did as he was told, his arms trembling from the effort of holding them up.

"Walter Ballard, right?" he said. "Is it okay if I call you that, instead of Will?"

No answer, the barrel of the gun still pointing at the two kneeling men. It was less than eight feet from Clare's head. He wouldn't miss.

"My name's Robbie Kett, you probably remember that. Can we talk for a minute?"

"No," said Ballard. "There's no time."

"There's plenty of time," said Kett, still holding his ground. "Walter, what are you doing here?"

Ballard's shadow shifted inside the booth, a quick peek through the window.

"There's nowhere to go," Kett told him. "You're surrounded. But I guess that doesn't matter, does it?"

"No," Ballard said again. "I'm almost done."

"I'm sorry about your son," said Kett. "I'm sorry about Sebastian, I truly am. He didn't deserve what happened to him, but it wasn't their fault, Walter."

"What the fuck do you know about it?" Ballard shouted back, his voice muffled by the booth, strangely distant.

"They weren't there for him, they didn't give him the help he needed, they made him feel like his life wasn't worth shit. They're as much to blame as anyone, and now one of them is going to die, just like he did."

"This is bullshit!" yelled the other man, Stibbe. "I wasn't even there, I didn't—"

"Stop lying!" said Ballard, almost a shriek. "You were there, both of you. You didn't care, didn't give him a chance to find justice, you just abandoned him and it fucking *broke* him."

"It wasn't me," Stibbe wailed. "I had nothing to do with it!"

"This is the fucking problem," said Ballard. "Nobody accepts fault, nobody admits they were in the wrong. Can you imagine what it was like? He was trapped in there, his leg was crushed by the door, it was mangled, and he was screaming for me, screaming while they tried to stop the wheel."

His voice was high pitched, almost a shriek.

"I can still hear him screaming."

"I'm sorry, Walter," said Kett. "I really am. But there's a better way of doing this. Let them go. We can open an investigation, we can—"

"Can what?" said Ballard. "Make it right? Bring him back?"

Kett licked his dry lips, the sun boring a hole in his skull, making it impossible to think.

"One in seven," he said. "That's right, isn't it, Walter?"

"Yeah," said Ballard. "There were seven carriages, the rest were broken. I should have known not to let him on, should have told him no. I knew something was wrong, I..."

He uttered a desperate, choking sob. A cry of absolute heartbreak.

"It was the last ride, the last one. I should have said no. I should have gone with him. He didn't even like them. He was fifteen, for Christ's sake, too old. He only wanted to do it because of his mum, because she always loved…"

Kett understood how broken Ballard was. He'd lost his wife. He'd lost his son. This was all that mattered. He was consumed by revenge, and one way or another, somebody was going to die today.

"You need seven, don't you?" said Kett, changing tack. "This doesn't work unless you've got seven people."

Ballard sniffed, the barrel of the gun dipping. Kett felt, rather than heard, the subtle shift of Gorski's team, and he braced himself in case somebody took the shot. Nobody did, the man still an amorphous shadow behind the dirt-smeared glass.

"You didn't give me enough time," he said after a moment. "But I knew you wouldn't. Doesn't matter. Odds are still the same. We all have a one in seven shot, just like Sebastian did. Pretty generous, all things considered."

"Let them go," said Kett. "Let's talk about this, you and me."

"Kett," barked Clare from the top of the stairs. "Enough. It's going to happen."

An object flew from the open door of the ticket booth, hitting the ground and sliding into Clare's knee. It was black and rectangular, the size of a book.

"Pick it up," growled Ballard.

Clare did as he was ordered, scooping the object from the ground.

"Open it, pick one."

Clare unzipped the object and lifted the lid. He gulped air.

"Pick one!"

Clare wiggled something out from inside the black case and held it up. It caught the light, glinting, but even from where Kett was standing it was clear enough what sat in the Superintendent's hand.

A hypodermic syringe.

"Now you," Ballard said.

Clare slid the case across the platform. Stibbe shook his head so hard his chins wobbled, his eyes so wide and so white they looked like headlamps. The sweat was rolling off him, pattering on the metal platform of the Ferris wheel.

"No," he croaked. "No, I won't do it, I—"

"Just do what he says, Jim!" said Clare.

"I won't," Stibbe said again. "I won't, I won't."

The bigger man pushed himself to his feet, swaying unsteadily, his face rigid with defiance.

"I won't," he said again. "You're surrounded, you need to put the gun down and—"

"Pick one!" shouted Ballard, his voice laced with hysteria.

Stibbe retreated towards the steps, his body tense.

"No, you won't do it, you can't do it, you—"

He broke into a clumsy run, launching himself down the steps so fast he lost his footing. The fall might have saved him, but Ballard was too fast. The barrel of the shotgun punched through the door and he fired a single shot, the force of it sending a concussive blast through the hot air.

The top of Stibbe's head erupted in an explosion of dark blood and brain matter. He dropped like his strings had been cut, momentum carrying his feet over his shoulders and leaving him slumped like a rag doll at the bottom of the steps.

Kett looked away, the shock of the man's death momentarily detaching his mind from reality, as if this was some kind of fever dream.

Somebody screamed, the sound of it quickly drowned out by the shouts of the armed response team.

"Drop the gun! Drop it now!"

But Ballard was still secure in the booth, the shotgun pointing at Clare again, smoke rising from the barrel. The air was full of the acrid stench of gunpowder, the mist of blood like a butcher's workshop. The Superintendent knelt on the platform, as calm as if he'd gone to pray at church. He'd closed his eyes, his breaths deep and steady.

He looked like a man who had accepted the inevitable.

He looked like a man who knew he was about to die.

"I warned you," Ballard was shouting. "I fucking warned you."

"He's dead," Kett said, hearing his own voice as if from a million miles away. "Stibbe's dead, Walter. You've had your revenge, you can stop."

"Doesn't work that way," he shouted back. "You know that as well as I do. They have to *choose*, they have to pick a number, just like Sebastian did. That's the only way. Luck."

Something thumped inside the booth, as if Ballard had just punched the wall.

"Fuck!" he yelled. "You're right. You're right. It needs seven people. It needs seven or it doesn't work. He's dead, this one makes two. I'm three. You."

Even though Kett couldn't see Ballard's face, he knew the man was looking right at him.

"You're four. I need three more. Get over here, right now."

"Wait," said Kett. "It—"

"One," said Ballard. "Two, I'll fucking shoot him."

"Okay!" Kett said, holding his hands higher. "Just wait."

"Three others, right fucking now."

"We're coming," said a voice, and Kett didn't have to look back to know who was following his footsteps in the dust.

He climbed the steps to the platform—seven of them, he realised, as if the world was playing a cruel joke. Clare had opened his eyes and was watching him with that same look of sad resignation. The needle was still clenched in his hand. Past him was the darkness of the booth, Ballard a deeper silhouette whose gun didn't so much as waver.

Only when Kett got to the top did he turn around.

Savage was halfway up the stairs, her hands in her hair. Next to her walked Porter, the DI glaring at the booth like he could kill Ballard with the power of thought. Duke came last, giving Kett a nod as if somewhere in that giant head of his he'd come up with a master plan. Behind them, Gorski watched with an expression of quiet panic, her team still slowly fanning out to the sides of the big wheel.

"You're a bunch of brainless tosspots, you know that?" said Clare.

"I know, sir," said Kett.

"Enough," said Ballard from his cloak of shadow. "Stop talking. You realise what's going to happen now, don't you?"

One of us is going to die, thought Kett.

"Lucky Number Seven," Ballard went on, that same edge of madness lacing his voice. "We're all going to play a game."

CHAPTER THIRTY-SIX

"Lucky Number Seven," said Ballard again.

The helicopter hovered overhead, the Ferris wheel rocking in the downdraught from its rotors. Seagulls circled like vultures, drawn by the smell of blood.

Kett took his position at the top of the steps, facing the audience of coppers like he was waiting for his own execution. Savage walked to his side, her face hard, her hands clenching and unclenching. She met his eye, and he knew exactly what was going through her mind.

We wait for an opportunity, then we take him out.

It was a solid plan, because Ballard only had one shot left in his gun—Kett hadn't heard him reload. He couldn't kill all of them, but there was no doubt he'd shoot one.

The same odds, Kett realised.

The same game.

But what else were they supposed to do? The booth was a good twelve feet away from where he was standing, and the Superintendent was in the way. It was too far, especially when Ballard swung his gun towards them.

"On your knees, all of you."

"Clare, sir," said Gorski, edging forward, her gun trained on the booth. "What do you want us to do?"

"Shut up!" said Ballard. "Shut your mouth or I blow his fucking head off just like his friend."

"Stand down," said Clare. "All of you. We let this play out. And get that chopper out of here."

"Sir?" said Kett, quietly.

The Super shook his head again.

"We let it play out," he said, quieter this time. "Do as he says."

Kett lowered himself onto his knees, the raised notches of the metal platform excruciating as they cut into his kneecaps. His back protested, almost cramping, and he leaned back as far as he could go. Savage did the same, followed by Porter, then Duke dropped down on Kett's other side so heavily that he almost knocked him over.

Gorski spoke into her radio, and a few seconds later the helicopter banked to the side, heading away from the fair. Without the world-ending thunder of its rotors, the world seemed impossibly quiet—just the endless calls of the hungry gulls.

"Don't move," said Ballard. "There should be six needles left in the case. You pick one each, you hear?"

"What's in the needles, Walter?" asked Kett.

"Doesn't matter what's in them," Ballard hissed. "All you have to know is that one will kill you, the other six won't do anything."

"You're playing too? Why?"

He was trying to delay the inevitable, and Ballard wasn't falling for it.

"Now," he said, jutting the gun through the door. "One, two."

"Okay," said Kett, the panic washing through him. "I'm doing it."

He leaned over and picked up the black case. It was a kid's pencil case, he realised, subtle silver stars and moons on the hard shell and a rocket attached to the zip. There were six syringes inside, just as Ballard had promised. Stibbe had never taken his. Each was filled with a clear liquid, and there was nothing on them to indicate which one might contain a fatal dose of poison, no sign of an unlucky number seven.

Kett hesitated for a moment, feeling that same sense of detachment.

It's not real. It can't be real.

The seagulls chattered as they landed on the rooftops. The heat on the back of his head was cooled by the salt-scented breeze. Now that the helicopter had gone, he could hear the sea and—the most surreal thing of all—the distant laughter of children. How long had it been since he'd brought his girls to the beach?

The thought of never being able to bring them again made him feel like he'd been punched in the stomach.

"Hurry up," snapped Ballard, dragging him back to reality. "Or I start shooting. Pick one."

Kett slid the needle on the left free of its elastic. It felt too light to be dangerous, but the point glinted in the sun like the blade of a knife.

"Pass it on," ordered Ballard. "Hurry up."

He handed the case to Savage, who extracted the needle on the right before giving the case to Porter. The DI's face was a knot of worry, his hand trembling as he took one of the four remaining syringes. He passed it back up the line to Kett, who held it out to Duke.

"Take one," said Ballard. "Hurry up."

Duke picked a syringe, but it slipped from his fingers and clattered to the floor. He bent down to reclaim it, struggling to get a grip.

"Now!" Ballard roared, the gun swinging towards the PC.

"I'm trying!" said Duke, fumbling the needle around the metal platform. "I've got big hands."

He managed to pinch it between his fingers, lifting it in a white-knuckled grip.

"Throw it to me," said Ballard.

Kett passed the case back to Clare, and the Superintendent slid it through the open door of the booth. Inside, Ballard sighed.

"It's nearly over," he said quietly, and Kett wasn't sure if he was talking to them or to himself. "Do it. In the arm. Has to be a vein and don't think I'm not watching."

Kett looked at the hypodermic in his trembling hand. He turned to Savage.

"We can take him," she said, just a whisper. "We have to try."

"I'll do it," said Clare before Kett could answer her.

The Superintendent had closed his eyes again, his syringe held in one hand, his other bunched into a fist by his side.

"Sir," said Kett. "There has to be ano—"

"It's the only way," Clare said. "Tell my kids I love them."

"Wait!"

But it was too late.

Clare clapped his hand to his mouth as if to suppress a sob, then he wrenched up the sleeve of his jacket and slid the needle into his arm.

"Sir, no!" yelled Savage, trying to get up.

"Stay down," said Ballard, jutting the gun towards her. "The rest of you, do it *now*."

Clare pushed in the plunger, all the way to the hilt. Kett wanted to scream at him to stop, wanted to rip the needle from his arm and throw himself on Ballard.

But he knew he'd be a dead man the second he moved.

"The rest of you," said Ballard, the whites of his eyes visible as he watched Clare. "The rest of you do it—"

He didn't need to finish.

Clare arched his back, his hands dropping to his sides, the needle embedded in his arm like an arrow. He opened his mouth and a spray of thick, white vomit jetted out of it, foaming on his shirt.

"Jesus Christ," said Kett.

He got to his feet, pushing past Duke and taking the Superintendent in his arms just as he collapsed. He was too heavy to hold and Kett dropped with him, both of them hitting the metal platform. Clare's body bucked and spasmed, more white foam exploding from his mouth. His eyes had rolled back in their sockets, his throat gulping as he tried to breathe.

"Sir?" Kett said, pushing his fingers into Clare's mouth to clear the vomit away. "Colin! Fuck!"

Savage skidded down next to him.

"Get him on his side, sir," she said, her tears burning bright. "We need an ambulance!"

"Let him die," said Ballard from inside the booth. His voice was calm and quiet, full of relief. "Let him die, or you go with him. It won't take long."

It didn't.

Clare's body grew rigid, a final breath bubbling through the foam on his lips.

Then he lay still.

"No," said Kett, the word a sob that punched its way out of him. He rolled Clare onto his back, bracing his hands against the Super's chest and managing to push down once before Ballard started shouting again.

"I said let him die. You touch him again, you die too."

"You can't do this," said Kett, the frustration and the panic and the horror screaming inside him. He sat back, his hands in his hair, while Clare's body slowly cooled in the sinking sun. "You can't do this."

The shotgun slid slowly out of the darkness of the booth, and Ballard followed. He kept the gun locked on Kett as he emerged from his hiding place, his face hidden by a balaclava but his eyes red raw with emotion. There was a collective rattle from the tactical team as they lifted their guns, but nobody was going to take the shot—not when Ballard's finger was on the trigger. They'd already lost two coppers today.

Kett lifted his hands, a tremor rocking his whole body. Ballard glanced at Clare, and even with the mask over his face Kett could see him smile.

"It's done," said Ballard. "It's over. I don't want to hurt anyone else."

"Put the gun down," yelled Gorski.

"Yeah, put it down," said Kett, his voice a husk. "There's nowhere else to go, Walter."

"Oh, but there is," said Ballard, backing towards the giant struts that held up the Ferris wheel. "I'm done. I can be with him again."

Ballard spun the shotgun in his hands, the barrel under his chin, his thumb looped through the trigger.

"No!" said Kett.

He pushed himself off, a sprinter's start that propelled

him across the platform. Ballard saw him coming, tried to turn the gun back around.

Too slow.

Kett thumped into him, sending them both sprawling. Ballard's shoulder hit one of the legs of the big wheel and he spun, the gun clattering to the ground. Kett kept hold of him, wrestling him, only to feel Ballard's fist strike the soft flesh of his cheek.

He let go, Gorski screaming as she rushed up the steps.

"Move out of the way, Kett!"

Porter and Duke were running over but Ballard scrambled away, hurling himself onto the ladder that led to the centre of the wheel. He scaled it fast, but not fast enough. Gorski loosed a shot as she came close, the bullet punching into Ballard's stomach and releasing a plume of blood from his back. He kept climbing, oblivious as Gorski moved in for the kill.

"Wait!" Kett told her. "He doesn't get to die that easily."

He grabbed the ladder and started climbing, the entire frame of the big wheel creaking in outrage. Blood pattered down onto his hand, onto his face, as Ballard wheezed his way slowly skyward.

"Stop," Kett said. "There's nowhere to go."

Nowhere except up. Walter was slowing, struggling towards the small maintenance platform that sat at the centre of the wheel. He grabbed the railing and hauled himself onto it, falling back against the metal spokes. He ripped the balaclava from his head, revealing a face that had crumpled into a knot of agony. Then he grabbed his wounded stomach with both hands.

"Enough," said Kett, climbing as swiftly as he could, the rungs of the ladder slick with blood. "Don't move, Walter. Don't make this any worse than it already is."

It couldn't be any worse, could it? Kett peered down through the cobweb of metal struts to see Savage performing CPR on Clare. A ring of coppers circled them, hats in hands as they watched her work.

Gorski and her team had fanned out to try to keep Ballard in their sights, their visors catching the sun like fireworks. Kett blinked the sparks from his eyes, a sudden roar of vertigo making him cling to the ladder like it was taking off.

"Sir," called Porter from the ground. "Leave him, he's trapped."

He wasn't, though. Ballard knew exactly where he was going.

"Leave me alone," the killer said. He stepped over the railing onto the giant upright spoke that held the topmost carriage. "Just let me go."

Kett hauled himself up the last few rungs onto the platform, the wind trying to blow him back off again. He had to be thirty feet up—high enough to make his stomach feel like it was turning inside out, high enough to kill him if he fell. Ballard balanced himself on the steep angle of the strut, using the support wires to keep climbing. Blood spilled from his torso, raining onto the platform below.

"You don't get to do that," said Kett. "You don't get to do what you've done then leave. He was a good man. He was the best of men, and you killed him."

"He was responsible," Ballard shouted back, the wind trying to carry off his words. "He killed my boy. They all did. They had to pay."

"They didn't kill him, Walter," Kett said. "Nobody killed him. It was an accident. It was... it was bad luck."

Ballard laughed, looking down.

"So you do get it," he said. "It's all luck. We play the

odds every single day, all of us. Sometimes you win, sometimes you don't."

Ballard's foot slipped, and for a moment it looked like he was going to drop. But he clung on, gargling as he struggled to get a foothold. Kett stayed on the platform, the other man almost directly overhead.

"The odds were rigged for Sebastian," he called down. "He never got a fair shot."

He was two thirds of the way up, but he was flagging. He stopped, bracing his feet on the wires and hugging the thick strut. His clothes billowed in the wind. Kett couldn't be sure, but it sounded like he was sobbing.

"You'd do it too," he said. "You'd do what I did if it was your kid."

"No. I wouldn't. Not like this. You think this is what Sebastian would have asked for? You think this is how he wanted to see you? You're his dad, Walter."

"I know," Ballard answered. "I just want to go to him. I just want to see him again."

There was nothing Kett could do to stop him.

"Robbie," came a familiar voice from below. "Let him go."

He didn't think it could be real, but when he glanced down through the crisscrossed wires he saw Superintendent Clare standing in the shadow of the Ferris wheel. His face was still white from the foamy vomit, but he stood tall and strong, and his eyes were clear. Savage and Duke stood next to him, shielding their faces from the sun.

"Sir?" said Kett. "What... *How?*"

Ballard had seen it too, a howl of grief from overhead.

"That's not possible," he said. "There was hemlock in that syringe, it... it should have killed you."

"Not me, you great, steaming tossbag," bellowed Clare. "I'm invincible."

"No!" Ballard wailed again. "You can't—"

He might have let go or he might have slipped, but Ballard was suddenly falling. Kett reached out for him as he dropped past the platform, managing to clasp a handful of the man's T-shirt—the impact dragging him into the railing and almost pulling him over.

He couldn't hold on, Ballard snapping free and hurtling towards the ground. His head struck one of the struts and he spun wildly, hitting the platform with a sound like a church bell.

"Shit," Kett said, dropping onto the ladder. "Shit shit shit."

Gorski and her team moved in like sharks, their weapons trained on Ballard. But he wasn't going anywhere, his body bent and broken.

Kett jumped the last few feet, landing awkwardly and limping towards Clare.

"Sir? How are you... What the hell happened?"

Clare's face twisted into a wry smile and he held up his hand. There was something in it, something small and pale, and the smell coming off it was distinctly coconutty.

"Is that..."

Clare nodded.

"Duke's cake," he said.

"*My* cake?" said Duke. "My homemade Bounty Surprise?"

"Yes," said Clare. "The surprise being it has the same effect on me as a needle full of poison."

He pocketed the rest of the cake and wiped his lips.

"You faked it, sir?" said Kett. "How did you know he wouldn't check?"

"How did you know it wasn't the needle with the hemlock in it?" added Savage. "It could have been the deadly one."

"Lucky Number Seven," said Porter.

Clare waved them all away.

"One in seven are good odds," he said. "I fancied my chances. And even if it had been..."

He looked at each of them in turn, considering his words.

"Better me than any one of you hairy tosspockets, am I right? I've done my time, I've lived a life. Besides, if I shuffle off this mortal coil then I never have to look at Duke's face again."

"What's wrong with my face, sir?" Duke asked, feeling it with both hands.

Kett turned his attention to Ballard, who was almost lost in a sea of police. The man lay on his stomach, his hands cuffed behind him even though he still showed no sign of movement. A puddle of blood had formed around his head like a halo. The Ferris wheel towered overhead and Kett found the point where Ballard had fallen from. He couldn't be alive after that, could he?

When Gorski peeled herself loose from the crowd, though, she had a grim smile on her face.

"He's breathing," she said, tucking her rifle against her side as she approached Kett. "I think you slowed his fall. You saved his life."

"More than he deserved," said Porter.

"No," said Clare. "This way he pays for what he's done. He doesn't get away with it. Any sign of an ambulance?"

"Inbound," said Gorski. "You okay, sir? I thought you were dead."

"That was the idea," said Clare. "Back in my university

days, I was quite the actor, I'll have you know. Played a few of Shakespeare's best."

"I thought jazz flute was more your thing, sir?" said Porter.

"I am a man of many talents," he said.

"But you liked the cake, sir?" asked Duke.

"Aaron, it was like some kind of tropical monkey had shat in my mouth," said Clare, fishing a scrap of coconut from his teeth. Duke's face fell, and Clare clapped a hand on the PC's shoulder. "But it saved my life, Constable," he said. "So I'll be forever grateful."

They all took a moment to look at Ballard. Kett couldn't imagine the pain that the man had endured, the horror of losing his son the way he had. He'd lost his mind, and so many people had paid the price.

You'd have done the same, he'd said. And Kett had denied it, of course.

But who's to say what you were capable of when all your luck had run out?

"Come on," Clare said. "Let's get out of here. If I don't get the taste of Duke's coconutty toss out of my mouth, I'm going to pop my clogs for real."

He stomped down the steps like he'd just been out for a casual stroll, marching across the shadow of the Ferris wheel and vanishing behind the shell of the dodgems.

"I'm still not sure I understand what just happened," said Porter as they watched him go.

"Me neither," said Savage.

"We got lucky," said Kett, making his way down the stairs on legs that didn't feel strong enough to hold him. "We got very, very lucky."

They headed for the exit, the laughter of the gulls serenading them as they went.

CHAPTER THIRTY-SEVEN

Wednesday

KETT PULLED THE VOLVO OVER TO THE SIDE OF THE bumpy lane and parked it behind Superintendent Clare's monstrous Mercedes. It was late afternoon and the sunshine streamed over the back wall of Erik North's stables, filling the car with golden light. Swallows darted in and out between missing roof tiles, almost too fast to see.

It felt like it should have been quiet here, but any hope of peace was shattered by the argument that was taking place in the back seat of the car.

"She's called Twinkle!" said Alice with some fury.

"No she's not," said Evie, a wicked smile on her face. "She's called Farty Butt Cheese."

"Farty Butt Cheese," echoed Moira, giggling.

"She's not! She's called Twinkle!"

"Farty Butt Cheese McPoopy Bandit Pants," said Evie, bursting into a hearty chuckle that was brought to a swift end by a slap on the arm from Alice. "Alice hit me!" she squealed, hitting her sister with both fists. "I'll kill you!"

"Hey!" Kett said, turning around to try and get between them. His back protested, everything threatening to cramp. Luckily, Billie was sitting next to him and she unclipped her seatbelt, sliding her top half between the seats and grabbing Alice before she could retaliate.

"They're winding you up, Alice," she said. "Just ignore them."

"I hate them," Alice said, almost in tears. "Why did they have to come? They ruin everything. It's *my* horse."

"Don't be sad," said Moira, putting a gentle hand on Alice's arm that was promptly shaken off.

"Yeah, don't be sad," said Evie. "Or you'll make Farty Butt Cheese McPoopy Bandit Pants Von Pompom Bum sad too."

"Right," said Kett as the girls kicked off again, a serenade of screams. "Everybody out."

He cranked his door open and climbed into the clammy early evening air, instantly engulfed by that not-unpleasant aroma of horses. He opened Evie's door and caught her as she jumped, plopping her down then immediately pulling her out of the way as their oldest daughter exited the car. Alice lunged for her, and she wasn't messing around.

"Enough," said Kett, Evie sheltering behind his back. "Both of you, or we're going straight home."

Alice shot Evie a look of unmistakeable violence that Evie returned, almost a mirror image.

Kett checked the Super's car, finding it empty. Billie had lifted Moira out, holding her tight as she squirmed to get free. Legions of crows chuckled at each other from the trees, clouds of them fighting for a roost. From the other side of the stables he could hear the gentle clop of hooves and the soft snort of a horse.

"You're sure Erik said we could come anytime we wanted?" Billie asked, lowering Moira to the ground. "I feel bad just turning up, especially as we were here yesterday."

"That's what he told me," said Kett. "Besides, Clare asked us to meet him here. Come on."

They set off towards the open gate, Evie bolting.

"Don't run off," he told her, sighing with frustration as she completely ignored him. "It's not safe, Evie, there are—"

She was gone, Moira too, both of them galloping through the gate between the buildings. Billie rushed after them, Kett following her into the wide courtyard that held the stables. Clare stood in the middle of the space talking to Erik. The Superintendent had taken off his jacket and had rolled up the sleeves of his shirt—a bandage around his forearm where he'd injected himself with the needle. He looked the picture of health, and Kett thought again—as he had so many times since yesterday—of him lying motionless on the platform of the Ferris wheel.

They'd come so close to losing him for real.

Southpaw, Erik's enormous horse, stood next to them, tethered to his stable door and swishing his tail to keep the flies away.

All three turned when they heard the Kett girls charging across the courtyard.

"Easy," said Erik, welcoming them with bright eyes and a soft smile. "You don't want to scare him."

Southpaw snorted again, as if deriding the words. Erik turned his smile to the horse.

"I wasn't talking about you, I was talking about Colin," he said.

Clare laughed quietly.

"There's not much in this world that scares me," he said, giving the girls a stern look. "But you three are on the list. Billie, Robbie, good to see you."

He greeted them with a nod.

"How are you feeling, sir?" asked Kett.

Clare didn't answer, his brow furrowing as he lost himself in the events of yesterday. He scratched at his bandaged arm, at the place where he'd slid Ballard's needle into his vein.

"Where's Twinkle?" Alice asked in a quiet voice, hiding behind Billie. "Why isn't she in her stable? Has she gone?"

"She means Farty Butt Cheese, not Twinkle," risked Evie, who was trying to look over the door of the nearest stable. Erik laughed.

"Twinkle is waiting for you," he said. "She's out back in the field."

"But Farty Butt Cheese is busy," Clare added, shouting into Southpaw's stable. "Isn't that right, Farty?"

Something metallic clattered inside the stable, and a moment later Porter leaned over the door. He'd taken off his jacket and his shirt and his vest was almost transparent with sweat. He was completely and utterly filthy, his face streaked with dirt, and he looked about as miserable as any man Kett had ever seen.

"Am I done?" he asked, breathless. He caught sight of Kett. "Oh, hey, sir."

"What on Earth are you doing, Pete?" asked Kett.

"It's called exercise," said Clare. "The old-fashioned kind. Otherwise known as hard work. And you're finished when I say you're finished."

"But why doesn't anyone else have to do it?" he whined.

"Because everyone else isn't you," answered Clare with a sadistic grin. "Now get scooping."

Porter groaned, slouching back into the stable.

"Bit harsh, sir?" said Kett.

"Nonsense. It's good for him."

Kett laughed.

"I hope it's okay that we're here."

"More than okay," said Erik, lifting his calloused hand in a wave.

"We had a great time yesterday," Billie said. "This place is amazing. Thank you so much, again, for letting Alice see your horses. She loves them."

"Not my horse," said Erik. "Hers. Yours. Twinkle is equally besotted with your daughter. Fast friends already."

Alice beamed, the closest thing to joy that Kett had seen on her face in a long time.

"Come on, I'll take you through. You can help me tack her up if you like. All of you."

Erik crossed the courtyard, the three girls giggling their heads off as they trod on his shadow.

"He's so..." Billie started, seeming to struggle to find the words. "Tall."

"Tall, eh?" said Kett, raising his eyebrow. Billie blushed.

"Yeah," she said. "You know, *tall*."

"I've never heard it called that before," he said. "Savage here?"

"And Duke," said Clare. "They're looking at the horses. You'd think they'd never seen one before."

"How's Savage doing, sir?"

"About as well as you'd expect, given what she went through. She's champing at the bit to get back to work, but I thought I'd give her at least a day off to recover. She needed a break."

He shook his head.

"I think we all need a break after that. I've never known anything like it."

Neither had Kett. He'd spent the day at HQ trying to wrap his head around why Ballard had done the things he'd done—and *how*. The man had been planning his revenge for seven long years, and the number of moving pieces was immeasurably complex. It would take weeks, he knew—months, even—to put everything together. And it would take a lot longer than that for the surviving victims to get their lives back.

The good news was that Ballard was still alive, although only just. He'd make it. He'd pull through.

And Kett still didn't know how he felt about that.

"I remember it," said Clare, his voice quiet. "Sebastian Ballard, I remember his case. There was nothing we could do, but he deserved more than we gave him."

He sighed, and before Kett could think of something to say to him he heard Savage calling.

"Robbie, sir!"

She appeared from the path that split the stables, Duke right behind her. They were both in civilian clothes, matching black Nike tracksuits and white trainers that had already taken a battering from the dirt. They still had their matching bruises, too, although they were less swollen now, and starting to heal. She leapt nimbly over a pile of wet straw and jogged up to them. It seemed like a million years ago that he'd dragged her from the garage, and he thought about how close he'd come to losing her, too.

But he'd said it so many times before. It's what the job demanded from you, it's what the job fed itself on. You had to give up a little piece of yourself to save everybody else.

"They're amazing," said Savage. "The horses. I've never really been a horse person, but I think that might change."

She smudged the sweat from her forehead.

"And Erik's lovely," she said. "He's so…"

"Tall," said Billie with a knowing smile.

"Yeah," said Savage, grinning back. "That's the word, tall."

"So tall," said Billie, and they both laughed.

"I'm tall," grumbled Duke. "I'm really tall. Taller than *him*, anyway."

"Yeah…" said Savage with a shrug, and the two women laughed again.

Duke pouted.

"I thought you loved me," he said.

"No, I said I loved Mr Peanut," she replied. "Whoever that is."

But she wrapped her arms around his waist, giving him a kiss.

"If you guys are talking shop, I'll go find Erik," said Billie, heading off.

"Speaking of talking shop," said Savage, letting go of Duke. "I'm not sure if you've seen it yet, but this is unmissable."

She pulled her phone from her pocket and handed it to Kett. The screen was a blur so he slid on his glasses, seeing a YouTube video of a sun drenched riverbank. She pressed play.

"Brace yourself, sir."

The camera swung around and Porter and Duke appeared, along with a very naked Asif Nasir. Duke was on the ground, Nasir straddling him and flailing around like a landed fish—his nether regions thankfully pixelated out. Porter grabbed Nasir's leg like it was a rope and hauled himself out of the water, lying in the mud.

"Jesus Christ," said Clare, who was craning over the

screen. "Another highlight for the Extreme Crime Task Force."

Porter helped Nasir up, both of them looking like they were about to fall back into the water. Then Duke clambered to his feet and yelled at whoever was filming, and the screen went dark.

Clare's eyes were bulging.

"I've never, in all my life, seen anything so bloody—"

"There's another one, too," said Savage, grinning. She took the phone for a moment, tapped the screen, then handed it back. "This one's even better."

Kett read the title of the video out loud.

"Norfolk man loses fight with seagull."

"What?" said Clare, reaching for the phone. "Give me that."

Kett stepped out of his reach, watching wobbly footage of Superintendent Clare on Prince of Wales Road. He looked like he was unwrapping a Bounty, but after a couple of seconds a seagull the size of a small car flapped down and snatched it out of his hands.

"I said give me that, Detective!" Clare barked, lunging again.

The seagull soared up, but not before Clare grabbed one of its feet. What followed was a flurry of wings and hands that lasted almost ten seconds before the seagull managed to pull free, the Bounty still in its beak. It escaped up the road, Clare's arms wheeling as he gave chase. They both vanished around the corner.

"That didn't happen," said Clare, finally managing to rip the phone out of Kett's hand. "That wasn't me. How do I delete things from the internet?"

He threw Savage's phone into the mud.

"Not like that, sir," she said as she picked it up, wiping dirt from the screen. "I'm sure nobody's watched it."

"Says 12,000 views," said Duke. "Not bad."

"Well that explains the seagull stuff," said Kett. "Did you get your Bounty back, sir?"

"I told you, it wasn't me," growled Clare. "And yes, I bloody did. No bird is going to beat me in a fight."

Kett laughed.

"Right," said Clare. "Enough dilly-dallying. I need to know how we missed Ballard? How did we not suspect Will Talion?"

"Because he was there when the bomb went off," said Savage. "We know that Sephie handed him a random box, there was no way he could have influenced her decision. If he'd got Number Seven, he would have died. People don't do that. They don't risk their life like that."

"Except they do," said Clare. "Why?"

"Because he wanted to die, sir," said Savage. "We saw that yesterday, when he jumped."

"It's more than that," said Kett. "It's more like he wanted it to be fair. Ultimately, his son died because he got in the wrong carriage. He had seven to choose from and he picked the one that malfunctioned. He lost his leg, and then his life. One in seven."

Southpaw clopped a hoof on the ground, nickering quietly. Kett walked over and let the animal sniff his hand with its velvet-soft nose, then he patted it gently on the neck. There was something immensely reassuring about the bulk of the horse, a kind of gravity that made him feel weirdly at peace.

"He wanted to give himself the same odds because it was only fair. He gave those odds to everybody he held responsible for Sebastian's death. And yeah, at the end of the day he didn't care if he died. He just wanted to see his boy again and take out as many people as he could along the way."

"What I want to know is how he found hemlock?" said Duke.

"Easier than you think," Savage told him. "It grows all over Norfolk, believe it or not. You just have to know what to do with it."

"And it *was* hemlock," said Clare. "Hay let me know. I've debated whether or not to tell you this, but the lethal dose was in your syringe, Kate. If we'd played his game, you would have died."

Savage put her hand to her mouth, shaking her head. Duke wrapped her in a hug.

"The other six were filled with saline," Clare went on. "They were harmless. Hay found numbers etched into the plastic case, too small for anybody to see."

"Thank you, sir," Savage said when Duke had let go of her.

"Bastard," muttered the PC.

"I called the hospital today," said Savage, her voice quiet. "I—"

"You weren't supposed to be working, Detective," scolded Clare.

"Sorry, sir," she replied. "I asked them about Will. Turns out he was discharged just after lunch on Monday."

"I didn't know," came a muffled voice.

Porter stuck his head over the stable door again. He was filthier than ever, so much straw in his hair that he looked like he was wearing a wig.

"Crikey, sir," said Duke. "Are you *rolling* in it?"

"No, I am not bloody rolling in it," Porter shot back. "Maybe you'd know that if you came and gave me a hand."

"Think of the calories you're burning, Porter," said Clare.

"I'll burn your calories, you old—"

"What was that?"

"Nothing, sir," said Porter, leaning on the door. "Will, or Walter—Ballard, whatever his name was—he was still at the hospital on Monday when I went to speak with Ben Reed. And he was there that evening as well. I just assumed he'd been there all day, because he wasn't a suspect."

"They checked their security cameras," said Savage. "He left and came back, twice."

"Shit," said Kett.

"That is a major cock-up," said Clare. "You lot are the Extreme Crime Task Force, you need to do better."

Southpaw nudged Kett with his heavy head, and Kett gave him another scratch on his neck.

"Sorry, sir," he said.

"It's done," said Clare. "It might not have made any difference. Ballard has been planning this for years. He's meticulous, he accounted for every contingency. He's been living a lie all this time while he prepared, working for Reed's company to cover his tracks and never leaving his son's chair. Not in public, anyway. He was light years ahead of us, and he only needed two days to execute his plan. He knew that by the time the police were even close to identifying him, he'd have done what he needed to do."

"Except he didn't plan for every contingency," said Duke, striking a movie poster pose. "He didn't count on us."

"Yes, thank you, Arnold Schwarzenegger," Clare said. "I was just about to say that, but in a way that didn't make me look like a tosspuppet."

"Sorry, sir," said Duke, deflated.

"He wasn't that meticulous," said Kett. "Not all of his

victims were involved with the fair. We already know Linda Mayweather wasn't working the night Sebastian got hurt, and two of the women who he trapped in the cars joined the council after 2015. They had nothing to do with it."

"But he needed seven," said Savage. "Seven victims each time, or as close as he could get, or it wouldn't work."

"Bloody nutter," said Duke.

"Thanks for your professional assessment," said Porter.

"Sorry, sir, but shouldn't you get back to your manure?"

Porter pointed a finger at the big PC, but Clare interrupted before he could say anything.

"Right, Duke, you can grab a shovel too. That stable over there needs a good mucking out."

"*What*, sir?" said Duke, horrified.

"First person with a clean stable gets a promotion."

Porter vanished back inside and Duke yelped, fighting to pull off his hoody as he lumbered across the courtyard.

"You're not really going to give them a promotion, are you sir?" said Savage.

"I am," said Clare. "Promotion from hairy tosspocket to regular tosspocket."

Kett laughed and Southpaw whinnied, nudging him again. He leaned into the horse, feeling the heat radiating from its body.

"*Are* you okay, sir?" he asked Clare. "That was some gamble, yesterday. You could have died."

"I could have," Clare said. "But that's the job, isn't it? Wasn't the first time I've put my life on the line, and it won't be the last. You play the odds every single day when you're a copper, and you can plan for some of it, but you can't control everything. Without a little bit of luck, we're all dead."

He laughed.

"The irony is I almost choked on Duke's bloody cake," he said.

"It wasn't that bad, was it, sir?" asked Savage. "He really worked hard on it. He used real coconuts and everything."

"He's put me off Bounties for life," Clare said. "I'll never forgive him."

They all turned to see that Duke had stripped off his T-shirt, his skin slick with sweat and his muscles bulging as he shovelled dirt into a wheelbarrow.

"What is he doing?" said Kett. "Digging a hole?"

"Does he know he's supposed to be clearing out the straw?" said Savage. "I'll tell him."

"No you won't," said Porter from inside the stable. He opened the door, wheeling his barrow out. "I win, sir. I win!"

"Congratulations," said Clare. "You're promoted. Chief shit shoveller. Right, I'm heading home. I need you all in first thing for a proper debrief. Good work, though. At the end of the day, we got him. Kett, you'd better go and round up your children."

"Do I have to?" said Kett, giving the horse a gentle pat. "I've found a better one."

Clare laughed, trudging across the courtyard and disappearing. Porter walked over, the smell coming off him making Kett's eyes water.

"Oh God, sir," said Savage, a hand over her mouth. "*Were* you rolling in it?"

"No!" Porter said, sniffing his armpit. "It's not that bad, is it?"

"It's bad," Kett said. "Go shower. I'll see you all tomorrow."

He walked around the horse, passing between two stables and finding himself on a dirt track. He had to stop for a moment because the view almost floored him—five or six paddocks leading down the hill towards a strip of distant woodland. The sun bathed the entire scene in golden light, while a gentle breeze made the grass ripple and the hedges dance. Four horses grazed sleepily, their tails swishing.

He took a breath and the stress and the horror of the case seemed to slough right off him, leaving him lighter than air. If he wanted to, he could have flown up to join the swallows that dashed and darted overhead. He could have flown forever.

Voices brought him back to earth, the clop of hooves and the birdsong-sweet giggles of his children. Erik appeared first, stepping out from behind a high hedge. He was leading a grey horse covered with dappled markings, and sitting on it, her smile like a lighthouse beam, was Alice.

"Look, Dad!" she shouted, laughing. "I'm riding Twinkle!"

"You are!" said Kett, walking over to join them.

Billie kept her distance behind the horse, holding Evie and Moira's hands as they tried to race ahead. They were all flushed from the heat, their hair tousled, but the smiles they wore were almost unreal.

Kett fumbled for his phone and took a hasty photograph of them all. Then he slid the phone back into his pocket and took a mental photograph too—one he knew would last just as long. There weren't many perfect moments, he knew, but this was one. He wanted to remember it forever.

"I've got some time, if you guys would like a lesson?" said Erik. "I'm not much of a teacher, I'm afraid, but I can run you through the basics."

"Please, Dad?" said Alice. "Please, can we?"

"Sure," he said, because there was no other answer he could give. There were dinners to make, rooms to clean, work to do—always so much work—but it could wait. It could all wait.

Alice leaned forward and wrapped her arms around Twinkle's neck, hugging her. Kett watched them walk past.

"I've got a little arena," said Erik. "It's not much, and we may have to fight the pigeons for it, but it will do the job."

Kett waited for Billie, lifting Moira into his arms and holding her clammy body against his chest.

"I don't think I've ever seen her this happy," Billie said, looking at Alice.

"Me neither," said Kett. He gazed down the hill and soaked in the sun, absorbing the incredible, unearthly peace of this place and feeling more at home than he had done in years. "I could live out here."

"In a stable?" asked Moira, and he laughed.

"Yeah, in a stable. Just make sure I have plenty of hay to eat. And the occasional apple."

The girls laughed, Moira pushing her hand to his face as if feeding him. He pretended to gobble her up and she roared with laughter. He put her down and she ran off with Evie, then he took Billie's hand and held it tight.

"Sometimes it just works out, doesn't it?" she said. "Sometimes life just lets you be happy."

They rounded the corner in time to see Twinkle walking into a sawdust-filled arena, Alice clinging on for dear life but still laughing her head off. Evie and Moira had scaled the wooden fence and were cheering her on in a rare show of support.

"Sometimes you just get lucky," said Billie.

"Yeah," said Kett, lifting her hand and kissing it. "Sometimes you do."

ABOUT THE AUTHOR

Alex Smith wrote his first book when he was six. It wasn't particularly good, but it did have some supernatural monsters in it. His latest books, the DCI Robert Kett thrillers, have monsters in them too, although these monsters are very human, and all the more terrifying for it. In between, he has published thirteen novels for children and teenagers under his full name, Alexander Gordon Smith—including the number one bestselling series Escape From Furnace, which is loved by millions of readers world-wide and which is soon to become a motion picture. He lives in Norwich with his wife and three young daughters.

Find out more at alexsmithbooks.com

Made in the USA
Las Vegas, NV
08 August 2023

75850640R00252